Chestnuts
of
Yesteryear

Chestnuts of Yesteryear

A Jewish Odyssey

Zvi Ankori

gefen publishing house
JERUSALEM ◆ NEW YORK

"Armoney Eshtakad" Translated from the Hebrew by Evelyn Abel.

Typesetting: Raphaël Freeman, Jerusalem Typesetting
Cover Design: Studio Paz

ISBN 965-229-318-0

1   3   5   7   9   8   6   4   2

Gefen Publishing House
POB 36004, Jerusalem 91360, Israel
972-2-538-0247
orders@gefenpublishing.com

Gefen Books
12 New Street, Hewlett, NY 11557, USA
516-295-2805
gefenny@gefenpublishing.com

www.israelbooks.com

Printed in Israel

Send for our free catalogue

For Ora

And our three daughters –
Gilatt, Gannit and Dahlia

For our three granddaughters –
Yarden, Oranne and No'am

And our four grandsons
Lee-Or, Or, Roi and Amir-Adam

That they may know where their roots are

Tarnów That Was

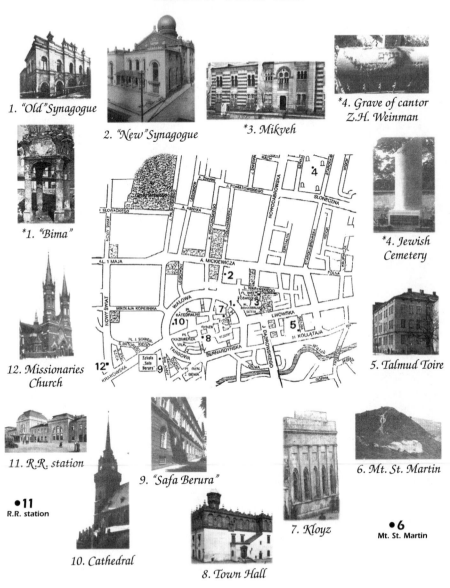

1. "Old" Synagogue

2. "New" Synagogue

*3. Mikveh

*4. Grave of cantor Z.H. Weinman

*1. "Bima"

*4. Jewish Cemetery

12. Missionaries Church

5. Talmud Toire

11. R.R. station

9. "Safa Berura"

6. Mt. St. Martin

7. Kloyz

10. Cathedral

8. Town Hall

* All that remains of Jewish Tarnów:
1. "Bima" of the "Old Synagogue"   3. Mikveh   4. Jewish Cemetery
4. Memorial Column, made of fragments of "New Synagogue"

Table of Contents

A Bouquet of Books
(A Word from the Author)

THE ENORMOUS BOOKCASE that stood against the left wall of the back room was the most conspicuous and imposing piece of furniture in the modest two-room flat where I passed my youth. Lacking all charm on the outside, it was nevertheless bathed in an aura, and imprinted upon its surroundings more than any other item that ever came to rest within the walls of our home. Little wonder then that as I leaned on the sagging shelves, I felt waves of friendship coming at me, and I reciprocated with unadulterated love – love of the chest itself and of what it harbored, whether the open or the hidden, at which I could only guess.

Time and time again, as I would draw out a book at random, rest it on my left palm and leaf through it with the fingers of my right hand, I was aware – both as a child and later, as a young man – of the debt of gratitude I owed this wonderful treasure trove that had always been with me, from earliest infancy, even before I could read. This awareness would neither wane nor vanish even after I found myself leaving home, nor would its impact ever diminish, even after there was no longer a bookcase at all.

The debt was manifold: for the pleasure that awaited me be-tween the covers of every book; for each tale, each poem granted me; for the excitement at every line, even those I found difficult to understand during my first hesitant steps along the pathways of literature; and for moments of grace and flights of fancy inspired by the bookcase. As I stood there, my hand tingling at the touch of each page of a book I had chosen, my eyes never stopped caressing the other titles beckoning from the shelves, a glance that signaled to them: "Wait for me, soon I'll call on you as well."

What spell did this plain, mundane piece of furniture weave on young and old alike? From the distance of dozens of years and thousands of miles, I try to look back and understand the spirit of those times. How did the bookcase become so meaningful a milestone in the landscape of my youth that I would regard it as the 'Ark-of-Arks' of my life, despite its lack of any special beauty or antiquity?

Above all, it must have been the enormity of the bookcase that so impressed everyone, its overwhelming presence affecting even those who set eyes on it for the first time. Taking up an entire wall, its grandeur for new onlookers lay chiefly in its magnitude, which dwarfed and obscured all other pieces of furniture in the two rooms of the flat. Even the solitary closet that stood next to it – and held the garments of a family of five – appeared ashamed of its own wretchedness, like a poor relation apologizing for taking up room next to so illustrious a kinsman. Indeed, no better proof is needed of the uneven scale of values that reigned in the home than the asymmetrical sight presented by the pair of cabinets: the one was defined by a regime of austerity and being content with little as far as material assets were concerned; the other, in contrast, marked by an insatiable appetite for collecting and sheltering spiritual assets.

While its disproportionate and ungainly exterior continued to astonish, since few private flats could support such a fixture, it was nevertheless a peek into its contents that provided the near unforgettable experience. Obviously, a quick opening of the double-winged, glass door could not really expose the rich contents of the bookcase; but it enabled one, if only fleetingly, to sense a secret and mysterious vibration from the overflowing shelves, which lent it an aura of surprise and promise.

The bookcase! Here, side by side, are sacred and secular, as far apart as heaven and earth, yet dwelling together in kinship as if complementing one another in some arcane covenant at whose origin and union I still wonder.

The bookcase! A bridge on which there met – and also clashed – two types of culture, melding to make our home the living, breathing entity I remember to this day. As a family project that began from what was, in fact, empty space (apart from the handful of books that each partner brought to the marriage), the bookcase was apparently planned as a neutral repository for the absorption of new acquisitions. The trouble is that by being the spiritual edifice of two architects – both strong personalities and each laying a different intellectual foundation, each having a distinct idea as to the nature of the future collection and its desirable course of development – the bookcase became not only a fertile meeting place, but also a stormy arena of conflict between two worlds: the one, my father's, was the realm of traditional Jewish scholarship with its unique blend of historical layers and topical divisions; the other, my mother's, was a splendid spectrum of universal literature, philosophy, history and art. That, in any event, is how the bookcase and its evolution struck me, with a child's innocent simplicity.

Here, now, are the ministering angels of two worlds: the large heavy tomes of the *Babylonian Talmud*, Vilna edition, printed by the Rom Widow and Brothers (in black cloth binding with black leather spines), purchased in 1920 to mark the occasion of my birth, with my name stamped on each volume as was the custom of the times, as if my father sought to immediately arm his son with a defense kit for his future battles as a Jew. Here are the Talmudic code of *Hilkhot HaAlfas*, by Rabbi Isaac Ben Jacob Alfasi, and the volumes of Oral Law, the *Mishnayot*, which had been purchased when Father was still single and had his own name stamped on them. They are obscured by the huge black rectangles of the *Shulhan Arukh* and the halakhic commentary of *Meginnei Eretz*, Lvov Press, and those, too, bear my father's name. The sacred books, the *seforim*, old and new, are arrayed in black ranks on the three middle shelves, like a rabbinical delegation anxiously reporting to a ruler in whose honor they have donned their shiny, black, silk Sabbath kaftans (*bekeshes*), instead of their everyday, coarse black *kapottes*.

On the shelf above the "greats" are their colleagues, also veiled in black but of more modest proportions: volumes of the *Humash* – the Pentateuch; *Mikraot Gedolot* – the Bible with multiple commentaries, and with the biblical commentary of the Malbim (Meir Leibush ben Yehiel Mikhal); the many orders of the *Aggadah* series of *Ein Ya'akov*, as well as an older edition of the same in three volumes; and two volumes of *Midrash Rabbah*. Near these stand the honorable prayer books (*mahzorim*) for the High Holy Days, in the Ashkenazi version, and the two-part "thesaurus" of prayers in the Sephardi version, *Ozar Tefillot*, printed by the Rom Widow and Brothers in that notorious year of 1914; they were given to Father as a wedding gift, two weeks before the shots rang out in Sarajevo. Father enjoyed the special communion with the Sephardi prayers, especially when the cantor and his choir excelled themselves in filling the air of the synagogue with their accomplishments. How wonderful a refuge the prayers proved to be from the coloratura of the songsters! More than prayers, they were a treasure of commentary and background with which Father could sit back comfortably, while the cantor delivered his idle trills and tremolos and, as Father put it, "aimed his prayer at the audience rather than at our Father in Heaven, thereby diverting the congregation's attention from the text to his own operatic talents as tenor."

All these books, and dozens more like them, represented to me "Father's world" – the Jewish heritage down the generations. whereas Mother's world denoted all that was foreign: Polish, German and French literature. Despite Polish-German hostility, here are gal-

lants of Polish prose and poetry nestled on a shelf shared with
such German muses as Goethe, Schiller, Herder, Lessing and Heine.
All of them preening in ostentatious bindings, their titles stylishly
stamped in Gothic gold letters. Against them and on a separate
shelf, a row of French writers have dug in their heels, outfitted in
thin paper ("typical of the miserly French," Father gibed), and requiring the ministrations of the Engelberg bindery downtown, to
also dress them in black. Even though the new covers were blank
and stripped of both title and grace, they nevertheless achieved
a sort of balance and I was glad to see that the "French" were no
longer eclipsed by the haughty "Germans." Also arrayed there in
case of need were Langenscheidt dictionaries for a variety of languages, hefty midgets in blue binding. All these (in Mother's elo-
quent phrase) "flew the flag of the wide world" and, through them,
she, high priestess of the shrine of that world, conveyed some of
"Japheth's beauty to the tents of Shem."

Between the sacred works defined as Father's sphere and designated by all (in Ashkenazi pronunciation, of course) as *"seforim,"*
and Mother's realm characterized by "foreign" alphabets – an in-
termediate block early on established residence on the shelves. The
language was Hebrew but the contents – secular. Most of these were
literary works, including both translations of general literature and
original Hebrew compositions, whether Enlightenment and na-
tional-revivalist writings, or the fruit of the first generation in the
new Eretz Israel. Next to these was the academic library: Hebrew
linguistics, Jewish history, philosophy and essays. How often I wondered which of my parents had been the moving force behind this
section of the library. After all not only Father, but Mother, too, was
fluent in Hebrew and an ardent champion of both the language and
literature. With obvious pride she would point to selected works
that she had bought prior to her marriage from the Hebrew bookseller in Krakow (Tarnów's Hebrew bookshop only opened in 1925).
She was especially fond of the ten dark blue volumes of Graetz's

Jewish History in Sheffer's translation, and the complete works and translations of David Frischmann, embossed in an old, gold hue with the figure of a sphinx, the upper part of which took the form of a bare-breasted woman. But apart from the early acquisitions which left no doubt as to the buyer's identity, I failed in my attempts to draw a clear dividing line between the books that Mother had planted in the chest since her marriage, and those that Father had added to the modern Hebrew library.

Only with the passage of time was I to realize that things cannot be separated as simply as it had seemed to me initially, and that the differences reflected by the two types of literature were clearly not confined to the bookcase, but represented a clash between the two parents as to the kind of home each wished to have. Only then was I to appreciate the puzzle of joining two cultures, when each was fated to be shouldered by one spouse alone; like a flesh burn was the wrestling, and as deep as an ancient well the pain, and darker than night the secret. It is a riddle worthy, perhaps, of taking its place alongside "the three or four baffling mysteries," that confounded even King Solomon, with that wisest of all men finding no answer (*Book of Proverbs* 30:18–19).

Since then, down all the roads that I have walked, I have carried with me a palpable sense of joy and pain, as it was both my fate and privilege to combine within myself the two opposing worlds of my parents. For though they were joined together and dwelt side by side all their lives, they never really achieved a true bonding of the spirit. Whereas I, inside myself, am able to sustain them in peace, merging them into my personality in complete and lasting harmony.

The bookcase! A mine of unfathomable depths that again and again continued to surprise, divulging its mysteries to all visitors. For behind the front row of books, two additional rows hid in the depths, invisible ranks filling the unseen space of six out of the nine shelves. (Only on the middle three shelves did the large tomes not allow room for additional rows of books.)

Little by little, curiosity whetted my appetite and lured my hand to invade the world behind the front rows and expose its treasures. Based on experience as a boy, I knew that there was no better time than the week before Passover for so thrilling a rendezvous: that week, all the books would be taken from the shelves to the balcony for their annual airing, which conveniently happened to coincide with the commandment of *bi'ur hametz* – the removal of unleavened bread. And the All-Merciful One in His kindness would shield the books and stay the rain on those days, protecting them from dampness or harm.

The yearly book-cleaning campaign in which the entire family took part, was conducted, of course, under Mother's baton. At a signal from her, each child and adult member of the household would take up a position next to a pile of books that happened to be assigned to him or her – whether by chance or by Mother for reasons she kept to herself – and proceed to banish a year's stock of dust. This was done by banging two books together; or by opening and slamming a book shut again until the dust took flight from the nest it had built itself between the pages; or it was done by running a soft, feather brush over leaves turned page by page and then along the outside edges; or by wiping with a dry or damp cloth; or by any number of other means that had become part of household tradition.

And how extraordinary! During this handling, more and more of the books that lay concealed in the belly of the bookcase were revealed to me, a hidden treasure trove unlike any other on earth. And one by one, I would etch their titles in my memory so as to return to them lovingly and page through them once more after the holiday.

The bookcase! A *mélange* of intoxicating bouquets founded on two basic scents: that of the thick paper of old presses, moldy and yellowing from a superabundance of years; and that of the new sheets – pale, devoid of expression – casting envious, gleaming-white glances at the mystery that had been books, until their own time came to be sprinkled with letters and to have literary character sealed by the printing press.

The scents of the different types of paper intermingled with that of the printing dyes which had remained distinct for generations. Thanks to this peculiarity, I learned in time – with eyes shut and by smell alone – to tell where and when each Hebrew book had been fashioned: whether by a Venetian studio four hundred years earlier or by the Rom Widow and Brothers in Vilna at the start of the twentieth century. Maybe it had been born at the press of Menashe Ben-Israel in seventeenth-century Amsterdam; or could it be Piotrków, Poland, or Fuerth, Germany, some two hundred years later? Or was it the fragrance of Eretz Israel that was trapped between its covers to inadvertently disclose the book's esteemed pedigree and crown its makers in laurels of awe?

Into this orgy of bouquets flowed also the aroma of old leathers and fresh glue from Engelberg and other sundry binderies, so that the early ancestors of scent spawned generation after generation of redolent offspring, distinguished from one another by whiff and era. But most powerful of all was the smell of dust. And more extraordinary still, the love of books – which was the very essence of our home – did not flinch at opening its heart even to the dust that enveloped every shelf and every book that stood on it in grainy, gray mantle and, moreover, to glean from it the perfume of fine oil, of nard, saffron and balm of Gilead, which only an initiated few ever had the privilege to inhale.

And so, each book emitted a unique and distinct fragrance – all its own and unlike any other book in the whole world. And this individual bouquet lent it a unique character – a physical nature – different from any of its companions on the shelf. Let it be said once and for all: the paper, dye, print, binding, glue and dust mixed all together in the whole of these components – they, along with the actual contents, of course – are the preeminent anima of the greatest of all human achievements: books!

Indeed, ever since I first discovered the secrets of the bookcase, it has not been my habit to take a book from a shelf and retire with it to a table for leisurely perusal. Rather, I stand leaning on the open shelf for half an hour, an hour, and even longer, holding the book to sense the feel of it, to penetrate beyond the printed letters and embrace the spirit caught between the covers; and all the while I open my lungs to breathe in the scent of it, along with the scents of the books around it, growing giddy on the bouquets...

This attitude towards books which I acquired in my parents' home and which, today, may be described frankly and openly as erotic, has remained with me throughout my life, no matter where I have lived or what I have studied or taught. And in all the libraries in the world where I might find myself standing and leaning on a shelf – be it at Oxford's Bodleian, or London's British Library, or the Marciana of Venice, be it in New York, Athens or Tel Aviv, or the reading room of the National Library on Givat Ram in Jerusalem – I am always reminded of that magical experience, as if I had lived it only yesterday: that unforgettable childhood experience and voyage of surprises into the recesses of the enchanting bookcase that resided in the dimness of the back room of my parents' home.

To my good fortune, several months after I immigrated to Palestine in 1937, my parents hit upon the wonderful idea of sending me most of the "important" books in the chest. (Ah! Where are you, the "unimportant" ones?) These, consequently, were saved from the inferno. This, my only inheritance – and the richest of all imaginable ones – my parents passed on to me.

How fortunate, too, that the shipment reached me before the outbreak of war and has remained with me to this day, despite the vicissitudes of time, wars and wanderings. And here they are, "Father's-and-Mother's-books," arranged in their full sad splendor in Jerusalem – where Father and Mother wished them to be, where Father and Mother hoped to see them again after their own planned immigration. Now, the books stand in my study opposite Mt. Zion and always before me, an open wound, bearing mute witness to a Jewish home that once was and is no more – a home materially poor, but rich in the best and noblest offerings of the human spirit: books.

In the twilight of my days, older now than my parents were then and sated with study and scholarship but never, ever with books, I have no bookcase such as the legendary piece of furniture that stood in my parents' home. Rather, my entire home is one large bookcase – open shelves wrapping themselves around walls from room to room and floor to floor, unhampered by either doors or divisions. And there is not a room in my house whose walls are not upholstered with books, nor a wall in a room that does not emit their strong odor. But the sum total of all the scents of the hundreds and thousands of additional books that I have acquired over the years – including those I myself was privileged to compose – yes, the sum total of all these cannot equal the unique, intoxicating bouquet of Father's books and Mother's books, which have seen me through from infancy to this day.

And with this bouquet in my nostrils I wish to live and create for as long as my breath allows. And with this bouquet, I wish to die when the time comes.

CHESTNUTS OF YESTERYEAR

1926, the year the book begins. The Wróbel children in Tarnów:
Mala (age 7.5) Hesiek (6), Gunia (1)

Time: *Friday noon, the end of summer, 1926*

Place: *The Wróbel home, second floor, Rosner Building, 9 Bóżnic Street, Tarnów – the second largest city in western Galicia*

The Plot: *Six-year-old Hesiek, son of Golda and Aazik Wróbel, is watching his one-year-old sister, who is asleep in the bedroom, the back room of the modest two-room flat. In the front room, which contains the kitchen stove, his mother is busy cooking and baking for the Sabbath. Suddenly, from the top of the clothes cupboard, where three plaster busts stand – Beethoven, Schiller, and Dante – the latter topples onto the floor. The boy is startled, even though he knows that Dante's head has long been fixed back on with glue, having most likely broken off in a previous fall. He calls out to his mother for help, but she either does not hear him or cannot come to his aid just yet, having too much work on her hands. Only after some twenty minutes does she deliver a response from the kitchen: she frees the boy of his babysitting duties and urges him to run down quickly (for the Sabbath will soon begin) to the old chestnut tree in the yard or to the city park to collect chestnuts from the ground. Only old chestnuts that had fallen off the tree the previous autumn can be crushed and made into real glue, having absorbed the damp from the rain and the snow on the ground before slowly drying out in the sun of spring and summer. Relieved of his concern for the baby, the boy bursts outside to look for such chestnuts, singing a song he has just made up:*

> *Glue we need for poor old Dante:*
> *Glue to stick his head back here –*
> *Chestnut glue for poor old Dante,*
> *Chestnuts few of yesteryear...*

Between the boy's initial cry and this final rhyme unfolds the story of the odyssey...

Oh, take me back to my childhood lure,
To days of song and infinite joy,
To golden fields and skies so pure
Beheld in rapture by an innocent boy.

Flourish once more, oh youth of mine,
Like the aurora and its halo that shine!
But can a flower upon hard rock bloom?
Will Sodom revive on its mound of doom?!
                    Saul Tchernichowsky

נא השיבו לי ילדותי
תור־השירים, גיל־עולמים
שדמות־זהב ושמי־טהר
וימות ילד, ילד תמים.

שוב ופרח, אביב ילדותי,
שוב כצפירה תופע בהלה!
אך היפרח צחיח־סלע,
סדום תבנה עלי תלה?!
                    שאול טשרניחובסקי

Polały się łzy me czyste rzęsiste,
Na moje dzieciństwo sielskie, anielskie,
Na moją młodość górną I durną,
Na mój wiek męski, wiek klęski;
Polały się łzy me czyste, rzęsíste.

I shed my tears, demure and pure –
For my childhood's idyll that longs for songs,
For my youthful years, so haughty and naughty,
For my age of manhood, of deeds and defeats –
My tears were flowing purely, demurely....
                    Adam Mickiewicz

— לשוא בלילות
משוע אליך ניבי.
כמו על הר הזיתים אעפיל לעלות
וקברות מעברי נתיבי —
                    רחל

– In vain through the night
My voice beckons you and craves:
As if climbing Mount Olives, the Eternal Rest Site,
With my path lined by graves, none but graves...
                    Rahel

Dante's Head

"Ma-a-a-a. The "head fell down again!"

From the all-purpose room at the front of the flat – a quarter of which was reserved for the kitchen and stove where glowing "embers merrily jumped – there was no response. As usual, the sun-drenched room benevolently continued to gaze from the heights of the second story onto the inner courtyard of the large block of flats, indifferent to the cry of panic coming from the adjacent room in the back. Only the Sabbath pot, which rested on one of the four stove burners, sounded up-and-down bursts and the bubbling of boiling water, letting you know that the chicken wallowing in its soup was desperately banging on the lid to escape, and that even if the fowl suffered a momentary defeat and retreated, it would gird its loins and try again.

In the back room, which contained only beds and cabinets, the boy stopped leafing through the book that he had pulled from the bookcase, as if he had frightened himself with the cry he delivered into the world. Unlike the front room, which radiated daylight, the back room was always dim because of the tall chestnut tree that rose from yard to roof and, half-way up, invaded the second-story window and painted the walls a dark green. But despite his sudden panic, the boy continues to do his duty, shooting frequent glances at the crib that holds the baby he was charged to watch. In vain, however, he waits for Mother's response and shifts his disappointed eyes between crib and doorway to that bright rectangular space between the two rooms whose double doors were always left open.

From his position near the bookcase on the left wall of the bedroom he cannot catch sight of Mother's movements, nor can he direct his view inward to the kitchen corner where the stove stands. But he knows instinctively that she is there, across the threshold, and that since her return from the market she has been busy with preparations for the Sabbath meal. And he also knows that the fire-stung victim of the pot and pillory of blazing metal has realized its fate and, with one last effort, beat its head in suicide against the armored lid that closed it in – and was silent.

For the past seven weeks, since the start of school vacation this summer of 1926, the boy has, of his own free will, stayed home every Friday morning to watch his little sister, while Mother gets ready for the Sabbath; and – just by the way – uses this opportunity to both rummage through the books and avidly follow her every movement in the kitchen, attending to or guessing at every stage of the work in progress. His sympathy – openly and without reserve – belongs to the repast trapped in the metal vise. The more time passes, the more this spontaneous, innocent championship somehow turns into personal involvement and solidarity with a fate hard and bitter. All too physically, he senses the bursts and bubbles emanating from the pot like the din of a lost campaign engraving zigzags on his chest. His mind's eye subjects the entire business of food preparation from any living thing to monstrous images against which he evokes an equally monstrous imagination of protest, crying out against the murder of any of God's creatures – the kind of cry that floats across to him night after night before sleep from the gaping black mouth of the skull-headed creature in a work by Edvard Munch. Mother cut out the picture from an exhibition catalog she had once purchased in Vienna and pasted it onto one of the square panes of the bookcase door, where it gapes to this day.

The boy remembers only too well when he first became aware of the fact of animal bloodshed for the satisfaction of man's appetite and how upset he had been. It had happened almost a year earlier, at the end of September 1925, just as his first month in the first grade was drawing to a close. The torrid air of Yom Kippur eve hung motionless between the apartment buildings of the Jewish neighborhood in Tarnów as he and Reb Aazik, his father, walked down to the river, holding in their hands a pair of *Kapparot* ("atonement") chickens, half dead from heat and fear. "How nice it is here," he murmured to his father as they left behind the stifling city. The boy was hard put to understand why his father did not share this enthusiasm. After all, the breeze was so cool and refreshing and lapped at their faces as they made their way down the path to the community-run poultry slaughterhouse. It was on the banks of the Wątok, not far from the stone bridge on which they (and other Jews like them) had eight days earlier observed the custom of *Tashlikh*, symbolically casting their sins into the water.

So kind and friendly was the breeze that it made you want to drop down onto the thick grass that grew wild on the riverbanks, for a respite from the heat of the day. Except that after a few moments, the boy dimly sensed what Reb Aazik had known from the start: the breeze was plainly teasing them, and the initial gust, that had so charmed the boy with its coolness and freshness, only masked a heavy trail of stench in its wake. The meaning of the stench and its source the boy was to discover only when he reached the building and stepped inside.

Since that lone visit to the slaughterhouse he seemed to choke in suffocation at the very sight of a festive dinner table bedecked with dishes prepared from living things in honor of the Sabbath or holidays. Here, look – here is the Lord of Vengeance, rising out of the reeking bog of the dark Wątok River that laboriously wends its way along the southern rim of his city, Tarnów, with its filthy waters seeping into and poisoning the town arteries. Here, here he is, the Lord of Vengeance, with the butcher's knife he plucked from the hands of Yekel the *shoyhet* (ritual slaughterer) at the community slaughterhouse. The white cloth laid on the Sabbath table grows redder, redder … bloodier…

Thus, entirely on his own, the boy arrived at a belief in the superiority of vegeterianism, even before he had an inkling that there was either such a philosophy or practice. Ah, but all his attempts to deny himself meat was met with no success, causing him frustration and shame. He longed to be a true vegetarian, but managed it only for brief spells, ending in a renewed sense of failure and despair. In this troubled state, he tried to imagine how Millek Lauber would find his way out of the difficulty. *It's all relative and depends on the perspective* – he heard himself repeating the familiar doctrine uttered by his neighbor from the same floor, who was five years his senior. Yes, there was a certain convenience and comfort in this simplistic Lauberian version of the theory of relativity, especially since the eleven-year-old philosopher who preached it was, for the child (the smallest boy in the apartment block), a friend and guide – an older brother in times of woe.

All at once, the boy feels a sense of relief and dual sweetness – a sober wisdom and acceptance of the facts of life – descend on him with all the serenity of a lullaby; almost as though the prisoner of the pot, sentenced to boil, had never uttered the cries of rebellion or groans of defeat that only a little while earlier had fermented the boy's blood as if a mighty battle raged between the angels of light and the angels of darkness. Now his ears hear only the tinny clatter of the lid itself: merry, joyous, heartwarming, as if a playful steam hand were amusing itself with the lid, bouncing it to a steady rhythm, up and down, down and clash, like the makeshift percussion instruments used at weddings by the brothers Mendel and Avrum Blatt.

The two Blatt brothers, tailor apprentices and *klezmers* from the working class neighborhood of Grabówka in the eastern part of town – along with their two other brothers and one of their three sisters, all of whom made up the famous Blatt Quintet – delighted audiences with their tricks and tunes by looping plates of tin and brass and lids of colored enamel pots, around a high pole. By stepping on a hidden pedal, they would set into motion an integrated system of springs – their own ingenious invention – causing the plates and lids to clash merrily and noisily like cymbals, up and down, up and down, while leaving their hands free to draw a bow across the strings of a violin or run their fingers along the keys of a clarinet. In this fashion they produced and delivered into the world the sweet and poignant melodies that earned them fame throughout Tarnów's Jewish community and even beyond, from Dąbrowa and Żabno in the northern part of the province, to Tuchów and Ciężkowice in the south, and from Pilzno and Dębica on the main road east to as far west as Wiśnicz and Bochnia on the outskirts of Kraków. The troupe even found itself hired for functions outside of the working class and outside of the Jewish community, with non-Jews, too, often calling on their talents for weddings.

"Maaaaaaaaa…"

The boy rouses himself from the waves of calm that had suffused him, almost drowning the reason for his cry in the first place – "The head is on the floor again!"

With a firm and sharp motion he waves away the memory of the last wedding, whose image lingers self-indulgently on his lashes, refusing to vacate the stage like the others – a merry Blatt Quintet celebration that had taken place about two months previously in the Schlissel flat on the floor below. Without waiting for a reply, he raises his voice for yet a third time towards the kitchen:

"Maaaaaaaaa..."

As was his habit of late, he finds himself hanging on to the word with true devotion and unrelieved longing. Choosing a high note from the cluster of notes attached to the roof of his palate, he rolls it forward to the front of his mouth so as to clad the first syllable in it, and draws it out soul-expiringly, just as he does with the *Ehaaad* [One] in *"Krishme,"* that is, the *Kriyas Shema* of the morning and evening prayers. Then, by bouncing the "a" of the second syllable, he sends it dribbling impishly toward Mother so that it may roll and land in her loving and mollified lap. A strange, sweet sense sets his flesh tingling, spreading through his whole body to the very fingertips. He is baffled by his reaction to the mere sound "Ma," which overzealously produces and invades his limbs with a sharp, unfamiliar excitement and a pungent potion of pleasure. Or, perhaps, to the very defiance of one of the explicit rules Mother had laid down for the entire household, namely that she was not to be addressed by any nicknames or other forms of endearment, no matter how disguised! Ah, how sweet the forbidden trill in his form of address to her! And what's more, to his own surprise, he finds that as blatant as his disobedience may be – he is not sorry, no, no, he is not sorry at all!

CHAPTER ONE

In Bed at Night

1

T HE ABSOLUTE BAN applied by Mother on displays of affection within the family left no room for compromise. Under the puritan regime that Golda Wróbel instituted, once the children were out of swaddling clothes, there was never again any hint of a hug or kiss within the home. "It is not proper for children of your age," she would check the six-year-old boy or his seven-and-a-half-year-old sister when they clung to her skirts in sudden fear or the desire for a moment's coddling, or they asked to join her in bed on a Sabbath morning, as they had done before the baby was born. Moreover, she rejected all the Polish or Yiddish names of endearment common among Jewish families in Galicia, allowing the children to address her solely by the rather coarse and anemic twin syllables "Ma-ma."

"Love has no need to fly flags," she retorted with typical finality to the criticism of her younger sister, Zippora, who found it difficult to reconcile the two forms of behavior that reigned in her sister's home: on the one hand, a tough outer shell and the strong arm with which Golda conducted family affairs; on the other, an exquisite lattice work of warmth and loving concern for her children and home. Zippora felt her misgivings doubly keenly, as she was a guest in her sister's home. After the death of their father, Zvi-Hersch Weinman, in Tarnów in 1920, she accompanied her mother and two brothers to Boston, regarding it as her duty as the unwed sister. The trouble was, that as a young woman of nineteen, she had already drunk the wine of Eastern European radicalism as embodied by the Bolshevik Revolution. This ideology had been tempered in her heart both by the hopeful fragrance of Redemption, borne then on the wings of the Balfour Declaration and British conquest of Eretz Israel, and the quickening scent of pioneering idealism, which the trailblazers of the Third Aliyah had translated into reality.

Little wonder then, that the attempt to transplant her to American soil failed. She was shocked by the unbridled incitement of the American government and press, and by public hysteria against militant labor unions and immigrant communities – incitement that reached its peak in the famous Boston trial of Sacco and Vanzetti. Zippora returned to Tarnów in 1923 to be welcomed with open arms into her sister's home. Her basic lack of sympathy, however, for the strict discipline she witnessed in that home, and Golda's refusal to respond to her criticism, soon drove her out. Within days she had rented a room of her own at the Burek, the lower market at the foot of the hill of historical Tarnów. As a result, the earliest scene to be etched on the boy's memory was of sitting on "Aunt Zippora's window sill," and gazing at the tumult of the marketplace, unfurled like a brilliant carpet across the square below.

Still, Zippora managed to live in her own room at the Burek only briefly, for, in 1924 her dream came true: she immigrated to Palestine and joined Kibbutz Beit Alfa in the eastern Jezreel Valley. As part of this idealistic company of young people who just marked their second anniversary of settling on the land, she hoped to realize the social values she had seen trampled in America and, at the same time, to take part in the Redemption of the Jewish People in their own land.

But her body could not support the climate of Palestine at the time, and she moved to Vienna with her life partner, Tula Koch, until the Anschluss uprooted them once again and returned them to Eretz Israel in 1938, where Golda's son and daughter now awaited them. All this time, Golda kept an anxious eye on her sister's travels and temporary resting places. The wounds left by old arguments had healed and shed their scars, and the love between the two sisters continued to blossom as before; indeed, to grow stronger, watered now by longing and distance.

"Love exists without words and on its own strength," Golda continued to challenge likewise the frank and daring admonitions of Irena, who came on her first visit to Tarnów since emigrating to America. She came in the spring of 1925 for the first birthday of Shulamitka (abridged to Mitka) – the eldest child of her brother, Dr. Yeshayahu Feig, and his wife, Rivka. She also attended the birthday party of Golda's younger daughter in August 1925, bestowing on the child a silver spoon similar to the one she had bought for Mitka. Disagreements this time lacked the personal rancor that had characterized clashes with Zippora, since Irena backed up her arguments against Golda's stern order not by getting mad as Zippora had, but with erudite discourses (punctuated now and then by an impressive Yankee "yeah!") regarding the progressive educational approaches developed in the United States, especially John Dewey's New Pedagogy and teachings on children's rights. Although Golda voiced resentment at the words – not necessarily because of their gist but because "they were said in the presence of children," (something she found hard to accept, which for Irena was a "matter of principle") – her instinctive appreciation of the new "Western" trends left her with a sense of respect for Irena's opinions and motives. Nevertheless, there was no relaxation of the house "rules," which Golda continued to enforce out of a profound sense of inner conviction.

Mother's word was law in her home, and there was no court of appeal. Only the baby, yes, the one at whose crib the boy-babysitter casts alarmed looks from his post at the bookcase – the baby who just this month turned one year old – she alone was exempt from the "rules," the duty of restraint applying neither to her nor those handling her. She was named Feige, after her great-grandmother, that woman of valor who, four generations earlier rolled up her sleeves to work alongside Reb Moishe Gokhban in the running of a distillery and inn in the village of Storzhov, on the plain of south Volhynia. Both were entrusted to them on the basis of an *arenda* (concession) from the village squire, Count Potocki, as was the way in those days. But not even this legendary woman, in all one hundred and seven years of her existence, had ever been awarded any sort of pet names, whereas her great-granddaughter, the only female in all the clan to be so "honored," had an affectionate diminutive tacked on to her from the very start: hardly an hour old and little Feige became Feigeleh and, then, under the influence of Polish, Feigusia.

Yet, as a dark gleam began to blaze more deeply in her eyes, and the pink flush of infancy merged with the green-gray-silver olive complexion of some former Mediterranean incarnation, as fresh black jetted her soft hair and wrapped the brown dusk of her pupils in a fan of long lashes, letting a veil of Jewish sadness descend on her face, so the name evolved to Feigunia, which, she herself later shortened to Gunia. And so it stayed.

What was true of her name, was true also of all the other manifestations of love connected with her. Here, too, the reins were slackened and freedom of expression swept the entire household in an enthralling tidal wave. As if by magic, it soon became clear to everyone that the hugs and kisses, nonsense words and indulgent cackles showered upon Gunia in public and so unstintingly, were not meant for her alone, even though heaven and earth will testify that she was worthy of every single one of them on her own merits. The truth was that the daily congregation around her crib served as a mailbox, collecting and delivering missives of love from and to every member of the family, and illuminating the home in a glow of affection.

2

The boy can't remember when exactly he resolved to get around the rule of "Don't call me Mamaleh" and "Don't call me Mamusiu." Actually, no special decision was necessary, since in his heart of hearts he had never consented to the rule and simply obeyed it outwardly. There was nothing for it but to wait for a ripe moment to present itself: a breach in his mother's defenses which would enable the "right word" to issue forth from hiding and turn things around.

He does, however, remember clearly the circumstances surrounding the moment the breach was revealed. As is so often the case, it, too, came about suddenly and by chance and was no more than a trifle; nevertheless, from the moment it was laid bare – a moment firm in his mind – all the laws of Creation changed and a great light burst forth!

It happened at the end of the first half of the summer of 1925, when Gunia was born. The last summer of complete freedom – the freedom of childhood which is set aside for play and fun. For the Lord of Time, as he was wont to do, had already laid at the bend in the road an inescapable ambush for the start of September – the First Grade of elementary school – with all that was exciting and alluring about it, and all that was frightening and constricting. Alas, in precisely this summer of climax, the vacation plans to which the children had so looked forward popped like a bubble and the entire family stayed cooped up at home through the heat of summer. Mother, hampered by her final months of pregnancy, could not take her son and daughter on vacation to Rabka – a brook-filled, sun bathed, lush resort in the Carpathian Mountains – as she had the previous year, and the one before that.

"No matter, Rabka will wait for us two years," she tried to placate the children, promising that in 1927, two years after giving birth, she would take them – all three of them! – to Rabka. She promised without truly appreciating what she was doing. She promised, forgetting that man is not the master of his fate and cannot make long-term commitments.

Meanwhile, all of the neighborhood friends, excited by the upcoming start of school, set out with their parents for a variety of vacation spots. Some went to Ciężkowice and the popular Pleśna, some went as far as the picturesque Poprad River on the Slovakian border, and some to fancier locations such as Krynica, Rytro, Piwniczna, Szczawnica and so forth. And so all of a sudden, one day the boy found himself entirely alone. Nor did Mala, his sister and playmate, put herself out to rescue him from solitude. She spent most of her waking hours at her classmate Siańka Berglas's house, whose parents owned a large toy shop on Wałowa Street and lived in the flat above. The Berglas flat had three advantages: it was in the center of town and so more or less equally far to go for all the girlfriends; it was very large and spacious; and it boasted toys the like of which had never been seen in the Wróbel home. For the girls, it had one more important attribute: since Siańka's parents were in the shop from morning to night, the home, relieved of their presence, provided not only a broad arena for play, but complete freedom for gab and gabble, clack and cackle, prate and prattle or just plain chitchat, whereas in the Wróbel home, Mala and her friends would not have been left undisturbed to their pursuits, wasting time in endless fiddle-faddling.

One of these friends Mala's brother remembers with a certain tingle – Tośka Herbstman: a beaming blond sprite, somewhat short and round, but with the face of a ripe peach. More than once, at school, she had looked his way in blatant challenge. He – one grade lower and two years younger – had been thoroughly befuddled and a hot blush rose on his cheeks, which soon doused that impossible liaison.

Another of the friends was Dora Wakspress, whose father owned a glassware shop on Fish Street. How the boy teased her, and, with the cruelty of children, tagged her "Mouse" for her small size and freckles. And how happy he was, seventy years later, to see her face again at the home of her older sister, Giza – albeit only in an old photograph from which merciful time had wiped clean the freckles. Giza and her husband Jucio Prowizor, had joined a Communist cell in Tarnów. Nor was Jucio your typical Jewish armchair Communist, who spent days in endless discussions of the "workers struggle" while "bourgeois" parents financed both studies and a seat at fashionable cafés. When the Communist Party took over Poland under the sway of the Soviet Union, the armchair Communists would cling to their key positions in the state machinery, adopting Polish names such as Malinowski, Szydłowski, etc. Not so Jucio. In his youth he had consciously chosen to be a manual laborer: "Let the *goyim* see that not all Jews are merchants, but know how to work just like them!" Nor did he change his name when Communism came to power; rather, in his official capacity, he was careful not to burden those of his race who had survived the Holocaust. Only towards the end of their days, rejected and betrayed by the regime they had so faithfully served, and mourning a dream that had died, did Jucio and Giza at last find a peaceful haven in Israel – the country they used to discredit as a rotten fruit of colonialism.

Tośka and Dora, both short, were especially dwarfed by a third, tall girl, whose first name had been dropped in favor of Flauma (abbreviating her unpronounceable surname Flaumenhaft). Enhancing the illusion of height was a mop of black hair that looked as if it was stranger to the teeth of a comb. Its ends, wiry like the tufts of a rope, did not, like plaits, fall softly onto her neck and shoulders, but stood up straight in wild abandon, curbed and checked only by the beret of the school uniform.

Most of Mala's hours during those long summer days were spent in the company of her three friends – all of whom were to perish seventeen years later in the Holocaust – and of their hostess, Siańka Berglas, a pretty, self-indulgent child who would later set up a home and family on Haifa's Mt. Carmel. Only when she returned in the evenings would Mala spare an hour or so for her younger brother. The boy, however, suddenly cut off from his friends, soon learned to appreciate the unexpected compensation that solitude had dropped into his lap: a warm and genuinely increasing closeness with his parents.

In the summer, Father had time on his hands. His pupils were off with their parents on vacation, leaving Reb Aazik with a mere handful who had to be prepared for their *bar-mitzvahs* in the hot months of Av and Elul. Nor had the top students left; three evenings a week, without any thought of reward, Reb Aazik sits and reads with these from the Rambam (Maimonides). The rest of the time is however free to devote to his son. Every morning the two of them sit down at the large table in the front room for a three-hour lesson in Bible and *Gemara* – practicing what they have studied that summer in the tractate of *Berakhot*: "He who teaches his son Torah is like one of its recipients from Mount Horev (Sinai)". And in the afternoons, Father would continue to instruct his son informally, while they went out for a walk. All this was in total contrast to the normal order of community education. Just as in secular schooling Aazik and Golda had advanced the entry of their five-year-old son into the First Grade by a whole year (or two, according to sticklers), so these two pressed ahead with sacred scholarship as well. They rewrote the counsel of *Pirkei Avot* (The Sayings of the Fathers): "At age five, reading and *Mikra* (Bible), at ten, *Mishna* (Oral Law)," and read instead: "At age three, reading and *Mikra*, at five, *Mishna* and initiation into a page of *Gemara*". From here on, they resolved, age was to pose no obstacle.

Only at the end of July, after a month's absence, did neighbors young and old begin to stream home from vacation spots in an ever surging tide. Latches and locks were removed from doors, windows and shutters flung wide open, and the sound of women's voices filled the air and courtyard as they regaled one another, from floor to floor, with reports of their adventures or, Heaven forfend, with heartbreaking laments about illnesses, accidents and other mishaps that had marred their vacations. Even sooner, and with more rejoicing, contact was renewed among the children and daily games and chatter were picked up where they had left off. Just as things had been before the break, they took turns playing on one another's home turf, in this courtyard, or in front of that gate; it took no more than a day or two and everything was back to normal.

That evening, too, at the end of July, 1925, was no different from those that preceded the vacation. In the shade of the old chestnut tree, in the courtyard of the large apartment block – Rosner House, at 9 Bóżnic Street, where the Wróbels lived on the second floor – the reunion of the neighborhood gang proceeded as usual almost to the very end. But just before parting, a surprising development took place. Engrossed in the final games of the evening, the boy heard, from the heights of the second floor, the cry, "Hesiek!" – a mother's normal call, summoning her child back to the nest at the close of day. In the same moment, at the end of the long balcony, in the rectangular space of the corner flat window, two shoulders appeared, topped by headful of hair: Golda's eyes raked the downstairs courtyard for her son.

"I'm here, Ma-aa, playing with the children," the boy turned his head upwards, towards the window that had emitted the cry. *Why is she calling me so soon* – he wondered – *there is still about half an hour of daylight left?* The next instant, however, he correctly assessed the situation: *if Mother is calling from the front room, it means she has just finished cooking, and supper is ready.*

In his mind's eye he sees the weekday evening scene at the Wróbels: the center is taken up by a large, plain wooden table, unadorned, resting against the wall opposite the door to the flat.

This all-purpose table, to the left of the stove, is where the boy sits every morning with his father during summer vacation, with the open *Gemara* before them, and where every Friday, Mother kneads the dough for her famous Sabbath *challes*, which have earned acclaim in the whole neighborhood. Now, this ordinary weekday evening, the table is covered with a white, vinyl cloth and set with four plates.

Father sits on the left side of the table: Mother, after serving the food, will sit down opposite, on the right; nearer the stove so as to reach the dishes more easily. He, the son, and his sister, Mala, sit along the width of the table, their backs to the door and facing the calendar map of Eretz Israel for the Hebrew year 5685, which was produced for the charitable fund of Rabbi Meir Baal HaNess. The calendar – a single large sheet attached to the wall – contains all the days of the current year. The boy's eyes, which have obsessively gotten used to reading all printed texts placed before him, even if they are the same ones day after day, knows the calendar down to the last detail, including the pictures of the four Holy Cities – Jerusalem, Safed, Hebron and Tiberias – at its four corners, and the Wailing Wall at its center. The Wall's stones sprout five imaginary, tall cypress trees and Golda will one day embroider this scene onto a red velvet *tefillin* bag for her son's phylacteries when he reaches *bar-mitzvah* age. "It's a good thing that *Rosh HaShana* is so close, and the calendar will be changed," the boy consoles himself, his eyes long bored with the repeated study of the same picture.

A second cry from the window confirms the boy's calculations: "Come home, Hesiek" – this time a command that brooked no argument – "Come up at once. The food is on the table. Father is in a hurry." Father was giving his lesson on the Rambam to his special group this evening, and everyone knew that Father did not like to be late for his classes. "Coming, Ma-aa, right away." Still, it takes another moment or two to part from the other children, after which he turns on his heels to race towards the stairs.

3

But he is stopped in his tracks by a sense that something strange and embarrassing has crept into the words of parting. And he has no doubt that the change concerns him personally, something that he either said or did in the last minute. The jeering glances of his three companions pursue him, piercing his back like iron spikes. Deciding on an instant counter-attack, he returns to the spot where he left them standing, bayonets in his eyes challenging them to a duel: "What's the joke, boys?"

Oddly enough, they are not put off by his head-on reaction, nor do they wipe the hint of mockery from their eyes. And instead of answering, they release a counter volley of their own, as if he owed them something: "What did you call your mother? 'Ma-aa'?" began Idek Weiss, who lived one block over, on Nowa Street. Despite his slight build, Idek was a year and a half older than Hesiek, but the two would stride together through four years of Hebrew elementary school and eight years of Hebrew high school, even belong to the same group in the Zionist-Socialist youth movement of Gordonia. They would found a new movement paper in Polish, *Naszym Torem* ("On Our Track"), and fill its columns with their own compositions. Idek was to immigrate to Palestine a year after Hesiek and study at the Haifa Technion.

"You called her 'Ma-aa'?" Idek now repeated, flashing some prominent teeth and hooting. The laughter shook his body so that it was hard to see how such a skinny vessel could contain so huge a quantity of giggles and not burst.

"You called her 'Ma-aa'?" seconded Monek Abramowicz, also a year older than Hesiek and living some three hundred yards away in the corner building. Monek, too, would spend years in the same class as Hesiek and Idek at the Hebrew elementary school, but in the end would drop out. A typical hanger-on was Monek: he would never dare start anything on his own, nor offer an independent opinion, but always follow someone else's lead. Still, he acquitted himself as a mouthpiece with such admirable conviction that he – and his audience – seemed truly to believe him to be the prime mover. Now, he stood safely behind Idek and, like an echo, released his own version: "Tell the truth, Hesiu" – he feigned curiosity – "The name you called your mother, is that her real name or did you dream it up?" The words are delivered to Hesiek, but his eyes remain fixed on Idek, as if waiting for a sign of how far to go.

The boy does not yet understand before what or whom he is supposed to defend himself, nor what cause he is meant to champion, but, should a fight be forced on him, his weapons are drawn and ready: "To whom it may concern," he deliberately resorts to formal address, "I call my mother 'Mama.' Plain and simple. It's my mother and I have every right to call her how I please."

Don't apologize! – an inner voice eggs him on – *You don't owe anyone anything! Attack is the best defense; scoff and give them all you've got!* "And what should I call her?" He obeys the secret voice. "Maybe, like you, I should call her 'Mamusiu,' which rhymes so nicely with 'siusiu'?" (A word parents whispered into a child's ear at bedtime, to get the bladder emptied before sleep).

In utter disdain, Hesiek proceeds to act out the regular nighttime ritual that takes place in every household:

– "Mamusiu, I don't want siusiu"
– "For pity's sake, do your siusiu"
– "I have no siusiu, Mamusiu"
– "Nu, siusiu now, siuś, siuśśś..."

He concludes with a stirring rendition of the sound made by drops cascading on the chamber pot.

"There's nothing wrong with 'Mama,'" Zyga Koszer interrupts the teasing. As usual, he chose his words carefully and knew how to deliver them with proper emphasis, as if the fate of the world hung on them. Zyga, who lived on the actual street of the nearby barracks, had already turned seven and treated the age difference between himself and his friends with the solemnity it deserved, even though in September, he, too, like the younger three, was to enter the First Grade at the "Safa Berura" Hebrew Elementary School. This gravity of Zyga's – where did it come from? Did it stem from a compulsive sense of mission inherited from his mother, the most energetic Zionist activist in town, member of every committee and delegation, orator at every assembly, hand in every project, so long as it served the Jewish and Zionist cause? Or was it the reverse: did it reflect a profound humility and shy integrity, qualities no doubt stemming from his father – a manufacturer and wholesaler of men's shirts on Pod Dębem ("Under the Oak") Square – a dead-eyed man in the shadow of a strong, energetic woman? Either way, Zyga's earnestness was sincere, never eliciting the ridicule that could greet a child pretending to be an adult. In later years too his freckled face would wear a cloud of constant sorrow that, from chin to hairline, hardened into an expression of untold suffering. This, at a certain stage in high school, would be considered thoroughly romantic, and be referred to – in the vernacular, of course, and with an important tone as – *Weltschmerz*.

These four friends would travel quite a way together in Hebrew school but, as they grew older, their ways would increasingly part ideologically: Zyga and Monek were to join the youth movement of the General Zionists, while Idek and Hesiek looked down on this party as *petit bourgeois* and joined the Labor Israel camp of Gordonia to hold forth loftily about socialism and self-realization. Paradoxically, it was "bourgeois" Zyga who quit school and, with typical serious-mindedness, learned a trade in anticipation of the Koszer family's immigration to Palestine in 1936. And in his Eretz Israel reincarnation, from his first year in the country until his death, he continued, as in his youth, to relate to work with awe as the supreme Zionist value, and by the sweat of his brow drew his bread from the earth on the modest farm that he and his parents established in Hadera.

"'Mama' is fine. Absolutely fine!" Zyga said again, calmly. By so doing he reproached his two friends for invading Hesiek's private domain, while he, in turn, turned aside the latter's challenge to all-out war.

"'Mama' is fine. One hundred percent fine!" He reiterated for the third time with authority, as if he alone had the right to judge and that was that. "'Mama' is natural and fitting. You want it with trills, that's fine, too; without trills, also good. The trouble is, Hesiu, you don't say 'Mama'. You probably want to say it and are sure that you do say it but, in fact, what comes out of your mouth is a silly combination of two syllables – 'Ma-aa' – which you obviously didn't mean. After all, you don't hear yourself, only other ears can hear you properly: our ears, for example. Or your mother's. And her ears, like ours, hear 'Ma-aa', which has no meaning – 'Ma-aa', and nothing else."

The boy was left open-mouthed and speechless with amazement. Zyga's words were so novel and unexpected, yet so convincing, that he didn't dare interrupt, but waited eagerly for him to continue. Zyga sensed the uncomfortable situation the youngest of his friends had gotten himself into. In yet another display of wisdom beyond his years, he decided to forgo all triumph and leave Hesiek a friendly opening for an honorable retreat.

"You don't have to take my word for it, Hesiu," he said in a half-whisper, with appeasing delicacy. "Get someone older than us – Millek Lauber, for example – let him decide. Ok?" And without waiting for an answer, he signalled to Monek to run to the Lauber flat (next door to the Wróbels on the second floor of the building) and fetch Millek.

"It may well be that nobody's at fault" – Millek's common sense sentiments were aimed at finding a solution without dealing in right or wrong. "The truth is, that when you come to say 'Mama' in everyday, normal speech, your lips, which form the first 'M', don't manage to close together again, so that without noticing, the second 'm' is swallowed up and out comes 'Ma-aa'. You should practice in front of a mirror. Roll the word on your tongue, run through the m's on your lips, you'll see."

You could have cut the ensuing silence with a knife. Twilight played with the canopy of the old chestnut, as if seeking to mollify it for the loneliness that would soon visit it when the children went home. *Well, it's worth thinking about,* the boy decided, but obviously this was not the time to test it. *No, not now. I can't stay anymore. Mother is waiting and Father is in a hurry.* And as his friends made their own way home, downcast and silent, as if rebuked, he turned on his heels and without wasting another minute on goodbyes, broke into a sprint – as if running away from something – to fly up the stairs. In seconds his quick footsteps echoed along the second-story railed balcony leading to the corner flat. A door was heard to open, and shut. A forlorn evening stillness descended on the courtyard at 9 Bóżnic Street, and on the whole world.

4

What transpired that evening inside the home, the boy never recalled nor brought up again. All that is known is that, to the surprise of his parents and sister, who had expected a report on his reunion with his friends, it was difficult to get him to say anything. He stared at the wall opposite him, perhaps seeing, perhaps not, the pictures of the four Holy cities in the four corners of the Eretz Israel calendar; perhaps seeing, perhaps not, the five cypress trees rising out of the stones of the Wailing Wall. Without appetite, he bit into the piece of bread before him, so that the *motzi* benediction over bread, which he had mechanically mumbled when he took his place at the table, would not have been in vain. After a while, without having tasted the food or opened his mouth in conversation, he asked permission to go to bed – and before he could even finish reciting a rushed *Krishme* in bed, drained and empty of all thought, he sunk into a deep sleep.

By morning the crisis was over. As if an invisible hand plucked him from the night just as the horn of Brach's brick factory went off. Except that, this time, something is different. The horn does not seem to issue from the high, red factory chimney, visible for miles around, nor does the boy seem to sense it from without. Rather, it is signalling within his own brain – that's where it takes shape, that's where the thousands and thousands of particles come together to form a single unbroken wave of sound and, from there, gain momentum to burst through and pronounce in his own voice from one end of the earth to the other: "That's it! Plain for all to see – the breach!"

Now, as his heralding voice echoes all over town, the horn of Brach's factory is joined by all the many other industries that girdle Tarnów in a red brick belt of toil: another factory for building blocks, founded by the wealthy Jewish industrialist, Reb Szajeh Silberpfenig; the brewery owned by Roman Sanguszko, the town duke; Schwanenfeld's distillery; Hollender's saw-mill; Schantzer and Dagnan's two steam-driven flour mills; and then Dora Fisch's first electric flour mill. Adding to the great bugle cry are the horns of the nail factory and *kopyciarnia* (a plant for wooden lasts), both also owned by Szajeh Silberpfenig. And the chimneys of these factories, and of dozens of smaller ones, emit a lingering toot, their calls intermingling, as if one chimney were telling another: "The breach! The breach! Here is the breach!"

And now the church bells join hands with the factories, opening their mouths in wonder and presiding with the peal of chimes over the factory horns. First and foremost among them is the old Carillon of the cathedral in the town's historic center. This is followed by the pair of merry bells from the twin spires of the Church of the Missionaries, established at the turn of the century at the end of Krakowska Street; and the small impish gong of the old wooden Church of the Virgin Mary on the banks of the miry Wątok River, across from the Jewish slaughterhouse and opposite the old

Christian cemetery. These are joined by the Bernardine bells, whose dull, irritating sound preaches endlessly, like their owner-monks who, in the eighteenth century, cloistered themselves behind a wall at the foot of the historical Tarnów hill. All these together send a festive note to the four corners of the earth, caroling in unison a hymn of joy and cheer: "*Kyrie Eleyson! Kyrie Eleyson!* The breach has been found!"

And they, in turn, are greeted by the choir of the "Great Synagogue," delivering an enthusiastic "Hallelujah" under the baton of Sokołowski and the supervision of Cantor Kamieniecki, while Ephraim Atlas, the neighbor whose voice has not yet broken, as usual cuts the air with his high, virgin soprano, and Rowiński, the thin, old bass, shakes the walls with deep vibratos that sink into the belly and shock the soul. These are answered by the choir of the Jewish Reform Temple, which also includes women (and, some say, even gentiles), to the accompaniment of an organ: "The breach! Look, a breach has been found!"

The breach! It flashes like lightning and fires the boy's imagination. The flame consumes his rest and makes him leap out of bed. Everything is so clear, so ridiculously simple, how is it he had not found the solution on his own? 'Ma-aa'!

'Ma-aa' itself was the breach! It was the ruse he had been looking for! And it had been here all along, within reach, only he hadn't known it. Now that it was exposed, he would apply it consciously, deliberately, and not by an accident of his lips' not closing! If Zyga was right, and this was the name that his mother always heard from her son's mouth without protesting – it opened up a rich range for expressing emotions, without defying Mother's rule not to heap endearments on her.

Indeed, everything, everything, to the limits of the imagination, could be expressed with this one elastic word – whether by lengthening either the first or second syllable, or shortening one and bending the other. Or leading one into the other and sending both off together, be it at a gallop or oh, so slowly; be it by breathing mischief into them or vibrating the vocal chords and squeezing them to tears. Yes, everything could be sounded by this lush treasure of surprising options: from divine craving and longing that soared up, to echoing moans of dejection; from unforgiving anger and rage to the serene greeting of a new morning in Mother's blue eyes.

Except that, now that a way has finally been found to pour out – one-sidedly and without limitation – what he has to say to Mother, he feels no real happiness. The "ruse," for which he has so long prayed and whose discovery so overjoyed him, suddenly seems to him sterile and embarrassing. In the absence of any sign or hint that the message has been received and the gift has pleased, the success of the "ruse" is, at best, partial and, in any case, disappointing. *Love that lacks the openness of response is marred by a deficiency that longs to be repaired* – this truth he would like to explain to Mother, slowly and patiently, as if he were the grown-up and she a little girl needing guidance. *Love needs confirmation, constant reinforcement, feedback, and there is no confirmation, no reinforcement and no feedback except by words or touch.* But the words do not come, and the touch is non-existent. Mother may not have protested, but neither will she respond, and there has not been the slightest sign to tell that she has received the message. And just as Reb Levi-Yitzhik of Berdichev was not granted a response in his famous talks with the Master of the Universe, which thus remained a soliloquy – so, too, the boy, the great grandson of the great grandson of that very Hasidic *Tzaddik's*, and the son of a mother who has sown in him great pride in his lineage – he receives no response to his imaginary, hour-long talks with her, departing his childhood with his secret wishes unfulfilled.

And yet, the many long hours the boy spent in his mother's company during the summer were free of all tension. He was with her for most of the hours of the day – apart from those of his walks or the *Gemara* studies with his father. Indeed new ties were formed between mother and son, strong bonds like the invisible seams she expertly stitched into old garments, laboring by the light of the paraffin lamp long into the night. Just as he drew closer to his father in that summer of 1925, whether through the *Gemara* lessons at the large table or during their candid talks while out walking, so, at the same time, his heart went out to his mother with increasing love and devotion.

Apart from Golda's daily care of the children and routine housework – which she was particularly adept at performing casually and with a dismissive smile, as though no effort were invested and the chores simply "did" themselves – most of her weekdays were filled with activity. Cool mornings would be spent at the Singer sewing machine that Father had presented her upon her pregnancy, whereas in the afternoons she would draw up a chair to the window and, in the brilliant light, lean for hours over her embroidery, a huge biblical Gobelin wall tapestry of "Eliezer and Rebecca," her special project for the last two years, since her son started learning Bible stories. "Look, how pure the golden desert is in sunlight!" She would instruct her son in the blazing colors that she wove into her work, trying to infect him with her own love for golden spaces and involve him in the creative joy of working with colors, as opposed to the gray, erosive, lonely task of mending clothes and socks – a job she put off until the night hours, when only the regular breathing of her sleeping children relieved its monotony. The Gobelin – so she said – would be placed in a gold frame and hung on the bedroom wall at the head of the two parental beds, so that the golden glitter of the biblical desert she embroidered and the luster of the golden frame would ease the dimness of the room, shadowed by the chestnut tree that blocked the sun. The Gobelin, her crowning achievement, was in fact highly original and radiated a simple warmth, even though its light did not have the power to dissolve the gloom. In any case, she did well to stick to her original drawing rather than be diverted by Doré's etching, a reproduction of which she discovered in an early edition of *Sippurei ha-Mikra* (Bible Tales) by Ravnitzki and Bialik.

Amazingly enough, between one chore and another, she also found time to prepare for the baby's arrival and initial needs. Here, however, in unusual departure from habit, she went out of her way to involve her daughter and son – no doubt under the direct influence of Irena (who advocated "children's rights") – and fostered their equal participation in the home. Thus, by working together, they aired the diapers and tiny garments of previous births that had been carefully laid away, washed and painstakingly folded. These had waited five years, concealed in the old wooden chest with the curved top and heavy iron hasps – the coffer that stood in the kitchen corner and had been a gift from her grandparents to her own parents. Golda's children loved to inhale the cloud of white naphthalene bursting from the cask when its three locks were opened – as if it contained the incense of enchanted, legendary worlds that had long hidden inside. As for Golda, the coffer offered up the sweetness of childhood at her grandparents' home in Storzów, the Ukrainian village where she had been born. Alongside the "native" articles to enjoy renewed use, was a bundle of "American clothing," the gift of Aunt Pearl from Pennsylvania, wife of Bereleh-Ben, the first of Aazik's brothers to set out for America. She had no more use for baby clothes – Pearl wrote to Golda in faltering Yiddish – for since the birth of her fifth child, Hanna, in 1920, she had been warned not to fall pregnant again.

5

"Let's paint the bedroom in bright colors for the baby," Mother suggested about a month before Gunia's birth. The bulging waistline left by her two previous pregnancies did not bode well as this term drew to a close – she mumbles to the oval mirror on the clothes cupboard, despairing of her corset which refuses to fasten. Defeated, she lets go of the string, and averts her eyes from the small chest with its photograph of a tall, attractive bride – herself – eleven years ago.

In other respects, however, she seems to delight in her pregnancy. Despite her fears, the skin of her face has somehow become clearer, and there is not the faintest sign of a mark, or trace of a freckle. Her full hair is shiny, emanating health, and her eyes are bluer than ever. In addition, bit by bit, there is the merest hint that her famous hardness is easing up somewhat, and slowly, slowly, without her being aware of it, her absolute assertiveness seems to be relaxing. Thus, as commanded by Irena, the three of them – mother, daughter and son – together choose the new base color for the walls, together decide on the form and color of the pattern to be sprayed on top of this, and together spend long hours watching over the work in progress.

To start with, of course, the room was emptied of furniture, except for the bookcase that rested on the left wall. Because of its size and weight, it was, with great effort, merely moved two footsteps into the center of the room to allow the painters' ladders access to the wall. It was draped in heavy lengths of cloth, spotted with every hue of color under the sun, and congealed whitewash splattered from previous jobs. Amused by the sight of the large bookcase – the pride of the apartment normally, suddenly turned into a golem, dressed in a shabby old coat of many colors – the boy found himself marvelling at the fantastic pattern of all the splashes of paint and whitewash that had landed on the cloth.

The paint and whitewash of an entire generation of Tarnów residents have left their fingerprints on these lengths of cloth, he smiled to himself, hitting on a silly thought: what if the colorful residues on the cloths were not random at all, but a conscious decision on the part of the painters' brushes, out to trick their handlers, or to rebel against both them and the monotony of the work? Or, maybe, by fashioning a spotty mixture of hues from the concoctions of skimpy, liquid colors, the brushes were mocking the clients' own poor taste?

Little did the boy know that the moment his doubting heart gave birth to the thought, was one of prophecy. How could he possibly imagine that, some fifty years later, when visiting the American exhibition at the Biennale in Venice, he would see similar cloths there – canvases virtually identical to the Tarnów painting covers – proudly draping the walls in awe-inspiring display? How could he possibly predict then that some day in the future, in the crowning glory that is Venice, he would suddenly come within earshot of the learned explications of two curators – an American and Italian – both exalting these canvases as the generation's revolutionary tidings in the plastic arts?

What an experience that painting day in 1925 proved to be! The boy had never imagined that a room's ordinary painting could turn into a display of love on the part of the whole family. Grasped in the hairs of the brush of Hazkl, the painter, the love climbed up and across a bedroom which had not felt the touch of paint for many a good year, and dressed the peeling wall cover in a new wrapping. A bright hue (pea green, as Mother defined it) had been unanimously chosen as the most suitable. When the paint was absorbed and the walls dry, Hazkl placed on the greenish surface large, square sheets, half stiff and lacking any color due to the many layers that had hardened on them from previous paintings. These, he and Mother referred to as "*shablonas*" (pattern molds).

How strange and wonderful – the boy gazed in amazement at each *shablona* – for it is precisely what is *not* there that breathes life into it. For their uniqueness had come into the world only as various shapes of various sizes had been cut out from them, leaving ordered replicas of voids and vacuums that appeared like open mouths praying for the colored water. In fact, when they were sprinkled with fresh, shiny golden dye – this, too, picked by Mother and the children – and the empty spaces sipped fully of the golden elixir and rows and rows of golden flowers began to appear almost magically on the greenish background as Hazkl placed *shablona* after *shablona* on the wall at regular, measured intervals and sprayed his gold on them. Thus they spread from wall to wall, covering the entire room, their golden stems intertwining from ceiling to floor.

While Hazkl wraps the walls in golden flowers, his assistant, Honeh, maneuvers his way to the ceiling to restore its whiteness. Perched atop a two-sided ladder as if he were straddling a horse – still, sure, as if man could not wish for a more comfortable saddle – his leg muscles move and urge the ladder forward, like a rider pressing a horse's shanks. Honeh gallops atop the ladder at a dizzying pace, tottering from one corner of the room to the other, his right arm outstretched with the paint brush as if raising a beacon or banner. And as his legs display hair-raising acrobatics, aimed mainly at entertaining or alarming the children, his hand starts to glide the moist brush across the ceiling above, back and forth, right and left, in constant motion and amazing skill. At this point his body appears to be cut in two, as if there were no connection between the playful lower half, and sober, professional upper half, apart from the belt.

From the heights of his perch, Honeh embarks on the systematic painting of the ceiling, slapping on fresh, white paint and swashing the whole area with it. His brush strokes vigorous and rhythmic, wash and white until the last of the spots is wiped clean. Only the memory of the paint job was to remain in the gleaming ceiling, its smell – the boy would remember years later – like the fragrance of Golda's Sabbath *challes*, kneaded and waiting to be baked.

At last, after intensively executing circles, while galloping atop the ladder from one end of the room to the other, Honeh places his weary brush into the paint can, which is swathed in layer on layer of hardened paint residue and, with open satisfaction, beholds his work. At the same time, from their position at the foot of the ladder, Mother and the children also cast their eyes up, sending Honeh an appreciative smile. Here it is – the ceiling – pristine and radiant as if arising from the bath, pure and festive like a holiday. Here it is – the boy was to remember eight years later, on *Shabbat Nahamu*, 5693, the year of his *bar-mitzvah* – for just as pristine, radiant, pure and festive was the white, silk skullcap presented to him by his teacher, Mr. Weinberg, after being called up to the Torah in the makeshift synagogue at "Safa Berura's" summer camp in the Carpathian Mountains. Yes, pristine and pure like the ceiling was the silk *yarmulke* – apart from two gray stains that spoiled its whiteness at the very moment of receipt, stains made by the two tears the boy shed at the thought that his father and his mother, because of Mala's pneumonia, were unable to hold the ceremony in their own town and unable to be at their son's side on his big day.

And yet, Mother was right, Golda's son would secretly acknowledge years later. Without words or speech, love rose like a blossom in the modest flat at the end of the long second-story balcony: it burst through every barrier, hung from every hook, dwelt at every corner. It bounced in the flames of the kitchen stove and was the spice and herb of every dish Mother prepared. It sustained both loaf and learning (*kemah* and *Torah*) at the large table, observed by the four holy cities of Eretz Israel on Rabbi Meir Baal HaNess's calendar; it listened to the *Gemara* melody of Father and son as they pored over the open book on the table, and it added the final sheen to the *challes* Mother braided on that table for the Sabbath. It kept the secrets of the old wooden coffer, adopting its iron hasps and three locks. And it rested on the sun-bathed windowsill in the front room and, at the same time, hung on the green canopy of the chestnut tree that lapped at the back room – the tree that was to overpower Mother's colorful Gobelin and golden frame and, in the end, sentence the room of beds and closets to its eternal and original dimness – a calm refuge from daily tumult, a sanctuary of books and their endless hidden treasures, a mysterious den for youthful dreams and fantasies, whose sap never did, and never would, run dry.

Yes, Mother was right: Love triumphed.

It blossomed, constantly rejuvenating itself, like the chestnut tree growing taller from year to year and reaching the roof of the building. "Look, this summer, the flares of hundreds of pink-red flowers are being rekindled amid the chestnut's foliage, just like in previous years!" The child casts his eyes outside the shaded window, marvelling at the cycles of nature as if he, personally, had been appointed their witness.

The blazing chestnut blossoms – an errant image flashes across his mind – *are like colored lights on the snowy fir tree in the Christmas cards celebrating their messiah's birth.* True, he himself has never seen a Christmas tree, but a whole slew of cards suddenly parades merrily before his eyes, the kind that at the start of December are distributed among the residents of the building by the old neighborhood mailman, whom everyone treats with the greatest respect because he is a veteran of Marshal Piłsudski's Legionnaires, and because he was wounded in the battles to free Poland.

The cards are meant as a reminder of the customary holiday tip that the mailman expects to receive from the Jewish residents. And the Jews do give, each as much as he can, not because of the festival, God forbid – *their* Noel, when the sound of Torah is silenced in all the *batei midrash* (study houses) in town and even the women stop reading from the special *Ze'ena U'Re'ena* composed for them, so that study of Torah would not be responsible for extinguishing the fires of hell decreed for *that man* – but out of respect for the civic new year. Jews, too, after all, reckon by it, alongside the Hebrew calendar, and some even follow the heathen practice of ushering in St. Sylvester's Eve with parties and music and dances.

Yes, Mother was right: Love triumphed.

It enveloped the five members of the family as if in the large, cozy *tallis* (prayer shawl) with which Reb Aazik wrapped up his son in synagogue when the cantor proclaimed "Coihaaaniim!", calling the *Cohens*, the priests, to the platform before the Holy Ark to deliver their blessing. They, with *tallises* covering their heads completely, lean forward, the paired fingers of both hands separated in a priestly blessing – the sign the boy is not allowed to look at during the prayer itself, but which he knows very well from pictures of priestly tombstones that he has seen in books; from time to time he even tries to imitate the sign, forcing his fingers apart, two fingers spread to the right, two to the left, but without success, probably (so he believes) because he is not a *Cohen*. Oh, how safe and pleasant it feels inside the *tallis*! The middle part of the *tallis* Father pulls up high, like a canopy, sheltering the head of the child, who is shaken by the power of the proceedings, while with one of the four fringed corners Father covers the boy's eyes, so that he will not peek and, God forbid, suffer harm from the splendor of the *shekhinah* (Divine Presence) hovering above the *tallises* of those making the blessing. This hidden, heavenly light is reserved for truly righteous *Tzaddikim* in the next world, and no flesh and blood is to behold it, here, in this vale of tears and live to tell of it.

6

While the wonderful, sun-filled days prior to the baby's birth followed one another tranquilly, the nights – oh, the nights – gave the boy no peace. In bed at night, he longed for Mother to come as she had done when he was small. He does not expect her to sing him a lullaby as she did then, for he is big now, five years old, and can sing all the songs by himself, and, after the baby is born, will sing Mother's songs to it, maybe even adding his own personal touch.

Nor does he want her to come and tell him a bedtime story, one of those fascinating tales that she used to make up every night, for he is already reading real books all by himself, in both Polish and Hebrew and, every Thursday, at Mother's bidding, even chooses two or three books for her at the "Safa Berura" lending library from a list she gives him, managing to read parts of them on the way home.

No, now he would expect her presence to take a different form: she should come in softly and sit down next to him and listen to *his* tales this time, tales that he, just like her, made up in his imagination during the witching hour which was neither day nor night and which, with a magic quill dipped in invisible ink, he recorded in his heart to tell to his own offspring at bedtime, and which one day he would maybe write down in a book.

And his mother (so he secretly prayed), who in youth had dreamed of being a poet, would listen attentively to her son's outpourings, her beaming face soft as a caress. She would run her fingers through his hair, as she used to do, or clasp a handful of wayward golden curls that had escaped the comb and, wordlessly, her eyes would bear witness: "Yes, you are a poet, my son. When you grow up, you will be a poet and write everything that I myself did not manage."

Then her fingers would trace the curves of his eyebrows and gently frame his eyes, and her laugh would roll at the old quip that she used to repeat each year on the third of Av – the birthday they both shared – that her son's two eyebrows and her own were so alike that they had been created in one image, twin sisters forever. And this, too, she would repeat, half in jest, half dreamily, on that extraordinary third of Av, when she was twenty-eight, and he, her son, was to come out into the air of the world, and she felt for a split second that his eyes had received a last dipping in the blue that lit up her own, and when they rose from the rinse, the color clung to them. Since then, a covenant of blue reigned between Mother and son, and a voice from heaven proclaimed that Father and the two girls, all brown-eyed, had no share in it.

In bed at night he imagined Mother calling him by name.

She would not choose "Henryk" nor its derivative nickname of "Henek," for both Mother and son, on principle, rejected the Polish equivalent of the Yiddish "Hersch," even though many Hersches in the neighborhood had readily adopted them. But even her choice of "Hesiek," which was a very common form, was not to his liking. He would happily have returned to the original "Zvi-Hersch," which he inherited from his maternal grandfather, Reb Zvi-Hersch Weinman. Curiously enough, it was Father who clung to "Herschl," after his father-in-law's name.

"No, no, if only she didn't call me 'Hesiek'" – his lips speak soundlessly. And an echo from the corner of his heart adds: "Nor even 'Hesiu,'" though the whistled "u" ending lends it a softer tone, more pleasing to the ear, and it is the name used by his friends in the neighborhood, and by Father's *Gemara* students at the *beis-me-drash*. Indeed, even today – after scores of years and at a distance of thousands of miles from Tarnów, light years removed from the Tarnovian way of life of those days – this is how townspeople still fondly call him.

In bed at night he waited for Mother to call him by name.

Would she call him "Hesio," as did the girls who lived nearby, and as the girls in his class would for years to come? Its sound was soft and caressing, and the "o" at the end seemed to hang open-mouthed in the air, like a curious question mark, unhappy with the overt and choosing to plumb the covert. The word was filled with latent longing and unrelieved yearning, leaving a taste for more, like sweet-and-sour lemon ice cream.

"Hesio" is what he is called by Rahela Spinrad, the pretty girl who sits next to him in elementary school; a star pupil with a sweet voice and red cheeks and wise, laughing eyes, *not at all like an orphan; if it weren't for her gray dress and blue pinafore I would never have thought that she was from the community orphanage,* he thinks, and is immediately ashamed of himself, as if he had been caught staring at a cripple. A cripple? Is that how an orphan should be regarded? *Oh, how tangled and twisted was the general attitude to this sorry subject* – the boy thinks every time he passes the handsome, two-story building on Kołłątaja Street, near Schantzer's flour mill, on the way to Mount St. Marcin – *and how embarrassing and cowardly the sense of guilt that assails people at the sight of another's misfortune!* Even though the Jews of Tarnów have been blessed in the welfare facility that they established in their town and in its director, Yitzhak Lieblich, who was also the principal of the "Safa Berura" elementary school, nevertheless, their reaction, of which they are no doubt unaware, is casting shamed looks at the windows of the building; they lower their voices as if they had sinned by allowing their children to grow up in the protection of living parents, while other children have been visited with the incurable plague of orphanhood.

After the Fourth Grade, Rahela disappeared from school, despite her excellent report cards, nor did she reappear for the entrance exams to high school, as did most graduates of her class. Her classmate wondered from time to time where she was, that laughing girl, and what had happened to her; but, to his shame, he reassured himself that that was the way of the world with orphans. Nevertheless, he avidly listened to spreading rumors that she read everything she could lay her hands on and was an active member of the *HaShomer HaTza'ir* Zionist youth movement in town, and never stopped dreaming of pursuing her studies, especially her voice lessons. Unwritten law is, however, stronger than dreams and it applied to her unmercifully, as to other orphans. Even Lieblich, the principal, who was well aware of her talents and thirst for knowledge, did not dare defy social convention. Only after sixty-three years was her childhood classmate to meet up with her again – now a grandmother and veteran member of Kibbutz Ruhama in the northern Negev, where she built a life for herself after immigrating to Palestine during the Holocaust. Her face, in the nature of things, would wrinkle somewhat, yet remain that of the wise child, and her eyes would shine as then, and her laugh would still challenge the world as then, as then…

7

Irena, too, calls him "Hesio."

"You must be Hesio," her face smiled at him on her first visit to the Wróbels' home in May 1925, as she handed him a package of games: "A gift from your uncle in America," meaning Ben-Zion, Golda's younger brother. In his youth he had already made a name for himself in Tarnów as a Hebrew poet and playwright, continuing his literary pursuits after emigrating to America and even publishing a first drama there, *Naftulei Kinor* (Torment of a Violin) in the Hebrew anthology, *Nimim*. Even though Irena's acquaintance with Golda and her home stemmed from her friendship with Ben-Zion, she conquered the boy's heart in her own right from the very first moment, because of her natural manner, which dispensed with the "ritual" pinch of the cheek or the "obligatory" pat on the head and, no less so, because of her decision to put an "o" at the end of his name, "Hesio". In awe the boy raised his eyes to her, as if wishing to see for himself how her lips softly rolled and musically lengthened the "o" and, at the same time, to casually inspect her: he saw an erect posture, golden braids twined "Gretchen" style around her head, and a camera that had no rival in town.

"This revolutionary Leica, made in Germany, 35 mm and 36 exposures per roll, was first shown last month at the Leipzig fair," she replied to his wondering gaze. "I bought it when I got off the ship at Bremerhaven. No one can compare with Germany in this field."

Her assumption that he, at his age, had a grasp of the technical details, flattered him (even though it was entirely unfounded; he acquired his first camera only twenty-five years later). Dizzily, his ears gleaned the English nuggets from her speech. The language, still strange to Central European ears at the time, nevertheless sounded soft and pleasant from Irena's lips, despite the listener's ignorance.

With the same charming naturalness she knocked on the door of the Wróbel flat on a gray-blue dawn of July 19, 1925 to take him, as she had promised Golda, to watch the sunrise from the top of

Mount St. Marcin on the town's southern outskirts; her intention was to make things somewhat easier for her new friend (and future sister-in-law, perhaps) in the last month of her pregnancy and to celebrate with the boy his fifth birthday. "I've come to save you from your loneliness, Hesio" – she declared when he opened the door, the pronunciation of the "o" at the end of his name sounding conspiratorial. The words, uttered in a whisper so as not to waken the rest of the household, embarrassed the boy for a moment – he had never seen himself as lonely and waiting to be saved – but he soon regained his composure and responded to the invitation eagerly.

He was especially pleased to find that the route she had chosen was laced with her own experiences at his age, as if she wished to pluck a page from an old diary, when her life had been a restless stream flowing through the valley at the foot of the hill between the dairy farm of Skrzyszów, the village of her birth, and the neighboring village of Gumniska, where her father had built a white log cabin, a stable for the horse and an apple orchard. All this had happened before Gumniska's annexation to Tarnów's jurisdiction and the building boom at the end of the First World War, which ate into the fields and pastures that divided the town from the hill. Their cabin was only a mile away from the white castle built by the Sanguszkos, the town dukes, who one hundred and fifty years previously had come down from Mount St. Marcin to the valley. In the evening hours, the girl would gaze at the castle's spiked iron fence for the merest hint of what went on in the brightly lit interior. In the blue of summer dawn, however, she would quietly slip out to scramble up the hill and reach the peak with the first red ray of sunrise, before her father returned from Skrzyszów with the zinc containers, full from the first milking, arranged in his wagon for the morning route; she would then climb up next to him on the wagoner's seat and help him deliver the milk from house to house.

Irena's choice of the hill as their destination was therefore not at all haphazard. The boy, too, had now absorbed enough of the

"American" educational slogans, which Irena vigorously affirmed in her penetrating discussions with Golda, to understand her motives. By inviting him this July dawn on her journey to her own childhood, to capture with her, as she had done then, the first red ray of sunrise, his new friend, who was twenty years his senior, was effectively dismissing the age barrier between them and establishing an egalitarian, friendly footing for the adventure awaiting them on the mountain.

Irena and the boy proceeded at a measured pace, arriving at the crest puffing, to stand still for a moment in satisfaction, open to the rising rays that began to banish the morning chill. Sitting down on a jut of the castle ruins, they silently beheld the still sleeping town. Irena had not seen this view since she had emigrated to America, and it stirred in her distant childhood memories. A thick, white cloud cut across the scene, so that the twin spires of the Church of the Missionaries in the left, and the silver dome of the "Great Synagogue" dominating the right seemed to be hovering above the morning mist, while beneath, the urban block itself was dissolved in fog. Only the two lonely turrets in the middle of the line – of the Cathedral and the old Town Hall – continued to pierce the gray skies in quest for the sun. Independently of each other, the thoughts of each traveled far and wide.

Irena described to the boy her adopted city of New York, and the tall buildings of Manhattan. It would take another twenty-five years before he himself was to live in New York City and appreciate what she told him, that the skyscrapers looked like brazen-faced thugs insolently making fists at Heaven. Not so Brooklyn Bridge and its neo-Gothic gates: it rose like a cathedral between sea and sky, reminiscent of Tarnów's twin-spire Missionaries Church, ascending, like that summer morning towards the sun, and rending the screen of mist with its two sharp points. She also spoke of the travel fever that assailed her every spring, shoving a camera into her hands and ordering her to tour the wide world. Now that the

Leica was joined to her wander lust, she was impatient to see what it would do on her travels.

Hearing her words, the boy also decided to share a confidence with his big friend: he had a very special collection. He didn't collect pictures of muscle-building athletes, like most of his male friends, nor of moving picture stars, like those his sister Mala hid among the pages of her books. Rather he collected pictures of impressive buildings, old and new, from different parts of the world. Unhappily, his collection was not growing as quickly as he would like, because so few children cared about the subject, that the pictures were hard to come by or trade. Still, he would go on collecting. Without meaning to hide anything, the boy did not reveal to Irena the main motive behind his interest in the gems of world architecture. No, it did not reflect a mere wander lust, but had to do with his study plans – when he was big, he meant to study architecture and city planning.

When they returned to the cabin at the end of the day, Irena gave the boy a birthday present: a stick with an ivory marble, as if depositing in his hands a wanderer's staff to realize his and her dreams. She also promised to regularly send him postcards from different places in the United States and from her imminent trip to Mexico. Little did they know then that the Lowe Library – perched on neo-classic columns in the heart of New York's Columbia University campus, whose picture, chosen at random, was to be the first that she sent to the boy upon her return home – would, years later, be the venue of his own academic pursuits.

"Hesio" – Irena summed up their outing, the "o" this time sounding like a secret code from a faraway world, the secret whispered by Mexico's ancient pyramids to New York's modern skyscrapers. "The day will come when you will travel the world as I do, face to face with the landscapes and buildings whose pictures you collect. Maybe, then, you will recall that on your very first tour – and you are only now beginning – Irena was with you. Will you remember that, Hesio?"

8

In bed at night he yearned for Mother to call him by name.

Zvi-Hersch Weinman's decision in 1908 to part company from the Ukraine and to remove to western Galicia, which, though also subject to Austrian rule, was clearly Polish in nature, shook up the family well and proper. Everyone felt that in agreeing to serve as cantor of the "Great Synagogue" in Tarnów, he had landed them in an irreversible maelstrom, an existence of which they had little knowledge and, certainly, no control. They were, however, not blind to the advantages inherent in moving westward. The position of head cantor in such an important town as Tarnów, the second largest in western Galicia, and at the grand synagogue that had been inaugurated that year as part of the festivities honoring Emperor Franz-Joseph's reign and as the Jewish share in the celebrations, could, without a doubt, elevate their father to the level of Europe's illustrious cantors and liturgical composers, all highly acclaimed at the time.

The change of residence, at the same time, was one of the dearest wishes of Golda, the cantor's eldest daughter. Sixteen years old, she regarded the removal to western Galicia as a breakthrough to the gates of Vienna, capital and spiritual center of all of Central Europe! The proximity to Vienna, which was only an overnight train journey away, was to pave Golda's way for visits to the lovely metropolis and its cultural offerings. Oh, to actually see the repositories of treasured paintings and sculptures, while the whole city had been transformed in the last decades of the nineteenth century into a virtual museum of living architecture! To see the best plays at the Burgtheater and attend operas at the grand Opera House! To hear concerts performed in the halls of the capital by the best orchestras and most important soloists and conductors!

Uprooting of the blue-eyed, music-loving daughter of the Ukraine from the cradle of her childhood and youth, and her replanting in the soil of western Galicia, was therefore an operation free of resentment or crisis. True, the thirst for Vienna, which Golda felt, was slaked in time. Conversely, there awoke in her a totally independent love for the town of Tarnów, which increasingly supplanted her Viennese expectations. From her enthusiastic visits to Vienna between 1908 and the First World War, and from the years during the war when the entire family moved there, she seemed to have had her fill of the bustling capital. In the end, all that she wanted was to return to the seclusion of her cultured, but quiet, rural town and raise a family.

And so she did. At the end of her Viennese exile in 1918 she returned to Tarnów to help her father rebuild his home and to build one of her own. From then on – apart from a trip to Vienna for medical reasons in the summer of 1927 – Golda never returned to Austria. From time to time, of course, she felt stifled and berated herself for all the things she missed by having chosen the provincial life, instead of settling in Vienna like her sister, Zippora. But these passing sentiments were never translated into action. She remained in the town of her father's choice, and the birthplace of her children, until the end of her days.

Upon the death of her father in 1920, two years after their return from Viennese exile, another powerful bond riveted her to the town in which her father settled in 1908. Over the coming years, every *Rosh Hodesh* (the start of a Hebrew month), she would announce out loud, *"ikh'geih zum tatten"* ("I'm going to Father") – and everyone knew where she was headed. Alone in the large cemetery and oblivious of other mourners, she would cling to the gravestone and pour her heart out before her father. Red-eyed, but inwardly calm, she would return home and continue to steer the cart of her life – until her next visit "to Father." Throughout that entire time she rejected all suggestions of moving where life might be better. Golda stuck to her guns: "Here is where my father's grave is and this is where my home will be!" In the end she would also refrain from following her mother to America. Four months after her father's death, her son would be born in Tarnów and named after his grandfather.

Thus, even though in later years she was to remember her Ukrainian childhood as the happiest period of her life, the scratch left in her by departure from the Ukraine was superficial and transitory. Quickly and without hesitation or too much doubt, she adopted her new country and, with typical enthusiasm, threw herself into reading and studying to deepen her knowledge of its geography and history, touring both town and countryside in ever-widening circles. The knowledge she gained from reading and trips, she systematically and doggedly imparted to her children with more than a modicum of rigidity, as was her way; and, as if consciously hardening her heart, she imposed on her household a complete separation between her own Ukrainian past and the western Galician present. This reality was the most important thing to her, and she resolved that her children, too, would completely absorb it.

And yet, despite her quick acclimatization to her new town and her ready adaptation to the air and vistas of her adopted land, a haze of Ukrainian mystery seemed to envelop the Wróbel home, its residents and narratives, and set it apart from the surroundings. Golda's Ukrainian childhood appeared to her son as an enchanted world of enigma, its colors shrouded in a screen of fog, and his desire to rip off the screen and penetrate to its true hues increasingly took over his imagination, like a dybbuk that would not let go.

The screen of fog may well have remained intact had not her son struck out on his own in school and read *By Fire and Sword*, the first part of Henryk Sienkiewicz's Polish trilogy, set in seventeenth-century Ukraine. He was captivated, as he read, by the Ukraine's charm, landscapes and people and, even more so its problems. His imagination began to form a legendary Ukraine, a Ukraine of wonder, Mother's Ukraine...

*

In bed at night the son would wish for the reawakening of the Ukrainian Golda from the hibernation into which she had sunk on her move to Tarnów, so that she might overcome her western-Galician double. It would then be a victorious Ukrainian mother who would call him by name.

Not "Henryk" or "Henek," like those who had fully assimilated Polish culture; nor "Hesiek" or "Hesiu," nor even "Hesio," like the names in a closely-knit Yiddish-Polish milieu which preserved Jewish vitality in conditions of creative balance; but… "Hesieńku" – the thrilling Ukranian intonation that has no parallel in the cadence of western Galicia – "Hesieńku… Hesieńku…" And in a moment of grace she would add in a whisper, "My darling son," – again, not in the Polish of Galicia – not "synu" or "synku," – but "syneńku, syneńku," – it's melody sounding like the twang of a bow string, delivering an arrow from one end of the world to the other till it drops, drunk on love, giving up its soul in happiness.

In bed at night the boy dreamed that his Ukrainian mother called him by name.

Moishe and Feige Gokhban Arendar family in Storzhov

CHAPTER TWO

Like a Dinghy on the Dniepr:
The Gokhban Saga

1

O N THE WAVES of Mother's plaintive melodies, the boy sought
to sail to her Ukrainian homeland. A thousand balalaikas sob in the
distance and a thousand fiddles answer to the tune of the "Dumka,"
the Ukrainian song Golda liked to hum:

Tam na górze jawor stoi	On a high hill a sycamore stands
Jawor zieloneńki –	Its canopy green, full sighing –
Ginie Kozak w cudzej stronie	Far from fields of home and land
Kozak młodeńki.	A young Cossack lies dying,
Ginie Kozak w cudzej stronie,	In sorrow his young breath fades,
Śmierć mu oczy tuli:	Like a dream his life dispelled:
"Proszę ciebie, moja miła,	"Hurry, girl, tell it at the gates,
Donieś to matuli…	And bid my Mama farewell…
"Proszę ciebie, moja miła,	"Hurry, girl, tell it at the gates,
Donieś to matuli…	And bid my Mama farewell…"

As the boy listens to the strains of the "Dumka," laced as they are by Moniuszko, the master of Polish opera, with an ancient Ukrainian tune, he is aware of the whistling wind that rises from the Ukrainian steppes, commanding him to escort the Cossack back to his homeland and place his body in the bosom of the far away Cossack Sitch. And how strange – with all that he has been told of the suffering of his forebears at the hands of the Cossacks – their misfortune nevertheless does not make his heart beat with hatred, nor his eyes spark with thoughts of revenge.

Like a sharp-nosed, shapely Tartar *chaika*, so the boy's soul – a boat on the waves of an imaginary river Dniepr – is tempted to escape the ropes that bind it, slip anchor and pursue the wind of the plains, to catch up with it only at the mouth of the Cossack Sitch itself. There, at the foot of the Zaporozhe Rapids, the waters of the Dniepr surge and swell like the mighty Sambatyon does on weekdays, as the children learned from their mother. Unlike the Sambatyon, which rests on the Sabbath, the Dniepr never stops raging, not on the Sabbath of the Jews nor on the holidays of the *goyim.*

Zaporozhe! Here it is, that spellbinding place and name, meaning "across the thresholds," and hinting at its location behind rocks on the slopes of the Dniepr. The Creator of the Universe scattered them so, whether in anger or absentmindedness, and laid them down like sills across the channel. There, they protrude above the water, the seven granite boulders, blocking the passage of vessels at this section of the river. And against these, seven powerful rapids, in insane fury, declare war on the sills. How futile! All attempts to navigate past are doomed to failure and the Dniepr, a major route to the Black Sea, remains blocked. Instead, the boats are drawn from the water and, like wounded horses, dragged overland along the banks. Only downstream are they put back again into calmer waters to sail out to sea. At this stretch of turmoil, the Cossack Sitch set up home.

… A wild and secret land is the Sitch: the haven of free, ruth-

less spirits who chose to settle in it, the bosom of rootless adven-
turers....A land of dream and nightmare is the Sitch: sanctuary to
every defector who ever deserted a battalion, every derelict escaping official punishment or fleeing someone's vengeance. ...A land
of mystery is the Sitch: the destination of ruined peasants whose
creditors were after their blood, and of serfs who could endure no
more from their overlords. ...To all of these – but, above all, to the
Cossacks – the Sitch was home and homeland.

The boy came across an apt description of the nature of the
place in the testimony of Nathan Hannover, a Jewish witness to the
events of the seventeenth century, when insurgents rose up against
the rule of the King of Poland in this untamed frontier region.
Nathan – who lived in Zaslav, southern Volhynia, in the Ukraine,
a mere arrow's flight away from the birthplace of Golda – fled
to western Europe for fear of the Cossacks and the massacres of
1648–49, which he experienced first hand and recorded, along with
testimonies collected from others, in a book that was first printed
in Venice five years after. *Yeven Mezulah* he called the book, a play
on words from the Psalms, for beyond its straight forward meaning of "miry pit," it hinted also at "*Yavan*" (Greece), the code-word
by which the Jews at the time referred to the Ukraine, which was
Christian Orthodox, rather than Catholic, and so subject to the
Greek Church.

In 1923, when the boy turned three and was initiated into reading and Bible study by his father, the latter stumbled upon a new
edition of *Yeven Mezulah*. The modest volume, which had just
been published in Berlin (Klal Publishing, 5683 – 1923), instantly
found its place on an inner shelf of the bookcase in the Wróbel
home. And here the boy discovered it on one of his seasonal "fish-
ing trips" into the depths of the bookcase. He was never to put it
down again, its pages growing worn from overuse. And it seems
to him – when scanning Hannover's Hebrew text or returning to
Sienkiewicz's Polish epic, *By Fire and Sword* – that the wild and

elusive wind of the steppes, which broke through to the south and reached Zaporozhe, lifts him up like a feather and places him under its wings and the two climb higher and higher..

Look! There it is, down there, the one, the only Ukraine!

See now how they soar, not just in space but time: gliding towards the Sitch as it was in the seventeenth century and circling over Khortitsa – that desolate isle, rising from the Dniepr, some twelve kilometers in length and two in width. And as they observe the teeming human hive on the island, the two notice hordes of people ringing a huge tree with a great canopy – this is the Holy Oak, sanctified for generations. In its shade rebel cries were issued against Poland's king and there, at the Sitch, fateful decisions were taken. Ah! The Cossack Sitch, so faraway and unfathomable!

As if frightened by what it saw at Cossack headquarters in Khortitsa, the wind makes haste to escape the trap and retreats to comb the Ukrainian steppes in all four directions. On its way north it will fly very low, bowing over the Ukrainian Kurhan hillocks – the burial mounds of past generations and "soul-stones" of past wars, strewn over the plains with no inscriptions to mark or identify the casualties resting in the earth.

The fallen and their timeless loss are mourned and eulogized only by a heroic *Duma*, sprinkled with *Kozatske Pisni* (Cossack hymns) and *Zaporozhske Psalmy* (Zaporozhe Psalms) as sung by blind *lyrniks* or *kobzars*, the minstrels who travel from village to village with their instruments – lyre or *kobza* – in hand. Or, they are mourned by the dramatic portrayal of valor by the *startsy*, old codgers who stand at street corners or in the marketplace spinning their tales. Pursued by fearful specters of ghosts rising from graves to avenge their deaths, the wind leaps from one Kurhan to another, one Cossack tent to another, leap, after leap, it flies on and on.

Changing direction, it veers from the northern route to the left, westward, saluting the row of Polish castles locked in their dreams of tattered majesty, and abandoned.

Shhh now… It listens: their domes and crevices still buzz with secrets of yore. Stunned by the memories, the wind lands a kiss on the sad cheeks of the walls and last of the towers which once defended Poland's eastern flank, and which still stoop over their surroundings like wounded eagles refusing to believe they will no longer fly.

And after completing its flight between the provinces of the Cossacks and fortresses of the Polish nobility, the wind will again turn to glide above the shabby, long-suffering Jewish towns. It will ferret out both renowned congregations and the nameless, forgotten in oblivion – and, with fingers dipped in their warm blood, it will record the story of *Yeven Mezulah*.

Upon discovering *Yeven Mezulah* in the bookcase, the boy understood that as far as he was concerned, as the descendant of generations of Ukrainian Jews, this purchase for the Wróbel home was different from any other. He imagined that Divine Providence itself had guided his father to buy and place it in the bookcase for safekeeping until such time as his son would find it. With this purchase, Father's role in *Yeven Mezulah* ostensibly ended, and Mother's began.

And rightly so. For the 1648 massacres had taken place in a part of the country that had been her cradle, the root of her family; the names of the towns and villages and rivers mentioned in the book were interwoven into the tapestry of her life, of her ancestors, and certainly of her son's. Except that the mother refused to be lured by her son's Ukrainian romanticism and, apart from humming Ukrainian tunes and following "the news from there" in the daily press, she refrained from turning her Ukrainian memories into a testimonial of torment for herself and her children. The more she avoided the subject, however, the more the son was convinced that there was some reason behind it, and that a deep dark secret lodged in the recesses of her heart. True, she had never revealed the motive for her hesitation; but despite the silence, her son finally managed to persuade her to shed her reservations and set aside time to read from *Yeven Mezulah* with him. And once she began, she could no longer go on refusing. After an evening or two of heartfelt reading, the fences with which she had surrounded herself began to crumble, whether consciously or not, and slowly, slowly, of her own free will, Golda found herself elaborating with more and more of her own personal input: oral traditions that had been passed from generation to generation in her family and etched forever in her memory from the stories of her mother, Sureh, and her grandmother, Feige.

Typically, she clung primarily to the memory of landscapes. She had absorbed these as a young girl, when her father took her on his concert rounds through the towns of Ukraine and Galicia, along with his singers and musicians during the Purim or Hanukka holiday seasons. These performances became possible in 1900, when Zvi-Hersch gave up his post in Starokonstantinov, Volhynia, and moved to Tarnopol in eastern Galicia, where the Jewish community undertook to finance both a choir and an occasional band. Thus, twice a year, for eight years (until the family's removal to Tarnów), Golda's eyes took in the vistas on both sides of the Russo-Austrian border and the hues that changed with the cycle of the seasons, from greenish fields at Purim to the rainy brown of Hanukka's leaf fall, when a tired, withering autumn hands over the scepter of command to young winter, sparkling white.

From this broad scenic pageantry – sliding unhampered from the Dniestr River in the west to the silver horizon beyond the far away Dniepr – Golda, quite naturally, developed a special love for the corn fields and forests of her childhood in western Ukraine. Unlike her son, who himself could not explain his vague longings for the cataracts of the Dniepr and Sitch, and even nurtured a forbidden fondness for the Cossacks and hopes and aspirations for Ukrainian liberation – Golda shrank the map down to her own private Ukraine.

Apart from one exciting expedition to the Black Sea – to Odessa, Kherson and the Jewish rural communities that rose there in the nineteenth century – she sketched in her mind a map of twin lands locked in an eternal embrace, Volhynia and Podolia: from the plains of Volhynia at the top of the map, to the Carpathian hinterland of Podolia at the bottom. This personal Ukraine, a sadly exultant, bountiful land, was ribboned with rivers – the southern Boh and its small son, the Bozhek; the Slutch, the Rov, the Sereth, the Kortchik, the Zbrutch, the Stripa and the Smotritch – and over and above them all, the Dniestr, the Tcheremosh and the Prut – coursing through her body like a breathing network of arteries, the rivers sparkle with joy and smile, in summer sun as in winter snowdrifts, irrespective of the blood shed over the generations, and flowing in the Ukraine waters.

The Volhynia experience had the greatest impact. It began with the long-standing, two-story inn that Grandpa Moishe leased in the village of Storzhov, like his ancestors before him. There, in the upper story of the house, on a sunny summer day, his granddaughter, Golda, opened her eyes on the world for the first time.

2

"You asked where Storzhov is, the village where I was born, and what it looked like in those days?" Golda picked out one question from the many her son bombards her with. But instead of an answer, she gave him a somewhat bashful smile: "And how can I possibly know? I was four years old when I left the village, and never went back again, nor could I ever find it on a map!"

Even though she failed in her efforts to locate the village in the atlas, her heart was forever to carry two pictures from her childhood: The one – Grandpa's house – "High and rising above all the other roofs in the village, the only two-story house there, standing on the main road opposite the point where the Kropivnia spills into

the Kortchik." The second picture: "a gaggle of white geese floating in arrow formation on the water and coming to rest opposite
Grandpa's home. To my eyes, the eyes of a little girl, the geese looked
like sailors in white, invading the shore and taking it with gusto."

The house – an old inn attached to a distillery – was not the
private property of Golda's grandparents. As was customary at the
time, Moishe and Feige Gokhban merely ran it on the basis of an
arenda, a concession acquired by Jewish tenants (*arendars*) from
the Polish landed gentry (the *pritzim*, as Jews referred to them) – in
this particular instance, from Countess Potocka and her son, the
Count. The connection between the Gokhban and Potocki families spanned generations. Moishe's forefathers had leased the inn
and the right to make and sell liquor to the peasants. And while
Moishe, personally, was saddened by the sight of wretched peasants drowning their hard-earned coins in their cups, he considered
it as an incurable evil to contend with; so that, in his time too, the
inn continued to serve as an alehouse for the village peasants, just
as in the past.

Unlike the downstairs, which was always shrouded in the smell
of liquor and breaths of dozens of drinkers, the upper story, that of
the inn, looked like another world. Its only connection to the tavern
was a railed gallery that gazed down on the alehouse below. The
three rooms at the right were reserved for the Gokhban family. Here
Feige gave birth to her five children: Meiyer and Rivkeh and Mekhyl,
who had already spread their wings and left the nest, as well as Lowe,
the youngest of the boys, and Sureh, the last of the daughters. After
Meiyer, the eldest, cast off the ancestral lore and set out for far away
Odessa, and Rivkeh followed her husband, Alter, to Zhitomir, and
Mekhyl and his wife, Layeh, moved to Proskurov, the young Lowe
finally had the first room all to himself. The second room was his
parents', and the third went to his sister, Sureh, who, at the age of
sixteen, married Zvi-Hersch Weinman, the twenty-three-year-old
cantor who ate *kest* (that is, boarded for free) with his in-laws, as

was common practice. For most of the month the young husband was away, spending three Sabbaths in different towns of the region; on the fourth, he would return to his wife at their room in the inn. Here, on the third of Av, 5652, that is, the summer of 1892 by *their* reckoning, the seventeen-year-old Sureh bestowed on her parents their first grandchild: Golda.

The fourth room was for the Ukrainian maids who looked after both of the inn's floors, while the other six constituted guest rooms and housed wealthy merchants from Volhynia, Podolia and Galicia. The latter would stop by on their way from Kiev and Zhitomir, going westwards to Rovno, and from there to Brody, a free-trade city on the border between Russia and Austrian Galicia. Or stop while traveling north-west, to Brest-Litovsk and further. To Golda, a small Jewish girl caught in a remote Ukrainian village, the mysterious merchants, who easily crossed borders and journeyed from country to country, embodied an enchanted world beckoning her to cross the waters and come within its gates. Her entire life she carried with her an awareness that these merchants – more than her own father, crowned by the aura of his monthly journeys through local townships – sowed in her a longing for the faraway, and she, who did not live to follow her heart in this respect, passed on the *Wanderlust* to her son who, in good time, would fulfill it for both of them.

Often, when there was a vacancy, Grandfather Moishe would take in without charge a Jewish wayfarer upon whom the Sabbath had come inopportunely, so as to spare him the danger of passing the day in the woods; or, he would invite a *moikher-seforim* (traveling bookseller) who, apart from trading in sacred texts, also served as a faithful postman for news of the Jewish world; or he would host a *meshulah*, one of those "emissaries" who prayed for the peace of Jerusalem and dreamt of redeeming Hebron, and trudged from place to place singing the praises of the Holy Land. No time at all passed between these colorful figures, each of whom in his own way broke the routine of Golda's Sabbaths, and they were soon crossing fiery swords with the rich merchants in stormy discussion of the news of the day – and the little girl sitting on her grandfather's lap and playing with the hairs of his black beard lent them a thirsty ear.

Indeed, until the end of her days, no matter where she was or where she went, she would carry with her the memory of the rural inn where she was born, including the final experience – the one that apparently erected the monument to Storzhov in her heart. It concerned a surprising night visit paid by the village lord and his noble companions to the inn. "Mounted on horses, they came." She would recall years later the impression left by that bewitched evening when she, the only child in the only Jewish family among two hundred and fifty Ukrainian families in the village, suddenly found herself witness to so unusual a spectacle.

"No doubt, back from the hunt or wanting a cup," the knowing Ukrainian maids said, blushing in excitement at the vision presented by the noble gentlemen alighting from their mounts and making their way to the front of the alehouse. A warm blush also washed over small Golda's cheeks, who was excited that the gentile maids let her hide behind the pillars of the upper story railing to view the proceedings below.

There they are now, four handsome Polish gentlemen with young Count Potocki, that well-known charmer of the village girls, the handsomest of all. Oh, how she envied her grandfather standing before them to speak with them face to face! It seemed to the child that, despite her distance, the aroma of their cologne wafted to her nostrils, so different from the usual smells of the alehouse.

But the Ukrainian girls had guessed wrong this time; it was not to down a drink with his friends that the *poretz* (village squire) had stopped at the inn. Concealed behind the pillar, Golda saw the Count rise to his feet, signalling to his friends to remain seated, and to Grandpa to follow him into the side room. In that room Moishe would confer with the Czar's officials who came for protection "payments," and Grandma would pore over the *arenda* accounts at the end of every month.

For a long while Golda's eyes remained fixed on the rectangular door behind which the two closeted themselves. Even though she had no way of assessing the actual amount of time that passed, she knew that their conversation was drawn out. The fact was that the peasants drinking in the alehouse had already left for home, and the maids who went to clear up after them had already returned to their room. When the door finally opened and Potocki emerged with his Jewish tenant to return to the main hall and his waiting companions, the sigh that rose from the latter reached the little girl all the way up in the gallery. The village squire looked just the same as he had before retiring to the side room, chatting just as gaily as before. But her grandfather, it seemed to Golda, was sunk in silence, and there was something different about him – something she could not really put her finger on because of the distance of her lookout.

At last the guests rose to leave, with Reb Moishe, torch in hand, lighting the way to the gate where the horses stood, and taking leave of them with submissive bows and a smile that even from far away looked forced and sad. Right after this she heard, as expected, two things: the hiss of bubbling water in the basin near the gate as the torch was put in to extinguish the flame, and the scraping of the heavy iron gate when it was locked up for the night. Then, in the twinkling of an eye, Grandpa appeared in all his height, standing within the archway of the main entrance as if in a picture frame, his clothes – the typical dress of Ukrainian peasantry – more prominently *goyish* than ever before. He stood still, wearing, as usual, a round, Russian peasant hat that always seemed to Golda to be an inseparable part of his head, and now gave the impression of sprouting the side-curls of his beard that ran down both sides of his face. From her perch above, the visor of his black hat, which always sat forward, added depth to his eyes and height to his protruding cheekbones, like the eyes and cheeks of a Russian saint.

The child studied Grandpa. His beard seemed to trail down his black Russian *rubashka* which was rolled up, peasant style, above his belt. Its edges, Golda knew, overlay the *tallis-koot'n* (small prayer-shawl) that he wore every day, the fringes invisible because of the Jewish *hallat* – a kind of black coat reaching midway down the boots – that covered all, thereby differentiating between Grandpa and the Ukrainians. "How does his black beard manage to stick out and not be drowned in the black *rubashka* and black *hallat*?" Golda wonders.

Pressing her whole body against the pillar, Golda watched Grandpa's every movement, which she knew from the sounds that reached her room every evening. He is about to start the nightly ritual of smothering the downstairs lights, making his way from lamp to lamp and tallow to tallow and carefully stifling the flame. For the first time Golda sees the scene she could usually only guess at from her room: now an overall darkness spreads through the downstairs hall as the upstairs lamp, the only one left burning all night, continues to drip blue-yellow beads, causing rings of shadows to bounce on the walls.

Shivering, whether because of the cold of the night or the dance of shadows, Golda broke into a cry of welcoming Grandpa with open arms as he slowly made his way up stairs. And though he was surprised to see that she was still awake, Reb Moishe could not have wished for a pleasanter greeting this evening than the embrace of his small granddaughter. He lifted her in his arms, and all at once, sharply and unthinkingly, buried his dark head in the groove between her neck and shoulder. For a moment Golda imagined an unexpected moistness wetting the collar of her blouse. A fleeting thought flashed through her mind, but she banished it instantly and firmly: her big, strong Grandpa could not possibly be crying. Trusting in his strength, the little girl wound her left arm around

Grandpa's neck, while her right fingers entwined with the hairs of his beard to play with them as usual.

Without warning, though, her hand froze in the mesh of hair as if she had seen a ghost and the terrible sight completely immobilized her. In panic she roused herself from her stupor, straightened up in the arms that held her high and pulled back her head for a better look at Grandpa's face, as if to make sure that her eyes were not deceiving her. All at once she understood the "something different" that had eluded her a little while ago about Grandpa's face, and which she hadn't been able to put her finger on.

It was perfectly clear, beyond any shadow of a doubt: the beard! Yes, it was Grandpa's beard that was different. Something had happened this evening. The beard, which was amazingly black despite his advanced age, and shot through as if by mistake with only a smattering of silver threads, had suddenly turned old. It was all white, as if in envy of the snowy geese on the Kropivnia and Kortchik. She has no idea how this came about: could it have happened gradually, as in the normal course of aging, without her noticing? Or did it come abruptly as a result of Grandpa's meeting with his lordship? Either way, the child can't wait to tell her father when he returns about the amazing occurrence of this special evening of Potocki's visit to Grandpa's inn.

3

It was late at night, two evenings after the unforgettable visit, that Zvi-Hersch, as usual, returned from his tri-weekly cantor's cycle through the towns of the region, happy in anticipation of a week at home with his family and composition work. There was one rule he had set himself: the first evening of his return was dedicated always to his young daughter – letting her chat to her heart's content, singing with her, telling her a story. As the setting to his story, he would often choose one of the Volhynia townships near

Storzhov. He would fill the account of the town with life and substance, telling Golda of the deeds of the Ba'al Shem Tov, the founding father of Hasidism, and of his disciples from one hundred and thirty years earlier.

Thus, sometimes Zvi-Hersch would tell of nearby Mezeritch, capital of Dov Ber, the Maggid and heir to the Ba'al Shem, and how he would dispatch emissaries to all the four corners of the realm to spread the tidings of Hasidism. Sometimes he focused on the nearer Koretz, which, like Storzhov, sat on the banks of the Kortchik and was known to the little girl from the family's trips there for the *Yamim Nora'im* (Days of Awe) – it was the town of the famous Reb Pinhas, among whose adherents Grandpa Moishe numbered. Or he told of neighboring Anopoli, where the Maggid passed away and was laid to rest, and where his disciple, Zussya, accomplished great deeds by "exiling" himself to the towns of Poland along with his brother, Elimelekh, who was to reign in Lezhansk and help lay the foundations of Galician Hasidism. Sometimes he would stick to Slavuta, which sat in the old forests on the Horyn River, where the son of Reb Pinhas of Koretz served as rabbi and set up a printing press for Hasidic works. The "Praises of the Ba'al Shem Tov" (*Shivhei HaBesht*) were actually produced in Koretz, in Yiddish. Zvi-Hersch told also of Shepetovka on the Huska, and how it so happened that Reb Pinhas had been called to the heavenly assembly from this very town, while going on *aliyah* to Eretz Israel. Denied the privilege of the holy soil, he, in death, sanctified the soil of Shepetovka where, twice a year, Moishe would prostrate himself at his graveside. At times Zvi-Hersch would marvel over the town of Polonnoye, where the Ba'al Shem Tov's disciple, Reb Yehuda-Leib, known as the Mokhiah, served and was buried, as well as where the Ba'al Shem Tov's elder disciple, Reb Yaakov-Yosef, took over the rabbinate from the Mokhiah and upon his death was buried alongside him. But above all, Zvi-Hersch sang the praises of Medzibozh, Mother of all Hasidic towns, lying in the hollow of the arc southward, at the gateway to Podolia itself, cradled in the river arms of the Boh and the Bozhek (hence its name), the head-quarters of the Ba'al Shem for the last twenty years of his life and also his burial place.

And from Medzibozh Zvi-Hersch set out for sites in southern Podolia, where the Ba'al Shem had first embarked on his earthly and spiritual journeys: Okopy, his native village, and the defense batteries that gave it its name; Tlust, the site of his first revelation; and between Kosiv and Kitiv in the Eastern Carpathian, where a mountain path opened to let him commune with his God and his soul, while his wife made a living carting loam in her wagon, and he poured water and flour into a pit so that the warmth of the sun could bake it into *matza*:

From Kosiv to Kitiv	*Fun Kosev biz Kitev*
A little bridge hangs about –	*Iz a brikeleh farhanen –*
Where the *Ba'al-Shem*	*Vi der Bal-Shem*
Where the *Ba'al-Shem*	*Vi der Bal-Shem*
To take a stroll did set out.	*Iz shpatsiren geganen.*
From Kosiv to Kitiv	*Fun Kosev biz Kitev*
A little wood hangs about	*Iz a veldeleh farhanen –*
Where the *Ba'al-Shem*	*Vi der Bal-Shem*
Where the *Ba'al-Shem*	*Vi der Bal-Shem*
To commune with God did set out.	*Iz oif hisboydedis geganen.*
From Kosiv to Kitiv	*Fun Kosev biz Kitev*
Little birds hang about –	*Zenen feygelakh farhanen –*
Where the *Ba'al-Shem*	*Vi der Bal-Shem*
Where the *Ba'al-Shem*	*Vi der Bal-Shem*
To learn hymn-singing set out.	*Iz lernen shireh geganen.*

In recounting all these, along with his personal impressions of the trips to these places, Zvi-Hersch managed to impart to his small daughter a picture of the Jewish township as a vibrant, living entity which, despite its notorious poverty, was a rich Jewish world: the Sabbath – its weekly day of rest; Jewish holidays – celebrated throughout the town; and the Yiddish dialect heard all about. Ah, the child dreamed to herself, how different are those towns with their hundreds of Jewish children, from the remote village of her own life! And how very much she would like to visit the wonderful sites where the early Hasidim trod! Her love of nature aside (she sighs), village life is hard for a lone Jewish child amid *goyim*. When she is bigger – her father offers his ready consolation – he will take her with him on his trips and show her all these places. And, he vows: once he receives a permanent posting in one of the Jewish communities, the three of them – Father, Mother, Golda – will leave the village and settle in a town, maybe even in one of the large towns, thus putting an end to loneliness! Little did Zvi-Hersch know, when uttering the same assurance that evening, that the spirit of prophecy had issued from his throat…

His placating words of promise could not always ease the distress Golda felt when waiting for his return, or protect her from loneliness. Thus, if he found his daughter locked within herself or enclosed in sadness, he would try to amuse her with tales of the wit and wisdom of Reb Herscheleh Ostropoler, whose famous escapades had taken place in the neighboring town of Ostropol after which he was named. Or, if he was in the right frame of mind, he would hum for her a new melody that he had composed on the way home and not yet jotted down in his notebook; on such occasions, she, the four-year-old child, would serve as the first – and best – "audience" on whom to test the "catchiness" of a tune.

But, most importantly, Zvi-Hersch would lend an attentive ear to what his daughter had to say and how she had passed the time in his absence – events whether real or imaginary would be retold and nodded at intently. These heart-to-heart chats would not stop with childhood, and Golda would always long to unburden herself before her father, even when she was grown up and married and would continue to carry on her conversations with him at his graveside.

"Children develop a sense of belonging to a place by learning the history of their immediate surroundings," Zvi-Hersch would expound to his wife the basic assumptions of his pedagogic approach, to counter her teasing about wasting his precious time in "idle talk" with "only a little girl." Ardently, and with a profound sense of conviction – combining the devotion of both a Hasid and dreamer of redemption with the openness of an artist – the husband and father rejected Sureh's skepticism. Whereas his tales were meant by their very nature to stimulate his daughter's imagination, his purpose was to lead her down her people's historical paths and open for her a window onto understanding the two aspects of Jewish existence: its weakness, on the one hand, which was the result of external constraints forced on the Jewish people, and its inner strength, on the other hand.

This weakness he disclosed to her when describing his trips through the Pale of Settlement, that frontier strip which Czarist Russia tore from the body of the Polish realm in the late eighteenth century. To prevent the spread of the Jewish population from the conquered areas into the regions of old Russia, the Czarist regime imprisoned the Jews within the confines of the Pale of Settlement, which was in reality an enormous ghetto. Nor did Zvi-Hersch shrink from telling the child, despite her tender years, about the persecution of Jews down the generations, from the massacres of 1648–49, some two hundred and fifty years earlier, to the terrors of the Haidamak Rebellion one hundred and twenty years later and the "Southern Storms" of the Odessa riots of 1881, about a decade before her birth. In 1896 he could not possibly foresee the Kishinev pogrom of 1903, the Petlyura horrors of 1919–1920, or the Holocaust of Ukrainian Jewry in 1941.

This bloodstained mosaic the father inlaid with the patterns of Judaism's inner strength and regenerative powers, especially the miraculous renewal of the Ukrainian Jewish communities destroyed in 1648. The perpetrators were sure that they had succeeded in wiping out the Jews forever, but not many years passed before the towns were reoccupied by Jews as before and, by the end of the nineteenth century, even had a Jewish majority. "All this," Zvi-Hersch explains to Sureh, "and above all, the story of the three spiritual upheavals of our times – Hasidism, hatched in our very own neighborhood, as well as the Enlightenment and *Hibbat Zion*, which were welcomed with open arms here – I have included in my talks with Golda. Thus our daughter may always know that her people 'lives and exists' though its blood has been shed and, what's more, it continues to spread its wings towards the freedom of spirit, even as its tortured body remains chained and manacled."

Golda spent a whole evening, a whole scented Volhynian evening, waiting eagerly for her father's return. When he came, Zvi-Hersch sat back in the armchair at his daughter's bed and nodded to her with bright eyes that he was ready to hear her out. Hardly a few minutes passed, however, when to his surprise and the child's irritation Grandpa Moishe pushed open the door and motioned to his son-in-law that he wished to speak with him urgently. "We will finish the story tomorrow, Goldenyu," Zvi-Hersch sought to soften the shock and the frustration that cast his daughter's head down and brought her to instant tears. "Tomorrow you will tell me e-ev-e-rything," he lingered on the "e" sound, as if opening the bundle of disappointment that had built up in her heart during his absence and replacing it with a pack full of new hope.

"Listen to me, Goldenyu," his voice searched hesitantly for words that could withstand the look of reproach she delivered unmercifully, "it really is very late." His efforts at appeasement, however, soon proved totally superfluous because of the child's exhaustion. Before he could even bid her "Good-night," a heavy, steady breath came from the head of the bed, heralding an end to the conversation.

Not until he turned down the wick in the paraffin lamp to dim the light, did Zvi-Hersch notice the void in the corner armchair, where his wife, Sureh, liked to sit in the evening to knit or just relax from the day's work. "She must have been summoned to her parents while I was talking to Golda, and I must have been too preoccupied to see her leave," Zvi-Hersch tried to reconstruct her exit, conscious that he owed his wife an apology.

At that moment he felt a coil of anxiety attach to the thread of his thoughts and disturb his peace, like the empty cans roving Gypsies tied to their moving wagons which rattled 'hollow' on the paving stones to banish the fearful silence of night and loneliness. "What can be so important to Reb Moishe that he has to gather the whole family in the middle of the night?" Zvi-Hersch wondered, gripped by a vague sense of unease. He soon pulled himself together, and leaving the room on tiptoe so as not to waken Golda, turned the door handle to his in-laws' room.

4

A warm midday sun beat down on Golda's eyelashes until she finally opened her eyes. No, this is not her normal bed, though the two full bags on either side of her are certainly soft and comfortable, just like the cushions and featherbed in her room; maybe her own bedding is even inside them. From the steady motion, the rolling from side to side, and the pounding of the horse hooves which filters to her from up front, she concludes that she is in a wagon, but as she is lying down, she sees only tree tops and has no marker to give her an idea of the size of the forest. The horizon is blocked by the solid back of Grandpa, who sits tall in the driver's seat, dressed now as a complete *goy*, without the black *hallat*. Golda looks back and is surprised to find her mother and father seated quietly on the coffer, their smiles rather weary and forced. She raises herself on her elbows and discovers that the road is taking them through a dark forest – a forest such as she has never seen but only imagined while listening to the tales of horror the Ukrainian maids liked to frighten her with.

A hundred questions assail her head, in no special order and so quickly one on the heels of another that it hurts. What is she doing on the bags on Grandpa's wagon? The last thing she remembers is talking with Father upon his return late last night, but she can't remember any details. She does remember that she was in bed already; could she have fallen asleep while talking to him and been transferred to the wagon in her sleep? She will no doubt receive answers to all these questions, but does not have the strength right now to get up from among the bags and clamber up to the coachman's seat to sit beside Grandpa, as she usually does, nor to crawl to the back and get up on the trunk with her parents. One thing she knows for sure: something happened. And just as that something made her leave or sent her away in the dead of night from her village, without her taking leave of her home or neighbors – the white geese – so, too, that same terrible something would not allow her to return to Storzhov or see Grandpa's house or the geese ever again!

The need to leave the village puzzled the young Golda, but did not surprise the adults. For fourteen years, the threat of expulsion had hung over the heads of Storzhov's only Jewish family, its execution being deferred again and again. The first order had been issued back in May of 1882, when Sureh, the youngest of the Gokhbans, had turned seven, and came in the wake of the Provisional Regulations promulgated by Ignatiev, the Russian Minister of the Interior, (dubbed the May Laws). The regulations confined Jews of the Pale of Settlement to town life, banning them from the rural countryside. Ostensibly, the rules did not apply to the pre-1882 Jewish village inhabitants, but the regime did not lack for pretexts to enforce them on the old-timers as well.

Year after year, Reb Moishe had succeeded in staving off his expulsion from Storzhov. The Almighty in His abundant grace – so he would say after his exile from the village, a wink beneath the visor filling in the gaps – had set a guard on every side: on his right, the Potocki dynasty, that noble Polish house that had become a legend among Eastern-European Jewry, rewarding the loyalty of their Jewish protegés (including the Gokhbans) by interceding on their behalf with the authorities; and on his left, a whole series of Russian officials who materialized for "spot checks," so to speak, generally on the eve of *their* holidays. Entering stern-faced and brandishing "official" papers, they would soon exit from the side room with a fresh flush on their cheeks, the whiff of liquor on their breath and – curiously – bursting pockets in their uniforms. And so the world continued to turn for fourteen years – facing threats and averting them – until the evening that Potocki put in an appearance at the inn.

"Unlike the other *pritzim*, the Potocki gentry were not only noble by birth, but made of noble stuff, and young Potocki was the most decent of them all," Golda told her son years later. From sources close to the regime Potocki had learned that a new expulsion order hovered over "his Jew" in Storzhov. This time, however, it was not the whim of a corrupt, local official interested in increasing his bribe income, but the initiative of the central government, affecting thousands of Jewish innkeepers and liquor-makers in the countryside. In such circumstances, the young squire – regretfully – could do nothing. This, then, was the reason for closeting himself with his Jewish tenant in the side room. The little girl now understood that the squire, who had formed a special relationship with her grandfather since boyhood, had hastened to warn Grandpa that the police were conspiring against him.

The urgent warning was in fact a great kindness. The breathing space it gave them before the decree actually descended enabled the elderly tenants and their son, Lowe, as well as their married daughter, her husband and young child, to make arrangements to relocate.

The first order of the day was to remove the young couple and child to safety. And, yes, every cloud does indeed have a silver lining: the emergency forced Zvi-Hersch to put an end to his procrastination and accept the cantor's post offered him in Starokonstantinov, or Old Cosentin as the Jews called it, even though the hiring committee rejected his demand to establish a choir for him. His dream of arranging his melodies for four voices, in addition to the cantor's tenor solo, would have to wait for a later time. Against this setback, however, was the pledge of the Cosentin Jewish community to award the candidate a spacious flat from public assets and equip him with a piano. The die was cast. Zvi-Hersch's promise to his daughter to leave the village came to pass much sooner than anticipated. Moreover, thanks to the advance notice, Reb Moishe would be able to drive the three to Cosentin in his wagon and still return to the village in good time.

The packing continued until early light. Old and young worked feverishly, as if they feared that a slack in pace would, God forbid, spiral them into dangerous thoughts. For the purpose at hand, little Golda was transferred still asleep to her grandparents' bed for the few remaining hours of the night, while Grandma Feige rummaged through every larder and drawer for sacks which had once stored flour, ripped them open into cloths and, by passing a rope through the eye of a needle the size of a stake, transformed them into two enormous bags. These were large enough for all the cushions and blankets and other bedding which Sureh meanwhile stripped from the beds and removed from the cupboards, as well as the winter clothing, furs and carpets; Feige would close up the bags with the same needle and coarse stitch, so that they looked like huge quilts.

At the same time, Lowe, the only one of Sureh's brothers still living at the Storzhov inn, would undo the coffer's iron hasps, remove its contents and bring it, empty, to Sureh and Zvi-Hersch. In no time at all the coffer, too, would be filled with goods, its solid sides suitable for storing fragile items, while the iron hasps promised to protect the Sabbath candle holders, Sureh's silver and jewelry, and the sacred books that Zvi-Hersch had bought from booksellers staying at the inn. Last but not least, it would welcome the notebooks which Zvi-Hersch had filled with his pearly script – his original melodies, first, and then the notes of those he had received from his father, Reb Ephraim, scion of a dynasty of cantors that had roamed northward from the Balkans and, upon reaching the gates of the fortified Podolian town of Bar, "had seen that it was good" and settled there.

Moishe would then lock the coffer – slowly, slowly, as if wanting to linger over the feel of the metal – and hand the keys to Sureh, who was wailing bitterly. "This coffer has been in our family for generations, through all its wanderings," he declared, conscious of the momentous circumstances, "Just like this *arenda* deed, which my forefathers acquired from the Potockis and passed on to their children, until it was my turn to inherit it. Until today, I believed that what I held in deposit was a treasure, and I guarded it inside the coffer like the apple of my eye." The rest of Moishe's words, as Golda heard them from her mother, remained firmly lodged in her mind, even forty years later: "Oh, how wrong I was!" He was penitent. "The landowners who grew fat on exploiting the serfs, exploited the Jews no less, enlisting them by the force of the *arenda* to do their dirty work. By serving the exploiters, it was the Jewish tenant who stood for the exploiter in peasant eyes, for it was he – rather than his squire – who was always before them. And what is our reward for all our toil? An evil regime, that ignored the novel nature of our settlement and our share in rebuilding the Ukraine after its destruction at Tartar hands, is now eager to obliterate all memory of our life here over hundreds of years! If that's the way things are, we have no choice but to pick up the wanderer's staff and go..."

For a moment it appeared – Sureh went on with her description – that the old man's voice broke and was silenced, as he succumbed to regret. But the weakness soon passed, even though that brief fraction of a moment had seemed to his onlookers an eternity.

"What we do have is tradition," Moishe recovered. "The *arenda* and the coffer, by their age embody our early settlement in the village, and are passed down from eldest to eldest. It is only right, then, that we follow the family custom and pass them on to Meiyer, our eldest. Unfortunately, Meiyer is not with us, nor are Rivkeh and Mekhyl, but only Lowe and Sureh, the youngest of our children. The *arenda* itself has now been terminated, and only the coffer remains; which means that the convention of the eldest is no longer valid as before and reality alone must choose the heir. In these circumstances, the only one that can reap any benefit from the coffer is the youngest of all. Reality therefore determines to bestow the coffer on Sureh, in the hope that after her life-span of a hundred and twenty years she will bequeath it to her daughter, Golda, in keeping with both the convention of the eldest, according to the tradition of our ancestors, and as a memento of this eventful night, to remember our exodus from Storzhov."

The night slowly made way to the pink harbingers at the gate of the east. Smoke rose from a number of chimneys, revealing that several Ukrainian women already were toiling over breakfast; for the most part, however, Storzhov's good citizens continued to sleep on. The wagon was loaded with the two makeshift bags and coffer, and after a hasty morning prayer the entire family went out to the gate of the inn – Moishe, Feige, Lowe, Zvi-Hersch and Sureh (with little Golda asleep on her shoulder) – six Jews, the only ones in the village, flesh of its flesh, and yet, ostensibly, from another planet. Bowed with pain and sorrow and exhausted from the night's work,

Feige and Lowe kissed the child's cheek, careful not to wake her, and fell on the necks of the two adults banished to an uncertain future. Those who stayed behind knew only too well, as did the elder who now brought up the wagon, that within a few days, they, too, would be exiled from here. Yes, and upon their exit, there would be not a soul to bid them farewell but, more likely, someone to see them out with thrown stones, even though they had been born here and lived here all their lives.

5

Often, even after four decades, Golda and her son would still reflect on impressions of that night's events, which Sureh had bequeathed to her daughter, Golda, and which, through Golda, became part of her grandchildren's heritage in Tarnów. Brave Grandpa Moishe's bitter accusations against the Polish establishment continued to ring in their ears like bells of warning. And the more she and her son examined the words, the taller and wider she remembered Grandpa's square back as it had appeared when she first woke up in the wagon and she, only four years old, could see from where she lay no more than his back and the nape of his neck. Sitting high on the wagoner's seat and uncommonly erect for his years, wearing the black Russian *rubashka* from which the fringes of the *tallis-koot'n* playfully peeked out, and the round Russian cap that grew out of his neck, he looked to her like the ship mast she had seen in the children's picture book Father had bought her on one of his trips to Brody – a proud mast, contemptuous of the storm all around – or like the mighty rock, also in the book, lashed by breakers but unbeaten; or standing tall like the oak outside the fence of the Storzhov inn, to the top of which she, Golda, dreamt of climbing to touch the sky.

This is how she would always remember Grandpa and, in the background, the old inn and its railed gallery which crowned the downstairs alehouse like a ring, and herself, the only Jewish child in the village, hiding behind a pillar and observing the goings-on below. Also in the background, the waters of the Kropivnia and the Kortchik which flowed together, and the fleet of white geese gliding to the green shore opposite. She remembers, too, the Ukrainian maids and their gay laughter and scary stories, and an icon of a holy Russian saint hanging on the wall of their bedroom, and their cheeks flushed with excitement at the sight of the noblemen visiting the inn. And completing the picture are the shadows dancing on the alehouse wall that last night, to the faint light of the paraffin lamp…

Reb Moishe's anti-aristocratic stance, which may have been puzzling, given the Potockis' special attitude towards him, seemed to Golda – and consequently also to her son – completely within character of the elderly *arendar*. After considering everything she had heard from his daughter, Sureh, the two decided that the man had been endowed with an inborn, intellectual integrity that enabled him to perceive the gentry objectively, even though he was on the receiving end of their favors. He had realized that the actions of the Polish nobility in the Ukraine were not the whimsy of individuals, but an institutionalized exploitation that could not fail to nurture deep-seated hatred in its victims.

At times, Golda would tell her son – after thousands of miles already separated them from the Ukraine and Grandpa's home, and many years after his passing – she would hear the old man pacing to and fro on sleepless nights, his restless spirit chastising both himself and his ancestors: "Any way you look at it," he agonized, and tormented a succession of predecessors, "if the system is vile, then the Jews of our times, including myself are at fault and put ourselves at risk by clinging to the *arenda* – just as our forebears did in their own time. And just as in 1648 their obtuseness brought Chmielnicki down on their heads, so in our own generation the system of *arendas* might, God forbid, provide cause for a future disaster."

The old man, however, was alone in his anxiety. The subjugation and poverty of simple Ukrainian folk remained at the bottom of the concerns of both the Czarist-Russian regime and the disdainful, urban, enlightened Ukrainians, who paid lip service to an exalted love of their country but shunned the salt of the earth peasant and his hardships. Nor did the peasant's lot disturb the rest of the Polish landed gentry, or their Jewish concession holders – apart from poor old Moishe, who bemoaned the situation but dared not break the chain of generations and shake off his part in the socio-economic order. And apart from Meiyer, the eldest and most talented of his children, whose diligence and spirit Moishe and Feige soon recognized, sparing no effort to send him off to Odessa in pursuit of higher studies.

Unlike his father, however, Meiyer, the philosopher, who with all his soul was steeped in the revolutionary ideas of his generation, did decide to take a personal step to change the miserable state of affairs: while studying in Odessa he joined an underground cell of revolutionary students, dreaming to offer up his soul one day on the altar of the revolution.. His stunned parents, hastening to restore him to his former ways, decided that there is no better remedy than marriage to distract a young man from revolutionary dreams.

In Zaslav, Nathan Hannover's birthplace, next to Shepetovka, live Yitzhik and Dvoireh, cousins of the Gokhbans, who have two sons and seven daughters. Reb Moishe, whose habit it is to drop in on the Zaslav branch of the family when in Shepetovka to prostrate himself at the graveside of Rabbi Pinhas of Koretz, sets his eye on the older daughter, Gittel, as a suitable bride for his son – an educated, pretty young woman, who outside the house gives her name as Gertrude, as is fashionable among the "progressive" young. Her parents tell Moishe about the manifestations of anti-Semitism in their town and their decision to emigrate to America. Even better – Moishe mentally adds another string to the bow he has devised to save his son – Meiyer being included, as Gittel's husband, in the party making their way across the seas; this would remove him still further from the dangers lurking in Odessa. The match is concluded with a handshake and on Yitzhik's next trip to Odessa, his daughter, Gittel, joins him.

Hopes of Meiyer's emigration fit in nicely with the prevailing family atmosphere. Everyone was highly aware of the terrible estrangement between the Ukrainian population and its Jewish neighbors, and alert to the cynical use made of it by the Czarist regime, exploiting it for its own anti-Semitic policy. A hint of it plagued the family consciousness on the eve of its exile from Storzhov – in the understated, apprehensive speculation that a stone or two might well be thrown at them on their departure – for deep in the hearts of all was a real fear of new pogroms. There were many who agreed with Moishe that "We have no choice but to pick up the wanderer's staff and go…" Thus, little by little, independently of the government's expulsion decree, part of the family arrived at the conclusion that it was necessary to quit the Ukraine. Like a pillar of smoke and a pillar of fire, the two trends – expulsion and voluntary emigration – now walked before the Gokhban camp and were to engender decisive changes in their lives.

6

Unaware of the passengers' distress, the horses obeyed the signals Reb Moishe transmitted with a flick of the reins and, pulled the wagon east along the main road to Zhitomir and Kiev. They enjoyed the rays of the rising sun only for a brief distance, for soon, at the junction of Novograd Volhynski, Moishe lightly drew in the right strap, and the horses responded with a sharp turn into the forest, which seemed to swallow them up inside without a trace of their approach. They now embarked on a narrow secondary route, the more eastern of the two dirt roads branching out south from the Zhitomir-Rovno artery, the two roads would meet up again at Starokonstantinov, Old Cosentin, the objective of his journey.

Bisecting the forest, the dirt road joined the starting point with the final destination at Cosentin, as if connecting Storzhov, the world of yesterday, which had crumbled, with the world of tomorrow, the unknown.

Unlike the road, however, which by its very nature encourages movement, the forest remained static for the entire journey, as if its soul had frozen in the trees. Like mysterious edifices , the forest blocks stood motionless at both sides of the road, so dense, that the tall, thick-leafed trees huddled together to become one. A persistent sun beat down on their canopies, eager to breach the cool forest darkness. But the forest is not prepared to give up its secrets. Almost as if tree with tree had joined hands to close their ranks with lock and bolt, indifferent to the identity of the four passengers whose wagon traverses the forest this morning.

The elderly *arendar*, who is as familiar with the roads of Volhynia as with the byways of his village of Storzhov, has resolved to reach Cosentin by noon the next day. He has, therefore, made his horses swallow up two thirds of the journey on the first day, proceeding along the eastern route of the course while still fresh. Towards evening, the wagon would escape the forest to greet a large lake, heralding the town of Polonnoye, where they are to spend the night. Before that, however, the men will go into the old cemetery for *Minha* (afternoon) prayers opposite the shrine of Reb Yehuda-Leib, the Mokhiah, and *Maariv* (evening) prayers at the shrine of Reb Yaakov-Yosef. Moishe gazes at Polonnoye spread out before him and sighs: "How is it that unlike other Ukrainian Jewish towns, this town – in which ten thousand Jews were murdered in 1648 – has still not regained, after two hundred and fifty years, its former strength, but has barely seven thousand Jews, even though it was blessed with two such *Tzaddikim*?"

After letting the horses rest in Cosentin for the remainder of the second day, Reb Moishe makes his way back alone on the third day of the journey, along the western route this time, springing the now lighter wagon northwest to Shepetovka, where he would prostrate himself at the graveside of Reb Pinhas of Koretz before spending the night with the family in Zaslav. In the evening of the fourth day the wagon would roll into Koretz – which was just west of the village of Storzhov, and cross the Kortchik bridge. Once the horses smelled the water and recognized the river as Storzhov's, and inhaled the fragrance of Koretz's famous fruit tree plantations, they could be trusted to navigate the rest of the way home on their own.

While the motion of the wagon swings Golda like a cradle, lengthening her sojourn in the world of dreams, the three adult passengers continued to cloak themselves in silence, each lost in his or her own thoughts, each with his or her own forecasts and fears.

"I, of course, am the biggest loser in this development," Moishe concludes to himself. "Feige and I, that is" – he quickly corrects himself, cognizant of Feige's partnership in managing the *arenda*. "What can you do?" He sighs, "It is not easy at our age to pursue a new livelihood. Perhaps our savings will see us through the few years that the Master of the Universe will see fit to apportion us."

His eyes precede the wagon along the dirt road that unfurls a narrow yellow carpet between two dark forest walls. "To tell the truth, how do you even know, you old good-for-nothing, that the expulsion is a disaster?" He chuckles, as the empty, tree-lined road prevents the horses from straying and allows him to sink into thought undisturbed. He dredges up an adage learned in early childhood and coined by Nahum, nicknamed *Gam-zu* ("This too"), who, dozens of generations back, dressed all sorts of woes and ills in an optimism all his own: "This, too, is for the good," – so much so that the saying became his trademark. "Who knows? Maybe the expulsion that has descended on us is 'also for the good.' Times have changed. The *arenda* has died. I, personally, its last master and slave, may properly shed a tear over it. But these young people – why should they bewail being rid of it? What can a Ukrainian village offer Jewish youth today?"

The habit of optimism, which was one of Moishe's marked qualities and spanned thousands of years to his friend and brother, Nahum Gamzu, held sway once more. "Yes, the expulsion forces the young to grow up overnight and make decisions. Take Zvi-Hersch, for example, our son-in-law. How he agonized, poor boy! What ambitious, big dreams he spun: to conduct a choir and orchestra and perform mainly pieces that he himself composed. And after all, why not? Is it a sin to dream? And if not now, when? It's just that suddenly, because of the threat of expulsion, he was forced, as husband and father, to make a decision. Has he buried his dream? In faith, no. Someone of his mettle will never give up a dream, but only defer it reasonably. One may be sure that one day Zvi-Hersch will make it to Galicia, to Vienna, to the cantoral centers…"

"And, maybe, for the others as well – it is for the best." Moishe continues to mentally organize the post-*arenda* Gokhban world. "Meiyer, God willing, will sail off with Gittel and her family to America, and Rivkeh and her husband, Alter, who were also destined to liquidate their business in Zhitomir, will follow soon after. Even young Lowe is busy fantasizing about America. As for Mekhyl and Layeh in Proskurov, their emigration must wait, both because of Layeh's last month of pregnancy and the betrothal of their two daughters to two "enlightened" young men (*maskilim*), who believe that the Ukraine still offers Jews a safe future and have no intention of joining the "Exodus from Egypt." I understand the parents' doubts. It is not easy to turn your back on your own flesh and blood. But the girls and the bridegrooms have decided what they've decided and, it seems to me, if even just for the sake of the newborn child, Mekhyl and Layeh will also leave for Boston in a year or two."

"H-m-m... Boston!" Moishe smiles. "Everyone talks about Boston. As if there were no room left in New York, and no chance there of getting an apartment or making a living. The fact is that whereas before, only a handful of German Jews, calling themselves *Fortgeschrittene* (Progressives) set their sights on Boston – now, thank God, our own people, too, have settled there and the Jewish community is as large as Polonnoye's!"

"And after all," he allowed on further reflection, "Maybe as far as I'm concerned it's also for the good. Didn't I make a vow on that brash, bitter day of *Rosh Hodesh* Tammuz that if Heaven helped me and I survived the fire that broke out in Koretz, I would shed the yoke that the *arenda* is and set aside time for Torah study in the town of my salvation? That's fifteen years ago! And only today do I remember my sin: because of urgent business pressures which are the lot and constant struggle of a concession holder, and pressure from the Lord and Lady, I submitted to the authority of flesh-and-blood masters, breaking my vow to the Master of the Universe. But now that the *arenda* has given up the ghost and I am about to be expelled from the village of Storzhov after decades of faithful service, it is time that I – man poor in deeds, shaken and awed – present myself before the Holy Ark in Koretz and make good on my vow."

7

All at once he saw the fire of June 1881 burning before his eyes as if it were yesterday. He had ridden that morning from Storzhov to Koretz to buy a number of leather sheets for the estate from Herschel the tanner on *Inter di Milln* (Mill Street). Suddenly, cries of "Fire!" rent the air all around: "Yidn, s'brent!", and within minutes the blaze had spread all over Koretz (most of whose houses were wooden with thatched roofs), and the town and its residents were trapped in walls of flame and smoke. Fire-fighting being what it was at the time, the blaze did not die down until it had consumed hundreds of homes and shops and their entire contents, as well as everything flammable in its path. Instinctively, the population sought refuge in the waters of the Kortchik, but twenty people never made it to the river banks and were burnt alive. Apart from homes, all the synagogues, Hasidic *shtiblakh* and *batei-midrash*, fourteen in number, fed the fire, including "the Old Synagogue," built in the generation after the massacres of 1648–49 as a monument to the community destroyed by the Cossacks.

Reb Moishe, coming out from Reb Herschel's tannery shop with the leather sheets, and wanting only to get back on his horse and return to Storzhov, found himself suddenly rooted to the ground in the middle of *Inter di Milln*, with every house in the neighborhood on fire, apart from Mill Street itself. No more than a handful of stone buildings remained; the Catholic-Polish church – unlike the Provoslav wooden *Tserkvyas* – as well as the homes of the local magnates, whose names every child in Koretz, whether Jew or gentile, could roll off his tongue: the Weinstock brothers and Yaakov-Yosef Horenstein. "Obscenely ostentatious," Moishe aimed scornful barbs at them: for even in the midst of the disaster that had befallen the town, Moishe, the follower of Reb Pinhas of Koretz, could hardly restrain his disdain for the exhibitionism of the wealthy Jews who copied the castles of the Czartoryskis and Potockis to the point of ridiculousness.

Now, however, his sense of the absurd was drowned in the thick smoke all around. Not far off he spotted the *Garbarsky Shil* (the Tanners' Synagogue) going up in flames and leaped forward through the ring of fire; protecting his face with the leathers he carried, burst into the burning building. Oblivious of the burns on his singed hands, he pulled off the charred door of the Holy Ark and gathered into his arms the two Torah scrolls at which the flames were already lapping. Then, wrapping them in his leathers, he ran to the ancient public well in the marketplace and dropped the treasure inside.

His example roused the populace. Jews, who only a moment before had stood by stunned and helpless, now also began to throw things into the well – be it Torah scrolls saved from the fire or household goods that they managed to pluck from the conflagration. And although that evening local *goyim* were seen milling around the well and pilfering articles of Jewish property that had collected there, the scrolls that Moishe had cast into the well were at the bottom of the heap and thus spared from looting. After the Koretz tanners restored the synagogue, the scrolls were returned to the building and placed in the new Holy Ark installed within its walls.

As a result of this incident, Reb Moishe won instant acclaim in Koretz. "*Sholem Aleikhem* (How do you do), Reb Moishe 'Storzhover'" – people would address him with respect and affection on his visits to town, be it on his regular purchasing missions, or with his family for the High Holidays and Passover. "*Der Storzhover*" – even without his first name – was now so sought after, not only by individuals for personal advice but by the community on matters of Jewish law and ethics, that Storzhov seemed to have changed from a remote, God-forsaken Volhynian village, into a spiritual wellspring and center of Torah.

The reconstruction and repair of the burnt homes and institutions destroyed in the fire proceeded at a remarkable pace, for three reasons: funding from Koretz' magnates and merchants; the broad assistance pouring into the town from all Volhynian Jewish communities; and no less important, the inner strength of the inhabitants of the Jewish town, who had known and overcome, trials and tribulations in the past. Thus, by the middle of the last decade of the nineteenth century, there were no longer fourteen, but nineteen, houses of prayer and study, and the voice of Torah was again heard loud and clear on the banks of the Kortchik. Reb Moishe followed the progress of the work on his visits to Koretz and, from time to time, even dropped in at one of the old-new synagogues or at one of the six Hasidic *Kloyzes* in the town being rebuilt, to linger over

Minha prayers or a lesson in Torah, without, however, getting involved in the disputes between the Hasidim and their opponents,
the Misnagdim, or showing preference for one Hasidic sect over
another.

This was the natural and accepted way of things for fifteen
years. But the expulsion from Storzhov in 1896 put an end to the
unspoken arrangement. The Storzhov hero's refusal to favor any
one faction was no longer tenable once it became public knowledge that the "last of the *arendars*" and his wife had decided to
settle permanently in the town of Koretz. Every group and sect in
town considered it an honor to offer the hero formal membership
under its wings or, at the very least, to have him regard the group
issuing the invitation as the permanent abode for his prayers, study
and charitable works.

Moved by these displays of affection and eager to satisfy all
without offending any of the good people who had his interests at
heart, Moishe decided to pray *Minha* at a different synagogue every
day, until he had covered all the prayer houses in a more or less
tri-weekly cycle (excepting the three Sabbaths). But as far as a permanent place of prayer was concerned, including for the Sabbath
and holidays, his mind was made up, firmly basing himself on the
tenets and comportment of Reb Pinhas of Koretz, his spiritual mentor. This *Tzaddik's* conduct was always before him.

Clearly, he could not sit shoulder to shoulder with the heads of
the community, those haughty, well-born, moneyed gentlemen who
lounged in the pleasures of the "Great Synagogue" or the "Great *Beis-
Medrash*". Hadn't his rabbi accused even the Vilna Gaon himself
of pride?! Nor did he wish to be part of rich Yaakov Horenstein's
synagogue, or sit with the magnates of the *Kobilinsky Shil*, and even
second- and third-level merchants and dealers at *Reb Usher's Shil*
made him flinch. He felt strange with them, even though his nega-
tive opinion of them had undergone a serious change since the fire
and in view of their generosity in rebuilding the town.

By the same token, he did not wish to join the town's Hasidic sects. Despite his identification with the Hasidic world view, he did not submit to the solicitations of the *Kloyz* of the followers of the *Maggid* of Chernobyl, nor the *Kloyzes* of branches of the Chernobyl dynasty. Three of these, named for the original seats of their Rabbinate, had set down roots in Koretz: the *Kloyz* of the followers of the *Rebbe* of Skvira, the *Kloyz* of the *Rebbe* of Trisk and the *Kloyz* of the Makarov Hasidim. He also avoided *Mekheleh's Shil* which served as a *Kloyz* for the Berezna'ites, and even refrained from aligning himself with *Reb Yankeleh's Shil,* even though this latter house of prayer offered a haven to refugee Hasidim whose courts had not yet re-organized after the fire. In all of these, he was put off – just as Reb Pinhas had been in his time – by the excessive body swaying during prayer and the vulgar, outward *hislahavis* (burning enthusiasm), when all he yearned for was the heartfelt faith of simple folk, regarding fanatic extravagance as pretence and falsehood. Hadn't Reb Pinhas accused even Yaakov-Yosef of Polonnoye of falsehood?

Reb Moishe's inclination was to adopt one of the small synagogues of artisans and manual laborers: either of the wagoners and porters, or the prayer houses of the tailors, shoemakers, hatmakers, or even the *Klezmer Shilkhen*, which was the little prayer house of the town's folk-musicians. His disappointment, however, was not long in coming: all too soon he got a measure of the spiritual shallowness of the different groups, and although he tried to explain it away as the result of fatigue of the hard-working members, he nevertheless had difficulty finding his place there.

Reb Moishe thus had no choice but to direct his lights inward, to the solitary study and meditation, denied him by his former occupation as *arendar*. "Oh, what I have missed by staying in Storzhov all those years, shouldering a heavy burden and toiling over someone else's estate, while for the redemption of my own soul I did nothing," Reb Moishe berates himself, his heart breaking every time he opens the *Gemara* and finds it hard to grasp the issue discussed. "From now on," he vowed, "I will sit from morning to night at the *Yeshiveh Shil*, poring over a page of *Gemara*, and at midnight I will seek seclusion at *Deym Ruv's Shilkhen* (the Rabbi's small synagogue) and immerse myself in the *Zohar* by candlelight." Nonetheless, it was the *Garbarsky Shil*, whose Ark kept the Torah scrolls he had so devotedly saved from the fire, that quite naturally remained closest to his heart. In it, the synagogue of the tanners, the old man desired to pray and study until the day of his death.

8

A mere few weeks had passed after Reb Moishe and Feige's resettlement in Koretz when there was a momentous development – a development that lent forceful weight to the old man's warnings. Terrible rumors suddenly rolled in from faraway Odessa, toppling Moishe's plans with a mighty turn: *Meiyer is d-e-a-d!*

How cruel of fate to stage so hair-raising a coincidence: on the very night that the stunned family grappled with the news of expulsion from the village – far away from Storzhov, in Odessa, Meiyer was confronting a Cossack cavalry regiment called in to quell a stormy student demonstration. Pushed by the full weight of Cossack and horse to the wall of a building where the demonstrators marched, Meiyer collapsed on the ground, his body torn by hooves that galloped forward. Along with the bodies of his fellow students, also shot and trampled by Cossacks, he was thrown into an unmarked pit, and denied even a Jewish burial.

Thus ended the dream of the Jewish idealist from the Pale of Settlement, to sacrifice himself on the altar of the revolution, believing that putting an end to the suffering of the oppressed masses, the "Jewish problem" would also "dissolve of itself." This general, tragic conception was typical of young Jewish idealists in the nineteenth and twentieth centuries. Like Meiyer, they were ready to shed their Jewish heritage for the sake of a universal ideal and "grease the wheels of the revolution," even though, on the whole, the revolution turned its back on them in victory and ultimately crushed them beneath its wheels.

Blessed be the Master of the Universe, who anticipates the remedy for ills and comfort for the mourner. The day before the elderly couple learned of the murder of their firstborn son, the happy news arrived from Proskurov that their daughter-in-law, Layeh, Mekhyl's wife, had given birth to a boy. So that when Moishe and Feige rose from mourning, they still had time to reach Proskurov: there, surrounded by near and dear, bereaved like himself, the old man had a chance to sprinkle a few drops of solace into the cup of loss by acting as *sandak* (godfather) to his grandson. Then, with a supreme sense of the continuity of generations, the slain uncle's name was given to the newborn nephew when he was brought into the Covenant of Abraham, and ever after was known as Meiyer.

Another moment of satisfaction awaited Moishe and Feige when they heard from Cosentin that Sureh, too, was with child and in the summer of 1897 would produce a brother or sister for Golda. Everyone hoped that the grandparents would be able to come to the *simhe* (celebration) – it would be their first visit to Zvi-Hersch's cantoral seat – and if the child was to be a boy, Reb Moishe would again be honored in the capacity of godfather. It was learned that Sureh too, like her brother Mekhyl, wished to name her son after her martyred older brother.

The year 1897, however, was no ordinary year. In February of the previous year, Theodor Herzl's *Der Judenstaat* (The Jewish State) had appeared in the German original, and in a number of translations, including Russian and Hebrew. In the autumn of 1896, a version of it even appeared in Yiddish-Daitch – German text in Hebrew letters – in Kolomyia, in Podolia. Whether in the original or in translation, the little book then and later so fired the imagination of the masses that in 1899 it was published as a sixty-six-page pamphlet in soft orange cover in Zhitomir in the Yiddish *mamme loshen* (mother tongue). *Di Yiddishe Medineh,* and could be acquired for as little as twenty kopeks. Herzl's tidings caused a stir also at the courts of the Hasidic *rebbes*, especially those whose curiosity had been whetted for the past decade by photographs of the new colonies in Eretz Israel, and even though most of them did not formally join the proto-Zionist organization *Hibbat Zion,* they spread the ideas of the back-to-Eretz Israel movement in impassioned sermons before their followers.

One such particularly assiduous *rebbe* was Reb Yohanan (Yoihintche), the youngest of the eight sons of Reb Mordekhai, the *Maggid* of Chernobyl. Unlike the eldest son, who inherited his father's seat as head of the Chernobyl Hasidic dynasty, or the other six who established their own realms in a series of Ukrainian towns and reigned high-handedly, some of them even amassing wealth, Yoihintche chose to base his court at a tiny townlet on the Serebryanka tributary, between Skvira and Cherkassy. In the past, the locality had been granted to a cavalry commander (*Rotmistrz* in Polish), hence the Polish name Rotmistrzówka, which evolved into the Ukrainian Rotmistrivka, and Rahmistrivka in popular parlance. The Hasidim, too, favored the latter form – perhaps because of its Hebrew-sounding opening syllable – and that is how the dynasty is known to this day, even far from the shores of the Ukraine.

Yoihintche guided his flock towards modesty and being content with little, towards love of one's fellow man, and love of Eretz Israel. Unfortunately, he did not realize his dream of *aliyah* to the land of Israel, nor did he live to witness the appearance of Herzl's book, for the Master of the Universe summoned him to His Seat of Honor at the start of spring in 1895. The fervor that swept up the Jewish communities upon the publication of Herzl's *Judenstaat,* one year after the death of the *Tzaddik,* and the hopes raised by the news that the "King of the Jews" was convening a first worldwide Zionist Congress at the end of August 1897, were among the clear signs of the times when Yoihintche's rabbinic mantle fell onto the shoulders of his four sons. Three of them, apart from Duvidl, the eldest, who reigned in Zlatopol, remained in their father's town.

And these are the three sons who rose to the challenge of leading the House of Chernobyl in Rahmistrivka, weaving into the broad loom of new hopes – of which Herzl was the prophet – the love of Israel and longing for Redemption that their father, Yoihintche, had bequeathed to them. Motteleh – who was very likely named after his grandfather, the *Maggid* of Chernobyl, and carried the scepter of leadership for eleven years – and his brothers, Nuhimtche and Velveleh who, at his bidding, made the rounds of the Ukraine's towns and cities, preaching love for the Jewish People and *aliyah* to the Holy Land. One unforgettable Friday, at spring's end 1897, Reb Nuhimtche, the *meshulah* (emissary), arrived in Cosentin.

Now, it was Zvi-Hersch's practice in Cosentin to invite home for the holy day any unfamiliar Jew he met in the synagogue on Sabbath eve, so that he might spend the day with the Weinman family in the spacious flat the community had placed at the cantor's disposal. On the face of it there was thus nothing strange in the fact that Zvi-Hersch returned from synagogue that evening in the company of a guest whose identity he did not know, yet who, despite his simple garments, was clearly not a simple person, as confirmed by his speech and aspect. Only during the meal, when the guest began to sprinkle his conversation with words of Torah and to sing unfamiliar Sabbath melodies, did his hosts realize that they had been privileged to welcome into their home the grandson of the *Maggid* of Chernobyl, the son of Yoihintche, the first of the Rahmistrivka *rebbes*.

Till late into the night Zvi-Hersch learned and memorized the different Chernobyl tunes that he heard from Nuhimtche, who had received them from Cantor Yosseleh-Hazzen, "the sweet singer of Chernobyl." Yosseleh served as *baal-tefille* (prayer leader) for the *meshulah*'s older brother, Reb Duvidl, who had set up his court in Zlatopol. On the following day, after the Sabbath morning prayers, the *meshulah* addressed the Cosentin congregation. He began by lauding all Jews who supported settlement in the Holy Land and, finally, perhaps as a hint of the new voices emanating from Vienna and stirring the curiosity of every thinking person in the community, he asked: "Are the Redeemer's approaching paces echoing in our ears these very days? Do they prophesy remarkable events that are about to happen in our world?" He stopped at that without any explanation, as if leaving everyone to his own personal reckoning.

On their return home, the guest was honored with a festive *kiddush* (ritual blessing over wine and food) in the presence of all the community leaders. After blessing and drinking the wine and complimenting the cake that the woman of the house had made and served, he said: "*Hazzente leiben* (Dear cantor's-wife, may you live long), you will give birth to a son who is destined for greatness. Happy is your lot, for the hour of his birth will be an hour of awakening and hope for the Redemption of Zion. It is therefore fitting that you name him Ben-Zion (Son of Zion)!"

A hush fell over the room. The *meshulah* kept still for some moments, his eyes seeing and unseeing, sending a ray of light through the open window to some imaginary point above the confluence of the Ikopetch and Slutch – as if drawing inspiration from there. It was now clear to the Weinmans that since Heaven had revealed to the *meshulah* that Sureh carried a male child in her womb who would grow up to be a great rabbi (for what else could "destined for greatness" possibly mean?) – the boy should indeed be called Ben-Zion. The father was nevertheless in for a serious disappointment, since Ben-Zion – although he was to prove proud of his name and even adopt it as his surname instead of "Weinman" – was to turn his back on the rabbinate and choose instead to be a poet and artist.

This put an end to Sureh's plans to name her son after her poor brother. Eight years were to pass before Reb Moishe – on his death-bed – would learn from America that another grandson had been born to him and called after his murdered revolutionary uncle: Meiyer.

The Rahmistrivka emissaries were seen not only to preach but to practice. When a daughter was born to Nuhimtche, during the very same period, he called her Bat-Zion (Daughter of Zion), a name that also graced Velveleh's daughter. The call of *aliyah* to the land of Israel, the *rebbes* of Rahmistrivka addressed primarily to themselves, and they responded to it wholeheartedly. The first to leave was the leader, Reb Motteleh himself, who moved to Jerusalem in 1906. Sadly, he lost his life in the Arab riots in the city in 1920. His two brothers, who had assumed the leadership of the dynasty in the Ukraine, did their best to preserve the heritage, but were unsuccessful due to the upheavals of the First World War and the Russian Revolution of 1917, as well as the civil war in its wake.

Petlyura's pogroms and the policy to eradicate religious ed-ucation and values in general, implemented by the Bolsheviks against all faiths and carried out with great ardor among the Jews by their *Yevsektsya* agents, rendered hopeless the life struggle of Rahmistrivka Hasidism on its home ground. As a result, by roundabout means Nuhimtche made his way to Jerusalem in 1926, followed soon after by his brother, Velveleh – the last of the Rahmistrivka *rebbes* who managed to escape the revolutionary pillory – and they and their sons and their sons' sons built up the last Rahmistrivka branch of the House of Chernobyl on the soil of Israel, where it continues to this day.

9

The Zionist awakening at the end of the nineteenth century, which united young and old, Orthodox and Progressive, nevertheless em-braced only a minority and did not slacken the pace of Ukrainian

Jewry's emigration to the United States. After all, Herzl did not advocate practical settlement in Eretz Israel, as did *Hibbat Zion*, but subordinated the Zionist act to the procurement of an official charter from the Turkish government. In any case, he offered no immediate solution to the distress of the masses for which large-scale emigration to America was the only answer.

Preparations for the voyage to the United States thus remained the chief concern of the heads of the Storzhov and Zaslav branches of the family – in keeping with Reb Moishe's resolve: "We have no choice but to pick up the wanderer's staff and go..." The Odessa murder, which replaced the longed-for marriage alliance with an alliance of mourning, did not stop the emigration process but rather fueled it. Nevertheless, the attempts of the two families to emigrate together failed, even though bereavement, pain and rage sharpened their resolve to leave and bound them irrevocably.

The failure to coordinate arrangements was due to the discrepancy between one family's practical and emotional readiness, and the other's. And little wonder. The entire campaign had begun in Zaslav without connection to the Gokhbans and long before disaster had snatched the fiancé from the arms of his betrothed. No wonder, then, that the Zaslav branch – Father Yitzhik and Mother Dvoireh, with their two sons and seven daughters (including Gittel) – had decided months before the Gokhbans to break away from the soil of the Ukraine, a soil which devoured its children, and they set sail for the New World.

The Zaslavers departed in two waves. The first group, comprised of the father and eldest son, left in the autumn of 1897; their task, in common with numerous generations of immigrants, was to get the lay of the land and prepare for the others to follow. Now, however – because of Gittel's bereavement and the folk belief that a change of place is the best remedy for sorrow – the eldest daughter also joined the first sailing. Not many months passed before the second group, too, arrived in Boston, so that within the space of a single year, the entire Zaslav family, numbering eleven souls, removed from Volhynia to America.

Unlike their Zaslav cousins – whose decision-making was greatly facilitated by the fact of their concentration in one town, even one house – the Storzhovites, some of whom lived in Koretz and part in Cosentin, Zhitomir and Proskurov, did not muster up sufficient strength after Meiyer's death to make arrangements with the speed necessary to join the Zaslavite party. Nevertheless, the idea of emigration itself constantly hovered in the air and was the topic of every meeting and conversation. The more the talking stage was exhausted and the acting stage approached, the more divided the family became among itself, with the European advocates digging in their heels, on the one hand, and the emigration candidates having their say, on the other. Prominent among the former was Zvi-Hersch, who saw his chances for advancement as cantor and liturgical composer tied to the musical tradition of European, rather than American Jewry, which, at the end of the nineteenth century, was still a desert in terms of its cultural consumption. This was clear to Reb Moishe, as well, who, while driving Zvi-Hersch and Sureh and Golda to Cosentin reflected with concern on the future of his offspring. Consequently, despite his call to emigrate, he acknowledged that it would be better for Zvi-Hersch to bide his time in the Ukraine until he could be offered a fitting post in Galicia or Central Europe.

The others, who *did* see themselves as potential emigrants, kept putting off their departure because of pressing needs of one kind or another. Thus, an unforeseen hitch in the liquidation of the business in Zhitomir forced Rivkeh and Alter to stay on for another few years. Mekhyl and Layeh, too, found it hard to leave for America right away – for one thing, their two married daughters refused to join them, preferring Proskurov to Boston; but even more because their last born was delivered on the eve of the bereavement period for Meiyer – and how could they take an infant on such an ardu-

across the great ocean – finally laid low the Vohlynian village lad
who had been raised on the fragrance of open fields and ancient
forests and the clear waters of the Kropivnia and the Kortchik. In
the spring of 1900, he took to bed – pneumonia – and found himself
hospitalized. Now, all that remains to complete the saga is a compassionate nurse – an Angel in White – dispensing love. But no angel
came. Who did come was Gittel. She came and stayed.

As is true of mythologies, the Storzhov-Zaslav mythology
does not bother to explain how Gittel learned that her young
cousin – younger than herself, and her fiancé's "little brother" – was
lying desperately ill in the Department of Contagious Diseases
at Massachusetts General Hospital. If the first version is accurate –
the one that places Lowe on the same ship as Gittel in 1897 – it is
safe to assume that at least some contact was maintained between
the lone boy and the Zaslav family over the three years, and there
would be no mystery in explaining how Gittel learned of his illness and, perhaps, even helped him to receive treatment. If, however, the other version is correct – which denies all contact between
the Storzhovite Lowe and the relatives who apparently immigrated
from Zaslav after him – one can only permit myth to order fate to
lead the young woman to her cousin's sickbed. Whatever the case
may be, in August 1900 Lowe married his cousin Gittel. And while
there was rejoicing among the entire Zaslav family – her father,
mother, six sisters and two brothers – he, Lowe, remained the only
Storzhov offshoot on American shores, despite the fact that his father, Moishe, had been the High Priest of emigration.

Feige's outlook on the question of emigration was, however,
diametrically opposed to Moishe's. "Emigrate? What for? Will running solve anything?" Undaunted, she followed the radicalization of
the anti-Semitic mood in Russia and the Ukraine and its practical
expressions, which resumed in 1903 – in Kishinev, Homel, and elsewhere. To all these she had one dogged response that bound up past
with present and was applied to all the tyrants of all generations,

from the 1648 massacres down to her own day; all had a single, all-encompassing name which, in her eyes, was the eternal symbol of evil: CHMIELNICKI! With militant and undiluted resolve, until her death at the age of one hundred and seven, she was in the habit of declaring: "All the Chmielnickis together will not succeed in moving me from here. In the Ukraine I was born, and in the Ukraine I shall die..."

Not so the young people. They had despaired of the Ukraine not only because of anti-Semitism but because of its apparent stagnation. Thus, Feige's opinion notwithstanding, the Ukraine increasingly emptied of Gokhbans. The first to leave were Sureh and Zvi-Hersch in 1900: Zvi-Hersch was offered the post of cantor at the old, fortress-like synagogue in Tarnopol, in eastern Galicia. Then, Rivkeh and Alter and their household left for America, followed by Mekhyl and Layeh and their young son, Meiyer, to be reunited with Lowe in Boston. Moishe and Feige remained alone, visited now and then only by Mekhyl and Layeh's daughters, who had married and remained in Proskurov. And when Koretz accompanied the "last of the *arendars*" to his final resting place in the autumn of 1905, not one of his sons was left in the Ukraine to say *kaddish* at his grave.

*

Feige lived on until the spring of 1925; she bequeathed her name to her great-granddaughter, born in Tarnów in the summer of that year. In the two decades following the passing of her husband – years of world war and revolutions and hunger and temporary Ukrainian independence and riot – she never stopped censuring the Ukrainian *goyim* for repaying their Jewish brothers with hatred instead of love. Be it Vrangel, Denikin or Koltchak, commanders of the White Guards who trailed behind the Red Army and, in passing, dealt severe blows to Jewish communities, or Petlyura, architect of Ukrainian independence, who co-opted Jews to his government even as his soldiers killed other Jews in Proskurov.

And yet, time and again the old woman proclaimed that she would never renounce the Ukraine, continuing to upbraid the champions of emigration to their faces.

But declarations are one thing and reality another. Like a dinghy on the Dniepr that has come unanchored and, with nothing to stop it, careens downstream, ultimately to smash on the granite, so Feige's love for "her" Ukraine galloped helplessly between cyclones of slaughter to be crushed on the rocks of Proskurov. Indeed, when the Herald of Blood in that town devoured her granddaughters and their husbands – young people who had regarded the Ukraine as their homeland and had not left it in favor of America – the old woman was sapped of all strength and declared in rage: "A country that does not treat its Jews as a homeland should, cancels their duty of loyalty." Then, to atone for her former censure of those who left the Ukraine, she took a vow of seclusion and sanctified her solitude, refusing, to her dying day, ever again to cross the threshold of her home.

Her death spelled not only the departure of one of the last native innkeepers and the stalwart spouse of "the last of the *arendars*," but also the disappearance from the Ukrainian landscape and records of the last person to bear the name Gokhban. While her daughters and granddaughters took their husbands' names, as was customary, her male descendants in America followed in Lowe's footsteps, allowing the whim of an official upon their entry to the country to change the family name to Goldman, which is how they are known to this day. Thus, when the hundred-and-seven-year-old legendary woman was lowered into the grave, she took with her both the family name and the Gokhban saga – the saga of a family who for ten generations had made the wastelands of the Ukraine fertile, with not a sign of recognition, nor regret at the obliteration of the name from the country's book of chronicles.

Aazik Wróbel and wife Golda, née Weinman

CHAPTER THREE

History from the Mount

1

THE BOY'S CLIMB with Irena to the top of Mt. St. Marcin early that magical morning in July of 1925 was not his first excursion to the crest. It followed a series of routine Sabbath walks up the mountain, which Golda had conducted with her children since the start of the previous summer, and which she had been forced to stop at the end of spring, when her advanced pregnancy began to hamper mobility. The walks, unfortunately, were not resumed for another six years, when Golda's son was already in high school and the nature of the conversations on these outings took a new form.

The hill held many charms for the children: the pleasure of the ascent itself, the moments spent gazing at the changing marks of the seasons, the game of picking out buildings from the urban block in the distance and, most of all, the delicacy of wild strawberries in cream dished up by the Red Inn at the top (payment being deferred because of the Sabbath to the following Monday and the branch in town). In planning the outings, however, Mother's aim was not merely to see to the children's enjoyment. Primarily, she wished to enrich them with a new stimulus: an initiation to history. The Mount, it seemed to her, was the ideal place to present the past as a pageant, with the crest and lingering castle ruins providing a natural stage, and the town below supplying a richness of scenery that no theater anywhere could equal. Herself an enthusiastic dabbler in history, she had, since leaving the eastern frontier, immersed herself in the mysteries of Poland's past and, on the stage of the crest, would unfurl before her children a continuing serial of episodes about bygone Tarnów.

"Children develop a sense of historical belonging by learning the history of their immediate surroundings." She repeated to Irena the pedagogic creed her father had applied to her in childhood, when he had arrayed before her a sweep of towns close to the village in order to endear them to her. "One should help children assimilate the story of their surroundings – in this case of Tarnów – by making it a personal experience. And since, quite naturally, children tend to identify with familiar landscapes, such as the streets of their town or a nearby mountain that is the common destination of their walks, it is easy for them to imagine the historical figures who once trod on these streets or this crest." With typical assertiveness, she went on to explain why she had chosen Mt. St. Marcin as her focus: "Historical interest moves from the near to the far; meaning, from Tarnów to the nation and the world; and Tarnów's history begins here, on this mount!" Unlike her father, however, who concentrated on Jewish communities alone, Golda sought to impart to her children the general history of their town and of the region as a whole.

And indeed, the boy waited in suspense, from one Sabbath to another, for the appointed outing and the next installment from Mother's story. Here, looking down at his town, he received from his mother his first lessons in history: the story of the castle that once had been and now lay in ruins, and the story of the people who lived in it, their spirit still haunting the mount…

To be sure, historical excitement took second place to the actual ascent from the plain to the heights, to the chain of hills bounding the town of Tarnów on the south and including Mount

St. Marcin – a chain that heralded the start of the Carpathians and was thus known as the Sub-Carpathian Sill. Stepping onto the high sill at the southern gateway to his town and gazing from above out into the distance, the boy felt a powerful wind jolting him straight into the kiln of Creation: at exactly this spot (so he imagined) it all began. With wave riding wave the primordial pattern of the mountain strip developed and spread out, shutting off Poland's south. Suddenly, the foundations moved, the plain shuddered, and began to swell, swell and knead itself into chains of hills; ridge clinging to ridge and ridge parting from ridge, each higher and wilder than the other. And the ridges sharpened into peaks, and the peaks stood straight and petrified into cliffs, and the further south they traveled from their Tarnów starting point, the higher they rose until they reached full stature and froze in place to become what they were – the Carpathians!

But when the boy came down from the mountain, the magic, sometimes, would evaporate, the spectacle of Creation fade and melt away, leaving only an ungainly, orphan hillock in sight, devoid of any special grace or grandeur, its name grasping the robe of St. Martin (Marcin, in Polish) – a remote French saint, who had brought Christianity to the pagans in the regions of Gaul some fifteen hundred years before. In the second half of the tenth century, southern Poland's early Christian missionaries no doubt invoked him to inspire the first village converts to Christianity. They praised his habit of sharing his robe with stray paupers, and persuaded the villagers to erect on the mount a small, wooden church to his memory and to name the whole hill for him.

To rescue his Carpathian dream once he came home, the boy's only recourse was to turn to the *Great Romer Atlas*, the treasure he shared with his mother: the two, thirsty for distant places and conjuring up horizons beyond the horizon, both liked to pore over the large book together and imagine the enchanted expeditions that the book harbored for its explorers. The Atlas was capable of rekindling the thrill of actually going up the mountain, so that as soon as the boy began paging through it, the hills and the mountains would sally forth and march towards him in procession. A talented magician was the Atlas, divesting the mountains of their three-dimensional volume and transforming them into amusing ribbons of color – denoting altitude, of course – so that the further south you looked, the more they changed, from green to yellow and from yellow to orange and from orange to brown until they enclosed, in a dark-brown arc, the bottom of the map of Poland.

To scale the mountain – the boy's spirit soars anew at every ascent – means to be the first to reach the top as morning light breaks, and to wave a greeting to the sun and wind and the secret of Creation sealed in the mountains. Obviously, on his first outings with Mother, when he was four, and on his morning trip with Irena, when he was five, he could not foresee that the sharp pinch of pleasure provided by the sense of being "first" would persist into his teens when, as a youth movement counselor, he would assemble his charges on the hill for their weekly group discussions; or when, in winter, he would drag up a makeshift sleigh and, with sudden devilry, send it down the snowy slope to the squeals of its passengers, his two sisters. It was even more impossible to foresee the overwhelming excitement he felt when preparing for a first hesitant "date" on the mountain, with beautiful Karola, a classmate at the Hebrew high school – a blushingly pure rendezvous far from seeing eyes. He did not know that the mountain would always guard his secret, just as it had guarded the secrets of hosts of other young people through the ages.

Harder still was it to imagine that the mountain would continue to cast its spell for him years after he left town, even though the Tarnów he was to return to, heartsick, after a generation's absence, would not be the one he had known from birth, with half of its population made up of Jews; it would be an alien, bloodstained city of Holocaust, the only Jews remaining being the slaughtered thousands – and numbering among them his own father, mother, and younger sister, Gunia – dumped into a mass grave in the bowels of Tarnów's earth.

Yet to this mountain – the last happy relic of a far away childhood – he was to sail again in the autumn of his years, to come full circle. Only having gained the top again after so many years, and drinking in the landscape lying in the sunlight and the vision of the town reclining on the horizon, would he feel fortified enough to come within the gates of the five-hundred-year-old Jewish district that was no more. Only then would he visit the obliterated courtyards and the site of the now vanished apartment building, where his parents had occupied a flat on the balcony of the second floor. Yes, only the tall chestnut tree survived, forlorn in its loneliness and lament.

Indeed, once upon a time, at the top of Mt. St. Marcin, there was a castle. Here, at the height of the Mount – maybe even at this very dew-drenched, grassy spot where Golda and the children went walking – there once, more than six hundred and seventy years ago, stood a knight called Specymir (Spytko, in local parlance) – a magnate of the House of Leliwa (pronounced "Leleevah"), who served as the lord of the fortress of Kraków, the capital city. When he looked about him, his chest puffed and swelled with the mountain air that he breathed into his lungs, as well as with pride and satisfaction: very soon now (he had learned from sources close to the royal household) the King was to mark off the village on the crown lands occupying the slopes of Mt. St. Marcin, and grant it to him. It was then that he meant to erect a grand castle at the top of the hill to bespeak the greatness and marvels of the House of Leliwa for generations.

Spytko's hopes of expanding his assets did have a foundation. After all, he was a senior nobleman with a key position in the royal court of Kraków. As friend and advisor to the ruler Władysław Łokietek, a scion of the Piast dynasty – the first dynasty of the kings of Poland – Spytko left his mark on every initiative for which he was summoned to the king's side: as warrior, statesman and politician. His greatest achievement in the internal arena was the rescue of the scattered Polish duchies from the crisis of splits and bondage that had plagued them in previous generations. At the end of this process, for which Spytko had prepared the ground, Łokietek succeeded in reunifying the quarreling duchies and, in 1320, was proclaimed King over all of Poland.

For one irksome threat Łokietek and his Tarnów advisor could find no solution in their lifetime, and three more generations were to pass before it would be resolved: the threat from the Teutonic Crusader knights, hanging over Poland's head like the sword of Damocles ever since these Crusaders had returned from their exploits in the Holy Land. In 1226, following repeated attacks by heathen Prussians from the Baltic shore on Poland's divided north, the Duke of the north – Łokietek's grandfather – conceived a mad plan to invite these German knights to the region in order to purge the Prussian inhabitants of paganism and so to defend the Polish frontier against their incursions. This foolishness was to cost the Poles and their neighbors dearly: on the pretext of preaching Christianity, the Teutonic Order built up on Poland's northern flank a mighty German force, whose growing aggression became a source of endless trouble. This force would not be overcome until the Polish royal dynasty changed, and a life-and-death alliance was sealed with a neighboring people to wage war in unison against the Crusader knights.

In 1328 Spytko's hopes were realized – so Mother tells the children on their first trip up the mountain, with the figure of the nobleman, in their eyes, growing tall as the mountain itself. That year, the King rewarded his subject and friend for his brave deeds and personal loyalty by permanently signing over to him, from among his own assets, the village lands that included Mount St. Marcin; at the same time, he encouraged Spytko to establish a town on his

estate and, two years later, in 1330, issued a charter to the town settlers, spelling out rights identical to those granted that year to the
burghers of Kraków, the capital. Thus began the construction of
the nobleman's castle on the crest of Mount St. Marcin. At that moment, the town, too, was born, joining together two neighboring
villages, and its name was proclaimed from the top of the mountain – *T-a-r-n-ó-w.*

<h1 style="text-align:center">2</h1>

Just as the boy allows his imagination to roam unhindered over
the geological mystery of the crest's formation, so he gives it free
rein with respect to the castle as well, breathing fresh life into its
remains on the crest and viewing it in all its glory, as it was generations ago. In his fantasy, he sees himself restoring the castle walls
and towers, and populating it with generously-whiskered footmen
in mail, saber-belted knights and elegantly-attired ladies, exactly as
he dreams it must have been then.

For here, on the crest of Mount St. Marcin, history began:
here the castle was built, fortified and maintained. In later generations – from the fourteenth century on – it would fall to a variety
of noble houses: the Leliwites, the Tarnowskis, the Ostrogskis, and
the Sanguszkos. Indeed, the narrative of its construction, development and destruction over the generations is written in magnificent,
enormous letters atop the crest, like an awesome hieroglyphic scroll
unrolled in full view of the sun. There they are, the wondrous letters,
written by the hand of giants – the ruins! Convulsed on the back
and side of the crest, their very presence proclaims both the hopes
nursed by the founding fathers and the deathblow delivered to the
castle by its final heirs. For after four hundred years, when political and military circumstances had changed, along with the tastes
and lifestyle of the nobility, the Sanguszkos abandoned the fortress
on the mount and moved down into the valley that separated the

mountain from the town. There, they erected a white chateau, its exterior neo-classic, its interior modern and comfortable. Moreover, as an act of charity, they permitted the old edifice to be dismantled and its bricks re-used for the construction of the Bernardine monks' church in town.

Thus was sealed the doom of Mount St. Marcin castle. It was not felled by the fire of savage Tartar torches; its gates were not breached by Teutonic Crusader knights; nor was it trampled in the seventeenth century by tides of rebellious Cossacks or waves of Swedish invaders. It is Time that ate away into its foundations, its ruin stemming from the changes that visited Poland and the world on the brink of the modern age, leaving nothing but ruins, vestiges of both its days of glory and its ultimate destruction.

Spytko, Lord of Tarnów, served the Piast royal house all the days of his life. In 1333, upon the death of King Łokietek, his patron, Spytko became advisor and confidant to his son and heir, Kazimir, the only one of Poland's rulers to earn the title of "Great," and be remembered fondly by his Jewish subjects as well. And when Spytko finally shut his eyes for the last time in the sixth decade of the fourteenth century, having chalked up much to his credit, including assets and honors – so Mother would end her story about Tarnów's founder – he bequeathed to his sons not only sizeable tracts of land, but a paradigm of loyalty and service to the crown and its sovereign.

In time, when the boy came to sum up for himself what he had learned from his mother about Tarnów's founding father, he had a sense that an important link was somehow missing from the idealized portrait of the man she had sketched – namely, his attitude towards Jews. The omission was doubly strange in the light of the praises she heaped on King Kazimir and his favorable policy towards settlement of Jews in Poland. How is it that, despite their close friendship, Spytko did not follow in his king's footsteps and invite Jews to settle in his own town? Why did no Jewish suburb spring up alongside Tarnów's early urban nucleus, as was true of Kazimierz – the Jewish district next to Christian Kraków and ever after named for Kazimir the Great? After all, from the very dawn of the Polish realm in the tenth century – and certainly in the fourteenth century – the sight of Jewish traveling merchants was not uncommon in southern Poland. To one of these itinerants, Ibrahim Ibn Yakub, who arrived from the Muslim world four hundred years before Spytko's time, Polish history even owes a debt of gratitude for the earliest description of its nation. What, then, hindered Jewish traveling merchants from putting down permanent roots in Spytko's new town, and why did no group of merchants manage to set up a permanent organized community in Tarnów around the time of its founding?

Jews, in fact, receive no mention in the city records prior to the fifteenth century and only a century later does the first evidence appear of a permanent, recognized Jewish community in Tarnów. Witness the parchment in the city archives, the first charter granted to the community in 1581 by the town ruler, Duke Konstantin Ostrogski (he, at the same time, established a new town on his Ukrainian holdings and named it after himself, Konstantinov, or Cosentin in Yiddish, the town of Golda's childhood and the birthplace of her brother, Ben-Zion). Witness the synagogue established during this period on the edge of the city square. And witness the gravestones in the old cemetery and the names chiseled into them of rabbis and leading Jewish figures from those days.

Still more confusing to the son was the enthusiasm Mother injected into her tales of the nobility's lifestyle at the top of the Mount. Even in his childhood – when avidly lapping up Golda's imaginative descriptions of the castle, and so infected by her vivacity that his own fancies would join hers to bring to life the moments of the castle's heyday – a sense of unease descended on him which, as a child, he had no way to articulate. Only years later did he realize what it was that had disturbed his peace: the gaping contradiction between Mother's admiration for the glittering set of mountain gentry and her strange obliviousness to the lot of the villagers, who had long inhabited the valley and were bondsmen to the castle. Didn't she know that the peasant and his family were serfs bound to their master's land, from birth until death, like so many work implements or farm beasts?

The boy's spontaneous revulsion reflected initially no more than an innocent, emotional identification with the people who tilled the soil of Tarnów by the sweat of their brow, groaning under the yoke of a cold-hearted aristocracy. But as boyhood made way for adolescence, his interest in history broadened and his critical faculties sharpened, so that the more he considered the later exploits of Poland's aristocracy in the Ukraine, the more skeptical he became of Mother's idealization of Spytko, in her attributing to him an unblemished integrity and supreme loyalty to the crown.

"What about his selfish deeds for the sake of his own clan?" the son once dared to interrupt Mother's romantic effusion. For a moment he froze in his tracks, stunned by his own audacity. But he soon recovered, forced to acknowledge that his outburst had been neither offhand nor unthinking; rather, it expressed a profound inner truth that had long been germinating and sooner or later had to find release. The challenge not only expressed his disapproval of the self-centered aristocracy, but vented his growing disappointment with Mother: how could she cling to the memories of power-hungry noblemen and exploiters, when she so admired Stefan Żeromski, prophet of Poland's social-protest literature in the first quarter of the twentieth century, whom she, like many others, considered the "conscience of the nation?" And how could she shut her eyes to the bitter fate of the Polish peasant and at the same time so admire the works of Maria Konopnicka, champion of the peasants, whose poems she not only recited to her children, but even asked her son to translate into Hebrew?

Świecą gwiazdy świecą	Stars shine down on a world in gloom,
Na wysokim niebie –	Skipping in sparkling hue,
Jeno nie myśl, chłopie,	But stay, oh peasant, do not presume –
Że to i dla ciebie…	That their light glows also for you…

And what of her identification with the dry sarcasm and pessimism of her beloved poet, as opposed to the hypocrisy and deceit of the self-satisfied intellectuals, who paid lip service to lofty brotherhood and class equality?

A jak poszedł król na wojnę,	Now the king went to war, primed and proud,
Grały jemu surmy zbrojne,	To the blast and blare of trumpets loud,
Grały jemu surmy złote	To the blast of golden bugles of war,
Na zwycięstwo, na ochotę.	For triumph and glory evermore.
A jak poszedł Stach na boje,	Now Stakh, the serf, went to war, too,
Zaszumiały jasne zdroje,	Greeted by clear brooks rippling blue,
Zaszumiało kłosów pole	Greeted by wheat spikes bowing down low,
Na tęsknotę, na niedolę.	Humming a song of lament and of woe.

A na wojnie świszczą kule,	Now in war, as in war, the bullets caper
Lud się wali jako snopy –	And men are reaped like sheaves and slain –
A najdzielniej biją króle,	And chief among slayers, the kingly saber,
A najgęściej giną chłopy...	And chief among the slain, the serfs enchained...

Yes, he would declare before his mother that, now that he had grown up and studied, he washed his hands of Mother's sweet tales "from the top of the Mount," for they were no longer consistent with his views.

But one wounded look from Golda made him hold his tongue: wasn't there an element of ingratitude in his rebellion, seeing that his basic concepts and early layers of historical knowledge, not to mention his very interest in history itself, emanated from her? So he kept his thoughts to himself and was silent. Nor did his mother repeat her praise for Spytko, but turned now to a new subject: the story of Queen Jadwiga – a story that continued to stir her son even after the passage of the years, just as it had stirred him the first time he heard it, as a child.

The Jadwiga affair marked a turning point in Golda's program. Until then, the chapters of history she had dramatized for her children on Mount St. Marcin were anchored in the annals of the city of Tarnów and its surroundings. Now that these were exhausted, she broadened her sweep, stepping beyond the local to embrace the national history of Poland. Thus, in seeking an appropriate setting and a faithful source of inspiration for the next stage of her program, it was only natural that her choice fall on the majestic city, connected to Tarnów by a mere two-hour train ride: *K-r-a-k-ó-w!*

3

Golda had no difficulty in guiding her son and daughter through the mysteries of the regal past of the old Polish capital. Consciously or not, the forays she shared with her children returned her to former days and the boldness of her youth. For, from the end of the summer 1908, when the Weinmans moved to Tarnów, she – a young girl of sixteen, encouraged by her father despite her mother's consternation – made it a habit to set out on the morning train for a whole day's visit in the historic city, returning on the last night train, intoxicated by all she had taken in. No wonder she resolved to break through "to the wide world" at least once a month. This is how she came to know Kraków inside and out. For a girl who had spent her first eight years in a tiny, remote Ukrainian village and a small Ukrainian township, and then another eight years in the provincial town of Tarnopol, Kraków was not only a revelation, but also a staging ground for her future sorties to Vienna.

At times the Kraków journey was devoted entirely to visits to churches, museums, galleries and the Jagiellonian University. Or she made the rounds of the old synagogues and cemeteries in the Jewish Quarter of Kazimierz. One way or another, no "Kraków Day" was complete without an excursion to Mt. Wawel (pronounced "Vahvel"), where the royal palace had just opened to the public. In the final third of the eighteenth century, when Poland was dismembered among Russia, Prussia and Austria in a series of partitions, and the monarchy was dismantled, the Wawel, which had fallen to Austria, became the barracks of the Emperor's garrison. It was rescued from this fate only in 1905 (although Austrian soldiers continued to be stationed there until 1911), and once it was renovated and its gates opened to visitors, it became a favorite attraction of pilgrimages to Kraków. Years later, Golda was still conscious of her good fortune in being among the first waves of visitors to the Wawel.

At other times, "Kraków Day" took an uncommitted turn, Golda's only desire being to walk the streets of the enchanting city and grow heady on its atmosphere. In a year or two, she became familiar with the bookstores and the latest literary offerings, had learned to peer into the Green Balloon – a literary café opened in 1905 at Mikhalik's Cave on Floriańska Street – and to lend an ear to fervent discussions of new trends in Polish literature or listen to young writers reading from their first works. Finally, she would queue up for a reduced ticket to Fredro's comedy at the Słowacki Theater, built fifteen years earlier on the model of the Paris Opera, or to a play by Wyspiański at the Old Theater that had reopened, in 1907, after being renovated.

But, under the wings of the historical and literary capital there emerged also another Kraków, that of the seasons. "Each season and its Kraków," Golda said as she shared her memories with her children. On her very first autumn visit in September 1908 she discovered the ring of green called the Planty – because it was planted on the foundations of the wall and embankments that had once surrounded the city. She delighted in the underfoot crunch and rustle of yellowing leaves that covered the aged wrinkles of Kraków soil.

With the passing of the shortening fall days and their really short winter successors – days on which the Planty ring sprouted a brilliant plumage of snow, glistening white like Golda's Volhynian fur – spring days of ever lengthening light began to urge the young visitor to stray beyond the familiar Planty belt. She would then embark on turbulent walks along the Wisła, her thoughts chasing one another, her mind a beehive of ideas – with dozens of poems begun on these walks, none of them ever to confront the emptiness of a sheet of paper. And dozens of travel plans across oceans and continents were conceived, in the full knowledge that these, too, would never be realized. Only years later was she to reveal the route of her imaginary journeys to her son as they pored together over the *Great Romer Atlas,* as if beseeching him wordlessly to fulfill her dreams.

From here on, summer weather would start to stretch the rays of the sun to their utmost, enticing Golda to extend her walks further, far beyond Kraków's historical nucleus – sometimes even as far as the Krakus Memorial Mound, which was bound up with the figure of Krak, the mythological prince who founded the first settlement there and gave it his name, or to the Wanda Mound, named for Krak's daughter. All that, while recalling the sweet tales about the princely father and daughter, and the scary stories of the cave monster lurking beneath the Wawel. To rid themselves of this affliction, Krak's sons (or a local shoemaker apprentice, according to some) resorted to a ruse, casting a sulfur-filled sheepskin into the lair as bait to poison the beast to death – legends that the mother would one day retell to her own children.

One way or another – whether in autumn leaf fall or winter snow, whether on the banks of the Wisła in spring or the memorial hillocks in summer – "Kraków Days" were festivals, with Golda proclaiming her loyalty to the two great loves of her life: a hover between reality and fantasy, which, to her, was literature; and a floating between past and present, which is how she grasped history.

Golda's youthful passion for her trips to Kraków, which were the envy of other girls her age – whose homes were less permissive – and her attempts to plant and even water this passion in her children while imbruing Kraków's landscape with the next chapters of the "History from the Mount," caused her son, years later, to attempt, lovingly, to unravel the knot of her opposing motives and actions, to understand the contradictions of her character. How – he asked himself – could the love she felt for the Ukraine, its landscapes, songs and people, be consistent with her roaring alienation from the Ukrainian nation? And how, on the other hand, was he to understand her open admiration not only for the culture, language and literature of the rival Poles – but also for their national aspirations? How could Mother's craving for the simplicity of the non-Jewish Ukrainian village and the charm of the Jewish small town in the Ukraine be reconciled with her yearning for the big city, which, alone of all places (she would tell her children over and over) could grant a man refined taste, a meaningful intellectual pursuit and complete esthetic enjoyment? The answer, so it seemed to her son, lay in a third love, that embraced the other two – Golda's love of literature and love of history – which she anchored at the one firm Archimedean point she so longed for: *Kraków!*

This third love she never voiced explicitly. But her son always sensed in her a slow, inextinguishable burning of the soul, stemming from the unresolved contradiction between this love and the situation of her life. It came to the fore one day, when he, a high school student now, finished reading, together with her, a translated short story (by Somerset Maugham, perhaps), about a native Englishman who suddenly vanished from home and turned up only years later in some exotic city, dressed and acting as one of the locals, and identifying, like them, with his adopted city, as if he "should have been born there" had not blind chance decreed his birthplace elsewhere. Mother's reaction remained deeply lodged in the son's memory: "Oh, how profound the truth of the story!" she sighed, and immediately bit her lips, as though afraid that she had, unintentionally, given away a terrible secret locked in her heart.

Only years later, after he was already far away from Mother and had severed his ties with Tarnów, did the son appreciate the enigmatic and fateful upheaval that the encounter with Kraków had wrought upon his mother's soul. For he experienced a similar turn upon making *aliyah* to Jerusalem, where he, too, felt – after having built his home in the city of his choice and being captivated by its landscapes, its atmosphere – that despite his love for the scenery of his childhood, he should have been born here, only here! Fortune played into his hands and he did realize what his mother, in her lifetime, could not.

Kraków was thus Golda's hidden truth. It bound up her love for the city with her sense of the unfulfilled, which mercilessly ate away at the life of this brilliant woman, potential poet and potential historian – her body sentenced to life imprisonment where it did not belong. Along with her body, her spirit too was incarcerated, as were her dreams, her hopes, and many talents, all of which never came to fruition. With all her natural love for the Ukraine, where she was born, Kraków was her chosen homeland; Polish, rather than Ukrainian, was her language; Polish literature was her literature and Polish heroes, her heroes.

When World War I broke out six years later, in 1914, Golda's expeditions to Kraków were temporarily suspended; and when they resumed in 1918, after her return to Tarnów from Viennese exile, they were attended by the anxious need to accompany her father to his weekly treatments at the Hospital of the Order of Bonifrati in the big city. In one fell swoop, the beautiful Wawel disappeared, as did the Planty ring, the Jagiellonian University, and with them the historical and cultural points that symbolized for Golda the Kraków she had loved. Similarly, Kazimierz, the Jewish Quarter, vanished in smoke, though located right behind the hospital. Suddenly, Kraków aged and shrunk before her eyes, reduced to the stretch of road between the train station and clinic, just as the body of her fifty-four-year-old father shrunk before her eyes to a shaking shell. All at once, in mid-summer, her beloved city got dressed in drab gray. For two years death knocked at the Weinman door, and for two years the weekly trips to Kraków succeeded in extracting another week's grace, until the spring of 1920 when the man finally collapsed, never to rise from his sickbed again. When his widow, Sureh, at the end of that year, emigrated to America with her three unmarried children – only Golda, the eldest (married) daughter of all the Weinman offspring, remained in Tarnów, wrapping herself in mourning as in a coat of mail, steering clear of the train station, deaf and blind to the allures of her beloved city, as though she blamed Kraków for the disaster.

Just four years later, when she decided to extend the sweep of "History from the Mount" and illustrate for her children episodes from the past at the actual site of their occurrence, did Golda recover from her gloom and resolve to restore to "Kraków Days" their former delight. From now on, the children joined her sorties by train, and their love for Kraków soon became a joint family asset.

But a hasty trip to Vienna in 1927 for medical tests informed Golda that she herself, now a mother of three, had to undergo treatment at the very same Kraków clinic that had cared for her father. The nightmares and anxieties that had assailed her on her trips with her father, returned sevenfold. They ripped the halo from Kraków's head and dressed the city in black again. Thereafter, every utterance of the city's name, even unconnected with illness, was accompanied by a surge of choked-back sighs, and a silent pinch of the heart. Only in 1931, when Golda returned to health, would Kraków return to the wide horizon of her life.

4

With the confidence and energy of a seasoned tour guide Golda ushered her two children from the Kraków railroad station to the shaded promenade of the Planty, leading to the dark-red wall of the Barbakan – a defense rotunda built at the end of the fifteenth century to serve as the buckle of the belt of fortifications that once encircled the city. There, she turned ninety degrees to the left and entered Floriańska Street through the waiting Florian Gate, the only one of the eight city gates to survive, flanked by four towers and the city armory.

Passing through the gate, the three instinctively raised their eyes to the church spires at the end of the street. Standing at the point where the street joined the city square, the Gothic basilica, named for Maria, was built in the fourteenth century in place of an earlier church, destroyed by Tartar hands in 1241. They waited until, in another moment or two, (the mother had carefully timed their arrival), the clock would ring to sound the hour, and then the children were in for a surprise, just as she remembered she had been on her own first visit to Kraków in 1908: the *Hejnał* (pronounced "Heynow"), a sad bugle knell emitted four times at the start of every hour from the higher of the two Marianic spires.

"This knell, more than anything else, captures the spirit of the city of Kraków," Mother whispers. "For hundreds of years it has opened the hour with an elegy for the watchman who, some seven hundred and sixty years ago, gave his life at his post at the top of the first church. At dawn, when he espied Tartar horses galloping towards the city, he trumpeted a loud clear warning to alert the citizens who were still asleep; at that moment, a single Tartar arrow split the trumpeter's throat, cutting off the sound and his life at one and the same time."

Leaning against the side of the Florian Gate, the children stood as if hypnotized. When the note broke off in the middle of the melody, they imagined that they heard the arrow penetrating the bugler's throat. Only after the four customary knells were sounded – one for each direction – did the three of them move from their spot, as though freed from the grip of a dream. The impact of the *Hejnał* stayed with them even when they reached the Marian corner at the end of the street and turned right to the main square. The melody, or the story behind it, perhaps, cloaked them in silence. Wordlessly, they passed before the monument to Mickiewicz, the Polish national bard, and proceeded to the Wawel, where they were welcomed by the statue of Kościuszko, the last of the freedom fighters of the old Polish realm. After an exhaustive visit at the royal palace and the cathedral, the final resting place of the kings of Poland, Polish heroes and national poets, the mother had the children sit down at the palace gate: "Here, through this gate, Jadwiga set out for her coronation at the church and, through it, in time, her coffin passed on her final journey."

Even though the Jadwiga saga had been told more than once on their Sabbath excursions to Mount St. Marcin, the children never grew tired of hearing it again and again, nor Golda of telling and retelling it. Now, as the story moved to its original setting, within the walls of the Wawel and against the scenic backdrop of the capital, they all felt it taking on new life.

When Kazimir died childless in 1370, Golda began, the four-hundred-year history of the Piast dynasty suddenly came to an end. Various ills had visited Poland during the reign of this first dynasty. Although its first two founders ruled over a "Greater" Poland – Mieszko, who led his realm to the bosom of Christianity in 966, and Bolesław the Bold, his son, who extended the state's borders, reaching as far as the Dniepr – they were followed by a period of anarchy and fragmentation, with Tartar incursions taking bites out of the country's flesh. It waited for the last two Piasts, Łokietek and Kazimir, to restore to the realm its former status. Yet an anguished question weighed on the court during Kazimir's reign and, even more so, after his death: how to ensure the continuity of the kingdom. In the battle for succession, the Spytko line continued the "Hungarian Drift" which Kazimir himself had advocated. Thanks to the Spytko influence and that of the southern magnates, Poland's crown was placed on the head of Ludwig of Hungary and he wore it until his death in 1382.

Despite his place as "the Great" in the annals of Hungary, Ludwig did not fulfill the hopes of his champions, the magnates of Tarnów and Kraków. A descendant (on his father's side) of the French Anjou line, one of Europe's distinguished royal families, he was to remain ever after an absent and remote king, as alien to Polish eyes as Poland's subjects seemed to him. Not unreasonably he is remembered as Ludwig "the Hungarian," regardless of his Polish roots and ties: his mother, after all, was an illustrious Piast princess – sister to King Łokietek! – and his mother-in-law, too, was Polish. The Polish-Hungarian alliance, however, though disappointing to its champions during Ludwig's lifetime, in its second manifestation bore out most of the expectations that had been pinned on it. This was due to Jadwiga, who turned her back on the Anjou tradition and identified with her two Polish grandmothers: she embraced Poland as her homeland, Polish as her language, and became a Pole to the core.

The saga of Jadwiga, the youngest princess among Ludwig's daughters, brought Golda back to Spytko, or rather to his three grandsons, who spearheaded the efforts to install Jadwiga on the throne of her new homeland. Two of them inherited Tarnów from their grandfather and, thereafter, they and their descendants were to be known as Tarnowski; in 1390 they had the honor of hosting the Queen at their castle on the mount, making her the first – and certainly the most admired – monarch to set foot on Tarnów soil. The third inherited his grandfather's name and the other castle that the grandfather had built at Melsztyn in the district of Tarnów, and was thus referred to in the chronicles as Spytko of Melsztyn, the name by which his grandson, too, would be known. The efforts of the magnates of Tarnów and Melsztyn bore fruit, and October 16, 1384 was designated as Jadwiga's coronation day – even though she was a child of only ten and a half.

The Wawel coronation! Even in Tarnów Golda found herself swept up in emotion when called upon to recount the story of Jadwiga's coronation and to act it out for the children atop Mount St. Marcin, based on details she had picked out from Karol Szajnocha's comprehensive work. How much greater her excitement now, when performing the drama at the Wawel itself, with the grounds of the palace and the domes of the cathedral providing a realistic and picturesque setting.

Here it is, the royal hill, the Wawel, casting a long shadow over the Wisła which runs at its feet. Here the hill glitters in the last autumn sun, on that warm October of 1384, just like today, this golden morning, 550 years later.

And here is the royal courtyard: only a little while ago it stood, with only a handful of tourists or a school group crossing it on the way to the palace. And now, look, with a wave of Golda's magic wand, the grounds are suddenly filled with scores of valiant soldiers, sporting swords and helmets, alongside princes of the church in clerical garb – the *crème de la crème* of the Polish realm, each and every one of them of rank and honor, and next to them, their Hungarian guests gracing the occasion with their presence. Here they stand now, in formation, row by row, for the ceremonial procession from court to cathedral.

And look how the magic powers of Mother's dramatic talents have transformed the courtyard, an invisible hand dressing the pillars in garlands and draping colorful rugs along the banisters of the three balconies that adorn the royal edifice's three floors and embrace the courtyard in three hoops from all sides. And the balconies teem with invited guests connected to the court, gathered together to observe the proceedings of a historical event unseen in the capital for the past half century, since that great day in 1333, when Kazimir was crowned king.

Listen! The castle trumpets have sounded their solemn call, and in the spire of the Maria Church in the town square the sad bugler's *Hejnał* has answered. The combined tones of these two set all the bells of all the churches in town a-pealing, informing the entire populace that the royal procession has set out for the cathedral. Now the boy chooses to shut his eyes and direct his vision inward – for long ago he learned from personal experience that closed eyes have the power to intensify and detect details that open eyes tend to gloss over. Thus, while listening to his mother's story, he prefers, as it were, to peel her voice from the body of the improvised drama she is presenting and attach it to the coronation scenes that his own imagination produces, screening them to himself via the projector hidden behind his shut eyes. So he hears the sounds and, one by one, joins them to the scenes – as if he were watching a silent moving picture to the accompaniment of a sound track, a joint production of his and his mother's – and they all parade before him at their actual setting and in real time: in the Kraków of then.

Behind the closed shutters of his eyelids the boy sees the one on whose head the Polish crown is about to be placed, and on whose flag the white royal eagle will soon spread its wings. Here she is, advancing slowly, a gold-fringed, purple canopy sheltering her, while she radiates the wise and serene beauty that astounded Teutonic knights and other foes no less than it charmed her admirers. Here she comes, approaching now, tall for her age and rising above all the other ladies of the court who surround her; her many-pleated royal brocade robe, gold-embroidered in Gothic style, spilling to the ground so that even the autumn breeze cannot play with its edges.

Here she is, princess of all princesses and queen of all queens, as if she had just descended from the "Tableau of Polish Monarchs" painted by the great Matejko (copies of which hang on school walls, including at Tarnów's "Safa Berura" where the boy studies it every day). In front of the purple canopy, four noblemen bear the four "holies" of Polish sovereignty to the Wawel altar, as if bringing gifts to a shrine: sword, scepter, crown and "orb," known as the "apple" because of its shape, and displaying a small cross on its head. The Princess will receive them when seated on the throne: the scepter in one hand, the apple in the other, the crown on her head and the sword belted at her waist. Even though his eyes are shut, the boy senses the identity of the scepter bearer, Spytko of Melsztyn, whose grandfather, Spytko, the founder of Tarnów, had once carried the crowns for the coronations of Łokietek and Kazimir! Unintentionally, the boy's eyes fly open to find empty palace grounds lounging naked in the afternoon sun, surrounded by naked balconies with not a trace of flower garlands or a single colorful rug.

5

The respect in which young Jadwiga held the Tarnowski brothers and Spytko of Melsztyn, their cousin, was due, first of all, to the decisive contribution of these knights to placing her on the throne of Poland. Their support, however, was understood also as incurring a promise for the future: namely, that the Piast granddaughter would put herself in the hands of the grandsons of the man who had been the confidant of the last two Piasts, accepting their counsel not only as a minor, but as she grew older as well.

In regard of this brilliant maiden, however, who was endowed with every virtue and had been born for greatness, the Master of Bereavement showed little consideration, neither for the scepter that Spytko had given into her hands nor for the crown that had been set on her head. Destiny? Just so. Indeed, in this vein, the boy grasped the Jadwiga tales that his mother rolled off in weekly episodes, whether atop the mountain or on trips to Kraków. To him, the Queen's life seemed to have been an endless chain of disasters against which no mortal – not even kings or princesses – can arm themselves, and which leave in their wake a trail of sorrow, the stuff of which Greek tragedies are made. Above all, the boy's imagination dwelled on the anguish of the last link of the chain, the link of death.

On July 13, 1399, catastrophe struck, leaving Jadwiga inconsolable. Her only child – an infant daughter and the successor she had longed for – died. Within four days, the Queen and mother herself keeled over and collapsed – from illness, a broken heart, or both? – at the age of only twenty-five. And, as if the Angel of Death had to show his true might, he aimed not only at the royal house but at the base of its power, extinguishing also in a single month the candle of one of Jadwiga's most important supporters, young Spytko of Melsztyn, the Queen's favorite of all his peers. In August, 1399, Spytko fell in a campaign waged on the banks of the Worskla, east of the Dniepr. And great as was the success of the Tartar Golden Horde there, so was the grief for the courageous nobleman, slain far from home.

The melancholy, however, which spread its wings over the entire nation, was merely the last station on the Jadwigan Via Dolorosa. From the moment that the young girl entered the wing specially prepared for her at the Wawel, she became aware that even though all were captivated by her charm and offered her the gift of their love, it was she who was the real prisoner; a prisoner in the hands of her advisors, the magnates of the southern district, including the knights of Tarnów and Melsztyn, who had enmeshed her in a grand political strategy which sealed the fate not only of their own generation but of many long generations to come.

The most pressing target was to remove the pressure of the Knights of the Teutonic Cross from the northern flank of the Polish realm. To this end, the architects of the new policy planned to conclude a pact with the only natural ally in the region – the Grand Duchy of Lithuania, which had also been on the receiving end of the lethal Crusader embrace. The realization of the southern strategy elicited a painful, personal price from Jadwiga. At the age of five, she had been betrothed and even conditionally married (as was the custom of royal houses then) to her childhood love, Wilhelm, Prince of Habsburg, an eight-year-old lad with whom she spent her early years at the royal court in Vienna. There, everyone, including the two youngsters, wished for their vows to be fulfilled.

This state of affairs was intolerable to the Polish strategists. From the moment that Jadwiga was no longer the most sought-after princess in Europe but became, before God and man, the crowned sovereign of Poland, the situation thoroughly changed. In her new status, her advisors could not imagine that their protegée would not annul the planned, personal and diplomatic liaison with the heir of the House of Habsburg. For, after all, the payment for the realization of the grand strategy was she, herself – Jadwiga! She was the great prize, the trump card in the political power play. On her body the strategy was to be erected. Her availability for marriage was the backbone of the plan; without it, there was no plan. Marrying her off when she came of age, at twelve, to Jogaila, who since 1377 had ruled as the Grand Duke of Lithuania (and had already agreed to all the terms in exchange for her hand), was to serve the Polish realm both in its current predicament and over the course of time. And if this meant that the girl had to stifle her first love and childhood fantasies that were incompatible with the new realities – so be it! Willingly or otherwise – she was to be sacrificed on the altar of Poland's grand strategy!

Yet the son, who, in the account of Spytko the First had interrupted his mother's flow, now too could not hold back his objections: "Did the ten-and-a-half-year old girl suspect that the entire strategy of the magnates had been woven before she was even invited to Poland, when she decided to plight her troth to Poland, did she understand that a yoke was being placed around her neck and a task imposed on her that overturned all her dreams? Did she have no misgivings that even her closest advisors, the knights of Tarnów and Melsztyn, regardless of their love for her, would not shrink from applying pressure on her and even threaten to use force?"

In Vienna and Kraków events gained momentum. From the summer of 1385, as the Queen's twelfth birthday approached, Habsburg diplomacy stepped up its pressure, demanding Jadwiga's release so that she could fulfill her marriage vows. When these efforts failed, Wilhelm, himself, arrived in Kraków with an entourage of knights and aides, and openly demanded what was his – his bride. He was firmly rejected.

Golda did not reconstruct any scenes from that day of Polish-Habsburg confrontation in Kraków, presenting the rest of the process as natural and predictable. The way that Golda told it, when the Queen turned twelve – the legal age of majority – she, herself, applied to the cathedral office at the Wawel and asked to record in the church register the invalidation of her old vows. On February 15, in the year 1386, Jogaila's Christian baptism was celebrated at the Wawel cathedral; hereafter he was named, in Polish, Władysław Jagiełło and is so remembered in subsequent records. Upon the completion of this religious-political act, the way was paved for the complementary stages, which also took place in pomp and splendor at the royal church: on February 18, 1386, the marriage of Jadwiga and Jagiełło – on March 4, Jagiełło's coronation as King of Poland, alongside his wife, Jadwiga. Amid the festive din, no one paid attention to the disappointment of a twelve-year-old girl and fifteen-year-old boy on whom fate had so graciously bestowed coronets, but to whom it denied what even the lowliest subject was granted: love.

About a year after Golda regained her health and the Sabbath walks to the mountain resumed, the son – now the same age that Jadwiga had been at her wedding – returned once more to the question of that fateful day in 1385. The discussion was prompted by a classroom history lesson on the topic of "Queen Jadwiga and Jagiełło." Although there was certainly nothing extraordinary about it, the boy walked out stunned by the details that the teacher had supplied and his mother had omitted. Overwrought, he returned home and reported his discoveries. To his surprise, the mention of the girl-Queen's struggle against her patrons had an electrifying effect on the mother. Could it be – he wondered – that she regrets the brief, inaccurate review she had presented to her young listeners, and decided, now that they were older, to communicate Jadwiga's desperate cry? Was her compassion stirred for the two lovers, when the Kraków rulers prevented Wilhelm from meeting the girl to whom he was duly betrothed, according to church and state law, and instead, sent him packing in disgrace? Did she visualize the shameful scene of Jadwiga's small fists banging against the sealed windows of her room, her mouth futilely crying out to be allowed to meet with her fiancé? And in her heart of hearts did she secretly applaud the axe that the Queen brandished over the wooden side door in order to break through and be with him?

"You mean, they locked her up in her room? The Queen?" The boy cries out, stunned by the affront to Jadwiga. "None of this is new," his mother tries to minimize the importance of his discoveries. "And on our next visit to Kraków I'll show you the house, where Szczepańska Street meets the city square and where Wilhelm (so they say) hid while waiting for his fiancée. But in all truth, there is no proof that this is what actually happened."

The drift is transparent. Mother employs a method her son regularly approves: checking the sources of information. "What you raised is neither visual nor auditory evidence, but late Habsburg propaganda which Długosz, the pro-Habsburg Polish historian, wrote. As opposed to this, there exists a contemporary Venetian chronicle which says that, at first, Jadwiga accepted the news of her marriage to the Lithuanian duke in silence – a natural, understandable reaction. But days later, after much prayer, she agreed to the alliance 'for the sake of spreading Christianity in Lithuania.'"

"But what did the girl, herself, feel?" the boy insists, seeing his mother avoid the question of personal feelings and merely recite bookish dredged facts. "What did Jadwiga think of her advisors, whom she trusted, and who betrayed and sacrificed her to further their own interests?"

Here, the boy senses, Mother's old hardness returns to speak from her throat. The memory of his own struggles from age five and six swells in his mind so that he is no longer sure if he is bemoaning Jadwiga's fate or his own, which for years has been to do battle with Mother's inflexibility. How wide the gap, and unbridgeable! While Golda dismisses the human factor, belittling its existence "in such a young girl" (just as her own mother, Sureh, had told her in her childhood), and while she emphasizes the concern that the advisors displayed for the realm, which, after all, was their job, he, the son, sees before his eyes not a Queen, but a girl of his own age, and feels for her suffering and fears, her suffering at having to relinquish her childhood love, and hidden fears at marrying a heathen, twenty-two years her senior. A savage, according to many accounts which add horrible descriptions of Jagiełło's physical appearance and actions!

"And what if, in guiding the girl-Queen, the ministers did ignore her feelings?" Golda asks defiantly. "Doesn't the general good take priority over personal whim? What weight do a little girl's fears carry, or any feelings, for that matter, which by their very nature are transient, against the eternity of a nation? It was Jadwiga's duty to subdue all rebellious inclinations and lovingly accept the verdict for the sake of a supreme state interest, which is a Queen's mission!" And, as if upon reflection, Mother adds quietly. "When love and duty clash, and a choice has to be made, duty always comes first."

The son is astounded. These were the exact words she had murmured in his ear in her wonderful French accent during the weekly instruction she gave him in French language, history and literature. At the last lesson, which was devoted to the great French playwrights of the seventeenth century, she dealt with a series of tragic figures in Corneille's plays and their pursuit of lofty ideals; they coped with temptations and emotions and, in the end, overcame them through courage and resolve: "When love (*amour*) clashes with duty (*devoir*), and Corneille's characters have to choose between the two," she summed up the lesson, little knowing that she would soon use these very same words with regard to Jadwiga's dilemma, "*devoir* always comes first!"

"Oh, how aloof and hard you hold yourself," the boy racks his mother in a silent dialogue conducted with himself. "Not only do you completely ignore Jadwiga, the child, and her yearning for happiness, seeing before you only Jadwiga, the Queen – but even Jadwiga, the Queen, you treat not as flesh and blood, but as a literary character out of Corneille's tragedies. Do you see history and life only through the mirror of literature? Is literature, in your view, the sum total of history and life at their best?"

Very strange, the son reflects, *here I set out to learn new facts about Jadwiga and the events of her life, and find myself uncovering hidden layers in Mother's spiritual world.*

Mother, however, does not allow him to sink into reflection but compels him to pursue the discussion: "Look," she concludes, "'poetic justice' compensated for the personal tragedy. In the end, Jadwiga was strengthened by the refining crucible of her queenly duties and, in fifteen years of reign (out of a total twenty-five of life), displayed maturity, statesmanship, leadership and courage beyond her years; and she is remembered evermore as the person who changed the course of history of the country that had become her homeland. By marrying Jagiełło, she imported from Lithuania to Kraków the Jagiellonian Dynasty, which is named for the first king and was the greatest to have ever ruled Poland. At the same time, to pagan Lithuania she exported Catholicism, its clerics and preachers being trained in the Kraków Academy under her patronage. By these actions, Jadwiga unified the two peoples to free their borders of their common enemy, the Knights of the Teutonic Order."

6

The Queen – so Mother began the final chapter of the Jadwiga story – did not live to see the ultimate fulfillment of the mission for which she sacrificed her personal happiness. Nor did her three advisors, the grandsons of the founder of Tarnów, live to reap the rewards of the strategy they had devised – for death gathered them all up before their time. Eleven years passed after the Queen's death before conditions ripened for the daring, military measure that would finally tip the scales between the Teutonic knights and the united Polish-Lithuanian army. In mid-July 1410, in the region known also today as Eastern Prussia – because the Germans wiped out the pagan Prussians who inhabited the area, robbing them not only of their lives and land but also of their name which they took for themselves – in the central buckle of the belt of lakes closing in on the Baltic shore, the die would be cast. In this deceptively pastoral scene, sown with fortresses from which Crusader knights terrorized the locals, the Teutonic force under Ulrich von Jungingen was confronted by two heroes of Lithuanian extraction: Jagiełło, King of Poland, and his cousin, Vytautas (Witołd in Polish), who replaced Jagiełło as the Grand Duke of Lithuania.

Confident of the superiority of Crusader weapons and craving instant and conclusive hand-to-hand battle, Ulrich was enraged by the prolonged delay of the united Polish-Lithuanian forces who, according to the Rules of War, were supposed to open the battle. Champing at the bit, he dispatched two mounted couriers, bearing two identical swords, in the typical cross form of the Middle Ages. The riders stuck their swords into the ground in the middle of the field separating the two opposing camps, and left them there, an insulting "token" from the chief of the Teutonic Order to the two commanders facing him: whether to mock the dearth of their armaments, or symbolize the true crosses to be erected at the day's end for the fallen king and duke. But when the eve of July 15, 1410 descended on the killing field, it exposed the utter defeat of the Teutonic Order. And as the red sun sank into the waters of the lake southwest of the village of Grunwald, a full moon rose from the lake to the east of the village of Tannenberg and its silver light combed the field: strewn on the damp earth, the elite of German knighthood lay in deadly embrace with the elite of the Polish and Lithuanian knights.

After the fighting died down, Witołd walked out of the command tent to take stock of his fallen officers, his arms-bearers lighting his path with their beacons. A thick, palpable silence crouched on the heaps of corpses, its oppressive presence in stark contrast to the day's battle storm with its cacophony of German cheers from the Knights of the Cross, pulsing blasts of Polish horns, and panting blares of Lithuanian bugles.

Suddenly, the field gave up its secret: among the piles of dead, the shape of an unusually large Teutonic knight was clearly discernable, sunk motionless in the blood-soaked clods of earth. Anxiously, hesitantly, the corpse was identified; anxiously, flinchingly, the identification seemed unbelievable. Yet the signs were all there – a huge body, ornate armor, a fine cape – confirming the truth of it. A beacon was lowered: yes, there is no mistake. That is – *he!* Vytautas stood still, gazing at the remarkable silhouette of the dead Ulrich von Jungingen wallowing in a puddle of mud and blood, and then slipped to his knees in a prayer of thanksgiving.

"Oh," Mother sighs, "how happy I was to find myself in Kraków in 1910 at the unveiling of the monument for the five hundredth anniversary of the Grunwald victory, and how I dreamed of visiting the Teutonic forts, of dipping my feet into the waters of the lake near the battleground and sense what it must have been like back then, when the world held its breath, wary of the final outcome of that fateful face-off!"

Not in her rosiest fantasies could Golda imagine that sixty years after embarking on her historical tales about the Teutonic Order, and the wonderful and tragic Jadwiga, her son would set foot on Grunwald's very soil. How could she possibly picture, in those far-off days, her son going up, on her behalf and in her place, to the enormous strongholds of the Knights of the Teutonic Order – to Malbork (Marienburg in German), and Kwidzyń (Marienwerder)? And how could she predict that he would visit Kętrzyn (the Crusaders' Rastenburg) and stroll amid the ruins of the "Wolf's Lair," the field headquarters against Russia erected by the chief Teutonic swastika crusader of the twentieth century – a headquarters that is a monument to the megalomania of a single man who dragged an entire nation and a whole continent into the abyss. Nevertheless, this development, which not even the wild-est imagination could conceive, became a reality after the Second World War, when Golda's son, guided by his mother's spirit, toured the strongholds that she had so longed to see, along with other sites in the northern lake district, from Olsztyn (Allenstein) and Ełk (Lyck), which are part of Poland today, to Kłajpeda (Memel in German), which was restored as Lithuania's port.

If this were not enough, reality surprised further with the dis-covery of remains of the Order's early Crusader past in the Holy Land. Indeed, seventeen years before the son was able to travel to the sites of Teutonic escapades in Eastern Prussia, he had a glimpse of their first Crusader arena, the site at which their original mission had crystallized at the end of the twelfth century and the begin-ning of the thirteenth: it had served as a hospice for nursing, and place of worship for German-speaking Crusaders, who felt ignored and tongue-tied in the prevailing French atmosphere of the overall Crusader entity in the Holy Land.

The unearthing of the Teutonic center in Crusader era Jerusalem was one of the many achievements of the generation of Israeli archaeologists following Jerusalem's liberation in the 1967's Six-Day War. Within weeks, while clearing out the ruins of the Jewish Quarter, which had been destroyed in 1948, comprehensive excavations were carried out, unprecedented in vigor and in the fruits they bore, a project that continuous habitation in the city had previously made impossible. At the corner section, where Misgav Ladakh Street meets the stairway down to the Western Wall, rem-nants were found of three Crusader buildings – a church, a hospital and a guest house. The complex was identified as the House of the Hospitalers of St. Mary of the Teutons in Jerusalem. Bare arches rising from the ruins of the hospital section, whose floor is now overrun with weeds, hint at the form that the edifice took eight hundred years ago, while next door, the German church has again slipped on its exterior of old.

The Jerusalem finds were indeed surprising, but Golda's son was no less astonished to learn of the continued existence of the office of the Order's supreme commander in our own day; this, he stumbled upon, while innocently strolling through the streets around St. Stefan's Cathedral in Vienna. Located on Singer Street, in a baroque building whose only claim to fame is that it once housed Mozart, the anachronistic institution is a mere shadow of itself, restricted today to religious, charitable works under the patronage of the Papal Curia.

Golda's son thus came full circle. It began with the walks up Mount St. Marcin in Tarnów, the trips to enchanted Kraków, and the stories Mother told about the brutal exploits of the Teutonic Order and the efforts to stamp it out. It continued with the son's visits to the sites that his mother never lived to see: starting with Jerusalem, after 1967, which gave up the Order's early secret; then, on to the militant strongholds of the Crusader knights in the Baltic belt; and ending with the last modest corner that remained of the Order in Vienna. And finally, where it all came together, at the son's desk in Jerusalem.

7

Enchanted as the children had been with Golda's tales of the events that led to the Polish-Lithuanian victory at Grunwald, as the son grew older he found it difficult to shed a sense of unease at his mother's treatment of the subject. He had no problem with the struggle against the Teutons or the Polish-Lithuanian alliance. His difficulty lay in his mother's virtually exclusive concentration on the changes that the union of the two countries visited on Poland, omitting what happened in Lithuania itself after the conversion to Christianity and Jagiełło's marriage and ignoring the dilemmas facing Vytautas, the leader who remained in Lithuania.

For starters, Vytautas was torn between the native idol worship – which focused on the figure of Perkunas, early Lithuanian god of thunder – and Catholicism. The latter came in two versions, both imports. The one was brought from Poland by the missionaries of Queen Jadwiga, his cousin by marriage; the other, Teutonic, burst in from Prussia. The first, both greedy and generous, spread the doctrine of the Kraków Academy and broadened the horizon onto an unknown culture; the other, by contrast, forced itself on the people, leaving charred earth and baptizing the tidings of Jesus in rivers of blood.

On the political level, Vytautas sought space to maneuver between the dynastic alliance with Poland – which his cousin, Jogaila, had concluded to become the Polish Jagiełło and make Vytautas the Polish Witołd – and strengthening Lithuanian self-determination, which he continued to champion, evermore remaining, in his own eyes and in the eyes of his people, Vytautas of Lithuania. Lithuanian self-determination did not draw its inspiration from the Wisła, but saw its historical and cultural core on the banks of the Neris and the Nemunas – the Wilia and the Niemen, as the Poles called them – and desired room to live and expand on the slopes of the Dniepr, in the steppes of the Ukraine, and as far south as the Crimean Sea.

In his mind's eye, the boy sees Vytautas, symbol of Lithuania, leaning after the battle on a cross-like sword – and rightly so, for it is to the bosom of the crucified that Jadwiga had brought him and it is in the name of the crucified that he set out for war. Indeed, when leading his Polish-Lithuanian army eleven years earlier to the expanses beyond the Dniepr, he was borne on the waves of Catholicism preached by the graduates of the Kraków Academy, who demanded that Lithuania, newly Catholic, enforce its mastery over the Christian-Orthodox Duchy of Moscow, to restore it to Catholicism; at the same time, they called on him to fight the Asian Timur-Leng and the Tartars of Crimea, who worshipped Allah and opposed Christianity with a vengeance. As a Lithuanian and a Catholic, he believed that in fighting for the cross he was assured the support of the God of the Cross. To his astonishment, he learned first-hand that his new God was as indifferent to the champions of His religion as to its detractors, and indiscriminately meted out grace and blows to both. And if there was no reward and punishment, as the priests promise, what was it all coming to?

Witold must have been pained by the memory of the tragic events of eleven years earlier: the death of the royal infant girl in Kraków, to whom he, Vytautas, had presented upon her birth the gift of a silver cradle; and in the wake of this calamity, the death of her mother, the mother and Queen, his cousin, Jadwiga, the one and only. And a month later, the defeat on the eastern tributary of the Dniepr. The Worskla River, on whose banks the decisive battle broke out in 1399, turned into a death trap for his army. Not only did the dream of subjugating the Muscovite Orthodoxy diffuse like smoke, but it was God's very foes, those with the cry of "Allah Akbar!" on their lips, who overpowered the elite of Christian knights! Among the fallen was also Spytko of Melsztyn, one of the architects of Polish-Lithuanian rapprochement, whom Vytautas had hoped to bring over to his side after the Queen's death. Even he, Vytautas himself, had escaped slaughter only by the skin of his teeth, fleeing as fast as he could to Kaunas-Kowno. And now the priests – they, who had promised victory – roll their eyes to heaven, not content with jeering at the defeat, but demanding that he make a thankful offering to the God of his Salvation: that he build a new Catholic church opposite the ancient Perkunas shrine! "Oh, how to bear all this?" – the son imagines himself hearing the leader's desperate reproach of heaven – "Which god really supports my country?"

Now, eleven years after the defeat, the body of his worst enemy lies at his feet. But does the actual victory provide an answer to the doubts that are driving him mad? For only he, Vytautas, knows the real truth. It was not a war against Muscovite Orthodoxy or against Allah's faithful that was declared at Grunwald, but a war of cross against cross, a German Catholic sword against its Polish Catholic sister: an unresolved battle, decided by a surprise break-through – whose? That of the Muslim Tartars with whom he, the Christian Vytautas, had, at the last minute, sealed a secret pact, concealing them until the critical stage and then launching them into the campaign.

"Who then is the victor of Grunwald?" The imaginary Vytautas now shouts into the boy's ear. "The Crucified, whose name both sides invoked in vain? Or Allah, who first destroyed the Christian army at Worskla, and now saved one Christian foe from the hands of another Christian? Or is it Perkunas – yes, Perkunas and none other, the god of thunder – that old Lithuanian rogue, who every morning opens the gates of his shrine at Kaunas to thousands of worshippers and, with a merry eye, beholds the rival church across the way, the church that the honorable Grand Duke of Lithuania himself had built for the Crucified, at the command of his priests, and he, Perkunas, laughs, and laughs, and laughs."

*

One day the boy decided to let his father in on the secrets of Mother's "History from the Mount." The father listened at length to the tales the boy had to tell, without interrupting even once. Encouraged by Father's silence, the boy unfurled the pageant of history that he had absorbed from his mother down to the last detail, even adding a personal touch from his own readings and history lessons at school. At the end of the long monologue, the father continued to stroll beside his son in utter stillness, whether to allow the boy to add more details should he so wish, or to carefully choose the words that would deliver the proper response for the occasion.

"You know, Herschl, what Maimonides has to say about historical accounts?" Father's voice, at last, broke the silence. The voice was soft, indulgent and melodious as always – maybe more so than always – but to the boy, this time, it sounded like the scratch of a nail on glass. *No, I do not know what Maimonides has to say about history nor do I want to know* – the lad bit back the defiant reply that blazed a trail to his lips, in order to prevent its escape. For a brief moment he regretted having invited Father into the exclusive province he shared with Mother, for, based on past experience, he should have exercised more care in approaching the danger lines that separated his two parents' worlds, knowing that in certain spheres there was no contact between their respective preserves. He soon reconsidered, however: no doubt, Father, that outstanding Maimonides scholar, has a valuable message to impart in the name of the great philosopher.

"Of course, eight hundred years ago Maimonides did not know the chapters of history you have just related," Father's voice was soft and clear, as if trying to set aside all grievances. "In Maimonides' time, Tarnów was only a tiny village and Poland was envisioned as behind the Hills of Darkness. Lithuania was steeped in idol worship and the Teutonic Knights had just settled among the other Crusaders in the Holy Land. But as far as earlier chapters of history were concerned, with which Maimonides was fully familiar, as well as with the chapters of his own time, the scholar's opinion was firm. Thus, in his commentary on the *Sanhedrin* tractate, his ruling was simple, determining on principle – remember this well, Herschl! – that the preoccupation with history and reading history books is no more than –

"– An idle pursuit, that's what these books are… from the tales of chronicles and the rule of kings… and similar things that come from these books, that contain neither wisdom nor practical usefulness, and are a waste of time."

CHAPTER FOUR

Zlatte and the Emperor's Horseman: The Wróbel Saga

T

1

HE SUMMER OF 1925, full of anticipation of Gunia's birth as it was, carved out a singular place in the son's emotional realm, one which stayed with him through adolescence. With the passage of time, several other layers of memory were added to the retaining wall of impressions and experiences, so that even after seventy years, that summer remains etched in the son's mind as one of the most enriching and wonderful periods of his life. And though the primary source of the special feeling was connected with Mother, it soon spilled over into a different channel. After a year that sealed real closeness to Mother, both because of shared activities in the home and the chapters of the "History from the Mount," her advanced pregnancy forced her to suspend the routine Sabbath walks, thus ripening the conditions that helped the boy discover his father.

Day in, day out, in the early hours of the afternoon, following a whole morning's study over sacred texts and a light summer lunch, Father and son would go out for a walk about town. For an hour or two, and sometimes even three, they would stroll along, talking at length – that is, Father would speak, while his companion listened attentively, here and there asking a question, or interjecting an appreciative remark.

In those hours of conversation, no two of which were alike, and in which no two ideas repeated each other, the son was palpably aware of blocks of talk building up in his mind and heart, layer by layer, and crystallizing into a complete, well-polished unit that fashioned the drift and modes of his thinking. Beyond the subjects and content themselves, however, the discussions afforded the boy – albeit, only dimly at the start – a first insight into the differences between the worlds of his two parents. Only after many years passed, and the adult son began to turn those hours over in his mind comparing the materials with which Father would develop his conversations, with the topics that Mother chose to dwell on, did it seem to him that he had got to the bottom of the differences.

Whereas Mother spoke of the impact of poets, whose works she would sing or recite, or related exciting episodes in Polish-Lithuanian or Jewish history, or enthusiastically laid bare the plots of operas she had attended in her twenties in Vienna and Kraków – the conversations with Father were never retrospective.

Over and over again – as if from a compulsive urgency or a gnawing, almost prophetic impulse of pessimism – the discussions dwelt on the problems of the present and the outlook for the future. They revolved around the danger hovering over Polish Jews, who went about their business as usual, oblivious of the catastrophe to come; they applauded the boldness of the Enlightenment in the preceding hundred and fifty years, and warned that its work was not yet done, in view of Eastern European ingrained Jewish conservatism; and they welcomed the revolution inherent in the Zionist message, but lamented the fact that even this inspiring message had not really shaken the Jewish people out of their inertia. Now and then, the talk strayed further – plainly, Father was conducting a monologue on the purpose of life and the secret of death, on the mysteries of the heart and the wonders of the mind, on God and on man.

The difference, however, was not only in substance but in what the conversations represented. Mother's talks reflected impressions that she had absorbed from the outside – with her mind, her senses, reading of literature and studying of scholarly works, from listening to music, attending theater or traveling to and gazing at beloved landscapes – impressions she absorbed voraciously, drew sustenance from and, later, fed to her children. But if you were to block their flow to her, she would dry up and wither; take them away from her and she would be stripped of resources, bewildered and bereft – for only thanks to them did her heart beat and eyes shine, only because of them were her conversations what they were. Father's conversations, on the other hand, buzzed with ideas that he had extracted from the recesses of his soul, all original thoughts mined from the rock of his personality; and even though they were anchored in his wide reading and the knowledge that he had gained over the years, they were refined from the dross in the crucible of personal reflection and offered up as a coherent doctrine, unembellished by quotations from the sources and independent of "higher" authorities.

He, the scholar, whose erudition was "like the water that covers the sea," had learned to rise above his fantastic store of knowledge and, seemingly, to wash his hands of it, looking at every problem with fresh eyes not yet dulled by the fat of excessive learning nor spoiled by the baggage of a smug book culture. From the depths of his mind he would draw pure, refined crystals of thought, that were core and nothing else, that went straight to the point rather than around it, that aimed at the gist, at the meaning rather than the description. And the refined, unalloyed thought was entirely his own, and he isolated it in pure form from the whole wide range of extraneous knowledge. Just so did Marie Curie-Skłodowska isolate pure radium from uranium (as was proudly spoken of at all Polish schools at the time, including "Safa Berura" in Tarnów, apropos the plan of the Polish scientist from Paris to establish a radium institute in Warsaw, the city of her birth). Just so did Michaelangelo redeem from raw marble the figures he saw in his mind's eye and transform them into sculpture. And so, too, did Reb Zvi-Hersch Weinman, cantor-composer and Golda's father, isolate from the thousands of notes running around in his head the one true tune that he sought – unencumbered by all his knowledge of music and all the compositions that he had heard and known in his lifetime – to give birth to it purely, in authentic and innocent originality. The same was true of Father: the ideas he developed were authentically his own – they existed because of him, not he because of them.

The outings themselves, no less so than the heart-to-heart talks conducted on the walks, were also thoroughly enriching. These were different from Mother's excursions. Village-born, Mother liked to take the children beyond the city boundaries, to sites that recalled the landscapes of her childhood. When the ascent of Mount St. Marcin became difficult for her, she would take her children to the wheat fields in the northern part of town and the little wood known as Piaskówka ("Dune"), for the sandy expanse it encircled. Here was a convenient and favorite spot for mothers and the sand games of their children in the daytime, and a romantic venue for the bonfires of Zionist youth in the evening.

Not so Father. Though also village-born, he nevertheless chose to wander to his heart's content within the inner city, between the walls of its buildings and along its populous streets, bored by the mere thought of "loveliness of nature" or "fantastic scenery." It was precisely his very closeness to nature's vistas in childhood and the seasonal labor on his parents' farm in the village that led him to the conclusion that nature is wasteful, sterile and "chases its own tail in boring rotation and pointlessness," not to mention that it is amoral, based as it was on the principle that the life of one living creature was drawn from, and nourished on, the death of another.

"Therefore" – as he saw it – "The main thing is man, and all that man creates materially and spiritually: how he, who is born willy-

nilly, and lives willy-nilly, and dies will-nilly, organizes his household, works and studies, educates his children and teaches them
to learn, and how he rises above nature's amorality by offering an
ethic of his own that sanctifies all living things and lends purpose
to the universe. This is the real drama, and scenic landscapes are
no more than the backdrop."

Unlike Mother, for whom it was a matter of principle to impart
to her children an historical perspective and faithful information
about their city's past, attempting to endear to them even the archeological vestiges of bygone days, Father's attention was not given
to antiquities but to living people. Indeed, he opened for his son
a window onto Tarnów's new neighborhoods, those that had been
built on village lands annexed to the city in the nineteenth century, in the era of accelerated urban development under Austrian
rule. Out of a whole series of new neighborhoods, he was particularly attracted to the working-class district of Grabówka – a former village on Tarnów's eastern flank, where thousands of Jewish
refugees, fleeing pogroms and hunger, had concentrated, making
it a reserve of cheap labor for Tarnów's Jewish industry. It was also
a nest of abject poverty, a hotbed of all the evils and malignant
plagues typical of disadvantaged neighborhoods. But Father never
explained – and the boy dared not query – the secret of Grabówka's
fascination for him.

Were his motives ideological? The son tried to solve the puzzle
years later. Did Father identify with the mute cry the neighborhood issued by its very existence, the odious-repulsive sight of its
lanes and the festering sore that it made in the body of the town?
Or, perhaps, was he impressed in his heart of hearts, by the mighty
political power radiating day by day and hour by hour from the
concentration of thousands of Jewish proletarians? These – even
without demonstrations and red flags – were known to both the
oppressive Polish government and the complacent Jewish bourgeois establishment as members of the Bund Party, a well-organized

Jewish-socialist party, which (like its sister party, the Polish PPS) maintained strike troops of armed heavies, who were not shy about using violent measures to defend themselves.

More probably, however, it was some distant childhood experience that had won Grabówka its firm place in Father's heart. In 1895, when he was only fourteen, Yitzhak-Isaac (known as Aazik), the eldest of Shloime Wróbel's sons, left Wisłok, his remote native village in the central Beskids, and roamed westward, alone, to the town of Tarnów. The lad was well aware of the difference between his own intent and that of the thousands of other Jewish youth who also flocked to Tarnów from the east: while the latter grabbed at Grabówka, the first stop on the eastern edges of town, and turned it into a berth of working hands for the town, Aazik advanced into the town itself, true to his intent to seek out a home of Torah. His choice was the decisive step of his life, for, had he acted like his fellow migrants, he would have remained as ignorant as they. Instead, he had accepted the decree of that one-of-a-kind woman – his mother – who had yanked him from behind the horse and the cow and sent him "into exile", to a seat of Torah.

From a distance of dozens of years and thousands of miles, Aazik reflected on this remarkable woman whose willpower had dictated a new direction for his life – Zlatte, daughter of Arinyankif (Aaron-Yaacov) HaLevi Binder of the town of Bukovsk, which was next to his native village. He would cleave to her image as he remembered it from the day of parting: a modest woman, neither particularly small nor tall, not pretty in any obvious way and certainly not educated, performing the work of the house and fields with brisk, busy hands and, despite the harsh conditions of the farm, meticulously guarding her personal cleanliness and purity. In his memory, again and again, he turns over every detail and every scene from the stories she used to tell him in a sad, melodious Yiddish – a lean Yiddish that she had to spice with pungent Ruthenian idioms whose meaning, to his sorrow, he, Aazik, has managed to forget in the years of his severance from the region. But never, ever would he forget her stories, and ever after would he be grateful to her for opening a window before him to her soul, to her past, and to her wise and fateful decisions.

2

Zlatte's mother, Rivkeh, died in childbirth and she, the orphan, never even saw a photograph of her. How strange – she would often wonder, from the moment she was able to think – that, in the absence of a photograph, none of her relatives had ever bothered to describe to her in words the image of the person who-had-been-and-did-not-live-to-be her mother, nor to tell her anything about her and her life. Most disappointing of all was her father, Arinyankif HaLevi (the Levite), whom she tried to look up to with all her might, being especially proud (without knowing why) of the title "HaLevi," which he carefully attached to his name. But he returned no love. Upon the death of his young wife, he apparently withdrew into himself, abandoning the day-old infant as if he held her personally responsible for the tragedy. Little Zlatte could not know if it was she whom, with his own hand, he had erased from the scroll of his life, or himself, who had been erased from the tablet of hers.

Either way, on weekdays Arinyankif worked at hawking his wares and each and every Sabbath he attended the Bukovsk synagogue, where, as one of the four Levites in the community, he was often honored by being called up to the Torah. But at night, the light of a single candle flickered in the window well past midnight, and Arinyankif's head, prematurely shot through with gray, was seen poring over an open book. "He's dabbling in *Kabbalah*," people said knowingly in hushed tones, wisely turning away from both the window and the danger, lest, Heaven forfend, there should be "harm in looking."

On the day that Zlatte reached *bat-mitzvah* age, which was also the twelfth *yahrzeit* of her mother's death, something happened. Arinyankif recited the *kaddish* for the dead at the early-morning prayers but, afterwards, he was not seen to open his shop as usual. Suddenly, without warning – he was gone, and no one could say what had befallen him. There were those who surmised that he had fled to America, latching onto a faint hint in a letter that had come from across the seas. Others, whispering from mouth to ear, bandied about the possibility that his spirits had failed him and he had strayed into the "bad business of conversion" – may the Lord preserve us! Thus – they related – he had been seen in a brown monastic habit, living the life of a recluse in some mountain ravine, with the Christians bringing him their sick and lame to be healed. Most of his acquaintances, however, hoped that he had made the pilgrimage to the holy city of Safed to prostrate himself at the graveside of the holy Ari, Rabbi Isaac Luria, the sixteenth-century *kabbalist*. He had gone – they murmured – to repair his soul through prayer, fasting and abstinence, and, God willing, was an advocate before the Throne of the Almighty, for his townspeople and family and daughter.

The vacuum left in the girl's life by her mother's death and her father's disappearance was filled by Surihenne (Sarah-Hanna) Wróbel of Wisłok, Zlatte's aunt by marriage to Haim-Yitzhak Binder, Arinyankif's brother in Bukovsk. (Surihenne would one day also be her sister-in-law, when Shloime, Surihenne's brother, took Zlatte for a wife.) No one knows exactly when or how Surihenne assumed this role. In any case, it was she who raised the orphan in her home, from infancy through childhood and girlhood, and she who led her to the wedding canopy. Zlatte, for her part, apparently did not waste too much thought in examining her original relationship to Surihenne; it was enough for her that, for as long as she could remember, she simply belonged to this home, and home meant only one thing: Surihenne.

When Zlatte came of age, Surihenne instructed her in the

commandments incumbent upon a Jewish woman and imparted to her the rudiments of reading from the *Zennerenne*, that is, the "*Ze'ena U'Re'ena*", an explicated collection of biblical tales in Yiddish, which Jewish women would read, on the Sabbath and on weekdays. But for most of the hours of the day, Zlatte was charged with caring for the chickens and the cow in the yard, like all young village girls – work that Zlatte would engage in also in the near future, in the yard of the house in Wisłok which was to be her home after she married Shloime, as well as in far different circumstances in the distant future…

Harder than the orphan's state, however, and the absence of parental love, was the loneliness, and this, more than anything else, left its mark on Zlatte's life until her dying day. She didn't blame anyone; it was simply that none of the members of the household, had they even thought about it at all, could say exactly what place the orphan occupied in her aunt's home in Bukovsk: whether she was an adopted daughter, or a little sister, or just a plain servant. Since in the absence of a clear status folks chose to cloak themselves in silence, a mute wall built up around Zlatte – unique and invisible to all, except Zlatte, who heard herself enclosed within it. Moreover, it was a wall that went with her wherever she went. And stayed with her both when asleep or awake. And lodged forever in her heart.

Beyond the distance of time and space, Aazik's eyes still well with tears in Tarnów at the thought of the terrible loneliness of the woman who was to be his mother, and of the heart-to-heart talks she would conduct with the cow and the chickens in Surihenne's yard, for there was nobody to listen to her but them, just as there was nobody to ever ask her opinion or take an interest in her pain, her feelings or desires. Questions such as these were never put to her, not in childhood, nor in adolescence, nor even when she was married off, a poor orphan girl, to her kinsman, Shloime, the youngest of the Wróbel boys, who had also lost his parents. Thus, she was not asked for her opinion when they shaved her head upon her marriage, as is customary among orthodox Jewish women, and placed a wig on her head instead of her long hair. The fact is that it would never have occurred to her to protest nor, had she wished to, would she have known before whom to protest. She did however wonder how it was that she was asked to do all this, while Shloime, who had been made to remove his beard during military service, continued to walk about clean-shaven like a complete and utter *goy*.

Admittedly, since Shloime's seven brothers had left the village of their birth, Zlatte too believed that the relatives had been right in their decision to make a match between the two orphans and, through their joining, save the farm. Indeed, the calculation was proved correct: the brothers having no interest in the property left by their father in the village, Shloime – the only one of the Wróbel boys to return at the end of his military service to live in Wisłok – inherited the whole farm along with the cabin built by his father, Yitzhak-Isaac, fifty years earlier, and Zlatte came into chickens and a cow that were now entirely her own. Except that in taking ownership of the chickens and cows at Wisłok, she had not anticipated that she would again be acquiring gentle-eared listeners as in Bukovsk and, that here, too, in Wisłok, her adopted village, the mute wall would rise up around her, even in her own home, and continue to enclose her to the point of suffocation, despite her marriage to Shloime, whom she dutifully learned to love as a proper Jewish wife should.

In the Wisłok farmyard, next to the wooden shack at the western entrance to the village, Zlatte would tell the cow and chickens about her tall, handsome, well-formed Shloime, who rode like a knight on his gray mare or harnessed it to the wagon to make the rounds of the villages, trading in horseflesh with the farmers. Ukrainian *shiksas* (gentile girls), she would smile without jealousy, rolled their eyes at him and scattered a trail of giggles behind the mare, while young, army-age *shkutzim* (gentile boys) gathered around him at the tavern in the heart of the village or at the inn where he spent the night during the week, set a bottle of liquor down on the counter and offered him one glass after another. And as his heart warmed on the drink and he warmed to them, he, in the fluent Ruthenian of a born *goy*, regaled them, at their request, with his escapades and adventures – which may or may not have happened exactly – in the cavalry corps of his majesty the Emperor. And for the umpteenth time, one of the young men would ask Shlamko (as the gentiles called him) to tell the story of the medal, which no one ever saw, since (as he explained) it could be worn only at military parades. And for the umpteenth time Shloime would readily recount how an imperial courier had turned up at his barracks and, while his comrades-in-arms and commanders sat on their mounts in three-sided formation, like an open gate, the courier read out in German a ceremonial order of the day, commending Master Horseman Salomon of the House of Wróbel of the village of Wisłok for his loyalty to the Emperor and his horsemanship, and pinned a red-and-white enamel medal on his chest in decoration for his courage and in praise of his exploits. And on Thursdays, when he returned from the Bukovsk market to his home in the village, Shloime would check his leather boots which always stood in the corner of the shack and carefully polish them with the black paste he had brought home from the barracks and shine the brass buckle of the bandoleer hanging above them, and eagerly wait for the printed notice to arrive in the mail and summon him to reserve duty in the annual exercises of the corps.

And all this time, his wife, Zlatte, looked after the household and cared for the farmyard animals and gave birth to nine children (three of whom died before they were a year old). And she gazed at Shloime, her husband, when he returned on Thursdays and her eyes lit up at the sight of his fine figure and bearing, and her heart wept – not for the infants who did not survive, nor for her own loneliness, of which Shloime had no inkling, but for Shloime himself. In two days time, in the morning, he would make his way to Sabbath prayers, passing the entire village from the wooden shanty at the western approach to Wisłok to its eastern edge, where the wealthy "high society" lived and maintained the synagogue. But her Shloime would not be called up to the Torah, as her father, the Levite, had been in Bukovsk prior to his disappearance, and no one would greet him with a *"Gut Shabbes* (Good Sabbath), Reb Shloime," for he still shaved his beard like a *goy* and it was common knowledge that he had never studied or opened a book, and had no idea what a *Gemara* page looked like, and could barely read from the prayer book.

"And the boys, tell me Shloime," Zlatte cries out mutely, bitterly reproving her husband as if he were before her, "the sons that I bore you in pain and good faith, the grandsons of Reb Arinyankif HaLevi, what is to become of them?" After the Sabbath, she vows to herself, she will take the two who have reached *heder* (school) age, Aazik and Bereleh, to Bukovsk, and arrange for them to live with Surihenne and study with all the other children at the "Red" *melamed* (teacher), the tutor in Jewish texts. And so she did, and her heart swelled with joy.

Except that after six months, Zlatte brought the boys back home, having found them, on a visit to Surihenne's, swarming with lice, runny-nosed, in filthy clothes and hungry. The taciturn, reserved woman, who had never complained about anything that affected her personally, could not remain silent when it came to her children. Intuitively, she sensed, too, that the *heder* learning was not up to scratch and, what's more, she noticed that the red beard of the *melamed* was also crawling with lice. On that day, Zlatte, the mother, gave the town of her birth a divorce bill, took herself off from the home of Surihenne, her aunt and sister-in-law, and, with every fiber of her soul, clung thereafter to Wisłok, her adopted homeland.

Years after these events, Reb Aazik, son of Zlatte and Shloime, having settled in the city of Tarnów and himself become a father concerned for the welfare and education of his children, recalled every detail of that tempestuous Bukovsk experience, when – in a rage and without asking anyone's leave – his mother burst into the *heder*, cast a look of disgust at the *melamed*'s red beard and, without uttering a word, removed Aazik and Bereleh from there. Then, in complete silence and offering no explanation, nor even stopping at Surihenne's for them to say good-bye, she marched the two of them straight home across a shortcut through the fields and only once they were inside the wooden shack did she inform the children of her decision.

Borne on the waves of time and memory, Reb Aazik reflects in amazement on his mother's audacity – an audacity that is astonishing to him even then and must have been all the more so before, in the conditions of poverty, want, loneliness and illiteracy of those days. The Bukovsk affair – he reconstructs what his mother must have concluded at the time – ended in frustration, but not in defeat. On the contrary, she now knew that she must not aim too low. She was determined not only to snatch her sons from the horse ring to which the Wróbel destiny seemed harnessed in perpetuity, but also to rescue them from the vise of Wisłok, their native village, and of the town of Bukovsk. Yes, she must remove them completely from both of these and resettle them at a seat of Jewish learning! Nor was this the reaction of a momentary anger – her son, Aazik, marvels in admiration – but a considered, calculated and resolute action. A revolution!

Without shrinking from the magnitude of the sacrifice that would be asked of her and of her sons – since their departure for a city of Torah held out the fearful prospect that they would remain there, permanently cut off from herself and the family – Zlatte rose up and went to battle. Her immediate campaign was on behalf of her sons alone or, at least for the fate and future of her eldest son, but there is no doubt that she was aware of the broader significance of the deed. She – to whom no one, apart from the cow and the chickens, had ever listened, whose opinion no one had ever asked, who had never been heartened by sound counsel or supported by a word of encouragement – understood, that in the long run, her battle was not only for the course her children would take but for the image and character of all the Wróbels and Binders, a battle to change the direction and development of an entire Jewish clan for generations to come! As if she had been touched by the hand of God, she set out, once and for all, to break through the equestrian phalanx of the House of Wróbel and erect, in its stead, a dynasty of scholars whose light would radiate on both families for generations: the first of the dynasty would be Aazikl – to be known in future as Reb Aazik! (She corrects herself with gratification.) And after him, his son, and so on in the generation after and the one after that, scholars every one of them until the end of time! Doesn't the *Zennerenne* tell about Abraham, son of Terah, who set out alone against the whole world and smashed his father's idols? Didn't Mattathias and his sons rise up to remove the idol from the Temple? Well then, an end to silence! Freedom for the imprisoned soul! From now on, the mother's muteness would come unravelled and her voice would be heard loud and clear. For now she is no longer alone. Yes, now, for the first time in her life, there is someone who listens to her. Now, Zlatte had an ally: her son.

In the ramshackle, wobbly, wooden shanty in Wisłok, mother and son spin a dream. Between the low of the cow, whose care has recently been assumed by Esther, the youngest – upholding the unwritten law of village life that everyone, according to age and ability, does his share of farm work – and between the neighs of the horse, on which Bereleh is even now bounding bare-backed to the open fields; between the cackle of the chickens and the wail of children running barefoot in the yard in long cotton shirts – the two conjure up a great dream, the dream of Torah! And yet, she is but a simple, Jewish peasant woman, who cannot even sign her own name and, as for reading, has never got beyond the *Zennerenne*, and he is but a Jewish village lad, barefoot and versed in hunger who, physically, may look like the scion of the Wróbel horse-trainers, but whose aspirations, curiously enough, have amalgamated with his mother's until he has vowed to realize them come what may: no more a horseman for the Emperor, like his father and grandfather before him, but (as in the Bible) "the chariot and horseman of Israel!" Oh, you god-forsaken, beggarly hovel of a distant childhood! You, that with the passage of years appear to have shrunk more and more as if collapsing under the weight of your own poverty and old age, and slowly sinking as into a grave, dug with your own hands to lie in and return to your ashes! Aazik will always remember you as a defiled homeland, invaded by poverty, want and hunger that soiled every bit of purity and innocence, just as he will remember the daring of his mother, who resolved to rescue him from it.

3

From the start, the Wróbel forefathers were cattle-and-horse traders who conducted their business on both sides of the Polish-Hungarian border. It is not known when or how they came into the region, nor where their permanent base or residence had been previously. Did they occupy the low-lying Carpathian ranges (known as the Beskids), where their descendants were found in recent generations? Or had they come from the south, from the large, established Jewish communities of the Balkans and Ottoman Turkey, penetrating northward through the mountain pass after trekking across Hungarian soil? Perhaps they had arrived in the tenth century from the southeast with the refugees of Khazaria, traversing the broad steppes and the waters of the great rivers? Whatever the case, there is no doubt that the political and territorial changes that periodically shook up this part of the world left an indelible mark on the Wróbels themselves, their dwelling place, and the nature of their economic activity.

Particularly decisive was the dissection of Poland by Russia, Prussia and Austria at the end of the eighteenth century, with Austria gaining southern Poland, a region extending along a stretch of the right bank of the Wisła River and spreading southward to the Carpathians. This association reached its end only at the close of World War I, after the three conquered regions were liberated and united in a new Republic of Poland. The name, however, that Austria had given to the region did not fall into disuse with the change in regime: Galicia – a reminder of an early Ruthenian duchy that in the Middle Ages had alternately been subject to Poland and Hungary, its center being the fortified city of Galich (Halicz, in Ruthenian and Polish). The region's attachment to Austria in the last third of the eighteenth century, even though the result of military conquest, created a new situation whose advantages could not be ignored by the bulk of Galicia's industrialists, merchants and intelligentsia: it wiped out the traditional Carpathian border and opened the great Hapsburg realm and Vienna, its capital, to the residents of Galicia. Galician provincial towns, even the relatively small ones, were now exposed to the tidings of accomplishment and intellect that hailed from the imperial capital.

Nor did these tidings skip over Carpathian townships and villages, such as Bukovsk and Wisłok. Influencing the trend of economic activity peculiar to the region, including the cattle-and-horse trade, they changed the lifestyle of the residents. True, the notorious catchphrase, *galicyjska bieda* (Galician poverty), embraced all ethnic groups; but, on the positive side, law and order were imposed on the roads, and both sides of the natural boundary, which had formerly been the haunt of highway robbers and smugglers, were now open to safe and regular traffic.

The improvement of safety on the roads, which was highly valued by traveling merchants as a whole, combined with another development that was particularly relevant to the Wróbels: by continuing to deal in cattle and horses, they had managed, over the years, to form ties with the new masters of the land and began to supply livestock to the imperial army as well. This bettered their economic situation for a while but, more importantly, to a large extent it determined the fate of the family and its affairs throughout the nineteenth century and at the start of the twentieth. For the transition from stage to stage – from supplying horses to the Austrian army as a straight, civil business deal, to the enlistment of individual family members for actual military service in the Austrian cavalry – was inevitable, and even natural; it was merely a question of time, especially as the Wróbels had made a name for themselves as champion riders and experts on the fine points of equestrian handling.

Two more factors facilitated the Wróbel integration into the imperial cavalry. One was their outward appearance. Taller and heftier than the average Jewish population in the Diaspora, their heads uncommonly large and hard as a rock, their noses straight, their eyes undaunted, and their bald pates gleaming in the midday sun, the Wróbel men, when clean-shaven and seated erect on their mounts, could very easily blend into a Slavic Galician regiment with not a trace of anything physical to give away their Jewish origins; like the Austrian Empire itself, the imperial army, too, was multinational and multi-lingual.

The other factor was their family name, so very different from the prevalent Ashkenazi surnames in Galicia. It was distinctly Slavic-*goyish* in form and, in fact, was a common *goyish* name, being the Polish word for sparrow, that simplest and most plebeian of rooftop fowl. "Probably, when they settled in the area, our forefathers 'borrowed' the name from their Polish or Ukrainian neighbors, just like the Israelites did when they left Egypt; what a pity that in this instance, it is all the poor Slavic peasants had to offer," Father, years later, would tease his son, whose curiosity had led him to a preoccupation with roots. He had more than once heard his son say how loathsome he found the biblical boasting about the "great wealth" of which the Israelites had bilked the Egyptians. On this occasion, Father explained, at the end of the eighteenth century, Emperor Joseph II – the "enlightened" son of Empress Marie-Thérèse, who in 1772 tore southern Poland away from the Polish realm – issued an order "in the name of progress" for his subjects to assume the "enlightened" surnames that were to be assigned to them, and no longer go by their fathers' names as was common among Jews and eastern Slavs. Peppering his explanation with various comments, whether indulgently humorous or painfully barbed, Reb Aazik had spoken of the scramble to acquire a "good name," and the corruption, villainy and sycophancy that held sway under the mantle of this "enlightened" directive.

Not much time elapsed before, in the first third of the nineteenth century, one of the Wróbels donned the uniform of the imperial army. It was Yitzhak-Isaac, Shloime's father, Yitzhak-Isaac the First: first of all the Wróbels to be known as such in official records and in family tradition; first of the generations to be born under Austrian rule; and first of the cavalrymen of the house of Wróbel to enter the Emperor's service. In addition: he was also the first Wróbel owner of an "estate" that was to be registered in his name in Wisłok. Indeed, cavalry service did not only dress the horse trainers of the house of Wróbel in a glory unprecedented in former generations, but also created a new basis of settlement aimed at tying the military family to its village land for generations. So, in keeping with official policy of the time, Yitzhak-Isaac was granted a small patch of land upon his discharge from the army, on the assumption that his offspring would follow in his footsteps as imperial cavalrymen.

The property was utterly barren and its owners powerless to bring forth bread from the earth; it would become all the more insufficient if the family had many children, as was the norm in those days. Another difficulty stemmed from its location at the western approach to the one-street village, in the Ukrainian-Slovakian section and cut off from the Jewish settlement at the eastern edge, a mile-and-a-half away, where the synagogue stood; the Wróbels were thus totally isolated from everyday contact with Jews and Judaism. Despite this, the grant could provide the young couple with both a holding to live on and a base for chicken and dairy farming, and Yitzhak-Isaac accepted the property gratefully and happily, hoping to bequeath the estate to his sons and his sons' sons forevermore. Neither the givers nor the recipients in the thirties of the nineteenth century – at the height of Metternich's leadership in Austria – could imagine that a mere three generations of Wróbels would stay on the land. For the winds of change would not only uproot the third generation from the land, but bring an end to both Austrian rule in the region and the very existence of the Habsburg empire in Europe.

The discharged cavalryman erected a wooden cabin for his family to live in, by the banks of a stream that supplied drinking water to man, fowl and beast and, further down, emptied its waters with great fanfare into the nearby Wisłok River. The river – one of Galicia's larger waterways which lent its name to the village and cast its spirit over the entire region – comes down from the Central Beskid mountains and turns northwest, leaving, on its right, Bukovsk and Sanok and, on its left, Rymanów (with its impressive synagogue and the home of one branch of the Binder-Wróbel family) as well as the villages of the tiny Łemki minority, which produced fine local woodcarvers. The latter sold wonderfully engraved, hand-made objects in the souvenir shops of the vicinity – such as the Łemki wooden plate, bearing three, large intertwined vine leaves, which Reb Aazik's son purchased in Rymanów in 1937 as a memento of the trip he made with his sister, Mala, to their father's native land. (The plate now graces the son's home in Jerusalem; its twin, purchased on the same occasion, is in Tel Aviv, at the home of the daughter, Gilatt.)

Further on, the Wisłok crosses the oil fields of Krosno, where the Tarnów-based partners, Wurzel and Daar, among the most notable Jewish industrialists in Galicia, built a factory for the manufacture of boots, galoshes, coats and other articles made of rubber and the by-products of crude oil. To the north, the Wisłok encounters a road from the southwest, from Nowy Sącz in the Western Beskid (known as Santz or Zans by Jews, and the cradle of the largest Hasidic faction in western Galicia), then veers with the road towards the northeast, to the city of Rzeszów (Reyshe in Yiddish), which sits on the main road and railway line that cuts Galicia from west to east. At Rzeszów, the river moves to the left of the road and railway, paralleling them on its way east, and leaving, on its right, Łańcut, with the Potocki castle and the nearby syna-gogue (that survived the Holocaust and was recently restored as a state museum). On its left, at a considerable distance, the river by-passes the town of Leżajsk (Lezhansk), which in the generation after the Ba'al Shem was the capital of Galician and Polish Hasidism. The founder of the movement was *Rebbe* Elimelekh, that fabled *Tzaddik* who taught his followers to be as joyous (*lustig, freilich*) as he, and who stars, together with his brother, Zussia, in legends and song (his grave is a site of pilgrimage for Hasidim to this day). Descending into the valley, the Wisłok finally reaches the end of its indepen-dent course and, brimming with its load of water, spills into the San, which separates eastern from western Galicia. In September 1939, the Wehrmacht invaded Poland, and the Red Army, on the basis of the infamous Ribbentrop-Molotov pact, marched west to meet the Germans near the San. The water line did for a time separate not only two powers and two armies but also two worlds – the world of life and the world of death.

The San, like the Wisłok, starts in the Beskids – albeit somewhat more to the east. First, it turns northwards and passes Lesko, home-town of Bezalel Kresch, "Safa Berura's" Hebrew literature teacher in Tarnów. Beyond that, in the neighborhood of Bukovsk, the river crosses Sanok (to whose *Talmud-Toireh* Zlatte transferred Aazik and Bereleh after the failure of the Bukovsk experience) and, proceeding further north for a while, makes a sharp turn to the east, meandering somewhat undecided as to the direction to take, and eventually lands in the key historic city of Przemyśl (the bloody front in the First World War to which Reb Aazik Wróbel was sent as a gunner and where he fell into Russian captivity). Only after reaching Przemyśl does the San choose its final direction and, sketching an arch to the left, vigorously carves out a diagonal southeast-northwest channel. From this channel it will stray no more. Thus, it will cross Jarosław, the historic market town and venue of assemblies of Polish Jewry's Council of Four Lands in the sixteenth and seventeenth centuries and, with the Wisłok waters in its belly, proceed along a steady, diagonal course towards the mother of all Polish rivers – the Wisła.

The Wisła gushes forth from the Silesian Beskid in the west, flashing eastwards (as the popular folksong says) "a youthful knee to make love to Kraków, prince of Polish cities," and marking the northern border of the district of Tarnów. There, it braces two of the best-known Jewish townlets in the area, Szczucin and Żabno, homeland to the Stutchiner Hasidism of the house of Horowitz and the Żabno Hasidism of the house of Unger, whose *Tzaddikim* dwell in Tarnów. At the same time, the Wisła takes up the Dunajec River, which cuts its way to it through the mountains and drops down to the valley, having sipped at Tarnów of the waters of the Biała, which now mingle with it. Up ahead, on its way northeast, the Wisła washes Tarnobrzeg, which, like Tarnów, was the private estate of the Tarnowskis. It had once been called Dzików, which is why the branch of Hasidism from the house of Horowitz that originated in this town would call its leader "the Dzikower *Rebbe*" even after the latter had moved his court to Tarnów. From here, the Wisła sets out to greet historic Sandomierz – the granary town of King Kazimir, who encouraged Jews to settle there in the fourteenth century – and after another brief stretch, spreads its arms to absorb the San and the river waters that have flowed into it en route, including the Wisłok. Along this section of its flow, until it meets the San, the Wisła, during the period of Poland's dissection, ran congruent to the rift between the southern edges of the Russian region and the northern border of Austrian Galicia – a rift beyond which Austrian administration had no dominion, and the spread of German as the official language, and of German culture and German values was thus halted.

After the meeting of the two rivers, the Wisła and the San resemble the uneven sides of a triangle with its base in the Carpathian range. At this point, the eye gives free rein to the imagination, perceiving the sides of the triangle as the sloping roof of the Wróbel shack in the village of Wisłok – the left slope (the Wisła), long and sunken with age; the right (the San), erect and young. And like in a children's storybook, a chimney rises from the apex of the roof. But instead of smoke, the intermingled waters of the two rivers burst forth at their confluence to flow through the Wisła's broadened channel northward, to the heart of the country – Warsaw.

Presumably, when Yitzhak-Isaac first built the family cabin, it looked different from what his grandson, Aazik, was to know as a child some sixty years later. Very likely, in its early days, the walls gleamed with fresh white paint and the roof sloped along straight lines, the left side not yet sunken or caving in, the way Aazik sitting in distant Tarnów, now remembers it. Nor had the layers of yellow thatch, that covered it from the very outset, faded yet or been brushed with rot or tainted by green moss. But – as at the end of the century, so at the start of the road – the floor of the cabin was made of packed earth in which the seasons of mud and the seasons of dust traced the annual calendar; and as at the end of the century, so sixty years earlier, the entire interior space was but a single room, with the parental bed in one corner, while the stove, which preserved its warmth, provided a hub for all the children, particularly in times of frost or snow, when the chickens and farm animals were also brought indoors to take shelter in the warmth of the embers.

As the number of children increased, however, to eight sons and one daughter, the grant became a garrote and the warm but small stove which gathered the family to it, a snare of poverty. This being the situation, there was only one escape: to leave. Indeed, seven brothers dared to gnaw through the ring that fastened them to the childhood hearth, tearing themselves away forever from the cabin and native village of Wisłok, and leaving Yitzhak-Isaac, the widower-father, with Shloime, the youngest brother, to their fate on the humble farm.

4

Seven left. But after breaking through to the ominous wide world beyond Wisłok's one and only street, no more than three achieved their aims. They built homes and raised families and children, and at least some of their grandchildren are known by name. The other four brothers, in contrast, vanished early on into an uncertain fate. One, it was claimed long ago, was seen in Vienna, wearing, like his father, Yitzhak-Isaac, and, later, his younger brother, Shloime, the uniform of a cavalryman serving in the Imperial Guard. The second brother, according to eyewitnesses, was spotted on the lower East Side of New York City and eventually got lost among the masses of Jewish immigrants who filled it at the end of the nineteenth and the start of the twentieth century; he then disappeared. As for the other two, not a whisper of information was ever received, nor the slightest shadow of a sign. In any case, no one bothered to record the names of the four for posterity and only a faint echo of their anonymous existence continued to hover in the memories of the elders of the tribe.

Of Yitzhak-Isaac's other three sons – Shloime's older brothers – whose whereabouts are documented, this much is known. Herschl refused to migrate too far afield so as not to, God forbid, burn his bridges. He simply crossed the Carpathian range and settled in

Medzilaboritch, the first Hungarian (and today, Slovakian) city beyond the chain of mountains to the south. The city, which despite its modest proportions satisfied Herschl's desire for urban life, struck the young man as close enough to the Wisłok home for him to maintain contact with the family and lend a helping hand if at all possible; and, hopefully, in exchange, to benefit from the warmth that parents – and the friendship that a younger brother, a vibrant sister-in-law and their handsome children – might diffuse even across the highlands. At the same time, the city was far enough away from Wisłok to give the young man a sense of complete severance from the village of which he had his fill and which had nothing left to offer him.

Among other things, Herschl set himself the task of cultivating the local Hungarian doctors and pharmacists and, through them, to recruit proper medical care for his kin; such care was not available in Galician villages at the time. Indeed, he achieved his goal: when they came to town for medical reasons, his relatives enjoyed a generous dose of assistance from him and a hearty welcome in his home. Zlatte, too, from time to time, would bring the children to Medzilaboritch – for check-ups, first aid and medical treatment – being sure that Uncle Herschl would not only procure the necessary medical attention, but would make the visit to town an unforgettable experience for her village children.

The second brother, Tevye (Tuvia), was also careful to retain contact with the family, although, like Herschl, he preferred city life to rural existence. Unlike his brother, however, he spent his entire existence in the familiar circuit of the Central Beskids, living in Sanok or Rymanów, towns that he knew from his youth. It was *his* actions, however, that were to go down as changing the fate of the whole Wróbel family. Himself shrinking from the hardships of migrating to a strange land and never daring to stray beyond the borders of Galicia, he nevertheless had the wisdom and foresight to understand that there was no point in encouraging Jewish youth to remain in this region of no prospects, and that they would do far better to go out and seek new horizons. Consequently, he encouraged his son, Burekh-Fishl to emigrate to America. Burekh-Fishl, who was to become known by the initials B.F., may have reached Pennsylvania as early as 1890, and was the trailblazer of the family in America and the patriarch of all the Wróbels and Binders across the sea. He is also the one who abandoned the Polish spelling of the surname and determined its current orthography – Wruble rather than Wróbel – to conform more closely with the English pronunciation. The Binders also opted for a new spelling, becoming Bender.

B.F. thus began the chronicles of the Wrubles in the new world. By correctly assessing the practical advantages of being an immigrant among immigrants from the same country of origin – albeit, a Jew among gentiles – he focused his efforts on the mining town of Exeter and other such locales in Wyoming Valley, Pennsylvania, the valley of coal mines, in which, to a large extent, Ukrainians, Slovaks and Poles from the Beskids – some of whom had been miners back home – found an occupation. Like all immigrants from hard-pressed countries, they had an urgent need for a safety belt of services and supplies – groceries, meat, haberdashery – that could be obtained on credit. B.F. rightly concluded that a Jewish immigrant from the Beskids, who could speak the miners' mother tongue and knew their ways, was better placed than anyone else to offer sympathy and assistance, especially if he, himself, as an immigrant had already gone through the first stage of absorption, had assimilated a first smattering of English, had acquired a good first idea of American habits, and had even managed to set aside some savings for his subsequent progress.

B.F. calculated his course most wisely. Well-liked by both Jews and non-Jews, and attentive to their needs and absorption difficulties, he came to know all inhabitants of the area, whether old-timers or newcomers, their problems and hesitations, and spared no time or effort in doing "favors" for people, "casting his bread upon the waters," as it were. He happily responded to appeals from Ukrainian workers to read them the personal letters they received in Ruthenian from wives or sweethearts, and gladly wrote replies on their behalf. (No doubt, in their native village, it was the priest who read and wrote letters upon request.) Little wonder, then, that this energetic man became a dominant figure in two worlds at one and the same time: he was the omnipotent *gabbai* (warden), managing affairs at the congregational synagogue that the Wrubles and their adjuncts built on the main street of Exeter, and he also entered the American version of small-town politics and, borne on the wings of popular support, was elected to a minor post in the Republican administration. All this made it easier for him to help his family, still across the sea, to emigrate and come, one by one, to this mining town, and set down stakes either in the same town itself or in one of the sister towns in the coal valley. And, despite the economic crisis and shifts that the region has undergone in the past few decades, with mines closing down and population shifting, many second- and third-generationers of Wrubles and Benders still live there, continuing to regard themselves as local citizens, even though Exeter's original synagogue has been sold and no longer exists, and the families have transferred their synagogue membership to the larger communities in the region, such as Wilkes-Barre and Pittston.

The only one of Yitzhak-Isaac's three sons to personally venture in his youth to emigrate to America – even before his nephew, B.F. Wruble, did so – was Nahmen, who may well have been the first member of the Wróbel tribe to cross the ocean. Unlike those of the following generation, however, who ever strove to unite the family in the new homeland, Nahmen, from the moment he stepped off the boat, ostensibly decided to obliterate all memory of his old home and dive into the sea of hope and suffering of New York's Jewish immigrant population. Amazingly enough, though, at some stage he surfaced. And more amazing still – he turned up in Pennsylvania of all places, on the edge of Wruble-Bender territory, in Dixon City near Scranton. Here, he passed away in 1925, his monument being the only Wruble headstone in the small Jewish cemetery. All his life, it seems, Nahman had covertly, and without betraying any sign of it, kept tabs on his brothers. Aware that they, too, had meanwhile immigrated, he gleaned crumbs of information about them, although they had no idea where he had suddenly sprung from, or how or why: was he prompted by longing, need, or a desire to establish a family with his brothers close by? Perhaps it was the latent homing instinct of a lost son that steered him to the families that his brothers had established on the new continent so that he might die in the bosom of loved ones, where there would be someone to say *kaddish* on his grave.

These are the events that befell the sons of Yitzhak-Isaac who left Wisłok in the nineteenth century. Surihenne, on the other hand, the only daughter, went no further than an arrow shot from Wisłok in marrying Haim-Yitzhak Binder of nearby Bukovsk. The two made a living from a *kretchme* (a tavern and inn) and an auxiliary farm with a dairy cow and chickens, creatures in whom Zlatte had always found her friends. Yet, their son, also known as Nahmen, emigrated to America around the outbreak of the First World War and busied himself bringing Jewish immigrants from Europe to America under the hardships of war. His son, Morris Bender, in Exeter, married Lily, the daughter of Ben Wruble, who was the second son of Shloime and Zlatte and brother to Reb Aazik. Thus, on American soil, the two families that had been intertwined in the "old country," now sprouted new shoots all over the new homeland.

5

After the sons of Yitzhak-Isaac scattered to the four winds, and the daughter followed her husband to Bukovsk, and he, Yitzhak-Isaac, became a widower, the one-room shack with the warm stove continued to shelter only him and his youngest son, Shloime. When the boy reached conscription age, Yitzhak-Isaac sent him off to the cavalry, where he himself had served and, now that his discharge drew near, he hoped that at least he, the youngest, would make his home in the Wisłok cabin, to be followed by children and grand-children. But the hardship of years and millstone of loneliness de-feated the old horseman. Shortly before his son's discharge from regular service, Yitzhak-Isaac took to bed, never to rise again. All alone, he lay on his deathbed, his eyes glued to the cabin door and longing for a miracle that would open it and deliver to him his de-mobilized son, sporting tags of rank on his sleeve and flashing the red-and-white medal on his chest.

In vain did he wait; in vain did he pray for a miracle. Miracles don't occur in the cruel social system where arrogant – or, at best, indifferent – urban officials control the lives of simple peasants. And so it was in Shloime's case: because of the unyielding bureau-cracy of "the system", the officials charged with addressing the personal problems of soldiers in the Austrian army did not give their attention to the urgent plea of relatives in Bukovsk that the discharge of Master Horseman Salomon Wróbel be advanced by a few days. Despite his father's critical condition, the wheels of "the system" remained bogged down and an early release was deferred. Yitzhak-Isaac closed his eyes for the last time in 1877, denied both the pleasure of welcoming his son as a returning hero and the gratification of leading him to the wedding canopy. When Shloime finally arrived at the village on the later date fixed by military offi-cialdom, his kinsfolk could merely temper the sorrow of orphan-hood and mourning with the joy of welcoming the young man back home, and concentrate on providing practical assistance for Shloime. After all, now, all alone in the world, he was about to as-sume responsibility for the land and the farm in which his broth-ers had no interest.

Meanwhile, day in and day out, morning and evening for a

whole year after his return, Shloime, the son, walked the mile-and-a-half from his shanty in the western part of the village to the synagogue that stood on the eastern edge to recite the mourner's *kaddish* in memory of his father. At the end of the year of mourning, the legless, amputee rabbi of the town of Bukovsk conducted a modest wedding ceremony for Shloime Wróbel and Zlatte Binder, and the assembled relatives wished them well on their new, joint course of independence. And so the father's dream was fulfilled – even though sadly too late, and without his own participation. On June 16, 1881, three years after the young couple moved into the shack, Zlatte gave birth to a son, who was named Yitzhak-Isaac after his grandfather, Yitzhak-Isaac the First: Aazikl his mother called him, or Reb Aazik Wróbel as he would come to be known, in time, in Tarnów, where he would set up home.

Thereafter, Shloime was to suffer from the same economic hardships that had visited his father, Yitzhak-Isaac the First, fifty years earlier, when he had built his cabin on the bank of a stream spilling into the Wisłok and set out – naively – to defy the frailties of his farm. A lost cause! For, from the start, the Wisłok farm was unable to supply the needs of a growing family and, from the start, all effort in this direction was doomed to failure. Oh, the blind, cruel cycle of poverty! Just as in the previous generation the cabin had been homeland to a debilitating want in Yitzhak-Isaac's nine children, so it would consistently and mercilessly impose that fate within its walls upon the next generation, serving as homeland to a debilitating want also in Shloime's and Zlatte's nine children (three of whom died in infancy).

His few moments of satisfaction – the only ones, perhaps – reached Shloime in a printed notice in the mail, summoning him to reserve duty in his corps. When this happened, he would again don his uniform in delight, pull on his boots and pin on his rank tags, excited to take part in the exercises of the Austrian army as a reserve cavalryman. As luck would have it, however, on his twentieth stint of duty – the final one allowed by law – the aging soldier suffered a riding wound to the groin and contracted a type of painful infection that leaves its victims highly handicapped.

Shloime's livelihood continued to falter irrevocably, and his family tottered on the brink of starvation. And, yet, the wound made not a dent in Cavalryman Wróbel's loyalty to the corps; surely, it was to the likes of him that the servant's words in the biblical verse apply: "I love my master... and I do not want to go free." Chains of love bound the cripple to his master, the Emperor, and he remained linked to the tradition of loyalty that he had inherited from his father: loyalty despite injury; loyalty without complaint or demand for satisfaction; loyalty, even in pain and poverty, until one's dying day! The son's loyalty to the Habsburg crown exceeded all that has been exalted in the most devoted of soldiers, surpassing even his father's, who, for his part, had meticulously fulfilled his duty for twenty years. Oh, worthy, how worthy the son, and worthy, how worthy his loyalty of Heine's pen; certainly no less so than the two grenadiers that returned to France from Russian captivity and whose loyalty to their Emperor, Napoleon – even as prisoners-of-war – was immortalized by the poet. And sorry, how sorry the crying indifference (or strident villainy) that prevented the military establishment from seeing its way to repaying its soldier, if only with a dram of basic decency, if not with any expression of gratitude, for utter and unswerving loyalty.

The cavalryman, himself, in his submissive way, did not protest against the indifference, neglect and abandonment, nor did he complain. Just as he refrained from reacting at the time to the arbitrary (or thoughtless) injustice that prevented him from reaching his father on his deathbed, so now, too, he bore his pain quietly and without remonstration and, as he had acted throughout the years of his service, he asked of his commanders nothing, not even the medical care that every soldier is entitled to by law. His superiors – whether out of haughtiness towards one they saw as an ignorant peasant on whom there was no point in wasting means or energy, or because they were guided, wittingly or otherwise, by a hostile attitude towards Jews, or, perhaps, out of fear that they could be sued for criminal negligence – did not exert themselves to arrange hospitalization or even provide financial aid for treatment at home. One way or another, the severe infection went completely untreated. Instead, the soldier was sent home, broken and unwanted, with a laconic declaration that upon the conclusion of the twentieth exercise, he had fulfilled his obligations and henceforth was exempt from reserve duty. Thus, a seal was put on the question of compensation.

Heavy privation, made shameful by real hunger, descended on the Wróbel family in Wisłok in the last years of the nineteenth century and the first decade of the next as a result of the breadwinner's physical impairment. His income destroyed both by tardiness in finishing the seasonal farm work and the inability to make the village rounds in pursuit of the horse trade, Shloime had no choice but to put his trust in the assistance of his sons and his daughter who had emigrated, at the start of the twentieth century, to America. At the end of 1909, after seven years of absorption pains in the New World across the sea, the young Wróbels succeeded in preparing the ground to absorb their father and bring him to American shores, along with Zlatte, their mother, and the child of their old age, born in 1901 in Wisłok and called Aaron-Yaacov, after Zlatte's father Arinyankif (or Jake, as he was later to be known in the American vernacular).

Incredibly, the main obstacle to the success of the rescue campaign was Shloime himself. All the troubles put together, both of poverty and physical suffering, did not manage to undermine the faith of the crippled cavalryman in his sovereign, Franz-Joseph, nor detract from his desire to remain in Galicia and serve the Emperor when the call came. A truly massive dose of inducement was required to get Shloime to consent to embark on the "Cleveland" – the ship on the Hamburg–New York line – and to cut himself off from Europe, from Austria and from his monarch: his sons had to formally promise to help their father return to Galicia when called to the flag.

The severance of the last Wróbels from Europe entailed a severance also from the eldest son who, years prior to his father's infirmity, had moved to Tarnów. When the "Cleveland" raised anchor and sailed for the New World, Reb Aazik remained behind, alone of all the family, clinging to his residence in the city of Torah rather than share in the total uprooting of the Wróbel clan from the Old World.

6

In the small mining town of Exeter, Pennsylvania, at the home of his son – known as Ben in America (which was short for Bereleh, although to his parents he would always remain Bereleh) – Shloime sits confined to a wheelchair, his face that of a very old man, even though he is merely fifty and hails from a family of men strong in body and mind and known for living beyond eighty. Surrounded by caring children, Shloime in Exeter is free of all worry and, sometimes, actually feels restored enough to choose to go to work. But while his body languishes on the continent of America, his heart dwells on the other side of the ocean, on the great parade grounds of his old barracks. He fancies that he sees rows and rows of horsemen of the Emperor's cavalry, all mounted on their chargers and primed for morning roll call, while he, the Master-Horseman, stands fast with his horse in the front row, in the role of the right signalman, while the other soldiers, horse and rider, all fall in accordingly. True, the more time passes the more he seems resigned to the fact that given the state of his health he would have no chance of doing a real job in the army, even if he had stayed in his Carpathian village. But he is convinced that in the hour of emergency he will be summoned to return to the Habsburg realm. No, the Emperor would not – could not – pass him over when he has a need for his professional expertise.

But as the days run their course, his health goes from bad to worse and in 1914 he must be urgently hospitalized. He is brought to Scranton, Pennsylvania, where his daughter, Esther Klein, lives with her husband, and hosts Mother Zlatte in her home. Shloime's condition is so serious that he cannot attend the wedding of his son, Mendel (Max, as he was called in America); thus, Max and his fiancée, Lena, make a pilgrimage to the sickbed at Scranton's Moses Taylor Hospital in order to receive his blessing.

After eighty years, Jake, the youngest of Shloime's sons and now himself very ripe in years, remembers how he, a *bar-mitzvah* lad, sat at his father's bed, a witness to the visit of the two young people: in the grips of a high temperature, the distraught father mumbled words that were partly incomprehensible, although the overall drift was clear enough to surmise that his fevered mind dredged up the memory of his own wedding day to Zlatte. His father, too, Yitzhak-Isaac, was not at his wedding because death had snatched him away, before his son, Shloime, was discharged from the army…

The language difficulties that always hampered communication between the patient and the medical staff and nurses at Scranton became an unbearable obstacle as his condition deteriorated. Also, the distance from Exeter, from his sons, from chatting with relatives and acquaintances in his own tongue, proved a source of endless frustration to Shloime. As a result, he asked to be returned to his son's home in Exeter. The request was granted; having lost all hope of any real recovery, the doctors saw no point in keeping the invalid in the hospital against his wishes.

At his son's home, Shloime is again granted a few weeks of grace, with some days that are better and some worse. On the "better" days, he sits in a wheelchair at the window overlooking the backyard of the family home. The residence built by Bereleh at

110 Lincoln Street, about a hundred paces from the corner of the city's main highway, is a typical American frame house: the shady entry porch boasts a swing, luring evening sitters to light a thick cigar and ease into tranquil talk with friends, while the glass door beckons inwards, to the family room and the kitchen; a wooden stairway inside leads upstairs from the ground floor to the bedrooms. Imbued with a special sensitivity for his mother, whom he loved with a child's innocence until the end of her days, Bereleh erected a barn in the backyard where Zlatte kept a dairy cow, selling some of its milk to the neighbors. What stronger remedy to make two aging villagers feel at home than a yard and a cow to ease the longing for faraway Wisłok?

At the sight of the overgrown yard and Zlatte's reclining cow chewing its cud, and of the paraphernalia leaning against the wall – a wooden stool and zinc container with an angular tin spout which Zlatte uses for milking – it seems to Shloime, who most of the time dozes and drowses, that he has just returned to Wisłok from a tiring trip and is sitting comfortably, as he used to do then, in the yard next to the cabin built by his father, Yitzhak-Isaac, eighty years earlier. His ears pick up the gurgling water of the stream flowing into the Wisłok River and he strains to remember if it is Thursday evening, and whether he has just come home from the Bukovsk fair.

For, if so, he must, as usual, go to the whirlpool, where the waters of the stream mix with the waters of the river to froth and foam and confuse the fish so that they lose all sense of direction and, of themselves, leap into the net; this enables him, without any effort on his part, to bring a fish or two back to Zlatte, whose skilled and capable hands will turn out delicacies for Sabbath eve and an additional portion for the Sabbath day. Evening falls and Shloime's eyes seek the smoke that should be rising from the chimney of the stove. The scent of village eve fills his nostrils: in a moment he will rinse his face in the stream and Zlatte will serve him potato soup for supper. Tomorrow is Sabbath eve. Sabbath in Wisłok... Shloime nods off again, a serene, satisfied smile softening his agonized face.

But there are also the "worse" days – which are becoming more and more frequent – when he lies in bed, burning up and aching all over, and all the scenes and landscapes and figures and faces and events of his life parade before him in one great muddle, without any order of time or place, so that he is unable to detect either where he is now or whose face it is that is leaning above him in concern and distress. In the grip of fever, his thoughts increasingly disconnect from reality and he seems to float like the "Cleveland," on which he sailed, for the first time in his life and against his will, across the vast ocean to reach the shores of this land – a land lacking all charm and splendor. But these thoughts too, drift without anchor or compass or direction, grasping, for as long as they can, at a broken reed of momentary memory or a crushed straw of unfulfilled longing whose traces linger on in the consciousness.

Meanwhile, since he took ill, his outward appearance has changed too: his beard has sprouted (even though he is ready to shave it off in an emergency if called on to return to service), and his face, which was always that of a Slav peasant's – large and full and round and copper-tinged – has shrunk, softened, become more delicate and almost translucent, as if a hidden light shone behind it, and ever so gradually, it has donned the expression of a scholarly Jew...

"That's how he might have looked all his life had he chosen a *Gemara* page instead of stirrups," Zlatte suddenly rends the magic mist enveloping the docile silence in the sickroom. The adamant pronouncement by the wife and mother is dipped in a sadness empty of all pity or empathy. The sons around the bed are stunned and at a loss for words at the note of resentment rising from her words like a foul vapor and relentlessly clinging to the walls of the room. But Zlatte will not budge. Refusing to soften her judgment in any way or to retreat behind routine clichés of grief that the pained glances of her sons might evoke, she studies the patient again and at length – and her eyes are apathetic and void, as if he were not the person with whom she has shared a bed for nearly thirty-five years, bearing him nine children; as if he were not the tall, handsome young man whose erect seat in the saddle kindled widespread admiration, nor she the woman who walked out to greet him with shining eyes while Ukrainian *shiksas* rolled their eyes at him and burst with jealousy. On the contrary, she seems to be deriving a strange pleasure from having managed to stun her listeners. She would like to tell them, the sons of this dying man, who was now no doubt doing some very serious soul-searching before his Creator, that their father had been a total failure, from the start of his illusory military eminence to the painful and ridiculous end amid the sores of his groin, and that his whole life – apart from siring magnificent children – had pointlessly and unforgivably fallen short of the mark. She would like to declare that she, at least – his wife, who had quietly borne his misguided follies, his insensitivity to her feelings and her loneliness, as well as his indifference to a Jewish education for their children – had no intention of ever absolving him.

It is hard to know if Shloime understands his wife's words, or even hears them at all. All his lights seem to be directed inward, to a blue vision inside his soul, and there is hardly anything – whether objects or words – to grab onto as a bridge to reality. The one exception is his prayer book. His eyes stray to the night table near the bed, where the prayer book rests; printed in Vienna, it is a small pocket version with a non-Jewish looking binding, which he received as a soldier, the gift of Austria's military rabbinate, and had brought back to Wisłok at the end of his service.

For the first year after his return from the army, he carried the prayer book every day to the synagogue in the eastern part of the village to recite the *kaddish* for his father, and it also accompanied him on the "Cleveland" en route to America. In fact, it is the only Hebrew book he knows and the first and only one that he has ever really owned. Since his illness, it has sat permanently near his bed and, to him, it epitomizes the essence of his Jewish existence. No, Shloime does not read it, nor does he pray, but from time to time he reaches out to run his hand over the page at which it is always open, the one before the last, page 469, that starts with the "Prayer for the Safety of the King and his Ministers" and concludes on the next page along with the prayer book itself. Another biographical quirk: this one Hebrew item is the final concrete object to tie him to his monarch, while the Hebrew prayer, which is the only Jewish knowledge he ever gained – and this, too, only haltingly – is the sole vehicle by which he conveys his loyalty to the Emperor:

"May He who grants salvation to kings (and so forth…) bless and watch over (and so forth…)

> our Master
> His Majesty
> Emperor Franz-Joseph I
> and Empress Elisabeth Amalia Eugenia
> and the Crown Prince –"

Nor is Shloime even aware that this version in the prayer book, printed in the nineteenth century, no longer fits the circumstances of the Austrian royal house, for the Empress Elisabeth, well-loved by all and fondly referred to as Sissie, whose name he remembers in 1914, was actually assassinated back in 1898.

7

In August of that last year of his illness, 1914, the canons began to roar in Europe, reverberating all the way to the American towns of

Pennsylvania. Since the United States was not yet involved in the war, permission was granted in this neutral country to subjects of the states that were at war to apply to their consulates and sign up to return and enlist in their national armies; true enthusiasts even set out on their own initiative for the ports of New York, Philadelphia or Boston to sail in patriotic fervor and at their own personal expense to Europe.

A new wind seemed to be up and it burst into Shloime's room in Exeter as well. Joy lit up his face and his eyes seemed to burn with a new light, totally independent of the state of his body. Here, the hour of emergency he had so prayed for had come, and the hour of emergency was also his finest hour. Now, upon the conscription of tens of thousands of service carts and supply wagons harnessed to horses and mules, and given that canons, too, were to be moved by horse power, let alone the cavalry itself, the Emperor would urgently require his services as a consultant for the military's livestock – a job he could accomplish easily and with perfect success even from a wheelchair. Now, there was no doubt that the Emperor would call on him, and when he did, he would find his old horseman ready and willing.

On each and every one of the "better" days in which Shloime forged another quasi-link to reality, he asked those about him if the call-up notice had arrived, summoning him to his homeland. He turned to Bereleh, but particularly to B.F. – in whose ability as a politician to "move things" Shloime, like a typical rustic, has complete faith – and asked them to inquire at the Austrian embassy in Washington or at the Austrian consulate in New York into the reason for the delay. And without any prior discussion among themselves, they all profess that they have already done so several times, making up excuses and promising that the matter is being handled and will soon be solved to everyone's satisfaction. And Shloime grins contentedly, and sinks back into his hallucinations.

Zlatte, alone, is disgusted by this game and refuses to take part in the deceit. At such moments, she turns her back on her sons and goes out to the yard to tend her cow, just as she tended the cow in Surihenne's yard in Bukovsk and in her own yard in Wisłok – she tends the cow and is silent. The mute wall, which she believed had crumbled and would never cast its shadow on her again, returns during this period to imprison her once more. And worse still: postal contact with Galicia, which was disturbed by the outbreak of war, is now non-existent because of the massive Russian attack on the region that has led to the capture of Tarnów by the Czar's army, and she has no idea how her son is faring in the arena of battle. No, she is not concerned for Franz-Joseph, like her sick husband, nor for his cavalry. The latter have no doubt already left their ridiculous, showy parades on the barrack grounds and are busy galloping on their horses, sweeping through and trampling towns and villages. Yes, the towns and villages are depicted in official announcements as "enemy" holdings, but she, Zlatte, knows very well that they are no different at all from Wisłok or from Bukovsk which are on "our" side – certainly, not as regards their poverty – and her heart goes out to their wretched inhabitants. No, she does not long for Franz-Joseph, but for Aazikl, her eldest son, whom she willingly lent to Torah and to sacred work – like in the *Zennerenne* story about Hannah, mother of Samuel – and left him, with a clear though painful mind, in God's old country across the sea… "Where are you now, Reb Aazik, pride of our family?" her heart cries wordlessly "Where are you, Aazikl, oh, Aazikl, my son? Have you fulfilled Mother's dream?"

November 22, 1914 was a gloomy autumn day. The leaves that had fallen to the ground now wrapped themselves in a thin sheet of frost, pretending to be white snow. Real snow had not yet fallen that year. Only thin, moist flakes flew here and there, like butterflies that had miscalculated time and ended up in trouble; lacking direction and turbid in color, the flakes wavered between dropping to the ground and sinking into the frost or evaporating into thin air. In the forenoon of that faded day, in the stillness of mourning, the family, now called Wruble, bore the coffin of Shloime Wróbel – first of the clan to die on the soil of the New World – to the site where the God of uprooted immigrants would also furnish true rest for this immigrant who, with the best of intentions, had been uprooted from his village.

The pallbearers crossed the railway track on the edge of Exeter and proceeded up to the elevated plot gazing out onto the Susquehanna – the plot that Exeter's younger generation had hastened to purchase in view of their father's deteriorating condition. Thus, with this first excavation of a father's grave, a Jewish cemetery was inaugurated in Wyoming Valley's mining town. And unlike his father, Yitzhak-Isaac, who had died all alone in his cabin, Shloime was laid to rest in the presence of four sons who recited the *kaddish* at his graveside. The ceremony passed in pensive silence. There was a sense that the interment of the family's first deceased in American soil, more than the building of homes and the settling into new jobs and a new language, symbolized a final break from the old country and the setting down of firm stakes in the new homeland.

Only as they began to make their way home did the tension lift somewhat, as people walked in groups of two or three making their first hesitant attempts at reminiscing. At some distance from the bridge, the four sons left the road along with several other mourners and, of one mind, turned towards a frozen dirt road alongside a dense thicket on the banks of the water leading to Coxton Yards; at this point the Lackawanna River descends from Scranton to flow into the Great Susquehanna River, so swelled at times that it floods the entire area for hundreds of yards. Here, a small slaughterhouse (the "beef house" in family short hand) fixed its location in a modest, single-story structure. The building did not fare well under the pervading dampness, which peeled from its front the cover of whitewash applied in the early days, and stained the other walls with brown mildew.

And yet, despite its dilapidated bearing and premature old age, the beef house was the model of a successful family venture, established by the first generation of Wruble immigrants on American soil and providing a respectable living to most of its members, including the second generation. B.F. and Ben (Bereleh) had invested in it not only the better part of their energy and means, but also a superior expertise which encapsulated the experience of generations in the care of livestock, shored up by the Wróbels from the start of their wanderings over the routes of the Carpathians and up to the current generation. It is hardly surprising that Shloime, too, shouldered the work of the "beef house," contributing no small share of his knowledge and training, even though his health did not permit steady work.

The benefit was reciprocal. Again and again Shloime would declare honestly and sincerely that, for him, this was God's little acre on American soil, adding, with a hint of boyish bashfulness, that only here was he able, for a while, to forget his disability and ignore his pain. This is where he would ask to be brought on the "better" days, when the suffering eased somewhat and he managed to find the strength to connect with people and reality. This, therefore, is where his sons and acquaintances now came, to silently commune with the story that Shloime had taken to the grave, leaving no one to tell it.

The Wisłok book was closed and sealed forever, they all felt. Shloime was gone. No more would he stretch out on the lawn that reaches down to the river, as he used to during the noon break on the few working days that he spent at the slaughterhouse. No more would he spend long hours, as he used to, gazing at the current of

the surging Lackawanna and its merging with the broad channel
of the Susquehanna. Nor would this sight ever again remind him
of those Thursdays not so long ago when, after the Bukovsk fair,
he would hurry to the exciting site of the Beskid, where the cabin
stream poured into the Wisłok. How confused the fish would grow
in the maddening clamor of the water! How they would rush to flee
the commotion of the willful waters and quickly escape by jumping
straight into the net which he, Shloime, did not even bother to lower
into the waves! And how calm they would become at the feel of
the net, as if they had reached the comforting conclusion that they
could do no better than sanctify Zlatte's modest Sabbath table!

Indeed, the memory of the violent clash between the two
Beskid water channels, which was a salient feature in the landscape
of Shloime's life, took merciless control of his last night as well. His
fevered body in the final throes of death, it seemed to Shloime that
he was again gliding on the waves of the stream towards the stormy
whirlpool, frothy white. But what at first appeared to be a galloping
stream, swept along by an inevitable, spinning acceleration to the
open abyss of the Wisłok River, abruptly took on the image of his
mare – the faithful grey mare – who strained her sinews in a supreme effort to deliver him to his destination; and the frothy sheen,
gushing from end to end, was merely the white beads of her per-
spiring mane, shaking with every last ounce of her strength. And
he, Salomon son of Eisig Wróbel, Master Horseman of his majesty
the Emperor, is galloping on his mare without saddle, or harness
or reins – contrary to formal military procedure but as he used to
in childhood – and his bare, sick knees, having suddenly recovered their strength, clamp the mare's powerful ribs with all their
might, and the fingers of his clenched hands, blue from the effort,
dig tensely and with convulsive determination into the mesh of her
mane as if fighting for their life. His drained, exhausted body feels
the warmth of the mare's flesh suffusing his own and, as he nestles
his head in the back of her neck, he hears a thunderous hammering,

and can't tell where the pounding is coming from – is it the blood of her arteries beating with a thousand drums into the distance, or his own blood swelling within him and smashing his skull? The two, horse and rider, now ascend and – with a final flexing of the muscles – break through the whirlpool's steep wall of water. And suddenly, the horizon opens and they glide along the calm, broad channel of the Wisłok to the blue meeting point of water and sky, and all is still , still, still… And his knees may now relax their pressure, and his clenched fingers open to let the hand drop calmly, softly. And he may rest, rest, rest….

*

Shloime died of acute ague in the early morning of 4 Kislev 5675, according to the Jewish calendar, at the age of only fifty-five. A year later the first headstone was installed in the cemetery of the congregation of Exeter and, to everyone's relief, remained the only one for several years. Unlike its companions, which came later, all of polished marble and shining glitter and dual-language engraved inscriptions, as is the custom in the new country, Shloime's retained some of the original roughness of the marble and the inscription on it was in Hebrew alone. By common consent, considering who he had been, there seemed to be no point in having an English inscription, for in his brief spell – less than five years – on American soil, Shloime had not absorbed any of the language apart from a few isolated words for everyday use, and never felt at home with the sound of it.

An anonymous versifier – some Hebrew teacher from Pittston or Scranton, no doubt, who enjoyed dabbling in rhyme and rhetoric in the Hebrew tongue – was hired to compose an epitaph that Shloime himself would certainly have found difficult to understand. Floridly phrased (and liberally sprinkled with unnecessary "yod"s) – boasting even an acrostic insertion of the Hebrew letters of Shloime's name – it states:

Our heart-joy stilled, our days bereaved…	שבת משוש לבינו והפך לאבל ימינו
The crown of our head mercilessly reaved…	לוקחה עטרת ראשינו
Thus, our heart of hearts aggrieved…	על זה ידווה לבינו
And our eyes forever tear-sheaved…	מים יורדות עינינו

The crowning glory in all eyes was the acronymic title *"mohorer"* – "our teacher and rabbi, Rabbi…" – that the composer prefaced to the deceased's name, a designation that very likely filled the hearts of his sons and daughter with profound pride and gratification. And after all, why not? The gratification of mourners over a departed is more important than a departure from fact. Headstones are not meant for those who have passed on to the next world, but for those who remain behind. So what if the title that was carved in stone is plucked from the air – like other blighted flowers of rhetoric re-peated as if by rote – and contains more than a grain of pretence? In the present instance, the pretence is innocent and heartwarming and harmless and hurts no one. Only Zlatte, the wife – consistent and uncompromising as ever – diverted her gaze from the epitaph, and with cold, dry, unforgiving eyes stared into space instead. She most likely could not have read the words in any case and, even if she could have, chances are she would not have understood them.

Not so, today, three generations later. When the Tarnów grandson – at a far more advanced age than Grandpa when he died – comes to reflect on honest, innocent Grandpa Shloime; and when he comes to review Grandpa's sojourn on earth, the sojourn of a life filled with the good intentions and naive faith of a peas-ant boy, and yet pointless and aimless from start to finish, just like the pointless and aimless dream he dreamed as both a young and a mature man, a foolish dream to return to join a war not his own for a country not his own....

And when the grandson sadly dwells on Grandpa's untimely death – which, like his life, was equally pointless and aimless – a death caused by the disgraceful sloppiness and criminal neglect of a haughty regime which Shloime served loyally and artlessly, and for which he was repaid with apathy and disparagement....

At that time, the grandson deals Grandpa a true kindness by affixing in this book the kind of epitaph by which Shloime, with every breath, must have longed to be remembered:

Here lies
Master Horseman
Salomon son of Eisig Wróbel
Master Cavalryman in the Guard of His Majesty the Emperor
Franz-Joseph's Horseman on American soil

Zlatte Wróbel and grave of husband Shloime (parents of Aazik)

CHAPTER FIVE

Reb Aazik's Song of Songs: The Wróbel Saga Continued

1

At the weinman family flat in Tarnów, only a few steps away from the "New" (or "Great") Synagogue, scores of guests from the town's various Jewish social circles gather in mid-June 1914. They came to share in the joy of Zvi-Hersch Weinman, the cantor at the synagogue, and in the joy of Sureh née Gokhban, his wife, on the occasion of the marriage of their eldest daughter, Golda, to the Torah prodigy, Reb Aazik Wróbel.

Both groom and bride made specific requests regarding the wedding arrangements. Aazik insisted that the Rabbi of Szydłów be asked to conduct the ceremony. The latter served on the High Religious Court of the Holy Community of Tarnów despite the opposition of activists from the Hasidic *Kloyz*, who accused him of being an irredeemable *misnaggid* (opponent of Hasidism) – indeed, the spokesman of the *misnagdim* in the town – whereas Tarnów was distinctly Hasidic; they further complained that he prayed at the *bis-medrash* at Fish Square rather than at the *Kloyz*, where his fellow *dayanim* (justices) attended services. The 'Szydlower' was however (the groom claimed), a true scholar after his own heart: erudite, keen-minded and moderate in his judgments. In fact, upon his demise at the close of the Austrian era, he would be eulogized (in German) as a *Talmudfuerst*, a "prince of Talmud," and as a justice untainted by zealotry: "his ways were all pleasing and his paths all of peace." By choosing him as rabbi, Aazik wished, apart from expressing his own personal esteem, to protest against the self-appointed Torah spokesmen who allowed the "prince of Talmud" to wallow in poverty in a bleak room in the Krenzler building at 4 Lwowka Street. "Shame! Shame," cried Aazik, "that because of rental arrears for the miserable room, the threat of eviction hangs like a sword above the 'Szydlower's' neck!" In vain. His protest fell on deaf ears. In time, the building overseer, Krentzler's son-in-law, was to throw the rabbi and his bedraggled belongings into the street.

The entertainment program for the wedding also deviated from the norm – not in what it contained, but in what it omitted – and this was at the explicit demand of the bride. Golda, of course, had the reputation of being a modern woman in view of both her unsupervised monthly visits to Kraków and her responsible job at her place of employment, where, because of her knowledge of foreign languages, she was in charge of foreign relations. There were, however, people who felt that "modern" stood for "rebellious," primarily because of her objection, on principle, to marriages arranged through the mediation of a matchmaker (although she resigned herself to their existence in the end and had no choice but to submit to them), and because of her insistence on her right, prior to her marriage and without a chaperone, to go for a walk in the company of her "intended" to size him up and gain an idea of his character. "Or is there some other way for me to gauge the character of my husband-to-be?" she would reply in open defiance to charges of "licentiousness" and, with a bitter smile, describe an experience that she had actually had: one day she was out walking in the fields with a young scholar, who was highly spoken of. When they passed a cluster of beehives with swarming bees buzzing all around, the young man panicked, lifted the edges of his *kapotteh* to protect his face, and beat a retreat as fast as he could. "Would the man's disgraceful cowardice have been exposed, or his alacrity in abandoning his intended wife to a dangerous fate come to light, if we had *not* gone walking together?" Such assertions of Golda's were compounded by her refusal to shave her head upon marriage and her repudiation of wearing a wig to cover the hair she would not cut.

If all this were not enough, Golda now put a veto on one of the inalienable hallmarks of traditional wedding entertainment – the jester (*badhin*) – for reasons she could readily furnish: the wit and quips of jesters rested largely on double meanings and innuendoes bordering on the vulgar. Consequently, the entertainment for the event was to be provided by two groups – the *Meshorerim* choir of the "Great Synagogue" and the orchestra that accompanied it – who successfully made the time pass pleasantly with songs and music. Generally, Reb Zvi-Hersch himself would have conducted both, but this time, considering that he was the host, the *Meshorerim* and musicians prepared the program without him. "Not only is it in itself a more respectable standard," Golda claimed with satisfaction, "but one that faithfully reflects Father's spiritual world and my own love of music."

Golda's critical attitude was the source of a good deal of anguish for Toivyeleh-*badhin*, whose fame had spread far beyond Tarnów's boundaries. He was hailed as a master entertainer and, especially, as a wizard of wisecracks and biblical verses that he deliciously bent to his wit. The absence of a jester, however, did not detract from the joy of Golda's wedding, and the merrymaking lasted well into the night. In fact, that day, for the first time, the Weinmans felt that they had fully integrated into Tarnów's Jewish community, which was known as a distinguished seat of learning but sealed and inhospitable to strangers. It was, after all, less than six years since Zvi-Hersch had moved his family here, having been invited in 1908 to inaugurate the community's "New" Synagogue; and this, following a routine concert tour during the *Hanukka* season in the course of which he, his singers and orchestra arrived in Tarnów and made a strong impression. The wedding celebration itself, no less so than the large assembly of participating guests, was proof that the Tarnów congregation had opened its heart to the cantor-composer who had won it over with his original melodies, just as he had earlier won over old congregations in Russia's Pale of Settlement and young congregations in the "New Russia" on the approaches to Odessa and the Black Sea, as well as the congregations of Eastern Galicia. Success smiled on the cantor and his melodies, and all the strata of Tarnów's Jewish community began to hum the Weinman tune for "*Mogen Avois*" on Sabbath eve, to enjoy "*Yoyshev Beseyser Elyon,*" and to pour its heart out before their Creator on Yom Kippur with "*Al Hato'im,*" the notes for which, as set down in Zvi-Hersch's own hand, were found by his grandson among the possessions left after his death:

In this hour of carefree rejoicing, could any of the guests possibly have foreseen that within two weeks, the pistol of an unknown revolutionary in a faraway Balkan city would jolt the world into war for the next four years? Could he have predicted that Tarnów proper would subsequently become immersed in suffering and loss of life and property, turning all the participants of the wedding party, including the bride, her family, and her groom, into refugees chasing a roof over their heads and a safe haven? The fateful shots that rang out in Sarajevo in this unforgettable month – June 1914 – not only took the lives of the Habsburg Crown Prince and his wife, but utterly shattered a time-honored way of life: a life of stability, law and order, economic planning and long-term saving patterns, in an atmosphere of confidence in the future. In short, as the shots of June 1914 reverberated from one end of the globe to the other and, in reaction, the guns of August 1914 ignited the whole world, the fires of war burned away not only countries and people but also the *Zeitgeist*, the spirit of the period – a period referred to by Aazik in Yiddish as *"di normale zeiten"* (normal times), while Golda and the entire French-speaking intelligentsia embraced the romantic-sounding label of *la belle époque*. Years later, Aazik and Golda would look back on that era with nostalgia and patent sorrow, as if mourning a paradise lost.

Disaster was not long in coming.

In November, 1914, the month that Shloime Wróbel passed away at his son's home in America, half a world away, Russian forces conquered Tarnów as part of a large-scale attack by the Czar's army on the Austro-Hungarian Empire. The Russians held the city until May 1915, a relatively brief period, but one indelibly etched in the collective memory of the city and its Jewish population. Indeed, a gust of fear and gloom rises from the memoirs of contemporary Jews when this time is mentioned. No few of them were struck by a capricious fate, failing to flee Tarnów before the troubles came and remaining trapped in the city. Their testimony is filled with hair-raising accounts of a two-fold suffering – as both a conquered population, and as Jews. The city Jews were on the receiving end of a special cruelty meted out by Colonel Kozlov, governor of the city, in the early months of the conquest. In this campaign against and abuse of Jews, the *nahayka* (Cossack whip) served as a constant weapon, and groundless lashings were a daily occurrence. One of the ruler's favorite targets were men with beards, side-locks and black *kapottehs*, whom his Cossacks loved to torment on a Sabbath morning as these Orthodox Jews innocently walked to prayers in *Kloyzes* and *shtiblakh*. And woe to anyone who dared complain the next day at Colonel Kozlov's office – such "defamation of the good name of the Russian military" invariably earned the denouncer a sentence of twenty-five lashes.

Nor did the Jews who had managed to flee Tarnów prior to the entry of the Russian army escape damage, from locals and conquerors alike: Jewish homes left locked by refugees were broken into with the express permission of the mayor, Dr. Tertil, on the pretext that they probably contained food stores that should be confiscated and distributed to the needy. These private homes, and others like them, were converted by the Cossacks into stables for their horses. The same fate awaited the Apollo Cinema, whose owner, Mr. Lichtblau, was a Jew; it, too, became a stable, while the nearby Helios Cinema, owned by a non-Jew, was allowed to continue functioning as before.

Despite the heavy property losses incurred by those people who had abandoned their homes and fled for their lives, the latter nevertheless considered themselves fortunate to have escaped the hands of the notorious Cossack troops. The refugees found temporary shelter in the Austrian interior, notably in Vienna, the capital. Among those who took flight were also the young couple, Reb Aazik and Golda, along with the rest of the household of Zvi-Hersch Weinman, the cantor: his wife, Sureh, their seventeen-year-old son, Ben-Zion, their fourteen-year-old daughter, Zippora, and the youngest of the children, six-year-old Ephraim. The enlarged family took up temporary residence in what was then known as Vienna's "external belt" (*Aussenbezirk*), on Feiergasse in the Sixteenth Quarter, and remained in the capital until 1918. So that the letter sent in November 1914 from Pennsylvania to Galicia, bearing the news of Shloime's demise – a letter, which in normal times would have taken about a month to arrive – found Tarnów under a well-entrenched Russian military regime. Thus, the letter never reached its destination. More than four years were to pass before Reb Aazik would receive another letter in Tarnów, advising him of his father's death in America.

2

For the first two years that the Wróbels lived in Vienna, they came to no harm. The only difficulties experienced by the young couple were those common in those times, which affected the population as a whole. These did not prevent Golda from totally immersing herself in the capital's cultural life, with which she was acquainted from her previous visits and whose pace was left undisturbed by war – what's more, she was escorted by someone who loved music even more than she did: her father. "It was a Vienna that would never again have its equal," she would sigh in Tarnów in the Twenties and Thirties, when, to the best of her ability and with typical passion, she would attempt to sow in her children her impressions of those days. With all her sympathy for the liberation movements of the peoples included at the time under the multi-national, multi-lingual umbrella of the Habsburg Empire, she found it difficult to accept the dwarfing of Austria after the Treaty of Versailles, which left crowning Vienna sitting like a giant's head on a midget's body. "Oh! Vienna, Vienna!" her eyes whispered nostalgically and inconsolably, so that one hardly knew if it was Vienna she mourned, or her own self, confined to provincial Tarnów, while her younger sister, Zippora, having left Palestine in the Twenties, showed the courage to settle in the Austrian capital. Indeed, the Vienna that she had known before and during the First World War, the creative force behind the *Fin-de-Siècle* greats, still hovered above her, with its boulevards and parks, its opera house and concert halls, its theaters and cafés, museums and art galleries, its *Prater* amusements and Wiener-Wald pathways. And yet, in 1918, Golda, with her usual clarity of thought, had already decided that the plenty and tumult of the big city had become alien to her, and that she had no intention of continuing to swim in their deep waters. A repeat visit to Vienna in 1927, in inauspicious circumstances, in fact sealed the chapter of "earthly Vienna" in her life, leaving her, the refugee, with only a hoard of memories. These – the memories of those wonderful years in "heavenly Vienna" – were to nourish and sustain her to the end of her days.

While Golda and her father, the complete musician, were able to enjoy the musical treasures that the Austrian capital lavished on its residents, Reb Aazik, because of his notable erudition in Talmud and Jewish law, made the generous acquaintance of the top Jewish scholars at the local Rabbinical Seminary. This academic institution, the most important for Jewish studies in Europe at the time, took the refugee scholar under its wing, but could not employ him as a regular member of the teaching personnel due to the general ban on public institutions adding refugees to their staff.

As a result, Reb Aazik was granted the formal status of a *Rabbinerkandidat* (rabbinical candidate) and, like the aspirants to office of other religions, was exempt from military duty in view of the spiritual post he was to fill among his people. In addition, the academy referred hopeful candidates to him for private lessons, which assured him a measure of economic comfort. True, Reb Aazik did not take part in the regular curriculum, as required by the exemption board; but this was because the institution's top Talmudic scholar, Dr. Aptowitzer himself, had decided that the Seminary had nothing to offer a student of the stature of the Galician guest, and released him from the curriculum, suggesting to him, instead, issues that he might study on his own.

The Imperial Police, however, were not impressed by the fulsome praise heaped on the prodigy by the elderly professor. In its eyes, the young man was just one of the tens of thousands of refugees who filled the streets of Vienna during this period, and his absence from the classroom was against the law. In 1916, when the city police raided sheltered housing and private homes in search of defectors and shirkers, and apprehended a group of young men registered as *Rabbinerkandidaten*, Reb Aazik was found to be one of them. He and his companions were detained at the Blindengasse jailhouse in the Eighth Quarter and charged with varying offenses:

some, like Reb Aazik, with not fulfilling the conditions of their exemption from military service; others, as impostors in order to evade conscription; and still others as undermining state security.

Oh, Shloime son of Yitzhak-Isaac Wróbel, Master Horseman of His Majesty the Emperor and recipient of the legendary red-and-white decoration which you were awarded for your loyalty – who will remove the dust from your eyes? You, who all your life offered up a sacrifice to your monarch in generous, immeasurable service, and, for as long as there was breath in you, hoped that your sacrifice would find favor – look now and see what has befallen your son, whom you named for your father, the first horseman of the House of Wróbel, no doubt dreaming that the child would follow in the footsteps of you both: he has been cast in prison and waits, in the lock-up, with deserters and malingerers for his sentence!

Day after day Golda would walk to Vienna's Eighth Quarter to visit Aazik in jail; at the same time, she would inundate the Government ministries with countless petitions and memos, attaching recommendations from eminent professors – in order to establish that her husband was innocent of deliberate evasion and explain the background of his inadvertent oversight. One day, when she arrived at the building, as usual, she was directed to the office of the jailhouse commander. There she was handed an official notice advising her that Eisig Wróbel (as the name was spelled in German) had been conscripted as a gunner into the Howitzer artillery and sent with his regiment to the Przemyśl front in Galicia. Thus, the third generation of Wróbels joined the Austrian army. Aazik's induction, to be sure, was against his will, unlike that of his father and grandfather, who had volunteered; nevertheless, despite the distress of his forced enlistment and the prison period that preceded it, the notice was also cause for rejoicing. It exonerated Aazik of all charges of evasion or impersonation or any other evil intent, which carried with them both calumny and heavy punishment in times of emergency.

Gunner Eisig Wróbel's contribution to the war effort was relatively short-lived. Hardly two months passed after he set out with his canons, when reports arrived from the Galician front that in a sudden Russian raid in the vicinity of Przemyśl, the heavy Austrian Howitzers had been surrounded and were now, along with their operators, in Russian captivity. After some time, an official confirmation arrived at Golda's home from the Imperial War Office, citing the locale of the Austrians' captivity in Moldavia's forest region, east of Kishinev. Depending on circumstances, Russian procedure sometimes was not to hold prisoners of war in restricted facilities under tight military discipline. Rather, it dispatched them to remote areas and to abandoned wooden huts on the edge of far-flung communities; there they could lead their own lives while providing a variety of services to local inhabitants in exchange for food. Such was the case with the group of prisoners that included Eisig Wróbel. Golda and all the Weinmans breathed a sigh of relief upon receipt of the first sign of life from Aazik and in view of the relatively comfortable conditions of his captivity. All that remained now was to hope for the best: a speedy conclusion to the war, the customary arrangements for prisoner exchange, and the soldier's return to the bosom of his family.

In the spring of 1917, the toppling of the Czarist regime in the tidal wave of the February Revolution, and the crumbling of the Russian frontline, paved the actual – if not formal – way for Aazik's return from Russian captivity. The roads buzzed with throngs, whether of individuals or groups, whether in uniform or civilian dress, whether on foot, horseback or requisitioned peasant wagons. Like boats on a stormy sea seeking anchor at safe shores, some were trying to rejoin their units, others, simply, to get home. Especially difficult was the situation of the Russian military units who were in a state of complete chaos and flight from the front. Moreover, the offensive that Alexander Kerensky tried to revive on the Galician front in May 1917, after being appointed Minister of

War in the Provisional Revolutionary Government, ended in failure. The road to the west, to Vienna, where Golda waited with her family, was finally opened, but it was distant and dangerous.

A variety of stories were told years later about Reb Aazik's doings during the period of his captivity, and especially about the warm treatment he received at the hands of kindly Romanian Jews, dealers in wood and fur, who were permitted by the military authorities to move about in Moldavia's forest regions. They had come to know the water-carrier, a diligent and reticent prisoner, whose strong build seemed to burst through the tattered rags covering his flesh, and whose torn shoes were bundled with straw against cold and damp. They knew that he was Jewish for they would see him in synagogue on the Sabbath and holidays, but his hefty physique and hesitant stance on the sidelines, removed from the congregation of worshippers, colored him, in their eyes, as a complete boor, totally alienated from the Jewish experience.

How great then was their astonishment when, one day, in delivering his pails to one of the esteemed families and finding a group of *yeshiva* lads grappling with a *Gemara* question they found difficult to understand, he approached the table, glanced briefly at the page and instantly explained the passage – firstly, at face value and then with added meaning from Rashi's commentary and, for good measure, from the *Tosafot* annotations to the Talmud; and all this, in the enthusiastic, scholastic melody of Galician *yeshivas*, ending with the rule-of-thumb opinions of Alfassi, Maimonides and Caro's *Bet-Yosef.* After completing the lesson, he rose as if nothing had happened, picked up his pails and, without a word, walked out of the house, leaving his listeners gaping and wondering if he of the forest were not, perhaps, one of the legendary Thirty-Six Just Men come to enlighten them with the illumination of Torah, or even Elijah the Prophet himself, who was destined to smooth out all questions and problems, and who had now come to instruct them in a page of *Gemara.* The news spread like wildfire and the towns in the vicinity started competing with one another in an attempt to convince Aazik that he would do well to remain in this country even after the war ended, and serve as their rabbi.

Reb Aazik (which is how he was addressed from then on) thanked them for the offers, but rejected them all. After all he had been through since the outbreak of war, he explained, he had only one desire: to be reunited with his wife and to return with her to Galicia. His admirers heard him out in disappointment, but understood and respected his wishes.

Meanwhile, however, the political climate had changed. The October Revolution brought down the Kerensky regime and pulled Russia out of the war among the nations but, at the same time, sunk the country into a bloodbath of civil war. Across the western border, the death of Franz-Joseph in 1916 and the Austrian defeats on the various fronts rocked the foundations of the Hapsburg Empire and stirred up the peoples living within its borders. Even in Moldavia's remote forest stretches, news flashed like sparks of fire fanned by a mysterious bellows, igniting small blazes into dangeous fires. Rumors flew in the air like wild bats, striking fear with dark information of Romanian nationalists attacking "individual Jews scattered in the forests." The memory of the pogrom of fourteen years earlier in nearby Kishinev began to dye the cauldron of rumors black and red, auguring the worst. In view of the three attributes that endangered the captive water-carrier – "Jewish, alone and unprotected in the forest" – the merchants decided to use their connections to free Reb Aazik from captivity. Now, however, it was the prisoner who asked to stay: before leaving for Vienna, he longed to use the opportunity of his sojourn in Russia to travel to Koretz to make the acquaintance of Feige, that living legend, and bring back regards from her to her daughter, Sureh, and her granddaughter, Golda.

Aazik was elated by his meeting with the woman of valor who had just marked her hundredth birthday, yet was nevertheless as lucid and vivacious as a woman of sixty. Feige, for her part, welcomed Aazik warmly and through him sent a gift back to Sureh, her daughter – a photograph taken on the occasion of the visit; on the back of it, in an incredibly steady hand, she wrote a note. The photograph, today, is in Tel Aviv, at the home of Sureh's son, Reb Ephraim Weinman.

On his return from Koretz, the merchants outfitted the redeemed prisoner with clothes and boots (the boots would play a role in the future), and placed a bundle of bills in his pocket, presented him with a silver watch as a token of their appreciation, and delivered him into the hands of a trusty guide. And so the prisoner returned home, to his wife, to freedom. On the first Sabbath after his return, Reb Aazik, in the company of his father-in-law, went up to the platform in the synagogue and, in a shaky voice, recited the prayer of thanksgiving, while Golda, along with her mother and her sister, shed a tear in the women's section. "Unfortunately," Golda summed up the balance sheet of her marriage, "until now, the story of our marriage overlapped with the tale of war. From this point on, the two diverged: the tale of war for us was over, and we emerged from it, thank God, alive and well. Now begins the joint, personal story of Golda and Aazik Wróbel."

All of Vienna was in upheaval. There was a smell of defeat and of great change in the air. The refugee community sat on its suitcases, ready for the final – and, perhaps, the hardest – campaign: going home. Thus, in the spring of 1918, even before the fighting stopped and the Habsburg Empire came to an end, the Wróbel couple and Weinman family joined the great stream of people returning home, and came back to Tarnów to rebuild their lives.

3

With the excitement that only liberated prisoners and surviving refugees are capable of appreciating, Aazik and Golda decided to inform the tribe in Pennsylvania – brother Ben, and Shloime and

Zlatte who lived with him, and through them, also the other brothers and the sister – of the good news. For one thing, they had both returned in good health and spirits to Tarnów after living through the dreads of war and innumerable upheavals, and were only now starting to build a life together – for the war that had broken out so soon after their wedding had uprooted them from their home even before they had had a chance to set it up. Their other item of news was formulated with high emotion, yet with necessary care and in a roundabout way for fear of the evil eye: early in 1919 – Golda and Aazik informed the family in America – the twosome expected to become three.

It took a month for the letter to reach America by sea in those days, and another month for a reply to come from across the waters, with the corresponding update on the affairs of the Wróbel family on the American side during the four-year period. The writer was Pearl née Bransdorf, who had joined the Wróbel tribe ten years earlier by her marriage to Ben. Over the next two decades, Pearl was to become pen-pal to her sister-in-law, Golda, who was also a Wróbel by marriage, and these two, adjuncts from the outside, were to maintain the intra-familial contact of the House of Wróbel on two continents.

Golda hastened to open the envelope that the postman had placed in her hands and merrily began reading out loud the somewhat hesitant opening sentences. "Our Pearl has a hard time writing Yiddish" – Golda smiled to herself. But her eyes, quicker than her reading, suddenly caught the sad significance of the words in the next lines. She now understood that the introductory stutter stemmed not only from Pearl's difficulty in expressing herself, but also from the writer's attempt to mask, or at least mollify, the gravity of the message she had been charged to transmit. All joy faded from Golda's face and, in a quaking voice, she began to stammer just like Pearl –

"Father Shloime..." – she broke off without finishing the sentence. Aazik instinctively sensed the meaning of her sudden silence, grateful to his wife for her sensitivity, and did not ask her to read on. In utter stillness, his face stony, as if he had known the contents of the message for some time now but had only waited for written confirmation, he removed his shoes and sat down on a low stool to observe, if only symbolically, the commandment of *shiva* (the seven-day mourning), whose time was already long past. After a while, he rose, put the black *gartle* (the prayer belt that was always in his pocket) around his waist, picked up his prayer book and left the house.

He directed his steps towards the city's eastern neighborhood, proceeding pensively though resolutely down Lwowska Street, about a mile's distance, until he arrived at the synagogue in the working-class neighborhood of Grabówka. Like a stick inserted into a swarm of ants, the one-room neighborhood synagogue lodged among the crowded quarters of the prisoners of poverty and hostages of want, living on the extreme edge of Grabówka. Here, at this place – after a four-year forced delay wrought by the shifting sands of war – Aazik chose to recite the *kaddish* for his father's death. From now on, for a whole year, he would walk to Grabówka to say *kaddish* at morning prayers – setting out very early, for the local workers always prayed upon rising, before going off to their daily employment – and he would return again towards evening for the *kaddish* of afternoon and evening prayers. In contrast to the Sabbath, when a hundred, or a hundred and fifty worshippers congregated for morning prayers and the *musaf* supplement, only a few men managed to attend morning prayers during the week and only a handful were free for afternoon and evening prayers at the end of a long day's work. Reb Aazik, as the tenth man to the quorum, would join a group of manual laborers that had just come back from grueling construction work, or stand next to the owner of a small grocery whose face was etched with the entire history of exile, and recite the *kaddish*, addressing his God in a way that he had never been able to do at the "Great Synagogue," where he had a permanent seat with his name on it.

"It is just like what happened to my father in Wisłok," Aazik thought sadly on his way to Grabówka, "when, because of the military's obtuseness, he arrived home within weeks of his father's death and only then began to say *kaddish*. Woe to the Wróbels down the generations, and alas! – the revolving wheel that spins our destiny! As if it did not suffice that in every generation we are hounded by recurring poverty, cleaving to recurring cycles of suffering and injustice – now, we have also been sentenced to a recurrence of "deferred *kaddish*," with the repayment of the debt of *kaddish* that we owe our fathers being painfully and bitterly delayed by the force of circumstance…

Possibly, in his heart of hearts, Aazik was hoping to repay also another debt, one more distressing and disturbing – the accumulated debt of twenty years' severance from his living father, ever since he, Mama's Aazikl, had gone into exile at the age of fourteen from Wisłok to Tarnów to slake his thirst for Torah. He was not actually apologizing for the physical detachment, for there had been nothing untoward about his departure itself, which had been encouraged by his mother, with his father, too, making no attempt to dissuade him from this course. But even though he had a clear conscience about the act of leaving, he agonized over having committed the sin of impudence, by cutting himself off completely from the world-view of the father who had sired him. Yes, it was pardon and forgiveness he was seeking for not having been sufficiently assiduous in observing the commandment of "Honor thy father" and, instead, insolently turning his back on his father's way of life and values. Brashly, he scorned his father's admiration for the glitter of *goyish* military service, abhorred his father's submissive, blind loyalty to the Emperor, and bemoaned his indifference to a Jewish education for his children. And maybe – just maybe, even though he had never given voice to his secret thoughts – he wished to atone for the worst sin of all, the sin of a son's ostensible betrayal of his father: for during those long years of separation, while his father was still alive, he, his firstborn, consciously and with premeditation had the audacity to cast about for an alternative father-figure among the community's scholars and leaders in Tarnów, someone who would serve as an example to emulate, compensating somewhat for his physical and spiritual distance from his natural father.

At the end of the year's daily recitation of the *kaddish*, Reb Aazik made it a rule to attend the Grabówka synagogue every 4th Kislev, the *yahrzeit* of his father's death and, from 1924 on, the year that Herschl turned four, he was to take him along as well. As his son watched, the father would conduct the day's prayer before the Ark and recite the *kaddish*.

Kaddish at Grabówka! "Why Grabówka, of all places," the son wonders, "why does Father go all the way to this remote, forsaken synagogue?" Presumably, Grabówka, though not the handsomest neighborhood, so fascinated Father because of its physical landscape, which reminded him of his native village. True, when he came to Tarnów as a lad, he had not settled in Grabówka, as did most of the refugees, but advanced into the city itself to the seats of Torah. But now, after an absence of twenty-three years from his village, when he returned to Tarnów from Vienna a married and learned man, his father's death may well have awakened in him a longing for his village. And, how strange – the fields, green ponds and village shacks that he found in Tarnów, on Grabówka's outskirts, conjured up suddenly in his mind the sights, sounds and scents of the Wisłok to which he would never return.

The two faces of Grabówka – breathtaking rural vistas on its edges and grueling manual labor in its core, knitted with a gnawing poverty – took Reb Aazik back to the cradle of his being, to the desperate want and the draining physical toil at his father's Wisłok farm, and embedded the figure of the father, whom he had practically forgotten, among the mass of poor, hard-working people of Grabówka.

Actually, the inevitable – almost compulsive – comparison between his native village and his adopted city had during his first year in Tarnów at the young age of fourteen, already caused Aazik to question the prevailing social order. And as the astonishing similarity between Wisłok and Tarnów grew stronger in his eyes, the questions had only increased. It seemed as though a hidden super-architect had drafted the blueprint for both, and that an eternal law from above had determined their character and that of their inhabitants.

The laws of nature governing Wisłok had always been clear to him, but he had believed them to be peculiar to Wisłok alone. From early childhood on, he had come to know that at one end of this one-street village lived the paupers, huddled together in want and hunger: Jewish paupers – Shloime, his father, Zlatte, his mother, and his three brothers and sister (another brother was born only six years later), packed and crowded together into a single, one-room shack – just like their Ukrainian neighbors, who also languished in squalor. In contrast, a mile and a quarter away, at the other end of the long street, stood the houses of the Jews considered well-to-do, and the small synagogue they kept, to which he used to walk with his father on Sabbath morning; and next to these, were the homes of the Poles who, since time immemorial, had owned the fields and forest patches, and were the proprietors of the local saw and flour mills. So the village of Wisłok had always been, Aazik had believed. So it was, and so it would be forever. But could it be, that the same was true of the city of Tarnów? Looking about him at his new city, and coming face to face with urban realities, the village boy was shocked to the core. "It can only be," he decided, "that Wisłok and Tarnów descended to the world arm in arm, and despite the obvious differences between city and country, the one is the mirror-image of the other."

Don't the paupers of Grabówka, who live in congested huts at the bottom of Lwowska Street, resemble the wretched poor of Wisłok's western corner? And doesn't the other end of the long street, in Tarnów as in Wisłok, harbor the "bourgeoisie" and the large stores, boasting eye-dazzling shop windows? What's more: in the fancy neighborhoods above the town, you will find the high-schools where children from "good families" are accepted as a matter of course, but it is doubtful that the son of a tailor or child of a cobbler will ever find his place there. Wisłok and Tarnów, village and city, are twin sisters – the country boy realized by juxtaposing the realities of his village with the realities of his adopted city and confronting the poverty of both. Want and hunger have no exclusive homeland. Want and hunger have the same face – in every place, at every time.

Want and hunger were only one side of the coin and it was not they that propelled Shloime's first-born son out of the village. For the realistic response to poverty at the end of the nineteenth century was emigration to America, a recourse which the young Aazik wanted no part of, even though his siblings resorted to it. Within a few years of his own departure for Tarnów, his siblings, too, left the village and made their way to America, prompted by motives that were clearly economic, and continued to ply their old trade there: they worked at purchasing and slaughtering animals for meat, and even built a small slaughterhouse on the outskirts of Exeter. Not so Aazik. His decision, in tune with his mother's desires, was primarily motivated by the wish to totally restructure the family's value system, and not in the expectation of economic benefits. This is why he did not join the workforce in Grabówka. In fact, for his first nine years in Tarnów, his physical circumstances underwent severe deterioration – harder even than the conditions of poverty at his parents' farm in Wisłok. The deterioration was astounding: not only did the boy end his days with real hunger grumbling in his belly, but he lacked even a bed on which to lay his head. Yet, as great as the boy's hunger was for bread and the longing of his body for a real, soft place to rest, his thirst for knowledge was greater still, and he was prepared to curb the natural yearning for momentary comfort and satiation so long as, in exchange, he could progress in his studies.

This thirst – for a life of reflection and self-immersion in books and scholarly discourse – which he hoped to slake in Tarnów, could not be satisfied by the resources America had in hand at the time. On the contrary: America was still a cultural wasteland, and even as it physically and economically absorbed masses of immigrants, it required constant injections of spiritual succor and enriching stimulation. The spiritual repository could therefore not be sought across the seas, Aazik concluded, readily adopting his mother's desire to radically reform the Wróbel family. However, whereas his mother was guided by the power of intuition, the son formulated his decision in ideological terms: the Jewish spiritual repository is here, in Galicia, in its magnificent Jewish communities and Torah centers, under the wings of its scholars, on the one hand, and its Hasidic *Kloyzes*, on the other. Yes, despite the scorn heaped on Hasidism by early proponents of the Hebrew Enlightenment, the Hasidic establishment in Galicia was supremely scholarly, its rabbis were men of wisdom, and its rabbinic jurists intellectual giants. Consequently, he, Aazik, a country bumpkin from the village of Wisłok, desired to remain here, in Tarnów, in the city of Torah, at the feet of its rabbis and scholars and, for as long as he breathed, to sip avidly from the spring of their wisdom, knowing that his mother, Zlatte, bore the burden of separation with joy and happiness, and blessed the Lord for granting her a son who yearned for Torah. Unwavering from this course, Aazik was to firmly reject the immigration papers and sea passage that Bereleh renewed and sent him from America every year. No, he would never relocate to America! If ever he did leave the Torah tents of Galicia and move somewhere else, it would be only to Eretz Israel, "where the air was edifying and its Torah, truth."

The dream of education – education without limit, education beyond every boundary, every fence and every taboo – is what slung the wanderer's sack over young Aazik's shoulder, stuck a walking stick into his hand, and sent him into exile to the seat of Torah, Tarnów; for only by the grace of knowledge could a prisoner of poverty and captive of want break out of the bondage in which his mother, due to no fault of her own, had given birth to him. Galician penury, however, had been mercilessly laid down by a cruel law – an unwritten, draconian law – and there was little chance of escape: "Only two of a city and one of a family" (in reverse to the biblical formula) would be able to realize the dream: the others, no matter how ardent their dream, would continue to flounder in the litter of their lives, doing their share to help realize the dream of the chosen one who got away. Bereleh, too, after all, had wished to advance in Torah like his older brother, and how bitter was his pain and the pain of his mother, no doubt, when force of circumstance compelled him to leave the *Talmud-Toireh* in Sanok, which the two brothers had both attended after the failure of the Bukovsk experience – to give himself over completely to maintaining the farm, while Aazikl continued to prepare himself in Sanok for the Tarnów *yeshiva*. In his sorrow, Bereleh blamed the dispossession of his right to study on his older brother, so much so that, when Aazik set out for Tarnów, he refused, at their parting, to shake Aazik's hand.

A few years later, Bereleh emigrated to America, where he prospered. Mindful of his brothers and parents who had remained in the "old country," he would make sure to support them for as long as they lived there, and rescue them from the vale of tears as quickly as possible, carefully preparing the ground for their absorption in the new country. In time, Bereleh had realized his error and understood that Aazik was not to be blamed for the termination of his own studies. Therefore, over the years, he made every effort to help his older brother and his brother's family, who had remained in Tarnów, just as he helped his other siblings. Yet, he never forgot his first dream, the dream of Torah. Nor was he ever able to over-come the stinging insult that accompanied the burial of that dream. Until his dying day on earth he bore the pain of the unhealed scar, and until his dying day he never stopped mourning the loss of his right to Torah and education. What Aazik felt about the matter, no one knows...

4

Dreams. Like Aazikl and Bereleh, dreamers of Wisłok and bonds-men of destitution, so every last poverty-yoked youth in Tarnów's Grabówka continued to be led astray by dreams – dreams that bud-ded and drew near, dreams that blossomed and drew nearer, and dreams that withered and fell away. For while it is natural for man and society everywhere to weave tapestries of hope and longing out of secret yearnings spun by dreams, there is no more fertile soil than the dunghill of poverty for dreams to bud in – or wither on. And Grabówka's poor dunghill was the most fertile of all. How is it that the learned economists and statisticians, who enumerated all the modern industries, businesses and factories developed by Tarnów's Jewish capitalists over the generations and by Grabówka's Jewish workers, failed to mention the largest and most vital of Grabówka's factories – the factory of dreams?

Thus, the four Blatt brothers, for example, wretched tailor's ap-prentices in the labyrinth of hovels around the neighborhood syna-gogue, dreamed to a beat so utterly different from the drone of the Singer machines they were sentenced to listen to six days a week at [A]Kiva's sewing shop. As they plied needle and thread, they imag-ined themselves twining the filaments of enchanted tunes from the magical strings of the violin in their hearts, and shedding a seething tear into the mouthpiece of a wailing clarinet. True enough, the day came that they did break out and realize the dream of music that nestled in their souls. Along with one of their three sisters, who worked as seamstresses in the same shop, they established a *klezmer* folk troupe – the Blatt Quintet – whose fame reached far beyond the boundaries of Grabówka and brought its audiences a Jewish joy that was bittersweet, a Jewish lament that laughed through tears. Also Shloime, the tailor, known as *Korpiel* (Turnip Head), whose ungainly body harbored the soul of an angel, and Simha Ruda – a porter known as *Byk* (Ox), because without any difficulty he lifted 250-kilogram loads onto his back – all realized their dream. While bending their backs to earn their bread, one over a noisy sewing machine, the other under massive burdens, they rose, straightened their backs and flexed their muscles, and ended up acclaimed soccer players on the Workers Sports team, *Jutrzenka* (Dawn), founded by the Bund – and a living example to all the other poor lads that their dreams were not without hope.

But the dream of dreams of Grabówka's dreamers, like that of Aazikl and Bereleh in Wisłok, and of the other dreamers in the bogs of beggary of all generations, was *education*. Every generation had its own dream of education. In the last decade of the nineteenth century, the country dreamers of the House of Wróbel could contemplate only one avenue – that of venerable and traditional study – so that when the eldest son paved a way for himself from stable and spade to the fascinating world of *lernen* (learning) he quite naturally arrived at the tents of Torah. This, in the next two or three decades, was no longer the dream of his urban brethren-in-distress. Now, bent over sewing machines and cobbler blocks, even in the forlorn back lanes of Grabówka, were those who spun dreams of learning of a different sort in a world that had begun to change with giant sweeps: the dream of a general education at an uptown high school – an education that opened doors, expanded horizons, offered choices and freedom.

But shedding the chains of hardship, want and hunger was no mean feat. And the fact is that by the mid-thirties of the twentieth century, only three youngsters from the far reaches of Grabówka went on to tenaciously nurture the impossible dream of carving their way to high school: Schmukler, Yahimovitch and Schiffer. For all three it was a tremendous achievement. Yet, Reb Aazik, who enthusiastically followed their progress and viewed it as an updated version of his own dreams, would hold up to his son the Schiffer family as particularly noteworthy, and the performance of the youngest boy, Haim, for beyond Haim's personal talents and perseverance, his accomplishments were the result of a concerted effort, the fruit of the toil of the entire Schiffer family.

Haim's father, an apprentice at Tennenbaum's Bakery on Pod Dębem (Under the Oak) Square, had died when the infant turned one, compounding the destitution and backwardness of generations with the irreversible hurdle of orphanhood. And yet the boy made it to high school, with his older siblings supporting him at every stage of the way. Guided by the rule that "one member of a family realizes the dream," they freed Haim of the burden assumed, as a matter of course, by every child in Grabówka as in Wisłok – of helping to provide for the family according to one's ability. To make up for the deficit left by the youngest brother's absence from the work force, the siblings shouldered extra loads: putting in hours upon hours beyond their quotas, they operated the Singers at Kiva's workshop in order to finance for Haim what they themselves had been denied: a great leap forward. And leap he did – he, the pauper and orphan – all the way to high school, and not just to any high school, but to the Third High School, with its stress on sciences and its vauntedly demanding level of studies and, of all the Polish schools in the city, the most restrictive in the number of Jewish pupils it accepted.

Beyond the practical assistance of his siblings, Haim drew most of his moral support and encouragement from his mother, Pesseleh Schiffer. Pesseleh ran a small grocery store up on Lwowska Street; her chief source of renown, however, was encapsulated in the title *di doktern* (the doctor), earned for her consultations in folk medicine to those who called on her expertise. And whereas the succor she dispensed during the week was aimed at bodily health, the arena of her sustenance on the Sabbath was the synagogue. The Grabówka synagogue had never built a women's level, allocating, instead, a narrow section of the main prayer hall's room-and-floor-space to be used by women; this section was separated from the main – that is male – province by a thin partition of slotted windows. In this limited strip of floor and air, packed in with some fifty hard-working women, Pesseleh enjoyed a place of honor and an unchallenged authority – she, Pesseleh, was the unordained *rebbetzin* of the women of Grabówka.

And such was the nature of her "rabbinical dispensation": every now and then during prayers, she would open one of the windows in the partition, stick her head through into the masculine realm, and deliver an agitated three-word alarm to the *tallis*-wearers, a mixture of questioning despair and a cry for help: "*Vi halt men?* (Where are we?)" – meaning, what page in the prayer book had been reached as of this moment by Yitzhakl the *shammess* (beadle), who led the prayers and was Torah reader for most of the Sabbaths of the year. From the prayer hall, an irascible worshiper standing near the window would furrow his eyebrows to deflect her brazenness with a nervous "Sha-a-a!!!", and bounce the relevant page number and starting word back through the window like a rebounding ball. At this point, Pesseleh would quickly leaf through her prayer book, which had lagged behind the men, to the right page and advise her companions accordingly. By the time she managed to find the right page, however, and line up line with line and letter with letter to locate the word, the men would have relentlessly run ahead in their prayers, forcing the cruel race to be repeated two or three times during the morning service and supplementary Sabbath prayers, in a relay of endless frustration. Nevertheless, the All-Merciful, who can read men's thoughts and is not a harsh judge of prayer-book reading, would, in His benevolence, requite the saintly woman. For as it says in *Pirkei-Avot* ("The Sayings of the Fathers"): "The reward of a *mitzvah* is another *mitzvah*," and whose *mitzvos*, if not Pesseleh's, were as copious as the waves of the ocean?

Reb Aazik's son puzzles over the fact that he never personally came across Schiffer in those days, even though he passed by the Schiffer shanty more than once, and time and again he heard Reb Aazik, his father, refer both to Haim and to Haim's mother, Pesseleh (who no doubt reminded him of his own mother, Zlatte, for the corners of his eyes would suddenly glisten with a tell-tale dampness). It may have been mere chance that they never met, even though the age gap between himself and Haim would have posed a serious impediment to any connection between them. After all, when Hesiek was accepted into the first grade in 1925, and this, too, a year ahead of his peers, Haim was already sprouting the headgear of a high-school pupil – the four-edged hat and red ribbon around it that identified him as a pupil of the Third High School. Be that as it may, their paths never crossed in their hometown. Moreover, in 1937, Hesiek, at the age of seventeen, left Poland and made *aliyah* to Palestine, and when the "Polonia" slipped anchor from the shores of Europe, the boy shed the Polish coating of his name like a snake sheds its skin at the start of a new season, and dressing both his first and last name in a Hebrew coat of many colors, vowed that his foot would never again tread on Polish soil.

A mere eight years elapsed since the youth arrived in Jerusalem, but six of these were war and Holocaust, a time in which the world turned upside down, as did all the plans made when the world of yesterday still existed. In the violent reshuffling of all systems, the vows made earlier also lost their meaning, just as it says in the *Kol Nidrei* prayer of Yom Kippur – "our vows are vows no longer, and our bonds unbound…" The young man, who had deluded himself that by making *aliyah* and Hebraizing his name he had erased his Diaspora past, ostensibly to be reborn in his own land, suddenly realized that not he, but a foreign, iniquitous hand had contemplated erasing his past and the past of his people, destroying his loved ones who, like precious stones, had been embedded in the crown of his personal and collective past. At such a time (he felt), despite the vow he had made, he had to return to his native town and the desecrated Jewish neighborhood, to embrace any remnant of the conflagration, and however possible, to rescue from the inferno any survivor and any refugee, whether related to him or not, and bring them to safe shores. Thus it happened, that he was the first person from Eretz Israel to arrive in his former city after the war, the city to which he had intended never to return.

In the autumn of 1945, the son of Golda and Aazik returned to Poland and came within the gates of Tarnów. He came as a Hebrew soldier, a volunteer in the Jewish Brigade of the British Army. It was a destination towards which he had been striding for five years: from the battles of El-Alamain and Libya, via Italy, Holland, the ruins of Germany and its death camps, until he reached the land of the Holocaust. He was fated to be one of the first two soldiers from Eretz Israel who, by a circuitous route, made their way back to Poland at the end of the war, even though the country was "out of bounds" to military personnel from the west.

5

The pilgrimage of the Hebrew soldier to the killing fields of his childhood city took place shortly after the German surrender, with pandemonium reigning all around and the survivors – emerging from hiding one by one or in small groups, or congregating for lack of any other choice at the horror-haunted camps – hoping and yearning only to find kith and kin.

It was not the soldier's first glimpse of the sights of the Holocaust or of the survivors. For, concomitant with his military role, he had spent most of the years of his service in the British Army doing volunteer work among refugees and camp prisoners, especially among children and youth: setting up and running Jewish schools in Benghazi and Rome; serving as the first free Jewish envoy to the liberated Ferramonti concentration camp in southern Italy, and running a training farm near Bari for Ferramonti youth prior to bringing them to Eretz Israel; organizing and rehabilitating individuals and groups and directing them towards Eretz Israel; secretly rescuing the refugees, whom their British liberators kept idly locked up in camps for political reasons; surmounting innumerable obstacles to lead them to camouflaged assembly points of the newly forming *"briha"* movement for "illegal immigration" to Palestine. But even though this welfare and rescue work demanded immeasurable stores of emotional strength, devotion, understanding and courage, nerves of steel and resourcefulness, it could not prepare him for his final personal confrontation, a confrontation that he – as son, brother and friend – simultaneously longed for and dreaded: the confrontation with himself in the face of the Holocaust of his city and the destruction of his parents' home.

Countless times, in an anxious procession of images, the young man tried to envision what he would see, how he would feel, how he would rage, cry, wail, upon his return to his place of birth, which had meanwhile become a valley of death – but, when he did come, in 1945, none of this happened. Mechanically, like a numb robot, he looked around him unseeingly; and in the noon hours of an autumn day he found himself, an alienated stranger, sitting on the train from Kraków to Tarnów, a leaden soldier in the uniform of a British sergeant. And, mechanically, numbly, unseeing, the robot alighted from the train, a programmed mechanism hidden somewhere inside him was moving his limbs as he began to stalk the streets that had been – was it a million years ago? – a living part of his childhood.

The robot had been well-programmed. From the moment he left the square in front of the Tarnów train station, he transmitted messages from his memory disk, which he himself obeyed with predictable responses:

* Advance in a straight line from the railroad station…
  /*continue*/

* Turn right onto Krakowska Street and walk up the street to the end…
  /*continue*/

* On the right – the lit-up ads on the wall of Duke Sanguszko's beer factory…
  /*continue*/

* On the left – the twin red spires of the Missionaries Church…
  /*continue*/

* On the right – The small *bis-medrash* where Father Aazik taught Hesiek *Gemara* in the morning…
  /*continue*/

* On the floor above – Auber, the second of Hesiek's three violin teachers…
  /*continue*/

* On the left – Mash Bakery. M-m-m… Hot buns for Father and son on their way to the *Gemara* lesson. Next to it, the Baum building. The residents are Father's students; they all made *aliyah* to Haifa…
  /*continue*/

* On the right – Mroczkowski, the photographer. Childhood photos. The classroom tableau in the photographer's window in May

1937, before matriculation exams. The flat of Beirysz Bursztyn, classmate and fellow youth movement member, and his brother, Mekhek. Their brother, Romek, one of the first Gordonia members to immigrate from Tarnów to Eretz Israel to repair the ruins of Hulda after the Arab riots of 1929...
/continue/

* On the right – the residence of Dr. Feig, physician of the Hebrew school and Irena's brother. The toy store where the kind doctor bought Hesiek a ball of many colors. Home of the teacher, Weinberg. The Weg sisters. The whole town rushed to see the banister, bent by Mother Weg's fall...
/continue/

* The studio of photographer Hutter, the socialist, liked even by his opponents...
/continue/

* The Silberpfenig home: the apartment of the Hebrew high school's first principal and of his sister, the teacher, Henda. The home of Janek Borgenicht and Idek Biberberg, Hesiek's friends...
/continue to junction/

* On the right – the *Urszulanki* girls: the St. Ursula Convent high school, focus of wet dreams and boasts of conquests by adolescent boys...
/continue/

* On the left – turn to the *Apollo Cinema*. On the next street: the *Marzenie Cinema*, which doubled as a concert and lecture hall. Oh, the first silent films! Oh, the concerts Hesiek heard there with his mother! Oh, Dr. Schützer's lectures!
/continue/

* On the right – *Gelati Italiani*. M-m-m, Italian ice cream. *Café Secesja*...
/continue/

* On the left – the *Skolimowski Café*. On the square, the salute stand for May 3 and November 11 parades. Eternal participant: an old man in blue uniform recognized as the Tarnów survivor of Poland's January Revolt of 1863, as evinced by the number "1863" on his cap...
/continue/

* On the right – the *Starostwo* (District Ministries). First passports, issued to Hesiek and Mala in anticipation of *aliyah*!
/continue and stop at the junction: two streets go off to the right/

* The nearest street: 3 St. Anna Street – the "Safa Berura" Hebrew school. The Dr. Spann lending library. Eva Leibel, the beautiful librarian. Mietek, the *shaygitz* (gentile boy), the terror of the whole street, stoning "Safa Berura" pupils...
/continue/

* The Temple, where Weinberg officiates as cantor – a prayer house avoided by Orthodox Jews, who wouldn't even walk near it...
/continue/

* The other street: Targowa Street – to the Burek Market and to *tashlikh*, i.e., throwing all the year's accumulated sins into the Wątok. Haber's Tavern. How happy the town was when his Communist son escaped from prison!
/continue/

* Across the junction – the shot rabbit, hanging at the entrance of Paluch's *goyish* shop...
/continue/

* Kazimir Square. The Mickiewicz monument. Adler's pharmacy with the angel. May first. The red of flags. Ciołkosz, the socialist leader, addressing the crowd in both Polish and Yiddish. Hesiek plays hooky to attend the rally. Detectives mix with the demonstrators. Fear… Like a true revolutionary, Hesiek raises a fist in socialist salute and sings the "International." Fear… In a moment a detective will come to arrest him. Fear… What's this? The detective doesn't care? De-spair!…
/continue/

* From there to the Rynek, the Central Square. The cathedral and the Town Hall. The grocery owned by Hannah, whose grandson, Buziek, is in Hesiek's class and youth movement group. The Baron and Spitz home – three generations of connection to Father. The Wald store, where Witos, leader of the Peasant Party, buys leather for his boots…
/continue/

* To Żydowska Street. The "Old Synagogue." Dudek Schiff, Hesiek's classmate, but not in the same youth movement; Father teaches him *Gemara*, and his brother and Hesiek both take part. After the lesson, a violin-piano duet by Hesiek and their sister, Gusta: "the Caucasian Suite"…
/continue – turn left from Krakowska onto Wałowa Street/

* On the right – the Hebrew bookstore of Tony Kanner and Abraham Weinberg…
/continue/

* The stationery store owned by the parents of Hesiek Schmidt, Father's pupil, and of Zyga, the younger brother, who is Hesiek's classmate…
/continue/

* Books and music notes, at Adolf Seiden's, impresario for the city's cultural performances. Tickets to concerts and plays. Portraits of famous musicians in the shop window…
  /continue/

* The bookstore of Fenichel, the Zionist sports functionary. Used text books and banned "help" books for Latin. Fenichel's bald spot is bigger than Father's…
  /continue/

* The Berglas stationery. Above the shop, the home of Siańka, Mala's friend…
  /continue/

* Pani Gelbowa, the embroideress. Proud of her son, a professor at an American university…
  /continue/

* Maschler's home. Luśka Maschler. Luśka. Lusiu. Lu – –!…
  /continue/

* On the left – a savings bank and a concert hall above it. Annual recitals by Professor Bau's pupils. First violinists: Hesiek Wróbel and Artek Schanzer. At the piano, Bau's red-headed daughter. Bold Schanzer makes eyes at her…
  /continue/

* The street going down to the First High School and the Seminary for novices of the Catholic priesthood (mocked as *biskupyaks*). Disgusting acne on their faces…
  /continue/

* To the Eternal Flame for the Unknown Soldier. To Piłsudski Street and the municipal park...
  /continue on Wałowa Street/

* On the left – Legionnaires Street. To the Sokół theater and sports auditorium. The home of widow Regina Fluhr, whose son, Nolek, is tutored by Hesiek. The flat of Dr. Schützer, director of the Jewish hospital and an outstanding orator. The residence of old Mordkhe Duvid Brandstetter, one of the latter fathers of Hebrew Enlightenment literature in Galicia...

* On the right – *City*, Weiss's Hotel and Restaurant. Lauber Senior works as a waiter there...

* On the left – the home of Dr. Spann, the city's elder Zionist. His children all have Hebrew names: Yehudit, Naomi and Zvi. Dr. Goldberg's flat. Reśka Goldberg. Resiu...
  /continue/

* The Metzger confectionary and its cream cakes, competing with Krumholz's cakes across the street...
  /continue/

* Police station and city fire station...
  /continue/

* On the left – turn off to Brodziński Street. To Niuśka Feld. Oh, Niuśka ... To Koenig, the old teacher, and to his daughter, Róża, Hesiek's First Grade teacher...
  /continue/

* To Ciechanowski, classmate and youth movement peer. How

everyone envied him when he made *aliyah* to Ben Shemen! To the Sobelsohns, Karol Radek's family. To Monek Leibel and the Second High School, which he attended. His father, a doctor, with a large bald spot...
/continue/

* At the corner of Wałowa and Brodziński – Wilhelm Spiro's paper store. His son, Szajek – one of the founders of Gordonia and among Father's students – a violinist. Szajek's younger brother – a pianist...
/continue, and stop at the corner/

* At the corner – up three steps, Izraelowicz's candy shop, Eder's ice cream store. The *Eskontowy Bank* of the wealthy Aberdam family. Widow Jortner's *trafika* (kiosk). Stamps and post cards. The mail box...
/continue/

* To the right of the junction – *Rybna* (Fish Street), leading to *Fischplatz* (Fish Square), the "Old Synagogue" and the large *bismedrash*...
/continue/

* The glassware shop owned by the parents of Dora Wakspress, Mala's friend. Blatt, the baker. His daughter, Dora, made *aliyah* to Kibbutz Deganya, along with Idek Sprung and Mendl Wax, Gordonia counselors. How proud everyone was that they were to be part of the collective in which the great A.D. Gordon was active...
/continue/

* Across the junction – Wałowa continues to Pilzno Gate. Wachtel's

restaurant. From there, to the left, to the end of Lwowska Street.
To Grabówka. Oh, the strolls with Father in Grabówka...
/*continue*/

* To the left of the junction – Goldhammera Street: Dr. Saltz, father
  of *Ahavat Zion* and *Mahanayim,* and one of Herzl's deputies at
  the First Zionist Congress...
  /*continue*/

* *Hotel Soldinger.* To Rutka Keller and Nasiek and Henek, her
  brothers, Father's students...
  /*continue*/

* Also on Goldhammera: to Wolf Getzler, head of *Mizrahi,* whose
  sons study with Father. To the Planty. First violin lessons with
  Rausch. Opposite, Professor Bau's Music School. *HaShomer
  HaTza'ir* center. The barracks, and a little way from there, Roh'ka
  Baiczer's squalid apartment...
  /*continue*/

* Turn right – to the Sanz *Kloyz.* The "Great Synagogue." The
  mikveh (ritual bath) ...
  /*continue*/

* Now turn left to Bóżnic Street. 9 Bóżnic – no, the number's been
  changed to 5...
  /*Come on, turn left already, LEFT, to No. 5 – HOME!*/

At the nearest entrance, on the right side of the street which is One
Goldhammera, stands a man. He is the first man that the robot
encounters. Can it be that the streets he has just walked through
were all empty? Were there no pedestrians at this afternoon hour

on Krakowska and Wałowa, the city's main streets? Perhaps there were, perhaps not. He, in any case, looked without seeing, without noticing anyone. And here, all of a sudden, stands a man. At the entrance. Short. Lame. Round-faced. Nearly bald.

Oh, God of robots and God of men! You, who, in your great benevolence, play pranks on and mock your children at their worst and most painful moments – knowing, in your superior wisdom that otherwise their hearts would burst from unbearable suffering – why, at this of all possible moments, did you cease your jesting and rip the robot's mask from its face? Why did you choose this, of all robots, to expose the whole truth about your satanic villainy? Did you wish to crush the robot, who posed as unfeeling, and reveal his flesh-and-blood being, bare and naked in all his pain and vulnerability – standing at the corner of this street that he had not seen in years, the years in which the world collapsed into abyss? Did you do it to remove the film from the eyes of the unseeing viewer so that he would finally gaze about him and realize that all the Jewish milestones he had scanned on his walk here were but old cobwebs, ghost files regurgitated by a memory disk and endlessly rechewed, when, in fact, man, you didn't see a thing – not a thing, for there is nothing here to see. Nothing remains. Nothing around you but ruin and destruction and the silence of a graveyard. The Tarnów you remember – gone! And still, as if after the eruption of a volcano, the earth on which you tread today is boiling, bubbling with blood, fluttering with fear, crying out unheard and hurting, hurting.

And he stands there, that man, at the entrance of One Goldhammera Street, only a dozen steps away: short, lame, round-faced, nearly bald. As if he knew that you would come. As if he took it as only natural that you would come. As if he had waited there during all those years of darkness and horror just for you. How can you raise your eyes now and look into his face? You, who during all these years were a free man, and even though you went to war with weapon in hand, the hell that he lived through is something you will never even be able to imagine?! Why, of Tarnów's twenty-five thousand Jews, is it he, of all people, who awaits you? He, the first person at the gates of hell, your neighbor and old friend, your "older brother," Millek Lauber?!

Twenty-five thousand Tarnów Jews? One room was enough that evening to assemble all those who survived and returned – some fifty people – and most of these, too, were from the vicinity, rather than from Tarnów. Rumor spread through the town and everyone gathered to see and hear the soldier, son of Tarnów, come from the free world, from Eretz Israel. The audience contained only three people whom the soldier knew personally. A fourth Tarnowite was there, whom the soldier had not met before, but whose name he knew very well; as the chairman of the Committee of Tarnów Holocaust Survivors he welcomed the visitor. Thus, twenty years after his walks with Father in Grabówka in 1925, Hesiek belatedly made the acquaintance of Haim Schiffer of Tarnów's Grabówka, except that it was now a totally different Tarnów – a Tarnów without Jews.

Forty-four years passed after that meeting, before, in March 1989, in the United States, Golda and Aazik's son met Haim Schiffer once again. At Schiffer's modest but pleasant apartment in Wayne, New Jersey, the two sat and reminisced. There was only one topic that, by unspoken agreement, they avoided – their first and last meeting in Tarnów in 1945. Or, maybe, it was the other way around: maybe that is all they did talk about, dwelling on it without stop, wrapping it in reams of words, cloaking its memory in a flow of oblique anecdotes, that made certain they did not touch the thing itself. Yes, only that – that one, single encounter in the vast graveyard that Tarnów had become – is all that they talked, and talked, and talked about. Without words. In silence…

6

For seven days and seven nights in 1895, Aazik Wróbel, a lad of fourteen, walked from his village of Wisłok, by way of Rymanów, to Tarnów. That very route, though in the opposite direction, would forty-two years later be covered by Reb Aazik's daughter, Mala, aged eighteen-and-a-half, and son, Hesiek, aged seventeen, who, on the eve of their *aliyah* to Eretz Israel, wished with all their might to see the landscapes of their father's childhood; for to Poland, so they had decided, they would never return. This time, the trip took only three days and nights, because at its start and finish – from Tarnów to Rymanów and back – the road was now paved for regular transportation. Downcast by the visions of poverty in the western section of the Beskid village in which their father had grown up as a child, yet elated by the scenery he had traversed back then on makeshift roads when guided, like the fowl of heaven, to his desired destination, daughter and son returned from the trip thirsty to compare their impressions with their father's memories.

Unlike his daughter and son, however, who had been charmed by the vistas, Father's glance was fixed not on the mosaic of mountains and forests but on a mosaic of hopes and anxieties inside his soul. Thus, despite his children's curiosity, he could not, in 1937, share with them his impressions of 1895. He merely acknowledged, with a bashful, apologetic grin to veil his embarrassment, that in his mind he had seen a high mountain opposite him, protruding from the horizon, and the mountain moved neither to the right nor to the left during the entire journey. It was not a Carpathian peak that separated him from his destination (he explained to himself in those days), but the roof of the fabled *bis-medrash* of the renowned Reb Moishl Yehuda Yekiels Apter, to whom he was going, and the *bis-medrash* rose high above the hills, and little Aazikl of Wisłok had to conquer it come what may. Only when he reached Tarnów, did the boy learn that the rabbi did not have a *bis-medrash* of his own, and that his students divided their time between his private flat and the central *Kloyz*.

Nevertheless, his first meeting with the celebrated Tarnów sage, sparse in build and austere in habit, was, to the sturdy village boy, both an hour of revelation and an hour of decision. From the moment that he went up, in holy awe, to the first floor of the building and knocked at the door, he wedded his fate to the kingdom of books and, from then on, in this kingdom he was evermore to be both king and bonded slave. The expectation of this first meeting had held also an added excitement, a question mark constantly hidden deep in his heart which he, in his wisdom, did not permit to come to the fore – akin to the sentiment revealed in the *Song of Songs*:

"I charge you... that you stir not up nor awake love till it pleases it."

Now that the fateful meeting with his future rabbi had actually come to pass, the latent excitement suddenly awoke from its apparent hibernation: here, in this frail body in the armchair opposite, resting his black *kapotteh*-sleeved elbows on the tattered, old upholstery of its arms, sat the singular spiritual giant of the generation, one of the greats whose amazing breadth of knowledge and keenness of intellect lent light not only to the *yeshiva* world but also to the Hasidic courts; the magnitude of his learning earned him the recommendation of the great *Tzaddik* of Sanz, and of his son, Reb Yehezkel of Sieniawa, who had included some of Reb Moishl's Responsa in his own book. Can a country boy from Wisłok hope that one day he, too, will rise on the ladder of Torah?

The first time that Aazikl of Wisłok sat in front of Reb Moishl he felt as if in a dream. And he, an innocent youth, did not know at that wondrous moment whether his eyes, his earthly eyes, were actually seeing the material reality that enveloped him, or whether he only imagined this while gazing inward to his soul. Or, was his heart gripped by a sudden anxiety – the embodiment of all the anxieties unconquered by his fervent prayers? For, by a mysterious process of incarnation, the man sitting opposite him, diminutive in form yet huge in spirit, suddenly donned a hefty, strong and proud body, and the beam of light that illuminated the man's face made it clear to the boy, that it was no longer the great scholar whose fame so daunted him, but rather Shloime, yes, Shloime, his own father and sire: his face clean-shaven, his copper-shiny bald pate burnished by the Carpathian sun. And the armchair opposite – an ordinary homey armchair in which the great rabbi sat, resting his black *kapoteh*-sleeved elbows on the tattered upholstery of its arms – was no armchair at all, but an elegant saddle, adorned on both sides by the Habsburg eagles and gleaming with the brass buckles of the straps.

And his father, mounted on his white, well-groomed mare, sits erect in the saddle like a knight of the legends of old, radiating pride and confidence, from the golden shoulder pads whose fringes fall softly onto the upper seam of his uniform sleeves, to the black boots that sparkle like the marble of an imperial monument. All at once, Aazik sees his father offering him the brass stirrup ring that glares blindingly as he invites him to place his foot within it, to lift himself onto the saddle and to hold onto his back. His eyes whisper: "Don't be scared, my son, I am your father and you are my first born. Come up and I will be your Master-Cavalryman, showing you in lieu of the seventy faces of Torah, the seventy faces of horsemanship and you, too, will be a Master-Cavalryman like me, and maybe even an officer, if you will it with all your mind and body." But, look, without warning, a village aroma fills the air, saturated with the scent of fields and hay, caressed by a refreshing breeze from the stream's clear waters and mingled with the sour steam of horse sweat and droppings, and with the chimney smoke rising from the cabin stove at evening. And the lad's eyes mist over with the pain of remembering and longing – Wisłok, Wisłok, Mother!

At the moment that Mother's image meshes with the tapestry

of village odors, Zlatte's face, gaunt and stern, emerges from the evening vapors in sharp and deafening contradiction to the rider's complacent face, which boasts confidence and self-importance. The contradiction is unendurable, like the very juxtaposition of the two faces themselves. In a wink, the vision of horse and rider dissolves into the bookshelves that drape the walls from floor to ceiling, and Aazik finds himself once again in front of an ordinary homey armchair whose tattered upholstered arms, as before, support black *kapotteh*-sleeved elbows, and from the head of the armchair, as at first, a pair of eyes gaze out at him, and they are the good, wise eyes of old Reb Moishl Apter. And the boy rouses himself from his day dreams in a storm of emotions, feeling with every fiber of his being that he belongs to Reb Moishl and has always belonged to him, even if he were unaware of it – just as a son belongs to a father whom he has never seen – and never, never again will he belong to the cavalryman on the horse. Therefore, he must act – instantly! – for this was a divine moment, a moment of grace that might never return and must not be missed.

Then, mustering strength of spirit, he overcomes his anxiety and awe and in a clear voice which he did not know that his throat was capable of producing, he exclaims: "Accept me, my Rabbi! For with my mother's blessings I left family, village and home, and came to you trembling and fearful, and it is you whom I will follow, and even though I am unworthy – teach me your Torah, Father mine!"

"Father mine?" he hears himself, stunned. The words had slipped through his lips as if waiting for the right moment, unwittingly stealing into his speech and taking the place of "my Rabbi," which is how he had initially addressed the old man. "Father mine?" All at once he felt a sense of calm descend upon him, unlike any he had ever known. Yes: Father mine. The words had been articulated and could not be unspoken. And he, Aazik, son of a horseman who was the son of a horseman, had reached the point of no return and was at peace with himself. At last, he had a father...

Indeed, in the twenty-four years that were to elapse from the day he left the village to the day he started reciting his daily *kaddish* in Grabówka, the son would neither mention his father nor bring him to mind. And even though he would return to Wisłok in 1909 to take leave of his parents prior to their departure for America, in his heart of hearts he would know that he was returning only to Mother, that he would miss only her, and only to her would he wave at the Tarnów Railroad Station when his parents' train stopped there for three minutes en route to the port.

Unmoving, Reb Moishl continued to sit in the armchair for a moment or so, embarrassed somewhat. He could not recall a similar case. Generally, his decisions were quick and firm and, to date, he had had no reason to regret a single one of them. But now – something unusual had happened to him this morning. Only moments earlier, he had questioned the village candidate who had wandered in from Tarnów to study with him – no formal examination, of course, but casually, so as not to confuse him – and he had, in fact, concluded (though he had not yet told the party involved) that the boy was not yet at a level qualified to join his group of students. The rabbi would certainly not reveal his considerations but, clearly, even if the candidate was thought to be advanced in Bukovsk and Sanok terms, he was the merest beginner by the standards of Tarnów and its *yeshivas*, even if not an outright boor. Yet, now, the rabbi changed his mind. Something in the lad's ardor reminded him of his own, which had guided him in his youth, when, even though he was the son of a simple, hard-working tradesman, he had succeeded through ardor, perseverance and, perhaps, a measure of luck, to break through the cruel ring of poverty that had mercilessly and constantly closed in on him, and dared take the leap that had brought him to where he was today. Yes, he would accept the boy into his group. There were precedents: Rabbi Akiva, who was a shepherd... Resh Lakish, a circus gladiator... and Reb Aazik, son of the horseman of Wisłok...

As soon as he amended his decision, the rabbi was comfortable with it and banished all doubt from his heart. He relied on his sixth sense, and this sense told him that a great Jewish scholar might well sprout from the boy. He explained to Aazik the schedule of studies: the whole group assembled at the rabbi's home for two half-days a week, when methods of study were taught and each student was assigned a personal topic; on Thursday evenings, students were tested individually on the assigned topics; the rest of the time would be devoted to *lernen* (study), whether alone or in pairs at the *Kloyz*, and *lernen* was one of those things that had no measure and no end.

This, then, was the system that the rabbi employed with his students, imparting a methodology that rested on two pillars: memorizing the material – a laborious process for which there were no substitutes, nor tricks, nor omissions, nor shortcuts, but only "study, day and night"; and independent thinking beyond the subject-matter itself. This dual practice, lauded by Galicia's greatest rabbis and *Tzaddikim*, was meant to train Reb Moishl's students for all and any themes that they might encounter in the future on their own. In the words of one contemporary, the Hasidic rabbi, Shiyeleh (Joshua) Horowitz of Dzików, the father of the last Dzikower *rebbe*, Reb Alterl, who reigned in Tarnów from the end of the First World War: "He who studies with Reb Moishe Yekiels knows *lernen.*" Thus, that week, Reb Moishl announced to his ten top students: "We are being joined by a lad who has neither studied nor memorized and is virtually an *am-haaretz*, an ignoramus; but go easy on him, for he will surpass you all. There, you have been forewarned."

7

Without any possessions Aazik reported to the gates of the *Great Kloyz* in Tarnów, and without possessions he was to remain for the entire nine years that the *Kloyz* was to be his house of prayer, his

house of learning, his home. In the right corner of the *bima* platform stood the lectern on which his *Gemara* lay permanently open,
flanked on either side by a candle that was lit every evening. At first
the boy was allowed to use the lectern, the book, and the candles
out of public respect for his rabbi, Reb Moishl. Later, the situation
continued out of growing public respect for the *yeshiva* boy himself and for his monastic way of life, owning nothing in the world
but his Torah. Summer and winter, in cold and in heat, all his days
and half his nights would be consumed by the fervor of learning at
his lectern and, in the evening, he would remove his shoes to stand
barefoot on the cold floor, so that the chill of it would prevent his
weary eyelids from succumbing to the temptation of dozing. This
would be recounted years later in Haifa by one of Reb Aazik's top
students, Mordekhai Spitz, whose father, Reb Shol, was the same
age as the lad from Wisłok and met him when he first entered the
Kloyz. He brought him home to his own father, Leibtche Spitz, who
took the lad to his heart and exerted a profound influence on his
life and views.

Aazik's personal needs were minimal. Having no bed to rest on,
nor a roof of his own over his head for the few remaining hours of
the night in which to catch a short nap – the hard, narrow wooden
bench at the *Kloyz* would mercifully absorb the weariness from his
bones and draw a film of calm over his eyelids. Hidden behind the
farthest table, only this wobbly bench, slated for firewood, compas-
sionately marked Aazik's nights and guarded his tired breath. At
first light, the lad would hurry to the *mikveh* to wash the traces of
fatigue from his body and return to put on his phylacteries, while
the rabbi's daughter peeked out at him through the cracks. Every
day, secretly, she left for him at the sink a plate of leftovers from her
father's kitchen – his only meal on weekdays – and, sometimes, also a
bundle of clothes from the charity storehouse. Only on the Sabbath
and holidays would Aazik be invited to wealthier homes for *kiddush* and to partake of the *cholent* stew. At such times, a host with

a soul might occasionally ask him a question about Jewish law or legend and, as he started to reply, a great light would fill the home as everyone listened open-mouthed to the lad's learned explanations. In time, Leibtche Spitz was to invite his son's friend to dine at his table permanently on the Sabbath, and a unique friendship was to bind the two, despite the great difference in their ages. At the same time, the fowl of heaven would bring tidings of the boy's wisdom also to those who had no connection to the *Kloyz*, and he began to be addressed as Reb Aazik the *avrekh*, despite his young years (personifying the Sages' interpretation of the word *avrekh* – "an elder in wisdom and a youth in years").

Old Moishe Stiglitz – who lived on Żydowska Street (The Jewish Street) in Tarnów and after the Six-Day War settled in the restored Jewish Quarter of Jerusalem's Old City – remembers to this day what his father told him about Reb Aazik in those days. The father, Reb Wolf (nicknamed Voftche), had in his youth been one of Reb Moishl Apter's more veteran students who were instructed by the rabbi to accept the young stranger from Wisłok into their midst, and who came to appreciate his special endowments. Years later, Voftche, a father now and a respected member of the community, used to point out Reb Aazik to his son in the distance – as the scholar walked in the street with the ever-present *Gemara* under his arm – depicting him as worthy of emulation and commendation: an unlearned boy from a God-forsaken village who, by sheer will, diligence, perseverance and personal talents had risen to become the town prodigy and Reb Apter's top student. "And like my father," Stiglitz tells Reb Aazik's son years later when they meet in Jerusalem, "many other parents did the same, indicating Reb Aazik as a prime example and, what's more, by virtue of living in the same town as he, they even saw themselves as sharing in his glory."

And just as from the day that Aazik started studying with Reb Moishe, he sealed a covenant with the life of scholarship, never to turn his back on learning; so, too, he sealed a covenant with Tarnów, the city of scholarship, and would never leave it. Nor would it ever occur to him to return to the spiritual wasteland of his village, even if this meant a complete break from his parents. Yes, the break was irreparable and inescapable – this he understood from the moment that he waited at the Tarnów Railroad Station, waving farewell to his parents, who were traveling by train to Hamburg to board a ship for America, as the train stopped for three minutes. With composure and sober resignation, he stood there, as if he were not personally involved, for the three minutes that seemed an eternity, knowing he would never again see his mother and father, just as he would never again see his brothers and sister, who had crossed the ocean eight years earlier. From now on, he was alone.

In this strict regime of self-discipline and perseverance, Aazik would let nothing keep him from *Gemara* study; this was to be his conduct even years later when he no longer needed the *Kloyz* as a place to live, and day in, day out, simply set aside special times for Torah study there. His communion with his *Gemara*, then as in his youth, would totally detach him from his surroundings to the extent that nothing and no one, no matter how important, would be allowed to distract or disturb him.

This was clearly remembered by Daniel Leibel – one of Reb Aazik's older students and subsequently a linguist and member of *Davar*'s editorial board in Tel Aviv – who, fifty years later, would tell Aazik's son the following true story: one day, in February 1914, the Zionist leader, Nahum Sokolow, arrived in Tarnów to participate in a Zionist conference. Dubbed by the press "the prince of Jewish culture," his presence left an indelible impression. To the distress of his hosts, however, the atmosphere in the city was clouded by a false charge leveled at Sokolow by Polish nationalists, who accused him of belittling the Polish national freedom struggle, even as he fought for the redemption of the Jewish People. Despite the tense atmosphere, Sokolow asked to take a moment from his busy schedule to visit the *Kloyz* and meet the "Tarnów prodigy" whose praises he, too, had heard sung. To everyone's astonishment, however, Reb Aazik – immersed in *lernen* and true to his practice to have no contact with anyone while studying – did not lift his head, not even for Sokolow. The guest took no offence. In silence, he beheld the prodigy as he rhythmically swayed back and forth and intoned the canticle of *Gemara* with devotion. He understood.

"Reb Aazik's chant," listeners would whisper in awe, wary of raising their voices lest the moment's magic be undone and the melody dissolve. In time, a new custom took root on the square and streets around the *Kloyz*: men and women passing by would briefly stop in their tracks and lend a ready ear to the tall *Kloyz* windows that were fixed on both sides of the Holy Ark and opened onto the street. From the mighty chorale of student voices bursting through the windows, they soon learned to single out that one special voice that seemed to be borne on, rather than sustain, the wings of song. Hypnotized, they would listen to the soft, ardent song-of-songs and, closing their eyes, imagine it spreading its wings to rise and soar above the entire town. And a smile of gratification would suffuse their faces, an other-worldly gratification, as if they, too, had sprouted wings like the wondrous melody and, severed from worldly woes and daily hardships, ascended with it, higher and higher, all the way to His footstool, blessed be He. And at this sublime moment of exultation, someone might quietly recite: "Blessed be He who shares His wisdom with those who revere Him," and the lips of the bystanders would inaudibly reply after him, "Amen, Amen."

The sense of wonder at "Reb Aazik's song-of-songs" lingered long after Aazik had left the *Kloyz* and made his living as a teacher at the Baron de Hirsch School, supplementing his income by tutoring the children of wealthier families at their homes. To hear the song was a unique experience, remembered decades later by the sisters of Reb Aazik's private pupils, who eventually told his son about it. Thus, in Tel Aviv, to this day, Rutka née Keller recalls how she sat in the adjacent room of the spacious family flat, hearing, through the half-open door, Reb Aazik lead her two brothers, Nasiek and Henek, in the melody of *Gemara*. In Bnei Brak, Erna née Schmidt, spoke of the long, delicious moments she enjoyed, sitting hidden and unseen in the corner of the room, listening to the *Gemara* lesson being given to her brother, Hesiek, and his friends; Reb Aazik's melodious voice would then gently spread and embrace the apartment's entire interior. In faraway Texas, her niece, Hanka née Schmidt, used to reflect on Reb Aazik's unforgettable song, which reached her ears as he tutored her youngest brother, Samek. In Haifa, Eva née Spiro, remembers how she insisted on sitting openly alongside her brothers, Szajek and Hezkel, like one of the pupils, fully inhaling the hymn that seemed to anoint the text with a paradoxical libation: headiness and solemnity at one and the same time. She even managed to absorb something of the issues being studied, by learning to distinguish between the many hues of the music and thereby recognizing the nature of the discussion. Yes, those who heard Reb Aazik's heart-song, even if only once, carried it embedded in their memory forever.

8

After being widowed from her husband Shloime in 1914, Zlatte, was to live on in America for another twenty-eight years, her heart both rejoicing and pining for Aazikl, her firstborn, from whom she had been cut off forever. Indeed, she cried her heart out for joy when she received a letter from him. It was their first communication since the outbreak of the war, in which hostilities between Austro-Hungary and Russia had condemned them to silence and "no news." Now, after a treaty had been concluded by the warring nations, she hoped for more frequent postal contact between herself and her son.

Having wandered for several years from one son's home

to another in the mining town – from Bereleh to Mendel and Arinyankif (as she continued to call her sons, Ben, Max and Jake) – Zlatte left Exeter and the irksome-petty tensions between herself and her daughter-in-law, Pearl, and in the Thirties moved in with her daughter, Esther, in Scranton, Pennsylvania. This was a modest home, given the Depression in America, yet it was a virtual palace compared to the Wisłok shack in which Esther and her five brothers had grown up. In her daughter's home, the mother lived on to a fine old age, enjoying a modicum of fulfillment. True, the separation from her sons was hard on her, but, at the same time, also relieved her of pressures from them: for though they supported her in dignified style and desired her comfort with heart and soul, among themselves they saw her as a bothersome, obstinate old woman, clinging tenaciously to memories of the past and refusing to adapt to a life in the New World. It was the fondness of her grandchildren that filled her life with a luminous ray of light. To them she was a strange but kindly *Bubeh*, who seemed to have come down from a fabled realm. Her speech was a riddle, sometimes faltering, sometimes curious; her clothes, too, were strange, sometimes ridiculous, sometimes picturesque, like those in story-books; and her head was covered by a faded wig from days of yore. The *Bubeh* would sing and hum to her grandchildren not only wonderful Yiddish lullabies from the "old country," such as *"Rozhinkes mit Mandlen"* (Raisins with Almonds), but also wordless tunes. And amazingly enough, on the nearby streets, little non-Jewish Ukrainian boys and girls would have remarkably similar tunes sung to them by Ukrainian and Slavic *babushkas*, whose children had immigrated to America from the same Beskid landscapes as the local Jewish immigrants.

B.F. Wróbel (now Wruble) had been right in his forecasts, and his predictions had come true. While the non-Jewish Slavs worked in the network of coal mines in Wyoming Valley, Pennsylvania, and the women were employed in the silk spinning mills that opened in and around Scranton, the Jews, who knew their language, ways and needs from neighborly relations in the "old country," began to supply them with services: a neighborhood grocery, a local slaughterhouse, a small corner kiosk selling haberdashery and cigarettes for adults, toys and sweets for the children – all this, on credit until the upcoming weekly pay-day at the mine or the factory. Once again the time-honored counsel of the Sages: "Go, and make a living from one another," proved its wisdom in its application. As the economic and human interaction between the two sides brought them closer and closer together, they soon began to discover the degree to which prejudice and the incitement of Church priests had clouded the similarity and the kinship that bound them as human beings. This realization could not always wipe away the fanatic heritage of the "old country". Yet, corroborated by the living example of other ethnic groups who had integrated alongside one another in America, the new realization began to lay a solid foundation for a shared life of freedom, on the basis of norms popularly dubbed as "the American way of life."

Every Sabbath eve, in her room, Zlatte lit nine candles: six – as a blessing for a long and good life for her six children who had married, assumed responsibility and established families of their own; and three – in memory of the souls of the three infants that had been snatched away from her in their cradle. And she knew that her Sabbath candle had stood Aazikl in good stead and protected him from harm in that terrible war, and would continue to protect him in the future as well. For hours at a time Zlatte relaxed in the rocking chair on the porch of the shrub-lined wooden house, with the *Zennerenne* that she brought with her from Wisłok.

Worn with use, the book lies open on her lap, but she does not read from it. In her mind's eye, she turns the yellowing pages of a different book, the book of her life, and her eyes gaze about and fix on the hills dipping and dropping to the Lackawanna. She takes no notice of the ugly scars and ravages left by the predatory methods of strip mining, but sees other hills instead – the green Beskid hills of the Carpathians that glide down joyously to the Wisłok and its tributaries.

In this mood of illusion and reminiscence, Zlatte's thoughts would go out to her beloved son who, like her, spurned the treasured delights of America, yet, unlike her, refused to be tempted by them, remaining behind with his family in Tarnów. "Tarnów? What sort of city is it? What kind of life does it provide for her son?" the old woman suddenly cried out after four decades, guided by the simple faith that a mother's heart can affect the course of events. She agonizes over not having considered his situation previously, and a pang of anxiety gripped her. She feels that she must rush to his side to protect him, forgetting that her son was already a married man with children of his own, whom he most certainly worried about as she did over him. Tarnów! All she ever saw of the city – and this, too, while passing through, many years ago, on her way to the ship in Hamburg – was its name, painted in large black letters on a white sign above the railroad platform. And she remembered her son standing on the platform for precious moments, alone in the world, waving a white handkerchief, until he vanished from sight. "How thin and pale his face was, and how sunken his brown eyes" – she remembered. And her heart weeps.

On December 6, 1942, with the United States now thoroughly embroiled in war, and initial details about the catastrophe of Polish Jewry starting to filter through to the American press from across the seas, Zlatte died in her room in Scranton, at the age of eighty-two. Her body was laid to rest in the Jewish cemetery of Exeter, and a polished-marble headstone, engraved in both English and Hebrew, was set upon her grave, next to Shloime's plain, unpolished tombstone. For as long as there was breath in her body and her mind remained lucid – so, Aazik's son heard fifty years later from Jake, her youngest son who had come to America with her as a child and was always attentive to her needs – her lips, on her deathbed, uttered the name of her eldest son, trapped in conquered Tarnów, with no savior come to his rescue. "Aazik, my Aazikl," she mumbled briefly: her beloved son, the son who did not remain hers, for she herself had pledged him to Torah, making him the first scholar to emerge from this rural family. "Azik, my Aazikl," she reiterated, and then corrected herself, "No! *Reb* Aazik! Reb-Reb-Reb Aazik." And with a mother's pride, mingled with the adoration of a simple village woman, she gurgled the honorable title that had been earned by her son and whose honor reflected on his mother and the whole family. As 1942 drew to a close, Zlatte had no idea about the fate of her son, but was certain that the candle she lit on his behalf every Sabbath eve would save him from this world war as it had saved him from World War One. And blessed be the God of ignorance, who, in His mercy, protects mothers in His world and takes their souls when the time comes without taking from them their last hopes for the welfare of their children.

*

What did Shloime and Zlatte, protagonists of the early generations of the Wróbel saga, leave behind? Property they did not possess. Ornaments did not adorn their one room. Their clothing was plain, not a single item worth keeping. Even the letters written by Aazik and Golda to Zlatte were not placed into her hands personally, but delivered to Bereleh-Ben's address in Exeter, for she, herself, had difficulty reading them and, certainly, in replying to them. A few letters written by Aazik and Golda did come to light in Ben's attic, and Sarah, Ben's eldest, who continues to live in her father's house, graciously restored them to her cousin, the son of their authors.

And yet, a number of items do remain as an eternal memento of Zlatte. One is a photograph taken in America, showing the old woman seated in a dark skirt and a white Sabbath blouse, her wig on her head and her look bespeaking faith and resolve. An earlier photograph, taken back in Galicia and kept by Aazik and Golda, was lost with the destruction of the Wróbel home in the Holocaust. But the six brass candle holders, in which Zlatte inserted the Sabbath candles, one for each of her living children, have remained to this day. Four are kept by her beloved granddaughter, Bobby, daughter of Jake, under whose roof Zlatte lived during her final period in Exeter. The other two were taken by her great-granddaughters, Sharon and Sandy, the granddaughters of Esther Klein, the only daughter of Shloime and Zlatte, in whose home in Scranton the old woman spent the last years of her life. (The candles for the souls of the dead children had probably been placed in some makeshift device rather than holders). The great-granddaughters also took over the soup ladle – a mute testimony to the modest, strictly kosher meals Zlatte would prepare for herself. The clay milking jars, however, remain in the attic of Ben's house, an echo of the days that Zlatte milked a cow in her son's yard. Also two of these clay vessels Sarah presented to her cousin to be preserved in his Jerusalem home in remembrance of the grandmother they share.

And what was left by Shloime? The coffer that stood in the Wróbel home in Tarnów contained an Austrian photograph of Shloime in the uniform of a cavalryman of the Imperial Army – a picture that Shloime was certainly proud of and by which he would no doubt have hoped to be remembered: clean-shaven and bald, his head gleaming like the helmet lying by his side, one leg bent and resting mischievously on the point of his boot, while his eyes look straight at the camera, similar to the gaze of a right-signalman during roll-call – a photograph signifying "honor and majesty" as defined by the army of those days. Hesiek, Shloime's grandson, who knew his grandfather only from stories, liked to look at the photograph during his childhood, even though his parents' reluctance to show it did not elude him. Shloime's idea of honor and majesty obviously stood in direct contradiction to their own, or perhaps the captured pose was too *goyish* for their tastes. In any event, the photograph ended up like the one of Zlatte: both were lost in the destruction of the Wróbel home in the Holocaust. Shloime's grandchildren in America also remember such a photograph, but no copy was found among Zlatte's possessions. Could it be that Zlatte took out her rage on her husband's photograph, thereby seeking to eradicate his memory, for it embodied all that was contrary to her view and all that she refused to forgive him for in the last years of his life?

Thus, only one item of Shloime's remained: the small military prayer book which he guarded carefully, keeping it next to his sick-bed in the final months of his life and reaching out to shelter it be-fore he presented himself to his Maker. The prayer book came to light together with the letters from Aazik and Golda in the treasure trove of the attic of Ben's house. Sarah, who restored to her cousin his parents' letters and deposited in his hands two of their grand-mother's clay milking jars, also gave him their grandfather's only prayer book. And so it came about that the single item to survive the early generations of the Wróbel saga properly rests at the home of Shloime's Jerusalem grandson, opposite Mount Zion – though it is doubtful that the grandfather even knew of the site's existence, and certainly never mentioned its name or dreamt of laying his prayer book there. However, fate again tricked its servants. The volume of *Zennerenne* – the only book that Zlatte brought with her to America and always kept open on her lap when sitting at home, morning and evening, so that it seemed to become an integral part of her body and personality – of this, not a trace remained. Whereas the only material legacy that was to come to embody Shloime's memory in future generations was… a book, even though the man had never read a book in all his life, and even though the simplest prayer had a hard time settling on his lips.

And, yet, who is to say that Shloime was defeated all across the board? For his Jerusalemite grandson, who also chose the way of books, as his father had done and his grandmother had hoped the family would continue to, nevertheless also continued the family's military tradition – albeit in a completely different direction and out of totally different motives. While Shloime and Shloime's father, Yizhak-Isaac, willingly donned a cavalry uniform, and while Reb Aazik, Shloime's son, was forced to bear the burden of a gunner's uniform – all three of them served masters of a country not their own, and wore uniforms not on behalf of their own people. Not so the fourth generation: from the moment Aazik's son made *aliyah* to Eretz Israel, he joined the ranks of the Hebrew Haganah and, thereafter, the duty of service to defend his people dovetailed with each and every stage of his Erez Israel life. Thus, at the outbreak of the Second World War, he volunteered to serve as an Eretz Israel soldier in the campaign against the greatest enemy the Jews had ever known, and after five years of service on various fronts reached even Tarnów, the province of his childhood. Not much time passed before, in December 1947, he donned a uniform for the third time to fight for the rebirth of Israel and the founding of a Jewish state in Eretz Israel, continuing to do reserve duty for twenty years, like his grandfather and great-grandfather in their time. Thus did the son of Aazik-son-of-Shloime-son-of-Itzhak-Isaac realize the dream that his father had dreamt but did not live to see fulfilled: to plant his home in the bosom of a land whose bookish-image he had cultivated his entire life and bequeathed to his children and students.

CHAPTER SIX

Gates Pure and Impure

1

IN GOOD CHEER, Reb Aazik guides his son, Herschl, to the broad gully of Lwowska Street, towards the Grabówka neighborhood. "The Lwów-bound Street," as the main artery of eastern Tarnów was known, followed the historical route that cut through southern Poland from west to east, passing through Tarnów and arriving at Lwów. By shortcut it took no more than ten minutes to cross from the Wróbel home on Bóżnic Street to Lwowska.

"There was no Bóżnic Street yet in 1895 when I arrived in Tarnów from my village," the father reconstructed for the boy how this small street had managed to bind him with ties of loyalty, and captivate him with a thousand overt and covert fibers, to become the center of his life and world. But in the early days, it was still a god-forsaken area: neither the street, nor the two buildings that were to become the hallmark of the neighborhood several years later yet existed – the synagogue, dubbed "New" or "Great," whose silver dome stood out from afar, and the "new" ritual bath. Aazik was to pass thirteen years in Tarnów before the synagogue was inaugurated; the initiative for its construction had dated back to 1864, but a wretched ban hampered the building's completion until 1908. The massive back wall of the building, along with the other

235

prayer houses that cleaved to it, gave the street its Polish name *Ulica Bóżnic* (Synagogues Street), a name which has remained to this day, though there are no longer any Tarnów synagogues or Jews to worship in them. The ritual bath, too, opened only in 1904. Its ornate Moorish style was considered by nineteenth-century European planners to be Semitic, which is why they deemed it fitting to so dress the public buildings of the only ethnic community in Europe that was patently Semitic: the Jews. "It's interesting that the opening of the new bathhouse, rather than of the new synagogue, had such an immediate impact on my life" – Aazik surprised his son with his recollections.

Until then, for his first nine years in town – when he had no room of his own to live in, but spent both day and night at the *Kloyz* – Aazik would go for his morning ablutions to the old ritual bath, which from the earliest times had stood at Fish Square.

"The fact that the old bathhouse fell into disuse was not a matter of choice," he says bitterly. "The town fathers, displaying a remarkable obtuseness towards the sensitivities of their Jewish residents, took over the area for the erection of public toilets. The proximity of the latrines to the synagogue and adjacent study house – two key Jewish institutions which had been housed in the fine, historical building for more than three hundred years – not only disturbed the hundreds of worshipers and students engaged in holy pursuits there, but dealt a ringing slap in the face to the entire Jewish community, a community old and important by any criteria, as confirmed even by official (Austrian and then Polish) records which showed the Jews comprising about half of the town's population."

"Unlike the bathhouse," Aazik reflects frankly on those faraway times, "the Great Synagogue, despite its size and grandeur, made no real impression on my daily routine for the first few years after it opened." Even though he had been inside the synagogue on occasion and admired its beauty, and even though he had once or twice listened in obvious enjoyment to both Zvi-Hersch Weinman – the cantor who had inaugurated the synagogue with his stirring melodies and his choir he, Aazik, recited his daily prayers at the *Kloyz* and, later, at the *bis-medrash*. Only upon his marriage to the cantor's daughter in 1914 was his fate, once and for all, bound up with the new building and street.

The Grabówka journey begins with the labyrinth of lanes separating Bóżnic Street from Lwowska, and a series of what Yiddish slang referred to as *lokhs*, that is, "holes" – breaches in fences, hidden arcade passageways and crowded alleys leading to the main street. The lanes throbbed with religious, social, cultural and economic life far beyond the physical space available to the residents. There, Jewish boys grew up who, in time, were to earn public acclaim for their talents and daring: from their ranks were to spring rabbis and scientists, violinists, chess and soccer players, philosophers and men of action, revolutionaries and Zionist pioneers.

And like roses amid thorns, dark-eyed, sharp-witted Hebrew girls blossomed there, blazing trails to a new woman's status in Jewish society. You could meet them among the artists and builders, the declaimers of Bialik, Mickiewicz and Tuwim, the readers of Dostoevsky, Romain Roland and Żeromski, and among the passionate debaters of the theories of Marx, Borokhov and Lenin. Some of them joined the Third and Fourth Aliyot, fearlessly emigrating to Eretz Israel as pioneers, in order, with their toil, to make the desolate country bloom and lend their shoulder to the new, social and national experiment of kibbutz life. Only a decade and a half earlier had the kibbutz taken its first steps at Deganya, Merhavya and Bet Alfa – and who was to say where it would lead? And on that bitter day of the eclipse of God and man, you would see the girls among the ranks of partisan fighters in the forests of Poland and Lithuania, waging a bloody, futile struggle, gun in hand, against the Nazi conqueror – and, as survivors, you would find them on the decks of ramshackle, stealthy ships, ready to take on the British war fleet for the right of Holocaust survivors to drop anchor at their homeland shores.

Though the *lokhs*, too, teem with people like all the other lanes, and their yards house stores, workshops, taverns and even a small Hasidic *shtibl*, their main purpose is to provide residents of the Jewish neighborhood with shortcuts to the main street. Two of these alleyways, serving Bóżnic Street and others like it, deposit pedestrians at 4 and 6 or at 16 Lwowska Street. The first alley bursts smack-dab in the middle of a main junction that hustles and bustles on weekdays and dons the dress of stillness and serenity on the Sabbath and holidays. This is the Pilzno Gate or Iron Gate, which leads from the east to the center of historic Tarnów. Apart from the two historical names, nothing remains today of what was the buckle of the town's belt of fortifications.

Until recently, the boy would happily accompany his father on his way to the Gate. Whatever the explicit reason for their walk – whether to buy a Yiddish newspaper or have a haircut – the father never overlooked the building on the left corner of Gate Street. His eyes seemed to caress the flight of stairs leading to the first story of the building, and he would have difficulty swallowing the bubble of excitement that burst from the depths of his memory and choked him up.

After all, for seven whole years, the hardest but most enjoyable of his years in Tarnów, he had climbed those stairs three times a week to reach the three-room flat on the first floor, and there dwell in the presence of the great Reb Moishl Apter, to drink thirstily from the spring of his teachings. And for seven whole years – so the father tells his son – he would leave the flat three times a week, after hours of study and learning, exhilarated anew each time by the encounter with wisdom personified; and, at the very same moment, even before he reached the street, he would already eagerly anticipate his return to Reb Moishl, his rabbi, and the acute headiness of the experience that would intoxicate him once more.

While the first floor of the building, and the memory of the man who spread his teaching there, could even years later rekindle in Aazik's heart a glow of holy awe, the ground floor of the very same building was, in contrast, utterly ungodly. Indeed, as if to differentiate between sacred and profane, the lower story housed Heilpern, the caretaker of the community bathhouse. Every day, at morning ablutions, Heilpern would greet Aazik by baring two rows of tobacco-yellowed teeth, affixing a false, jocose grin to his pale face and hollow "Good morning, Reb Aazik." Could it be that someone, whose occupation involved looking at naked bodies all the time, increasingly lost respect for his fellow man? Yet, if the attendant's greeting ever did contain a rare hint of respect, this was not due to Aazik's scholarly achievements, but rather to Heilpern's admiration for the accomplishments of the muscular village boy on the "upper level" of the bathhouse steam room, equaled only by the acclaimed performance of Heilpern himself.

In any case, of the ten measures of wicked mockery that descended to the world, Heilpern seemed to have taken possession of nine, and he spread them in all directions, his face bathed in an expression of spite and unforgiving resentment. Every morning he would stride among the dozens of men in their nudity, the contempt in his eyes saying what his lips dared not: "Here, now, my good 'gentlemen,' you who think of yourselves as such important personages and consider your wealth a license to hold an entire community by the throat! And, here now, also you, 'pious' scholars, whose lips bespeak honeyed nectar and whose words ooze pure olive oil! I am the only person in this town who sees through your secrets and knows you as you really are, all your naked faults and hidden defects, with your hernias and your unseen scabies masked beneath your *yarmulkes*! I, and only I, see you as God has made you – as naked and bare as the day you were born!"

Heilpern was followed by *der Roiter Alter*, the red-bearded beadle. Pining bodies frequented his door asking him to treat hernias that had overstepped all bounds and painlessly restore the unruly organs to their place. During the week, Alter liked to catch hold of adolescent *yeshiva* boys who were trying to check the growth of their beards by plucking sprouting hairs from their chins. But his special pleasure focused on Sabbath mornings, when he ran the rod of his gaze over worshipers, hastening, prior to prayers, to cleanse themselves in the bathhouse from the propitious Sabbath eve activity of "be fruitful and multiply." Whether or not the gossipmongers were right in their supposition that the Sabbath inventory of morning buttocks after nightly activity brought this testicle-infirm sinner to unmentionable arousal, shall remain a secret between his instincts and his Instigator.

While the son shared his father's holy awe with regard to the first floor of the corner building and his abhorrence of the tenants of the ground floor, it was another building on Gate Street that seemed to him to harbor greater pleasures. This building housed Boigen's kiosk, where the neighborhood children used to buy a joint ice-cream cone and carefully apportion out an equal number of licks. And there was the barber-shop run by Fishl, known as *der barbirer.* His was not just any barber-shop but, indeed, a highly important institution. Here, the moderately pious (including Aazik), would seasonally submit their beards to the dexterous scissors of the proprietor.

2

He was one of a kind, Fishl, *der barbirer.* True, the white coat that all barbers had to wear while working, according to a municipal by-law, appeared to blur his uniqueness and level him with all the other barbers in the world, but anyone with sense in his heart and eyes in his head could appreciate that behind this whitey white was concealed the soul of an artist, who viewed beard trimming as both a creative outlet and a sacred craft. Now, this is how Fishl went about his work: to begin with, he stepped back to fix a studied, penetrating gaze at both the mirror, before which the client sat awaiting his ministrations, and the client's reflection in it. Fishl's examination was of special quality: it was not one of those looks directed by the puffed-up artists of today, avid to "improve" on nature or deconstruct it cubistically as they see fit; nor was it a mocking gaze, like that of the bath attendant, who, from the constant sight of bare buttocks on his right and left, had grown apathetic to man's beauty. No, Fishl 's gaze was all humility and awe, a gaze that bespoke reverence for the Jewish visage, for this visage was the work of the Master of the Universe, in whose image it had been created and whose spirit abides in it.

After the preliminary inspection stage, Fishl sank into thought for a moment: how is he to restore to the man's face its original luster, marred now by the unbridled sprouting of facial hair? And how to accomplish the task to the best of his ability, and in keeping within the limits of Jewish law? Finally, hitting on the right decision, with a firm turn of the hand Fishl flings a sheet over the client's clothes, draws the sheet up beneath his chin, and ties it at the nape. He is now ready: his scissors in his right hand, and a long, narrow, black comb in his left. But before lowering the implements onto the client's beard, he ever so slowly tip-toes up to the barber chair, like a cat, while practicing with his scissors scores and scores of brisk clips in the air to the triple-time of a waltz – like some tribal rite of passage from childhood to maturity, or the dribbling warm-up of a basketball or tennis player prior to the opening shot.

At the end of the practice, and with appropriate caution, Fishl approaches the barber chair where his client sits sunk in the seat, the scissors not stopping to cut the air for even a second. "Three to four trios of air cuts for every cut of actual hair" – the son mentally records while observing the ministrations Fishl accords his father's beard, calculating how many hundreds of such movements will vainly find their way into the air before the barber achieves his objective.

Next, Fishl turns to the task itself: trimming wild bristles that have burgeoned uncurbed since the last haircut and culling them from the main body of the beard, while again and again inserting the teeth of the comb into the hair and snipping all protrusions from the comb, leaving only the base layer of the beard itself. The way is now clear for the shaping stage, granting the beard an individual character – whether rounded, should the client favor the Austrian style, or pointy, for those who choose the Russian fashion. This stage ends with Fishl again retreating in order to gain a general impression and stopping, with one flash of his scissors, the imagined waywardness of a solitary hair caught by his sharp eye in brazen delinquency. Now he scrutinizes the overall effect and sees (as in *Genesis*) that "it was good."

He then concludes with a series of sprays of fragrant water from a metal bottle, rhythmically squeezing the pink, pear-like, rubber ball, which is attached to the bottle by a tube that is also made of pink rubber. This final touch brings the beard-trimming ceremony to its proper close. "The watering is good for the beard's natural and tidy continued growth," the barber holds forth earnestly, as if he were an agricultural expert, in reply to any request to skip the aquatic sprays or their dubious scent, "and it also makes grooming and combing easier." Now Fishl is free to give his attention to any hairs that may have grown on other parts of the head, which he does by shaving. The razor, banned by Jewish law for use on face and beard, is now the choice implement for nape and pate. Such a close shave renders void all division between the forehead and the phylacteries head-box, and lends prominence to the side-curls, which differentiate between Jew and *goy* – the very same side-curls for which *goyish* children hound Jewish children in the streets.

And yet, despite Fishl's strict adherence to all the laws specified in the *Shulhan Arukh*, the ultra-Orthodox nevertheless prefer to give their custom to Gimpel's barber-shop, located on the other side of the street and lauded as "stringently kosher." The fault, most likely, does not lie with Fishl himself; the added trust enjoyed by the rival barber-shop concerns the fact that it is shut for business during "the Three Weeks." "How amazing it is – the *goyim* have nothing like it," Aazik tells his son. "For three weeks, dubbed 'between the afflictions (*bein hamezarim*)' – that is, between the affliction of 17th Tammuz, when nineteen hundred years ago, the *tamid*, the daily Temple offering, was annulled and the walls of Jerusalem breached, and that of the 9th of Av, when the walls of the Second Temple were torched – Yossl and Moishe and Yankl, and tens of thousands of others like them, in Tarnów and Warsaw and Yemen and wherever there are Jews, mourn, remembering Zion and our shrine which still lies in ruins."

Actually, *der barbirer* has the advantage over his ultra-Orthodox rivals and even they call on him for the other type of service he supplies – his expertise as *feltcher*. This expertise is highly acclaimed, so much so that even doctors who had studied at universities – those generally called *di doktoirim* – who walk about town bare-headed and never go to synagogue except on the High Holidays – even they call on Fishl in complex cases. Indeed, at the behest of the *doktoirim*, Father would rush to Fishl to seek his help whenever anyone in the family came down with severe grippe or pneumonia, or had high temperature from infection, for there was no better remedy in such cases than removing the affected blood, which was Fishl's particular expertise.

The removal of undesirable blood is accomplished by three methods: by virtual blood letting, which only elders, Jews and non-Jews alike, continue to practice as they had done for years; by leeching, that is, by exposing the patient's upper back – the part that encases and protects the lungs – and submitting it to the blood-thirstiness of black leeches, who cling and gorge themselves on the sick person's blood, until they drop replete and exhausted; and by *bainkes* (cupping), applying by vacuum glass cups to a languishing back, up to ten for children and twenty for adults.

Upon receiving an urgent summons, Fishl would leave the

barber shop open, place a chair in the doorway to inform customers of his imminent return and, without tarrying, speed to the patient's home with his black leather case, which always rested ready on the shelf near the cracked mirror. In this respect, he was just like a real doctor, just like Dr. Yekel and Dr. Trammer and Dr. Leibel, or Dr. Bloch-Merzowa, the pediatrician, the one who started going gray in her twenties, her salt-and-pepper head adding a daunting respectability to her grave face, whose eyes, too, were the color of ashes.

Doctors' cases, however, were not like *der barbirer's* case. The former contained stethoscopes and injections, thermometers and various medicine vials, an instrument to widen the nostrils and the ear canals (so as to permit an invasive peep inside), and a round mirror with a rubber ribbon that the doctor would put on his forehead, cotton wool and iodine for bandaging and, sometimes, even flat wooden sticks to press down the tongue and make the patient say "a-a-ah" upon opening his mouth, to expose the secrets of his throat. Fishl's case, on the other hand, disclosed a jar with leeches immersed in a dark liquid, or dozens of thick-edged, rounded glass cups that he placed in a bowl, as he asked the housewife to boil water for their sterilization.

Next to the bed of the patient, who lies on his belly with his upper back bared, Fishl removes from his case a tiny spirit container and sets it aflame, picks up a small rod whose end has been swaddled in cotton wool and dipped into an inflammable liquid, lights it and, with a skillful turn of the wrist, places it, aflame, inside a cup held diagonally near the patient's back. "In a split second, the fire will eat up the oxygen in the cup, and the glass, with a customary spring, will be sucked onto the back by force of the vacuum to cleave to the skin. The skin, trapped willy-nilly inside the cup, will now start to billow like a round cushion, mustering the affected blood and changing its color to purple" – this is the explanation the child received as he anxiously watched the cups being placed on his sister's back. But a year later, when Fishl would again be called to the Wróbel home, for fear that the son, too, now had pneumonia, he would command his rod of fire with such amazing agility that, even before the boy noticed, the cups already adhered to his back and the treatment was completed; at which time, his initial fears would be too embarrassing to confess.

Decades after these events, when the residents of Gate Street had already been snuffed out in the Holocaust crematoria of Bełżec, the son – by then, a seasoned researcher of Jewish history, who had spent years studying state documents and notary ledgers (from the fourteenth to the seventeenth centuries) in the Venice Archives – would be reminded of this faraway childhood experience: the para-medical treatment of the wonderful Tarnów *feltcher.*

In the course of his historical investigations, he would collect hundreds of original documents in Latin, Venetian-Italian, Greek and Hebrew, all of them mentioning the Jewish *ciruici* who inhabited the colonies of the Queen of the Seas, the Serenissima, and especially the island of Crete. The study of what to all intents and purposes were *feltcher* activities would transport the son on the wings of longing far, far back in time and place to the mod-est brother at Tarnów's Pilzno Gate, who most certainly had never heard of the *ciruici* and probably did not know how universally honored and important the profession had been in bygone gen-erations. And how sad that the son would never again be able to visit the skilled, Tarnów *barbirer,* who had saved him and his sister from pneumonia (a deadly illness at the time); and that he would never be able to tell him how warmly he remembered him while perusing the documents on his colleagues in Mediterranean lands. The latter had already been well-established and widely acclaimed as excellent practitioners, their names enhanced by the title of *ma-gister,* when Tarnów had only just begun to shake off its village sta-tus and become a town, having no organized Jewish community of its own, but only a handful of Jewish merchants who made the rounds of its markets.

3

And yet, ever since the boy visited Kraków with his mother and passed through the Floriańska Gate, and ever since he learned about King Bolesław the Bold who had banged with his sword at Kiev's Golden Gate, the term "city gate" – including Tarnów's, even though it had been dismantled, leaving behind only a street name – took on a new, concrete meaning in his mind. He stopped relating to the geographical name of the place, which hinged on Pilzno, the nearby and fortified city, preferring the name "Iron Gate," after Kiev's Golden Gate. In his imagination – and the boy tried to share this with his father on their walks – he saw bands of Tartars storming the gate and retreating. But his father remained indifferent. So that no matter how wonderful were his walks with Father through the neighborhood lanes, he instinctively began to show a reluctance whenever his father wished to lead him out to Lwowska Street through the *lokh* opposite the Gate. Instead he chose the alleyway that came out further down the street, at No. 16.

The boy had correctly assessed Father's opinion of Gate Street. In Father's view, the events that did or did not take place in front of the historical gate were of no consequence in the present, not even as a marvel of fancy. The real marvel was reality itself, as it unfolded here and now, with its primary significance resting in its living people. These humble people, who for lack of choice had been compressed into a paltry number of buildings, two or three on one side of Gate Street, and a similar number on the other side, and lived there or conducted their business there (usually inside the cramped home itself), "earning their bread," in the words of the Sages, "off one another." Thus, apart from Heilpern and Alter, the bath attendants, and Fishl and Gimpel, the barbers, and apart from Boigen's ice-cream kiosk, there was Kleinhaendler, who sold women's scarves and fabric leftovers; and Hochner, a wholesaler-retailer in shirt cottons; and Pariser, specializing in woollen cloth from Białystok; and Lenkowicz, importing fabrics from Łódź. And next to them, were the sons of Hiel-Meiyer Laufer of Grybów, who sold shoes and leather, thereby freeing their elderly father for his *mitzvos*: at Sabbath's end, he would make the rounds of the well fed, wealthier homes, going from door to door with a white sack slung over his left wrist, his right hand filling it with *halleh* remnants that he distributed to the poor during the week.

At Gate Street there was also a real store, that of Fishl Geminder, who occupied the flat above the shop, and whose red beard, which grew at a legendary rate, overflowed and served as a landmark for people coming to the Gate: "If Geminder is here, everything is here." The store sold cigarettes and tobacco, postage stamps and tax stamps, as well as newspapers of all kinds, and even a few little Hebrew books, affectionately known as *seforimlakh*. Also at the Gate was the flat of the late Reb Moishl Apter, taken over now by Yisifhaim, the rabbinic judge; this is where the local rabbinic court convened. Also there, was the flat of Haiml Troym, one of the two "Eretz Israel *gabbaim*" in town, who emptied the collection boxes of Rabbi Meir Baal HaNess twice a year and transferred the donations to the *Koilel Galizye* in Jerusalem. And even though, traditionally, the reward of a *mitzvah* is another *mitzvah*, the donors nevertheless received a small gift at the Jewish New Year: a wall Eretz-Israel calendar of the coming year, like the one hanging in the front room of the Wróbel home.

Whichever *lokh* it was, the exit from the labyrinth onto Lwowska Street always dealt a triple shock: the shock of light, the shock of noise and most powerful of all – the onslaught of traffic. The street was utterly congested, especially on market days, by the traffic of drays and wains (*fury* or *furmanki* in Polish) – carts in which villagers brought their farm crops to town; the carts were harnessed to struggling, plodding, brown workhorses that panted and perspired just like their owners. The sides of the carts were fashioned like ladders, to be moved or dismantled, as required, and padded with a thick, protective plait of unpeeled twigs. Squeezed among the carts were two-wheeled hand-barrows, each with a porter yoked by rope to its handles, his palms taking most of the weight of the load and steadying the vehicle parallel to the ground, while the muscles of his back and neck hauled it; sometimes, the reverse was true, the porter's arms propelling the barrow forward, as he braced his belly to keep it steady. Both carts and hand-barrows would give way to an assortment of carriages, pulled by horse power and constituting a widespread means of city travel.

The most common carriages were black *fiacres*, topped by leather stretched across arches overhead; the arched roofs were collapsible, but for the most part kept in convex position to protect the passengers from rain and snow in winter and the beating sun in summer. Harnessed to one horse, or sometimes, two, the *fiacres* moved about as a convenient passenger service licensed by the municipality, ready to traverse the length and breath of town at all hours of the day. Less common, but much more elegant in appearance, were the *bryczkas* – private curricles, gleaming brown or the color of light wood, whose double seat was raised above two high wheels hitched to a perfectly-groomed neighing horse.

On rare occasions, even a *kareta* – a black, ornate coach – would find its way to Lwowska Street, enclosed within itself like its distinguished passenger, aloof from whatever was happening around it. At times, the black *kareta* resembled a hearse, its sides punctuated by glazed openings devised by a planner with heart (or with a macabre sense of humor), so that an insistent, curious corpse might look out and reassure himself that he was not missing anything by forever quitting this vale of tears. The passenger, who most probably wound up here for lack of choice, or by mistake, sits concealed in a corner of the coach as if trying to cloak himself in its dimness. Thus, while he himself has found a retreat from the foulness outside, he shows less consideration for the horse, abandoning its nostrils to a bombardment of abominable stenches, exposing its eyes to a deluge of sights spilling onto the city street, and baring its ears to the mass tumult of simple, non-privileged mortals – human and equine alike – while he, selfish and pedigreed, saves his own delicate soul.

Motorized forms of transportation did not appear in Tarnów until the thirties, with the exception of Duke Sanguszko's car. He would astound the town – which was his ancestors' private estate – by tearing through the streets in an open car, and even hosting a national car race there. Nevertheless, the town "progressed with the times," establishing a depot for inter-city buses at the square near the entrance to Grabówka; within the town itself, however, horses prevailed as the dominant mode of travel. Little wonder, then, that only after coming to Palestine in 1937, did Aazik's son, at the age of seventeen, ride in a taxi for the first time, whereas his father, never ever sampled the taste of a car ride…

The various horse-drawn vehicles that Aazik came upon during his first encounter with Tarnów streets as a boy in 1895, were joined at the end of the first decade of the twentieth century by a tramway: a red electric car – inspired and initiated by Mayor Tertil – and boasting a half moon and a star on its sides. The *mikveh* loungers explored a host of idle explanations for the similarity between the town emblem and the emblem of Islam, while others sought small comfort in the color of the emblem, which was blue and white.

Fiddlesticks! German in origin, it was the historical emblem of the Tarnowski nobility and they bestowed it on their "private" towns: on Dzików, that is, Tarnobrzeg (meaning "Tarnowski Beach") on Wisła's right bank; on Tarnopol ("Tarnowski City") in eastern Galicia, where Zvi-Hersch served as a cantor prior to settling in Tarnów; and on Tarnów itself – the jewel in the crown – in whose cathedral, inside Italian marble sarcophagi, rested the fathers of the dynasty, including the great military commander, hetman Jan Tarnowski.

The imported Italianism of the Tarnowski tombs was of no interest to Aazik. But his son – who was charmed by Italy's language and culture, and would spend a good deal of time there as a soldier and activist in the rescue of Holocaust survivors and, later, as an academic – from early youth closely followed those Italian artists (especially Padovani) who had arrived in Poland back in the sixteenth century at the invitation of Bona, the Sforza princess. As Queen of Poland, Bona's name was bound up with the last of the Jagiellonian kings: with Zygmunt the Old, her husband, and Zygmunt-August, their son, who was the architect of the Lublin Union of Lithuania and Poland in 1569. Golda admired the foreign queen not only because she had brought to Poland artists from her own country, but also because she had built a fortified city on the eastern frontier and named it Bar, after the Italian city of Bari. In Bar, three hundred years later, he who was to become Golda's father, Zvi-Hersch Weinman, would be born.

Ah, Bar! What Polish reader does not know the heartbreaking line – "*Bar Wzięty!*" ("Bar has fallen!") – which concludes the first volume of *With Fire and Sword* and its unfolding history of the Polish struggle during the Cossack Revolt of 1648. To Sienkiewicz's dramatic description, Golda added (as did her son) the story of the massacre of the Jews of vanquished Bar at the hands of the rebels, as related in *Yeven Mezulah*. In time, when the Jewish community of Bar was rebuilt, it was greater in number than any other ethnic group in town, and its builders included Golda's ancestors, who had come from the Balkans. When she told her son about these things in his childhood, Golda had no way of knowing that it would be he, the descendant of the Bar re-builders, who was to come full circle. For two of the son's rehabilitation missions in World War II would be anchored in Bari: in a village next to Bari he would set up a training farm, *Rishonim* (The First Ones), for youth who survived the Holocaust, and from the port of Bari he would send his charges off to Palestine. As for Bar itself (today in the independent Ukraine), it would take another fifty years before the son was able to get there as well and see the sites that Zvi-Hersch had described to his daughter. But in vain would he search for the past: – not a shred or trace of Jewish Bar remained.

Yet, in his childhood, despite his keen interest, the Wróbel boy did not manage to see the Italian sarcophagi in the Tarnów cathedral. True, unlike the parents in ultra-Orthodox homes, the Wróbels did not consider it unseemly to visit the historical churches of Kraków. Tarnów's cathedral, however, remained forever blocked off, for it would never occur to a Jewish boy to publicly cross the threshold of a church in his own town. Thus, only in 1985, forty years after the end of the war, was Aazik and Golda's son, at the age of 65, to visit, for the first time in his life, the inside of the historical cathedral in his native town. There he saw the Italian Tarnowski sarcophagi, preserved in the cathedral for four hundred years.

Tarnów's tramway planners naturally laid down a single track along the same main streets that had bisected the town from west to east since the day of its' founding. So the tram passed through Krakowska, Wałowa, and Lwowska in their entirety, from the railroad station at the town's western entrance, up to its eastern boundary at the end of Grabówka. From afar, the boy liked to stop and watch the tram accomplish the bend at the bottom of Pilzno Gate, entering Lwowska from Wałowa, as a massive burst of yellow-blue sparks, sent flying into the air, heralded the approach of the electric car.

"There is something exciting about the naked exposure of electricity," the boy whispered to his father, hypnotized by the hail of sparks; in those days, electricity was still shrouded in an aura of mystery and most of the homes in the neighborhood, including the Wróbels', were not connected to the city grid, but left to the mercy of the kerosene lamp. In the evening, the streets of the Jewish neighborhood were engulfed in darkness and Jewish children groped their way to *heder* (one room school), carrying their own light, in the shape of a tiny tin house with a candle in it.

Exciting and also scary, Aazik's son continues to reflect on the mysterious phenomenon, without revealing to his father his anxieties about the terribly splendid power of electricity. To complement the sight of his eyes, the boy commands his sense of hearing to listen to the merry din of the tramway as it quickly spills down Lwowska and is swallowed up in the haze enwrapping the edges of Grabówka. The sound will be audible in the distance for another moment, before it finally drowns in the tumult of the city and fades.

Tarnów's Jews shared the favorable opinion about "Tertil's tramway," and numbered among its faithful users, even though they retained from the war years a serious account to settle with the mayor. For it was Tertil who had ordered his officials in 1914 to seize the stands and stores of the Jewish residents who had fled to Vienna, on the pretext that the food that the Jews had ostensibly left behind was to be distributed to the hungry. In so doing, he had in fact abandoned the personal effects of the Jews to all takers. Upon their return to empty stores and homes, the Jewish refugees received some compensation for the commercial goods that had been placed during the war under the supervision of commissioners. But the wrong done them was not rectified nor their private belongings restored, belongings of which they had been robbed via an implicit license from the city.

Nor were the three pianos which vanished from the Weinman flat – communal property and supposedly protected by law – restored when the cantor returned from Vienna at the start of 1918, even though they were essential for Reb Zvi-Hersch's ongoing work, both as composer and cantor, and as instructor and choir conductor. Two years later, in 1920, Reb Zvi-Hersch Weinman, at the age of 54, passed away in Tarnów from a terminal illness and a broken heart, and who knows if the illness preceded the broken heart or vice versa, or which of the two delivered the death blow. From that time on, the purchase of a piano – an unattainable goal in the circumstances of the times – became Golda's fervent wish, a wish she imparted to her son. Days turned into months and months turned into years and only much later, twenty-five years after Golda's death, was her son able to realize her dream, when he was himself the father of three daughters learning music. What a pity that Golda did not live to see the piano at the home of her granddaughter, Gilatt, in Tel Aviv, and that not only her granddaughter, but also her two great-granddaughters, Yarden and Oran, tinkle on the keyboard; or the piano in Jerusalem at the home of her other granddaughter, Gannit, whose son, Lee-Or, now plays it as well; or the piano acquired also for No'am, daughter of Dahlia, Golda's third granddaughter. With these three, the son hoped to dress the bleeding wound left by the piracy of the three pianos of Zvi-Hersch, his grandfather, during the First World War.

While the lingering grudge Tarnów's Jews nursed against Tertil did not have an adverse effect on their actual attitude to the tramway itself, opposition of another sort to its continued operation gained increasing momentum over the years, and continued to preoccupy the city fathers. The opposition derived from the town treasury, which warned against the tram's financial unfeasibility and pointed to its growing deficit due to the costs involved in the maintenance of the rail and the running of the cars.

Nevertheless, not a single public figure dared – even for the sake of remedying the city's financial situation – to touch this one item that had virtually become Tarnów's commercial symbol. For everyone knew that the real compensation for the budgetary deficit lay in the emotional realm. Witness the tram (so all believed) and witness the Tarnów emblem on its sides: their town was becoming more and more like the great city of Kraków, which boasted a tramway of multiple lines; and so Tarnów, too, would soon be a big city like its sister. Only when the Germans entered Tarnów at the start of the Second World War, was the line stopped and its cars dispatched to Germany. Tramway traffic was never resumed in Tarnów, and probably never will be.

At the end of Lwowska Street, which was also the city exit to the east, and near the Grabówka synagogue, which stood out from the surrounding huts, was the *Remiza*, the end of the line and the tramway's city car barn. And "blessed be He who gives power to the faint" and material fatigue to the rail and cars, so that they require a yearly maintenance check. And how amazing – the town's Jews would chortle with a wink – of all the days in the calendar, it was the Jewish New Year and Yom Kippur that struck the town fathers as the most urgent dates for repairs, and they announced a shut-down of the tram service and the removal of the cars to the car barn for upkeep duties. So that even though camouflaged by technical reasons, the annual cessation of the tram service during the Jewish High Holidays provided Jewish Tarnów with some cause for poor man's joy, a minute crumb of gratification that the city was ready to throw to her Jewish residents in silent acknowledgment of their relative weight in the tram's clientèle and their share in the city's income.

4

The *lokh* through whose dark outlet the son chose to be deposited at 16 Lwowska Street had three virtues: it enabled access from the Jewish neighborhood to Rotenberg's Tavern (while the tavern's real customers, the *goyim*, entered it from the Lwowska side); it provided entry to Feivel Blazer's leather shop, which catered to Jews and non-Jews alike; and it spewed out pedestrians straight into the heart of Lwowska Street, near the entrance to Grabówka.

And all this to the chagrin of the town fathers, full of power and self-importance, the soles of whose feet had never ever been defiled by the miasma of the Jewish alleyways, and who had nevertheless decided that no self-respecting town should have even a single, solitary, out-of-the-way lane without a designative street-sign. As a result, in their ignorance, they named this *lokh Ulica Zamknięta*

(The Shut Street), and fashioned an appropriate sign at its corner; even though every Jewish boy knew that this was not a street, but a lane, and that the lane was not a dead end, but teeming with life and never shut down. Be that as it may, no one ever paid attention to the signs in any case, and everyone called the alleyways collectively by the Jewish epithet of *pishgesslakh*, meaning, unambiguously and un-euphemistically, Piss Lanes.

These three services, however, were not the site's sole virtues. As is fitting for a Jewish locale, the lane miraculously managed to rise above the reigning filth and set aside a tiny spot for reverence as well – for the *shtibl* of the Boyan Hasidim no less, the followers of the *Rebbe* of Boyan in Bukovina, who were acclaimed as the crème de la crème of Hasidism. Another of the poor street's touted virtues was the lovely Jewish girls it sprouted amidst the rubbish, most notably Eva Leibel, whose name became a byword for beauty and who is well remembered to this day. Eva was the daughter of David Leibel, a teaching colleague of Reb Aazik's at the Baron de Hirsch School, who was careful to spell his name according to Hebrew, rather than Yiddish, orthography and to pronounce it in the Sephardi ultimate-stress pattern, Dahveed. David was a high-ranking member of the Leibel clan, for the strengthening of which his loins gave forth a respectable and durable offering – three male and six female offspring, whom he raised to perfection in the *lokh* of 16 Lwowska.

On the right side, a hop and a skip away from the courtyards of 14 Lwowska and 12 Lwowska, the monotonous click and clack of machines at work began to fill the alleyway – the presses of Engelberg's Print Shop, operating out of quarters in the yard of the Rosenblut building at 10 Lwowska Street. Engelberg's is the largest of the three Jewish printing concerns in town, turning out high-standard publications in the three languages with which Jewish Tarnów is familiar – Polish, Yiddish and Hebrew.

In 1928, Tarnów's Zionist Organization would entrust to

Engelberg its new publication, the *Tygodnik Żydowski* ("The Jewish Weekly"), a Zionist periodical that started out as bilingual – Yiddish and Polish – and ended up only in Polish. From 1933 on, the weekly would also open its doors to the budding literary attempts of Hesiek Wróbel and, in 1934, after Bialik's death, would publish a full Polish version of Bialik's poem *"HaMatmid,"* which the boy, who was 14 at the time, translated from the Hebrew. The periodical would continue to appear until the outbreak of the Second World War, closing only upon the arrival of the advance German force into Tarnów on September 7, 1939.

The metallic rhythm of the printing presses wholly harmonizes with the other sounds streaming out from the same courtyard at 10 Lwowska Street. Despite the distance of two courtyards, the echoing sounds penetrate the *pishgessl*, rolling from one end to another. These are the sounds of Torah study by passionate, black-garbed *yeshiva* students, their voices mounting, hallowed, masking the stench of the lane and the vulgarities and drunkenness pouring out of the tavern, as if the desecration were Esau's but "the voice, the voice of Jacob." In a separate building at the back of the yard, in a flat raised about half a story above the entrance level, the Żabno Hasidim study and worship. They are the followers of Reb Eliezer Unger, the noted *Żabner Rebbe* – scion of a dynasty claiming kinship to Reb Elimelekh of Lezhansk, one of the fathers of Galician Hasidism – and it is he who holds sway in Tarnów, where he has established his "tisch" or table. It was said of Eliezer, that he had been blessed with two legacies: from Reb Naphtuly of Ropczyc, his paternal great-grandfather, he had inherited his erudition, whereas the rabbi of Rozwadów, his maternal grandfather, as well as Reb Moishe Hurvitz, his father's father-in-law, who stemmed from the same small town, had bequeathed to him the poignantly sweet melodies of Rozwadów. And the grace of these two – the erudition and the melodies – drew throngs to his door, with the Hasidim even opening an additional *Żabner shtibl* in the marketplace. There the proprietors of stalls and stores could pray on weekdays without having to miss the market's opening hour and lose out on the early-morning merchandise that the villagers brought to town.

As right as rain, everyone acknowledged that Eliezer of Żabno, who keeps alive the accomplishments of his father, Reb Shulim-Duvid – the first rabbi of the dynasty to move from his native town of Żabno in the northern part of the district of Tarnów to settle in Tarnów proper – is among the most popular folk-rabbis in town. Every Sabbath and holiday, waves of worshipers flock to Lwowska Street: simple folk from Grabówka, in holy company with a handful of learned men whose erudition has not swelled their pride; and when these two groups join the core of veteran Żabno Hasidim, the modest space of the Żabner *Kloyz* is packed to overflowing, so that many of the worshipers have to spill out onto the staircase and even half a story down to the level of the courtyard itself. Nevertheless, by cocking their heads upwards and straining their ears to absorb each and every note of the rabbi's prayer, they, too, on the force of the rabbi's merit, would be privileged to hear a flap of wings – the wings of the Divine Presence spreading in blessing above the heads of the congregation and sheltering them from all evil.

And when the rabbi's voice is heard
The joy of Sabbath and festival descends on all
Joy fantastic, joy ineffable –
Erasing from the heart all boundaries – the joy –
Dismantling all divisions between here and there
Voiding all fences between there and here
Until they are stripped of the mantle of this world.

And then it wraps them all – the joy –
Wraps those who have tasted of its delight
Wraps them in mercy, in the fringed shawl of virtue
Which is wholly Spirit, wholly Soul

And sets on all lips a melody – the joy –
Of the matchless melodies of Rozwadów
The Rozwadów melodies of ancestral legacy.

And the melody, the melody merges with the joy
And the joy, the joy is merged with the melody
Until they are one.

And now it impels – the melodious joy –
Impels their feet to float above the ground
Feet that dance on the course of clouds:
One two three, one two three –
Two steps forward, one step back
And again – two steps forward and one step back
Like the evening breeze
Stirring day-dreaming spikes of ripening corn.

Here, now it commands – the love-thirsty joy –
Commands the dancers to join hands:
Hand in hand
Wrist to wrist
Arm on arm
Shoulder to shoulder
Close, close, like a single body
In the reel.

Here, now it compels – the intoxicated joy –
Compels those present to shut their eyes
Those dark eyes of snuffed light
To shut them tightly, to shut them and wish
In painful addiction, in total self-forgetfulness,
That the hidden light may be rekindled.

At the same time it will sprinkle – the merciful joy –
Dew of cool sweat on feverish brows, breathing life in them.

Here, now, see how it paints – the addictive joy –
A warm blush on pain-etched faces, wrinkled in despair.
And like a blossom it rises – the joy of Sabbath and festival –
And blooms like a rose on their pallid cheeks
And, like Aaron's staff, every organ will bloom along with it
Every bone of the earthly body of dancers
A body that has become Soul.

And in this body-less state the joy will grow inside them
And swell sevenfold, and increase seventy-fold
In its devotion to *the One, none so unique*
Who has no bodily form, and is not a body
And who is infinite in His unity.

And stunned by the force of the song – the singing joy –
And drunk on the wine of dance to the limits, the limits
It will be consumed in its own fire – the blazing joy –
And the ashes of its consumption, finely-finely ground
Will be strewn over the aromatic flowerbeds of Hasidic souls.

5

It may be safely assumed that the most passionate adherents of the Hasidic dynasty which kept alive the Żabno name issued from the ranks of Żabno's poor, and that it was not monetary honoraria or their equivalents that they offered up to their *rebbe*, as was customary, but rather their naked, simple, stinging poverty. These followers, whether Żabnoites by birth or marriage to pious daughters of Żabner Hasidim, displayed an unreserved loyalty to their *rebbe*. Day in, day out, with ready heart and closed eyes, they followed their leader, both while he still lived in his native town and when he decided to move his "table" to Tarnów. No few of them clung to him, body and soul, tearing themselves away from small and intimate Żabno in spite of predictable, personal and financial obstacles, and removed to the heart of the big city along with their adored *rebbe*.

And just as the *rebbe*, a true *oizer dalim* (helper of the poor), identified with the downcast and hard-pressed – as opposed to those haughty rabbis who rolled in wealth and lorded it over their subjects – so he also served as a trusty mainstay for the women of the town, who struggled under the yoke of their burdens. It is thus hardly surprising that the Żabner *rebbes* earned the undying devotion of the local women. The latter, it seems, who won the hearts of out-of-town, arranged suitors, were able to direct the love of their spouses not only at themselves and at setting up home in their native town but, in most cases, also at their holy *rebbe*, the young men assuming the onus of loyalty to him and his dynasty, as if they themselves had been born in Żabno, like their wives. And when the women received the *rebbe*'s blessing to remove to Tarnów, they did not shrink from the hardships entailed, even if this was a course they had to take on their own, as in the case of widows. Undaunted, they undertook to eke out a living at their new place of residence, despite the added impediment of their widowhood.

So it was with Shayndl Klapholz of Żabno, who had brought her groom from Santz to the *rebbe*'s townlet. And, when the husband died in 1912, she roamed after her *rebbe* to Tarnów along with her six children, the youngest of whom, Monek, was only four years old. The struggle for bread was a daily affair, and even the children had to take an active part in it. Nor were their initial living quarters anything but inauspicious, and Aunt Kornmehl, who owned a large building on the other side of Lwowska Street, is to be commended for having allowed them to occupy one of the three small flats of the residential, barrack-like hut – the *oficyna* – in the courtyard.

And yet, Shayndl considered herself very fortunate for the privilege that had come her way: to live near the saintly *Tzaddik* and under his lustrous aspect. Less than two years after her arrival, however, in the autumn attack of 1914, the Czar's army conquered Tarnów.

Unlike numerous Jews, including the *rebbe*, who immediately departed by train for Vienna, Shayndl tarried and, in the end, was forestalled from leaving by the enemy's bombing of the railway station; thus she and her children were caught in the hands of the Russian conquerors. Only in 1916, a year after the retreat of the Cossaks, did the *rebbe* return to his court in Tarnów and, with him, the light returned to Shayndl's life. From then on, she would again cross Lwowska Street every Sabbath and holiday, walking a mere five minutes to come within the gates of the Żabner *Kloyz* for an hour's prayer and exaltation. And how happy she was when, after a few years, she managed to move from Auntie's cottage to the first floor of 12 Lwowska, drawing physically closer to her *rebbe*'s home. From then on, the balcony of her flat afforded her a view of the courtyard at 10 Lwowska, where her honorable spiritual leader held court, and brought her within earshot of the voices of the *Kloyz* students on weekdays and of the prayer of the *rebbe* himself on the Sabbath and holidays. During this period, one after another, the Klapholz children began to make *aliyah* to Eretz Israel and, like the eldest, who had already immigrated in 1920, Hebraized their surname to Ezioni. In 1934 it was Shayndl's turn to ask for her *rebbe*'s blessing prior to her *aliyah*. The last to immigrate, in 1936, was Monek, the youngest of the boys, who, as Dr. Moshe Ezioni, would, years later, be appointed to Israel's Supreme Court.

In the Meth family as well, the women had the upper hand in preserving the family's loyalty to the Żabno court, despite the allures held out to the younger Żabno males by the courts of other *rebbes*. For – so remembers Zvi Ezrahi, alias Herschl Meth, an outstanding educator at a state-religious high school in Tel Aviv – other well-known Hasidic sects began to beguile the young Meth boys with tales of the miracle work performed by their *rebbes* and called on them to break out of the closed, narrow Żabno circle. Interestingly enough, though Tarnów had no sect the equal in influence of the Santz Hasidism, the Meths were particularly captivated by the romance of the Hasidic dynasty of Bełz, which produced the popular song "*Mein Shteyteleh Belz*" (sung in Polish as well as in Yiddish), and fired the imagination of many. To this day, Ezrahi clearly recalls his exciting, youthful visit to Bełz prior to his *aliyah* in 1937, and his feet remember the feel of the wooden "sidewalks" placed across Bełz's mythological *blotteh*, the impassable mud at the approach to the large building which contained the *yeshiva* and the home of the Belzer *Rebbe*, scion of the renowned Rokeah dynasty.

Nevertheless, as intriguing and exciting as were the forays into other Hasidic worlds, the Żabner *rebbe* would always remain the absolute ruler of Żabner souls and bodies: on weekdays, the Meth males would pray at the small *Żabner shtibl* that opened at the corner of the marketplace, and on the Sabbath and holidays they would walk to the *Żabner Kloyz* at 10 Lwowska. All this because of the allegiance of the women of the family, natives of Żabno: because of Bluma, who had married Yaacov Meth and shown him the way to Żabner Hasidism when he settled in town and, even earlier, because of the grandmother, Ruh'l-Shayndl, who had also been born in Żabno. As far back as the 1870s Ruh'l-Shayndl had succeeded in rooting her husband, Avruhm-Nissn Wasserstrom, in Żabno soil, fastening him to the congregation of followers of the old Żabner *Rebbe*.

She was a valiant woman, Ruh'l-Shayndl, and it was her mind that determined all the decisions affecting the Meth household. At the close of the nineteenth century, Grandma and Grandpa Wasserstrom made *aliyah* to Eretz Israel in order to cherish the soil of the Holy City of Safed and inhale the very same air that, in the sixteenth century, had been inhaled by the master *kabbalist*, the holy Ari. But then came the First World War and the death throes of the Turkish regime in the land: persecution, expulsions, hunger. And when Avruhm-Nissn died of hunger and was buried in the ground of holy Safed, Ruh'l-Shayndl cast a glance about her and vowed not to end up like the old widows of Safed who lived out their lives alone amid the tombstones facing Mount Miron. Far better, once the war abated, to return to Galicia, to be reunited with her daughter and spend her remaining days under the wings of the Żabno *Tzaddik*. So, when the British drove out the Turks from the Holy Land and the sea routes to Europe opened once more, Ruh'l-Shayndl spent the last of her savings on a passage overseas and returned to the bosom of her family in Tarnów, the town to which the *rebbe* had transferred his "table."

The saintly Ruh'l-Shayndl thus spent the last years of her life exactly as she intended: in prayer and purity, the *rebbe*'s blessed proximity anointing her head with the dew of tranquility. And just as she was blessed at the end of her days with a life of holiness and grace, so she was fortunate that her passing from this life was also marked by holiness and grace.

On one of the last nights of Elul that herald autumn, while listening, at the women's section of the Żabno *Kloyz,* to the tune of *seliches* (Penitential Prayers) from the *rebbe*'s holy lips, a vein burst in her brain. A few weeks later, without regaining consciousness, she departed to paradise and was laid to rest in Tarnów's cemetery. No one heard her last words and no one knows which level of Hasidic *hislahavis* (enthusiasm) she had attained for her blood to swell so and burst its vessels. Only this was related after her death: that a smile of happiness never left her lips during the entire time she lay in a coma, adding a delight and softness to her face which had suddenly shrunk and was like that of a small, innocent Żabno girl with her whole future before her. There were those who expressed surprise at the smile, for the saintly woman could surely now expect her bones to "roll in her grave" on the way to the Resurrection in Eretz Israel when the Messiah came to Mount Olives where the dead would rise. And it was well known that "for *Tzaddikim,* 'rolling' was a sorry affair"; whereas, had she not returned to Europe, she could have been spared the 'rolling' and been buried alongside her husband in Eretz Israel, which, the Sages have already said, is like "being buried under the Altar." As against these, however, others said that the smile came to her by the grace of the *rebbe* and by virtue of her unswerving loyalty to him, to the extent that she had even abandoned the commandment of settling in Eretz Israel, and because of him, chose Żabno and Tarnów over Safed. But, perhaps, both were wrong. Perhaps the saintly woman's smile conveyed her sense that she had enjoyed the best of both worlds: basking in the splendor of the *rebbe*'s face and pure prayer, and having also cherished the soil of Safed in former times. For once the dust of Safed adheres to one's sandals, it can never be removed and counts as if one has ever after continued to dwell in Eretz Israel.

The Żabner *rebbe*'s following also included Pesseleh, Haim Schiffer's mother, the leader of the women's section at the Grabówka synagogue. Despite her great sense of responsibility, Pesseleh, during the Days of Awe, would leave the companions who relied on her guidance and, escorted by her son, walk the long and wearying way up Lwowska Street to the Żabno *rebbe,* to hear the mellifluous Rozwadów melodies that had been part of her childhood. This the widow did every year, praying in her heart that, by virtue of her *rebbe*'s melodies, the gates of heaven would open and her song, too, would reach the ears of the King of Kings. At that moment, the voice of her late husband would also be heard from the Garden of Eden, and the prayer of both would rise on the wings of the Rozwadów melodies, soaring to His glorious throne, blessed be He. May it be God's will.

Haim Schiffer, unfortunately, could never observe the biblical commandment of honoring the father he had never known, for the latter had quit this world when Haim was only a year old. He was therefore doubly careful to observe the commandment of honoring his mother: thus, he props her up as she puffs and pants up the road to the *rebbe's* courtyard on the morning of *Rosh HaShana*, the Jewish New Year, lugging a folding chair for her to sit on. When they arrive at 10 Lwowska, he takes pains to seat her next to the women, at a spot from which she can hear the prayers and the singing and, perhaps, even maneuver into her line of vision the tip of the *rebbe's spodik* (tall fur hat). After assuring himself of his mother's comfort, Haim quickly takes his leave of both her and the Hasidic world in the courtyard to sprint across Lwowska Street. Thus, he ostensibly cuts himself off from one domain and lands in another – on the wide football field behind the Bund House, near the Grabówka junction.

The band of boys he meets will have already been there for some time. And while Haim joins in the drill of kicking the *szma-ciok* (the home-made rag football), his ears apprehend, through the open windows of the Bund auditorium, snatches of a fiery speech by a Bund cultural activist, who, as he does every year, is now, too, giving a talk on "The Jewish Socialist's Attitude to Religion." The flocks of people filling the *Kloyzes*, *shtiblakh*, *minyunim* and synagogues at this very moment are (in the speaker's view) "evidence that religion is the opium of the masses." Hearing the murmurs of sympathetic reaction spilling through the windows, Haim has the impression that the audience – who, most probably would not have come to the meeting on this particular day if they did not, to begin with, agree with the speaker – are openly enjoying the snide remarks and disparaging references to one or another thinker, cited by the word-wizard to back up his assertions. Haim, too, avidly absorbs his words: for this afternoon, like every Sabbath and holiday, he will go to the HaShomer HaTza'ir movement "local," where the weekly group discussion, it may be expected, will also be devoted to the place of religion in our lives – and he would like to be able to quote from the material now reaching his ears. Yet, he feels no contradiction between his firm opinion on religion and the fact that he has just delivered his mother to the *rebbe's* court, or that, after prayers, he will go back there again to escort his mother home in dignity. For the two – religion and rebellion against religion – stride in inexorable co-existence through the streets of Tarnów, a co-existence whose architect was life itself.

6

The Żabno women, though they succeeded in molding the hearts and loyalty of their grooms to the local Hasidic dynasty, were not the chief mainstays of Żabno Hasidism. To the same extent, the movement was a magnet for men, drawn to it for the very same reasons that made it popular with the women. Both were swept up by its warm, folksy nature and its simple manners; both drew strength from the ease of its innocent faith, which understood human woes and weaknesses and did not make excessive demands; both felt *heimisch*, at home, with its basic equality and the fact that it was a small, modest, local product, like the "kindly, good neighbor around the corner," with whom there was no need for either pretence or secrets.

Such ease brought with it devotion: to the *rebbe* himself, to each member of his household, to his adherents wherever they might be, and to the earthly needs of the movement. This devotion, which encompasses everything and resolves everything, was best embodied by the figure of Reb Itche, whose full name was Reb Yitzhak-Wolf Hirschhorn. From the last quarter of the nineteenth century, when he was still in his teens, Itche, the youth, became very close to Shulim-Duvid, the prodigy-son of Reb Yaacov-Yitzhak Unger, rabbi of Żabno. As a new groom, Shulim-Duvid lived in Rozwadów at the time, boarding (or eating *kest*), as was customary, with his father-in-law, Reb Moishe, and Itche was always near at hand to see to his needs. And when the rabbi's son returned to his town with his wife, Itche, too, settled nearby, continuing to act as the young couple's steadfast steward and even marrying one of the local girls. In any case, when Shulim-Duvid inherited his father's court and his personal endowments led him to break out of the confines of the small town and increase the stature and drawing power of Żabno Hasidism many times over, Itche's status became more powerful as well: from personal assistant to the *rebbe*, he became the prime figure in building up the movement.

Upon the Russian invasion into West-Galicia in the fall of 1914, Reb Shulim-Duvid and his family fled to Vienna, as did many of the Jews of Tarnów and, quite naturally, Itche also moved there with his household, bearing the brunt of the refugee hardships of both families. After they returned from exile, Itche again settled near his *rebbe* in the city of Tarnów, rehabilitating and reorganizing the *rebbe*'s court and confronting the new difficulties and challenges engendered by the war. These included the collapse of the economic and financial systems as a direct result of the dissolution of the Habsburg empire and the severance of Galicia from Vienna; and the recurring manifestations of fanatic Polish nationalism and violent anti-Semitic outbursts, which also reached Tarnów.

Reb Itche's loyalty and self-sacrifice towards his *rebbe* were a model to the community and a cause for admiration, especially as it was obvious that, despite his being the general factotum and overseer in the *rebbe*'s home, his personal lot did not improve at all, and the meager living he eked out for his family dealt them a life of wretched poverty. In order to be within urgent call of the *rebbe*'s household through all hours of the day, Itche set up home in the Kornmehl building opposite the *rebbe*'s residence, in one of the three, tiny *oficyna* flats in the yard: alongside Shayndl Klapholz and her sons, and next to the Fuss family, whose eldest son, Aharon, was, like Monek Klapholz, to become one of the leaders of the *HaShomer HaTza'ir* youth movement in town and, in time, also like Monek, would study law at the Jagiellonian University in Kraków.

Apart from the general respect in which Reb Itche was held

because of his success as the *rebbe*'s personal *gabbai*, legends spread from ear to ear about the measures he took to safeguard the *rebbe*'s physical health and peace of mind, so that the latter could continue to compose his written works undisturbed. Thus, it was also told, whether with a wink or a great deal of unconcealed excitement, that Itche did not even shy away from deception, or withheld the truth on occasion, in order to cover for one of the *rebbe*'s sons who may have faltered; not because he agreed with the son's wayward conduct or supported his actions, but because he saw it as his duty to spare the *rebbe* all possible anguish that might be caused by his sons' misdeeds.

Indeed, while working to ensure the continuity of the Żabno dynasty and supervising the comportment of Eliezer, Reb Shulim-Duvid's eldest son, in preparation for the role he was to assume in the future, Itche had to think sharp and dream up stratagems of disguise almost every day so as to keep from the *rebbe*-father the actions of his two younger sons. These two, each in his own way and to one degree or another, had stepped out and strayed beyond the hallowed Żabno tradition. The middle son ostensibly remained within the realm of traditional scholarship, indistinguishable in dress or manners from anyone who entered the *rebbe*'s home; but in his heart of hearts he yearned to pursue a road beyond the Talmud issues trodden by every young *avrekh* in the Żabno *Kloyz*. In his mind's eyes, he saw himself plumbing the depths of Jewish thought of the sages of the Middle Ages, and first and foremost, of Maimonides, the Rambam. Dabbling in philosophy, however, was forbidden by long-standing bans, and in Żabno circles, as in the other Hasidic courts of Tarnów, was considered unthinkable; in any case, the *Kloyzes* had neither the books nor the teachers to satisfy the extraordinary intellectual curiosity of the *rebbe*'s son, who groped in the dark.

At that time, not far from the *rebbe*'s home, in the flat of high-school pupil Monek Lezer at Lwowska 15, Reb Aazik, Monek's

teacher, would, in addition to his regular *Gemara* lessons, devote one evening a week to studying Maimonides' *Guide for the
Perplexed*. And, how remarkable: even though Reb Aazik was an
avowed *misnaggid* and ostracized by the Hasidim, the *rebbe*'s son
began to slip away from his Hasidic study group, run across the
street between Lwowska 10 and Lwowska 15, and creep into the
Lezer flat in order to listen to Maimonides' words as explicated
by Reb Aazik to Monek (who, in later years, as Dr. Moshe Lezer,
would be the director of Haifa's central hospital which – even more
remarkably – would be called Rambam Hospital). "Reb Itche, on
such nights," old Dr. Lezer would tell Reb Aazik's son, "could only
say 'amen,' however reluctantly, and make up a proper excuse for
the son's absence."

Itche's snags in covering up for the second son, whose behavior
remained nevertheless anchored to the Orthodox religious world,
were nothing as compared with his trials in disguising the path
of the third son. The latter succumbed to *Haskala* (the Hebrew
Enlightenment movement) and was caught up by the socialist-
Zionism of the leftist Po'alei Zion Party, and who knows whether
the *gabbai* would have been able to keep the knowledge from the
rebbe had not the latter, Shulim-Duvid, fallen ill and been taken
for treatment to Vienna, where he passed away. At exactly this time,
the youngest son joined the pioneers of the Third Aliyah and, with
typical Hasidic ecstasy, immigrated to Eretz Israel, where he added
both his brawn and his intellectual prowess to the endeavors and
soul-searching of the *Gdud HaAvoda* labor squads. Before that, at a
suitable distance from home, he had shaved off his beard, snipped
off his side-locks, removed the hat from his head, and traded his
traditional garb for the blue working trousers of a pioneer and for
a Russian *rubashka*.

Despite his departure and renunciation of ancestral tradition,
the *rebbe*'s son never lost sight of the picture of his father's home.
Over the years, upon the evaporation of the pure socialist "end

of days" vision that the *Gdud* sought to realize in Eretz Israel, its adherents again went into exile to repair the world: some back to the Soviet Union, which from afar looked like a lighthouse of glad tidings, and some (including the *rebbe*'s pioneer son) to America, the *goldeneh medineh* (golden land). It was then that the rebel was suddenly filled with longing for the East-European Hasidic experience and began to publish nostalgic pieces in the American-Yiddish press, which were later expanded into books. At the same time, the *rebbe*'s son stuck to his rebellion and, remaining estranged from the Hasidic rabbinical affectations of lineage, would sign his name plainly and democratically: Menashe Unger.

Amid the schizophrenic immigrant society of New York, Menashe resumed his ties with old friends and acquaintances who had reached American shores from Tarnów, and especially with poet-artist Ben-Zion, Golda's brother, whose father's cantorial tunes Menashe had so preferred over the Rozwadów melodies, that he had used to steal away from 10 Lwowska to the "Great Synagogue." In their youth, the two friends would climb up Mount St. Marcin together and dream: Ben-Zion would read out his initial stabs at poetry, while Menashe would outline the blueprint for a new world in whose construction he would take part…

Aazik and Golda's son, in fact, met Menashe Unger at the handsome New York home of Ben-Zion and his wife, Lillian, and gleaned from his memory crumbs about his father, Shulim-Duvid, and his father's court. Menashe had kept a particularly warm spot in his heart for the *gabbai*, Itche, who, after the *rebbe*'s death, continued to protect the *rebbetzin* (*rebbe*'s wife) from foreseeable distress by entering into a variety of ruses to keep from her all information about the secular life-style of her youngest son. Illustrating Itche's maneuvers with an anecdote (that he later published), Menashe described a trip he made from the United States to Galicia in the Thirties: conscious of his secular appearance, he, with Itche's silent consent, pasted a beard onto his chin and attached false side-locks to the *yarmulke* on his head, and only after he passed muster under the discerning eye of the *gabbai* (who even straightened the *yarmulke* to make the side-locks fall near his ears), was he ushered in, in borrowed black garments, to the *rebbetzin*'s room. The Lord be praised! Like the eyes of Isaac the Patriarch, which had grown dim over time, so the eyes of the Żabno mother had dimmed with age and the ruse went undiscovered.

The eldest son, Eliezer, had to assume the yoke of rabbinical leadership as his father, Shulim-Duvid lay dying, and it was left to Itche, his right-hand man, to initiate him into the fine points of his role. When Shulim-Duvid's coffin arrived from Vienna in Tarnów, a long convoy of wagons and *fiacres* accompanied the *Tzaddik* on his final journey to the tomb of his forefathers in his native little town. Could any of his followers forecast at that time that Shulim-Duvid would be the last of the Żabno *rebbes* to be buried in the ancestral graveside, while his funeral cortege, along with Itche, his *gabbai*, and his son, the heir to his seat, would perish in the worst holocaust Jewry has ever experienced, and be denied a Jewish burial?

7

The tolerance Itche reserved for the *rebbe*'s sons in his charge was not duplicated in his attitude towards his own children. In grinding poverty, compounded by a premature widower's estate, the father strove to instill in his two sons the values that had always lit his path, with one son bringing him gratification and the other feeding him on bitterness. The first emulated the father in all his ways: God-fearing and a Hasid, twirling his side-locks, growing his beard, and joyfully accepting the responsibility of Torah and Hasidism; while the other, whose friends called him Alu, is remembered by Dr. Lezer, a high-school pupil at the time, as one who wore the *hallat* of a *yeshiva avrekh* and the wide-brimmed hat of a Hasid, but liked to retire behind the building to the rat-infested garbage mound where

Lezer taught him Polish – at his own request, of course, and without his father having an inkling of the dire heresy being committed.

"Alu defied his father and quarreled with him all the time," says Tulek Fuss, Aharon's younger brother, who lived in the same barrack-like quarters and after the Holocaust made *aliyah* to Israel. The echo of the arguments would reverberate through the thin walls and Alu's friends would lend an anxious ear as they closely monitored his battles.

The quarrels were followed by several instances where he ran away from home, and though neither the father nor the friends knew where Alu disappeared to, amazingly enough he found a secret refuge only a few steps away, at the home of Toibeh Fast, a deaf old woman who sat at the window opposite, mending furs. In the end, Alu helped himself to some of his father's cash and vanished.

Little wonder, then, that Lwowska's intellectuals were stunned in 1932 when they got hold of an issue of *Wiadomości Literackie* ("Literary News") with a photograph of an unknown Polish writer, Adolf Rudnicki, and a favorable review of his first work, whose title – *Szczury* ("Rats") – conjured up sights that were only too well known to the denizens of Lwowska and Grabówka. The eminent critic, Karol Irzykowski, prophesied that the new author, now only at the start of the road, would occupy a place of honor at the forefront of Poland's new literature. A mere glimpse at the photograph – the former neighbor, Klapholz-Ezioni, recalls – was enough to assure him and the other young people of Lwowska that the unknown star which had suddenly stepped onto Poland's skies was none other than the Żabno *gabbai*'s lost son, who had sought to erase himself and his original name from the skies of his town and, cloaking himself in a new identity, bounded into a world that was foreign to his father and his *rebbe*. Only then did the friends realize that the battle they had witnessed on the other side of the walls, at the miserable *oficyna* near the entrance to Grabówka, was not merely personal or the result of a generation gap, but a clash of cultures and world views that apparently could not dwell together under the same roof.

Irzykowski, the seasoned critic, was proved right in his discerning assessment. The talents of the young author did not disappoint, nor did the autumn of his years disgrace his springtime. Moreover, despite his rebellion and notwithstanding the borrowed Polish name, Alu remained true to his roots, for better or for worse. For worse – because traces of the miserable surroundings of his home in Tarnów, and the shadow of the strict father and doorkeeper of Żabno Hasidism never left him, and they are implicit in his works so that no Jewish Tarnowite reader can fail to spot or decode them. And for better – because his survival of the Holocaust marked a turning point in his views and works. Even though he was numbered among the top contemporary Polish writers, positioned at the forefront of a new literary current, *Kuźnica* ("The Forge"), the post-war Rudnicki rose and publicly declared himself to be a *Jewish* writer, a Jew who writes in Polish. Thus, he stayed on for some years after the Holocaust in the new Poland, so as not to allow Polish society to shirk the role it had played in the Holocaust of its Jews. And even though he himself had in his youth traveled far from the world of his forefathers, he never stopped demanding from the Poles a show of remorse for the Żabno-Tarnów home and world that had been destroyed.

After Shulim-Duvid's death, Rudnicki's father, Reb Itche, spent another twenty years in service to Eliezer, the *rebbe* whom he had raised from childhood, glorifying his name and the name of Żabno Hasidism as a whole. And just as the two never parted in life, so they did not part in death. On November 9, 1939, when the die was cast and the Germans set fire to all the Jewish prayer houses in Tarnów, an end was put also to all the ten Hasidic courts that stirred hearts in and around Lwowska Street, including the Żabno court. In the following months, preparing for the final extermination, the conquering regime uprooted the Jews from the small towns in the district, including the Jews of Żabno, and shipped them off to Tarnów.

The Żabno Hasidim, while aware of the strength and forbearance they derived from their *rebbe's* mere presence among them in times of woe, nevertheless urged him to flee underground into a bunker they had prepared for him in Żabno. A bunker in a town whose Jews were all gone – it was argued by people in the know – held out good chances of survival. But the *rebbe* refused to abandon his Tarnów flock. Just as he had lived purely, so he would die purely. Unlike the celebrated, powerful *rebbe*s of Bełz and the Satmer Hasidim, for example, or the great leader of the Lithuanian *misnagdim*, who, despite their vigorous preaching against departure, turned their backs on their obedient communities and ran for their own lives, some even leaving their wives and children behind – Eliezer Unger remained true to his past. He personally endured the catastrophe of Nazi bondage and extermination, and his soul was forever joined in eternal life with the martyrs of Tarnów and Żabno. His fate was shared by his kinsmen and colleagues, the other popular *rebbe*s who dwelt among their people in Tarnów – Leyzer Hurvitz, the *Grodzisker Rebbe*, and Alterl Hurvitz, the *Dzikover Rebbe*. The suffering and murder of these three *Tzaddikim* in Tarnów is documented in the memorial book, *Sefer HaKedoshim*, composed in New York by Menashe Unger, the youngest son of Reb Shulim-Duvid – the last of the *rebbe*s buried in Żabno – and a brother of Eliezer, the first of the slaughtered Tarnów *rebbe*s, the site of whose murder is unmarked. Just as, in his early writings, Menashe described the deeds of the *rebbe*s in life, so he devoted his remaining years to collecting evidence of their valor facing death.

While Eliezer Unger, the Hasidic *rebbe* of 10 Lwowska Street, was being sacrificed on the nation's altar, and his brother, in the land of the free, would only many years later finish documenting the extermination of the *rebbe*s in the Holocaust of Tarnów, another

Eliezer Unger would arrive in Eretz Israel. He was the son of the man known as Srul-Yossl Unger (uncle to the Lwowska brothers), who had set up a Żabno court of his own on Tarnów's Bernardine Street, at the foot of Central Square. Eliezer arrived in Jerusalem at the height of the Holocaust, an ember that had bolted the conflagration, bringing hair-raising testimony: the first live details of the atrocities he had suffered personally and from which he had escaped by the skin of his teeth. This report from hell shocked the Jewish community in Palestine but was all too soon drowned in a sea of verbiage and forgotten. The small community of Jewish settlers in Eretz Israel was, perhaps, too immersed in its own worries for the safety of its home under the looming threat of the Nazi invasion of Egypt or, maybe simply unable to grasp the unprecedented horror of total extermination. Ah, how sad that the earliest testimony of the Tarnów survivor did not rock the Jewish community in Eretz Israel as it should have, given the magnitude of the disaster…

8

"What a marvelous sight," Aazik reflected out loud, surveying the disgustingly filthy lane and simultaneously absorbing both the drunken bellows from the dirty tavern and the tune of *Gemara* from the Żabno *Kloyz,* along with the clacking of Engelberg's printing presses which are busily stamping holy Hebrew letters on large sheets of paper. "How marvelous a vision: the Divine Presence itself has spread her wings next to the Devil's camp to shelter her holy lambs and, while pure and impure enter side by side through the very same gate, each is a self-contained kingdom without any contact between the two."

This time, however, unlike his usually eager attentiveness, the boy both attends and does not attend to his father's words, not really catching his drift and certainly not the meaning of his florid formulation. An unbridled instinct, which he cannot even explain to himself, draws his eyes into the space of the tavern's dark interior; except that, despite his efforts and curiosity, his eyes see nothing apart from the ungainly shapes of unidentified heads that seem to be floating on waves of fog.

While still wondering at the puzzling, unreasonable sight – a wave of fog indoors!? – his nose tells him that it is not fog at all, but the cloud of an eternal stink that always hangs over the room. Mixed together in the musky cloud are the vapors of cheap wine and liquor from a dubious source, and the unsavory foam of measly beer combined with the tangy smell of *machorka* (the cheap tobacco peasants rolled in thin pieces of paper, sealing the paper with spit and smoking the product like cigarettes). This, however, is not the whole story of the unique fog of home spun odors, which never leaves the air of the dozens of taverns lodged in the lanes of Grabówka and around the lower marketplace, the Burek. On busy market days, the malodorous cloud thickens, sours and sharpens, enveloped by layers and layers of the outdoor scents that the peasants bring to town with them from the country – a close-knit weave of horse droppings, stench of pigs, dung of cows and the excrement of small cattle, the reek of urine and garbage and the air of stables and barns and pens and coops, of tar and rubbing fats for harness, belt and boots, the fetor of damp straw and moldy mattresses – and over and above it all, the stink of human sweat, which blends in with the breath of the many drinkers. Added to this are the burps and hiccups, the upshot of their drinking, which emit nauseating reminders of the cud of *kiełbasa* (the popular Polish sausage) and sauerkraut and lard and onions.

"The smell of *goyim,*" the boy lets out through his teeth as his face contorts with revulsion and an expression of open distaste. Upon hearing the words, the father stops dead in his tracks, like a horse stayed in mid-gallop on its hind legs when its ear is stung by a wasp, and, with a sharp movement, turns his full figure towards the boy. The son raises an innocent gaze to the father's face, overawed by the angry black of his blazing eyes, as if his eyes were black coals ignited by a sudden flame. No, no, these eyes of Father's are not the ones that he likes; he cherishes the ones that are bright and brown, and have a soft look that lights up with the serenity of wisdom and forgiveness. After all, what was there in the four words that he had uttered to madden a calm, reserved man like Father? Wasn't "the smell of *goyim*" said often enough about pork eating or drunkenness – with some disparagement and condescension, though no insult intended? So why should Father be so upset?

"Don't you ever let me hear you speak such slander again, Herschl!" Father thunders, which is so unlike him. Only after a moment does he regain his composure and manage to restore to his voice its soft, melodious tone, even though he continues to treat the subject with the greatest of sternness, stressing his words as would a teacher to a pupil: "Never! Say 'an abominable smell' if you must; or 'a foul odor' if you wish – I agree; but under no circumstances will I allow you to single out people with a specific identity and condemn them as having a characteristic smell. Just imagine the child of a non-Jewish family catching a whiff of our Sabbath dishes, which he is not used to, and turning up his nose to casually remark 'the smell of Jews.' Would you think that right? Would you think that true? Would you like it?"

"But is there no difference between the smells?"

Reb Aazik was too angry to pursue the discussion, particularly as he realized from his son's question that the boy did not really understand what he was getting at. He left off the matter for the moment, cutting the air with a firm downward wave of the hand as if to say, "Drop it. Not now, please. We'll talk about it another time," and continued to stride in silence to the end of the lane. The boy regretted the incident, but did not know how to convey his sense of contrition to his father.

Upon exiting from the dim alley, as if from a tunnel, onto the expanse of the main street, father and son required a few moments to absorb the shock of light delivered by the bare, hot afternoon sun lying in wait for them at the aperture of 16 Lwowska, so that they could adjust to its blinding glare. Blinking, but satisfied, as if they had overcome some unexpected ordeal, they found themselves treading briskly towards the junction and the start of Grabówka on Tarnów's eastern side – as near as a breath yet light years away, as if it were a different planet. To the right of the junction, from the small square that the Jews would call *Holz-Platz* (Wood Square), streets branched off to a series of Jewish institutions: the court or Reb Alterl Hurvitz, the *Dzikover Rebbe*, the modern cubic school building of the *Talmud-Toireh*, the Bund House, the "*Ochronka*" (community orphanage) and the Baron de Hirsch School, which was also known as the *Yavneh* School and was where Reb Aazik taught. Beyond these, a dirt road came into view, which led to Schantzer's flour mill, the Wątok Bridge for *tashlikh*, Starkman's yard of workshops, where the *HaNoar HaZioni* Zionist youth movement would one day take up occupancy, and finally, to Mount St. Marcin.

While the open spaces to the right of Lwowska Street provided the area with a green breath of air, the right, narrow strip along the street itself, going east, sprouted a dense row of homes, factories, stores, workshops and stands, and only way down the slope, near the *Remiza* and the Grabówka Synagogue, did a wide field open up, the *Kapłonówka*. Its expanse had raised generations upon generations of soccer players and once a year hosted the giant tent of the Staniewski Circus with its wagons of animals. A cheeky eastern wind toyed with the distinguished uptown dwellers, delivering the odors of circus-animal piss and droppings straight to the nostrils of the town leaders, and informing them, "The circus has arrived!" And in the still of night, animal howls and roars rise high in the air to strike terror into the whole town. For long weeks, the children reveled in the circus experience, the sweetest of which was the very act of sneaking in without a ticket, while Hesiek, whose parents did not allow him this form of entertainment, was consumed with jealousy and curiosity. Only sixty years later, when he and his wife made a sad trip to Poland, and his tour of Zamość happened to coincide with a visiting circus, whose tent was pitched at the edge of the historic battery, did he permit himself a visit – a late and singular compensation for the circus experience he had missed in his far-off childhood.

As opposed to the variety on the right side of Lwowska Street, the left side opened onto a large, sun-drenched square, formerly known as *Hazer-Platz* (Pig Place), because the square once served as the pig market for the villagers who brought their livestock to town. In the race of progress, however, the site would become the town's first bus station and be known as *Plac Wolności* (Freedom Square). And yet it would have done better to retain its name of old forever, for human swine in the Holocaust were to turn it into a horrific hub of expulsion and carnage, and the blood of Tarnów's Jews still cries out from its soil and will not be silenced.

9

From there on, it was – Grabówka.

The boy, walking anxiously alongside his father in the warm afternoon sun, sensed the unconcealed looks of affection directed at Father from all eyes, looks of respect and admiration, of gratitude and friendship. As they passed through the narrow lanes, to the rhythmic and monotonous sound of clacking sewing machines which – apart from night-time, and apart from the Sabbath and holidays – never cease their activity; and as they peered into the buildings whose doors and windows were wide open to relieve, if only a little, the suffocation prevailing inside during the blazing summer months, Reb Aazik, as was his way, greets each and every worker: the tailors and seamstresses, the cobblers, tanners and milliners, the barbers and laundry men, the wagon drivers and porters.

And they – the tailors and seamstresses, cobblers, tanners and milliners, the barbers and laundry men, the wagon drivers and porters – respond with genuine fondness.

Sometimes, on these outings, Father would learn of the approaching *bar-mitzvah* of one of the workers' sons. And, without even being asked, he would offer to instruct the lad in the ceremony without remuneration – and this, with an innate simplicity and a pure modesty, never making the recipient feel that he were accepting a gift. Or, while chatting with a barber, he might discover that the latter was finding it hard to make ends meet; at which point, Aazik would lower himself into the dipping upholstery of the old barber chair that had seen better days and, without any such prior plan, ask for a "head shave" – that is, a close cropping of the ring of thin short hair that surrounded his huge bald spot – despite the fact that he had received an identical haircut only a week ago in similar, unnecessary circumstances. And should he be in the vicinity around the time of afternoon prayers, he would take the boy into the *Roiteh Shil* (the Red Synagogue) of the porters, wrap his prayer belt around his waist and take his place like one of the porters alongside the strapping congregants – "Look at him, as strong and tall *vi a domb* (as an oak)," the men would whisper and turn their heads – and together with them, he would pray with true intent and devotion.

Strolling amid the shacks and yards, the boy senses that in that one afternoon hour he has learned from his father what ten pages of *Gemara* pressed into his head during a whole week of mornings could not impress upon him – namely, that there is no society, be it the poorest of the poor, that is free of distinctions and divisions, and that even the population of Grabówka, which occupies the bottom of Jewish Tarnów's social ladder, has its own internal differences and rifts, and that below the bottom of every ladder there is always a lower bottom, and that the lowest of the low chose to lodge far away, at the edge of Grabówka, next to the neighborhood synagogue.

Here you will find the always-hungry, decent family of tailors that spawned the mute and exhausted *Shtimme Matl*, whom fate abused no less than did her clientèle, leaving her stuck at the bottom of the ladder of her profession. And right next to them, opposite Rotkopf's bakery, the Blatt family huddles together, the one whose musician offspring managed to lift themselves somewhat above the grayness of their lives. Here is the sewing shop of Itche Haber, all of whose sons and daughters work there from morning to night, and next to it is Kiveh's sewing shop; here, bending over his work is Shloime Korpiel, the tailor, whose mother, Rubinowa, begs for alms, she and her three cohorts controlling the route from Lwowska to Wałowa.

Here now is the workshop of *der lumer Arin* (Aaron, the lame shoemaker); and the single room of the porter of porters, Hiel Ruda, who fathered seven daughters with the help of his wife, Ronia-Rubinowa's niece, who begs along the same route with her aunt and the two others – and two sons, who are porters like their father. Both parents and nine children sleep on the floor of the room, which is sometimes shared with unwanted guests. Indeed, one night (according to Grabówka mythology), a desperate rat appeared – apparently even hungrier than the Rudas who were stretched out on the floor – and bit off the big toe of the youngest boy, Simheh. Nevertheless, the boy grew up to be a man and stands firmly on his two feet, even without a big toe, working as a porter like his father and, as a matter of course, even playing soccer in the uniform of the workers sports club.

Also opposite the synagogue lives *der meshiggener Arin* (Aaron, the mad porter), a porter poor and wretched to the marrow, whom God and man paid a double kindness: God drove him crazy so that he would not grasp the direness of his circumstances, while the *gabbaim* of the neighborhood synagogue, all men of compassion and mercy, married him off to a poor orphan girl when she came of age, collecting a few złotys for them and throwing up a wedding canopy in the dead of night, no doubt to prevent the two miserable persons from seeing each other in the dark, lest they sink into utter despair, God forbid.

The more that time passed from that childhood experience, when the boy went about plumbing the farthest reaches of Grabówka in the company of Father and was exposed to the vivid social mosaic that composed the neighborhood, the more his wonder grew, and as a mature adult he began to ask the complex questions which, as a child, he had not known how to ask. How did it come about? Even if Father's attachment to the neighborhood could be explained by its surprising similarity to his native village, this still did not explain the source of the warm, personal contact that he developed with the residents of the neighborhood. This Torah scholar and prodigy, erudite, sharp-witted and without equal, this enlightened man whose life was flavored by study and in whose eyes the ideal image of Judaism was circumscribed by *lernen* –studying and gaining knowledge – what did he have in common with the residents of this neighborhood, most of whom lacked a basic education? How did he, of all people, pave a path to Grabówka's simplest folk, developing a warm tapestry of relations with them, and how did he, of all people, become the object of a love they requited in double measure?

Now, in old age, with his parents' home gone and Grabówka gone, the son turns back to those faraway days, diligently attempting to join line to line, detail to detail, traces of impressions and snatches of occasional conversations, bundling them all together into a single tale. In summation, he concludes that the tapestry of the extraordinary relationship between his father and the inhabitants of Grabówka was not woven overnight but evolved through many forms and phases before it reached the high level of closeness that he remembers from the Twenties and Thirties. For the first twenty-four years – so the son reconstructs Father's path – from the day that he arrived in Tarnów in 1895 as a fourteen-year-old

lad, until the year of saying the daily *kaddish* at the Grabówka
Synagogue, when he was already a married man of thirty-six, the
proletarian neighborhood at the edge of his adopted city provided
him with food for thought – riveting him with hidden currents
far more numerous than those that met the eye: the neighborhood was so near, so near and structured as a concept, and yet so
off-putting, even frightening, as a life framework. Actually, until
then, despite Aazik's fascination with the neighborhood's parallels
to Wisłok, Grabówka itself – not its alleyways and shacks, but its
people – had remained totally unfamiliar to him. His intellectual
interest, during the small breaks he allowed himself from his preoccupation with *Gemara*, was aroused by the model, rather than
the human experience, by the shell rather than the guts. He perceived the neighborhood as a case study, an instructive diagram of
ages-long, hierarchical habitation, a metaphor for the maze of partitions which both divide and unite the human family, rather than
as a living, breathing body in its own right. Moreover: in observing
the neighborhood, he saw its whole as a single unit, his eyes only
dimly grasping the thousands of living components that made up
the whole – each a riddle, each a self-contained, absorbing book,
each an entire universe.

The turning point came only after the World War, upon the arrival from America of the news of his father's demise in Exeter. Via
his daily walks down Lwowska to the Grabówka Synagoue to recite
kaddish and in his conversations with the people he met on the way,
a unique accord was slowly knit – Reb Aazik's intimate accord with
the neighborhood, with its people, rather than with the block of its
homes and streets alone. And it, the living neighborhood, with its
young and old, its men, women and children, seemed to suddenly
respond to the touch of his hand and open up to him, like a blossom
concealed in a crevice opens to the rays of the sun. The experience
of this living and unexpected encounter was like a revelation to Reb
Aazik – surprising by the very fact of its existence and surprising by

the new face it donned each day – and he longed to know it better and more closely, in all its facets and fine points.

The gist of the new experience was not the discovery of a populace whom cerebral world reformers, with an indulgent wink, would dub *prosteh Yidn* (simple Jews), but an attempt on the part of the observer to break through labels and reach beyond the prejudice that fashioned the general attitude towards them. Indeed, once the labels were shed and the prejudice attached to Grabówka's people as a whole was erased – a prejudice that was a direct object of their poverty and life of dirt, neglect, rough manners and ignorance – in its stead, their true nature was revealed: warm, open folk despite their difference, deeply rooted in Jewish (though not necessarily Zionist) consciousness, endowed with a robust instinct for survival, an intoxicating lust for life, a rare fighting spirit, and a luscious sense of humor, flying in the face of their poverty.

Did Aazik, as he roamed through the neighborhood, moved and excited by his discoveries, cast about for new opportunities to draw nearer these Jews and present them, as they were, to his son, to endear them to him as well? Had he decided, hereafter, not to permit the scholar in him to hide behind the armor of *Gemara* and shun them for their ignorance; nor to permit the Hebrew "savant" in him to uproot them from his heart for their roots in their Yiddish folk heritage; nor to permit the father in him to conceal them from his son – but rather to tutor the son to fully understand and confront the social phenomenon they presented, just as he tutored him to confront a convoluted Talmudic issue?

The son has no doubt that the Grabówka outings sowed his own strong love for manual laborers and that, under their impact – not merely because of ideological preference – the die was cast, with him deciding, at the age of thirteen, to join a pioneering-Zionist worker youth movement. He would choose Gordonia – a movement whose social make-up in Tarnów (as in the other hamlets and towns of Poland and Romania) was mostly simple folk and working class, along with a handful of intellectuals. Enchanted by the figure of Aharon David Gordon, the latter adopted his social-ist – not Marxist – "religion of labor," rather than blindly follow the young elitist locals, who, out of fashionable extremism, and maybe also in order to salve their own conscience, willingly gave them-selves over to the tyranny of leftist doctrines. In the same spirit, after his *aliyah* to Eretz Israel, the son would for years teach at the workers' seminary without recompense, while, at the same time, as a new immigrant and an apparent simple laborer, he earned his bread from grueling work behind a hoe on the few days allotted him by the Histadrut Employment Service. Even when invited, two years later, to join the salaried staff of the official school board, he chose to teach at and run schools for working youth, volunteering his Sabbaths, Bible in hand, to explore Jerusalem and its environs with the youngsters.

And it may well be that, in making his way years later as an his-torian, it would be the memories of Grabówka that would lead him to devote part of his research and teaching to Jewish craftsmen in past generations. *What a paradox*, the son marvels, *that the topics of my scientific work are so far removed, both in themselves and in their interpretative methodology, from Mother's way in history and, this, despite the fact that it was she who first whetted my curiosity for the profession. Not so Father: despite his dismissive-Maimonidean attitude to historical narratives of any shape and form, he exerted, indirectly and unawares, a decisive and lasting influence on the fields and direction of my professional interests.*

How sad that all trace has been eradicated of the fantastic contribution of Jewish craftsmen to Galicia's industrialization on the threshold of modern times. And, ah, how sad that not a ves-tige has remained of the textile and confections center that Jewish entrepreneurs set up in Tarnów with their capital and effort, and founded on Grabówka's Jewish labor force. Both the one and the other, proletarians and capitalists, transformed, amid bitter class struggles, a dormant rural town into a growing, urban center; and woe to both, the one and the other, proletarians and capitalists, that their internal struggles would prove so clearly trivial in 1942 when, as *Jews*, they would be led together to their tragic death.

10

The tavern on the *pishgessl* at 16 Lwowska was packed with villagers at this warm afternoon hour. Earlier, after hawking their wares, they had quickly made the rounds of an assortment of stores: some went into "Plon," the cooperative store of the Popular Farmers Party at the Burek, and came out, proudly carrying a new, shining metal farm implement purchased there; some bought seeds at Weintraub's, the crowded Jewish store in the municipality building; and some, to their disadvantage, stopped at the corner of the street next to a sleight-of-hand con artist offering *"Para-nie-Para,"* an odds-or-evens game for fools, of which there is no shortage at marketplaces. But all would finally end up marching *"do Hany,"* to Hannah's grocery at the Rynek, in the building "under the shaded arches," the ancient *Podcienie.*

Hanna, Queen of the Rynek! Bustling merchant, mother of daughters and mother-in-law of sons-in-law who all worked in her shop, and grandmother of Buziek, a classmate and youth movement peer of Hesiek Wróbel – she ruled the roost as mother, as mother-in-law, as employer, as queen. She, the matriarch of all the male villagers in the district: a compassionate eye that knows them all by name and remembers the names of their wives and children; an attentive ear that hears their heartfelt wishes, while the secrets of their souls are bared before her as before a priest at confession. Yet, unlike the recipients of confession at the Bernardine Church at the foot of the Rynek, she, the Jew, offers her interlocutors practical solutions to their problems rather than penitence by reciting so many more "Pater Nosters." Here now, they have entered her store, burly giants hanging on to her every word as if they were her children and she their mother. And she will sell them coffee and tea and sugar and seeds and salt – the exact amount to the last grain with no need for scales, but with her "sense" that never errs, and which enjoys universal trust.

Laden with their acquisitions, the villagers then rush to the grounds, where they left their *furmankas* (horse carts), to place their purchases on the wagons. Now, free of their loads, they can head for the taverns with a determined step, amid merry male camaraderie. Father and son, on their daily outing, catch sight of them, a band of men approaching Rotenberg's tavern in the *pishgessl*, doubtless so as to join those who have already gained a head-start on them by so many minutes and so many bottles. Together now, round after round, both the early birds and late-comers are ready to down their fill of liquor: leaning on the counter – first round; crowded around bare tables stained with beer and freckled with black burns from the impromptu stubbing-out of cigarettes – second round; third round, fourth, fifth, sixth – until a drunken stupor loses the count.

The fistful of bills held by the husbands (and reluctantly meted out to by knowing wives) is quickly burnt up, along with their intestines, livers, lungs and brains. But they have not had enough yet, and until the last bill they will continue to drown themselves in inebriating drink – with a ravenous resolve, with a sad-nervous resolve, with a resolve which is both enjoyment and despair, both a heartfelt desire and a decree of fate, both a lust for life and a will to die…

The sun gradually abandons its burnishing of the brass orbs that hold the crosses of the Missionary Church's twin spires on the western approach to the city – probably longing to commune with Kraków, prince of its dreams, somewhere beyond the western horizon. A gust of a cool northern wind suddenly gushes in from the area of the "Great Synagogue," converting the alleyway into a corridor, through which it propels its way to Lwowska, somewhat clearing the lane of its stench. In a little while, they will get up – they, who came in here strong and full of vigor and are now in the grips of a pathetic wooliness – and, huddle by huddle, they will make their exit towards the alley. There they will stand in a row, like a well-trained firing squad, their faces to the wall and, as if by command, empty the warm, foamy liquid of their bladders into the repugnant, filthy gutter. Relieved of the pressure by having fired their loads, and semi-sober thanks to the northern breeze, they will begin with faltering, wavering steps to thread their way back to the waiting drays at the nearby *Holz-Platz*. And as they walk, they lean on one another and prop up one another and kiss one another and weep and laugh in turn on one another's shoulder and fill their mouths with the profanities of rowdy, lecherous ditties until their throats are parched…

Near the *furmankas* the women are already cooling their heels, gritting their teeth and delivering a mute curse. With the wisdom of foresight, they have allowed their husbands only a tiny portion of the earnings collected from the sale of their produce, each woman bundling the lion's share into a small pouch which hangs on her chest, hidden away in the cleavage behind the folds of her blouse.

Nor were the women returning to the village empty-handed: they would emerge from Yankel Meth's stand in the Rynek, and Srul Wind's store at Pod Dębem Square, carrying several lengths of floral fabric for a skirt and some white cotton for a blouse; at Weissberg's or Eder's haberdasheries on Wałowa Street they would buy a variety of goods and wool to knit for the coming winter, as well as a bar of scented soap – a rare indulgence and the realization of the simple fancy they had been imagining for several weeks.

When the men arrive at the wagons, a fleeting glance is enough for the women to size up the situation. Registering no surprise, they move into a pre-rehearsed drill. Like soldiers reconstructing battle exercises in circumstances defined as dangerous, they perform all necessary actions efficiently and skillfully, with the faithful, mutual help dictated by the sisterhood of women in woe. With well-trained hands and, as a matter of course, amid double-edged jests and giggles, they fling the husbands – two women per man – onto the wagons, every man to his wagon, and drop them like sacks of potatoes onto the straw pallets behind each wagon seat; within minutes a mighty snoring rises from the belly of the wagons, shaking their sides.

*

At that very moment, with dusk sallying forth from the horizon and creeping towards the weary city, the church spires let loose clusters of pealing chimes, simultaneously vibrating and agitating like the hail of sparks scattered from the friction of the tram shaft against the electric cable above. The bells herald the approach of eventide and vespers, time for the third "Angelus," the reminder of the tidings that an angel brought to an anonymous Jewish woman two thousand years ago. At once, the village women pick up the whip and reins and, to the chorus of a stinging *"viyo,"* urge the horses to start moving down Lwowska Street towards home. At the exit from the city, some distance away from the tram garage and Grabówka's synagogue building, they descend towards the high, roadside crucifix which has stood there for generations, and, without sparing a glance for the figure hung on the crucifix, mechanically cross themselves, once, twice, and more, and with eyes shut murmur *Zdrowaś Maryjo* ("fare thee well, Mary!") – the Polish version of "Ave Maria". For this is the way of Polish Catholicism: the son is affixed to the cross, but the worshipers, especially the women, direct their hearts at his Jewish mother, the black-faced, black-haired, black-eyed queen of Poland who reigns in Częstochowa – a Black Madonna in a land of blue-eyed, fair-haired *shiksas*.

The evening communion with Maria lasts only a moment. Grabówka's nearby synagogue is lit up and the monotonous melody of the *maariv* (evening prayer) spins its filaments around the silence. And while nightfall worshipers genuflect in "*Modim anahnu lakh…*(We give thanks unto Thee)," the village women finish crossing themselves and return to their seats on the wagons. And while the Jewish worshipers "bow and prostrate" themselves in "*Aleinu,*" the closing prayer, the lash of a whip and the terse, firm call of "*viyo!*" can be heard from the front wagon – meaning that the hour is late and one must make haste while the glow of the sun still lingers above the horizon. And all the *furmankas* stir from the spot and glide in single file towards the twilight.

CHAPTER SEVEN

The Wages of Zealotry:
The Neighborhood

1

T HE RASH OF OBSESSIVE SORTIES into Grabówka's byways, which Reb Aazik and his son conducted day after day in the summer of 1925, could not fail to rumble through the community. The interest of friend and foe alike was not specific to Reb Aazik and his son. For there was nothing in this town that escaped the eyes of others, and everyone knew everyone else, especially in the new, eastern part of the city: every woman's nose was trained to whiff what was cooking in her neighbor's cauldron; and every wholesaler calculated who was to be the next unlucky retailer to go bankrupt and no longer to be given merchandise on credit; and everyone knew who prayed where and to which *rebbe* he made a pilgrimage during the Days of Awe; and everyone carefully checked whose son had shed tradition, Heaven forefend, or been ensnared by Zionism, and whose daughter had gone astray or joined the Communists; "and the street has eyes and the walls have ears and there is law and there are judges."

Conversely, it could be presumed that a Jewish scholar whose métier was study would not make a mockery of Torah but "look before he leaps." In consequence, any stroke different from the previous day's, and any step diverging from routine – such as Reb Aazik's recent conduct – gave rise to questions and astonishment amid the various factions in the community, delivering into the dense neighborhood air arrows of idle assumption and conjecture, and of such-and-such interpretations and counter-interpretations.

Indeed, sternly and chidingly, the erudite eyebrows of gallant, self-appointed guardians of communal social order shot up, and eyes schooled in the surveillance of other people's behavior – to make sure that it was actions *leshem shamaim* (for the sake of Heaven) – kept fervent tabs on the two, father and son, who in broad daylight wore out their shoes in Grabówka's scorching road dust and wasted away precious time on the idle pursuit, God forbid, of vain street jabber with the illiterate.

What message – the keepers of the faith at the *Great Kloyz* grumbled in unease – was this reserved man, who did not stand on dignity and generally despised all bombastic pronouncements, transmit by his provocative forays; and this, a decade and a year after having slammed out of *Kloyz*, the first "home" to welcome him, and having joined the *bis-medrash* at Fish Square? Was it not enough that he had embraced the Shydlover rabbi – that heretical *misnaggid* who had found shelter at the *bis-medrash* and from there incited against the *Kloyz* – and invited *him*, of all people, to his wedding and asked him to perform the marriage rites? Now, Reb Aazik was again heaping scorn on the *Kloyz* by striking an unholy alliance with the most complete ignoramuses!

At the same time, people who took a favorable and anxiously sympathetic view of Reb Aazik's grievances in the community arena, and who had always identified with his struggles for more openness, more sensitivity to others and more attention for the weaker segments of society, had nothing but condemnation for the hypocritical attitude of community leaders towards the Torah prodigy who had sprung up in their town.

"Der illui fun Turne (the prodigy of Tarnów)" – see the "big

shots" slap their bellies in self-righteous conceit at the sight of the lad that had landed at the *Kloyz* in 1895, a country bumpkin with a mere trace of Torah and now, thanks to them of course, a distinguished scholar, totally immersed in Talmud and utterly removed from the affairs of the world. Basking in self-importance, they would draw a silver snuff box from the back pocket of their *kapottehs*, take between thumb and forefinger a pinch of the tangy-aromatic, deep-brown substance, and inhaling deeply – with artistic panache – insert it into fillip-seeking nostrils to produce a smug sneeze: how happy the community whose leaders had raised so keen and erudite a Torah scholar as the "prodigy of Tarnów"!

The "prodigy of... Tarnów"? How so? Was he, the Wisłok *yeshiva* student, not a stranger in their town, without home or family; how come *they* claim him as one of their own, when it is common knowledge how shameful their attitude is to refugees or to plain ordinary newcomers, people who have been streaming to their city in swelling numbers? True, some immigrants were considered desirable. Thus, from the middle of the nineteenth century, and especially at the start of the twentieth, Jewish Tarnów became a loadstone for "choice" wandering Jews – starting with the varied range of Hasidic *rebbes*, many of whom moved there from their own towns and set up court in Tarnów; continuing with Hebrew authors and teachers, several of whom were to make a name for themselves in the Jewish world; to wealthy sons who settled there due to marriages made with prosperous, local families and who were supported by Tarnów fathers-in-law according to the custom of *kest*. The latter, after a few years of relatively easy acclimatization, tended to forget their previous status, which was similar to that of other newcomers, as well as the fact that their fathers or grandfathers had not been born in this town, and they, too, began to relate to more recent immigrants as interlopers. For there is no surer way of joining the solid majority than by aping their manners and, like them, showing contempt for the weak; and one can always find someone much weaker than oneself, towards whom it is not difficult to cultivate a sense of superiority.

Alongside the "privileged" desirables, there were also refugees whom the community leaders regarded as a nuisance. Nevertheless, Tarnów's geographical location on the *Kaiser-Weg* and main railway line – the two chief routes of Jewish refugees wandering from east to west – made it necessary for the factotums to either host a way station or serve as a final destination for the less popular elements as well. One class of refugee – the kind that required temporary arrangements – comprised Jews who had fled from Russian territory (especially after the Kishinev pogroms of 1903): stripped of all means, the latter would stop at various stations in Galicia en route to ports of departure from which they hoped to sail for America. Wave by wave, they arrived by train in Tarnów, where they lived out of suitcases and had to be provided with shelter, food, clothing and funds – and, above all, with a warm heart – and be furnished with a train ticket to Kraków, their next stop.

The other type of refugees, who hoped to fully integrate into the community, fell into two groups. One included Jews who, usually without their families, had left behind towns and villages to try to achieve in the developing industrial city of Tarnów not only a sufficient living for their own needs, but a base for a permanent home to which, in time, they would bring over their kin. It was mostly they who worried both the town fathers and the Jewish leaders, for they bloated the town's problem population, adding a new layer of homeless and hungry to the long standing local proletariat that, for years, had huddled together in Grabówka's disgraceful conditions. The second group requiring absorption was composed of *yeshiva* students like the prodigy from Wisłok, prepared to bury themselves alive in the tents of Torah. The Wisłok youth and dreamers like him, who chose Tarnów because of its reputation as a Talmudic wellspring, made the pilgrimage with pockets empty but hearts full of anticipation and faith. Both, the job seekers and the Torah hopefuls, looked to the local Jewish community council; and the cries of both for the most part fell on deaf ears and callous hearts.

"A *fremder* (a stranger), *a pshivlik* (an on-hanger)" – the locals wickedly branded the newcomers, their words intoning derision, rejection and even hostility. Young Aazik, too, on his arrival was marked as "*der Ruteiner*," labeling his origins as predominantly Ukrainian and tagging his spoken Yiddish as Lithuanian-Ukrainian.

The "prodigy of Tarnów"? Blackguards! Did the community fathers really think – whether out of magnificent obtuseness or ignoble hypocrisy – that by attaching the name of their town to the prodigy they wiped out all the want, neglect, loneliness and agony that had been his portion since coming to the city, and continued to be his portion despite the praises sung in his favor? Did they hope that this cheap, verbal ruse absolved them of their duty, without their actually having furnished the youth a warm meal by day and a proper roof over his head by night? Hogwash! It was not the town that ennobled him, but the boy who ennobled the town! True, the lad had known poverty back in his village as well, but village poverty was tolerable, not contemptuous of its victims, whereas in Tarnów Aazik became an expert in the lore of urban poverty, which was immeasurably worse than its rural sister – dastardly, villainous poverty that leaves its victims wallowing not only in want, but in loneliness. Yes, such were the wretched conditions in which Aazik lived for his first nine years in Tarnów.

"Disgraceful!" The Zionist students, organized in Tarnów's Bar-Kokhba circle, challenged both the Orthodox and the assimilationist community establishments, accusing them (without specific reference to Aazik) of ignoring the plight of the refugees and of turning their backs on the supreme precept that "all Israel are responsible for one another." Indeed, as the Zionist movement matured in the first decade of the twentieth century and the concept of "working for the present" and "conquering the Jewish communities" crystallized, the students' energies would be propelled headlong towards a socio-political plan of action that was to revamp consistently the face of the community and its leadership. Alas! These developments came too late to affect the lot of the lonely *yeshiva* student from Wisłok or enable him to forget the suffering, want and physical agonies he had experienced during his initial foothold in Tarnów, when the *Kloyz* served both as a framework for study and a physical scaffold for life, for better or for worse.

Bodily agony was, in time, compounded by mental anguish. The patronage of Reb Moishl, the most outstanding scholar at the *Kloyz*, certainly furnished the student with effective protection, and none of the people who had anything to do with the institution dared to openly take issue with his sponsorship. But this same patronage also spurred the jealousy and xenophobia ever buzzing for receptive ears, and a medley of rumors ever welcomed by vile lips thirsting to publicize them. And so it was. When "the Rutenian" was in his third year in Tarnów, at the age of sixteen-and-a-half, a train of slurs began to trail behind his back, concocted by master zealots and thickening steadily. The watchdogs and hunting dogs of zealous orthodoxy began to bark in menacing unison: "This prodigy, who was dropped into our midst out of nowhere, is not flesh of our flesh but a *misnaggid* planted in the orchard of Tarnów's Hasidism, his learning reeking of the foul odor of a Hebrew Enlightenment devotee – *maskil*."

The situation became even direr after someone testified that he had seen Aazik at a farewell assembly for the first ten emigrants to make *aliyah* to the village of Mahanayim in Eretz Israel. "Obviously, not only the fire of Enlightenment, but also the blaze of Zionism, had licked his *kapotteh*, and the two together singed its edges. One could thus no longer remain silent: "It was time to act for the Lord;

for they have made void Thy Torah," – and the sooner action was taken, the better!

2

The canon of zealotry had issued forth from the *Great Kloyz*. Founded in the nineteenth century, the Tarnów *Kloyz* had been planned as both a central and a unifying institution, serving the Jewish neighborhood's expansion over rural areas annexed to the city. And a central institution it did become, as envisioned by the founders, its influence exceeding the zealous nucleus that gained ascendancy and dominion over it. From the start, the large hall was built both as a synagogue and a *bis-medrash*. At the same time, its appearance, its tables, its walls, were all so ugly and shabby that it seemed to be deliberate – as if the planners, jealous of the well-known formulation in *The Sayings of the Fathers* that warned against wasting time on praising the beauty of "a tree or a plowed field", had rephrased the dictum to warn: "who so studies and interrupts his study to say, 'how fine is this table, how fine this wall,' it is as if he sinned against his own soul."

Here, every Sabbath, a crowd of more than five hundred worshipers assembles, led by all the "*sheineh Yidn*," (the beautiful people), each and every one of them either "community dignitaries" and "high society," on the one hand, or Torah scholars, on the other. Attached to these were the "simple Jews," eager to bask in the warmth of *Yiddishkeit* at least on the Sabbath. The *Kloyz* is packed also on weekdays for evening prayers – especially since the end of 1923 which saw an increase in the number of people who began to stay behind after prayers to peruse "the daily page of Talmud," as suggested that year by Rabbi Meir Schapira: that is, to get through the Talmud in seven years by studying one page of *Gemara* a day. Nevertheless, even *Kloyz* regulars do not regard the institution as their exclusive place of prayer; they also worship (and even serve as cantors, if their voices are pleasing enough) at other major prayer houses and other *minyunim* or *shtiblakh*. Thus, on weekday mornings they recite the *shahris* (morning) prayer in the *Ashkenazi* version at the *bis medrash*, or each man goes off to his own *shtibl*, and at sunset they close the day with the *minhe-maariv* prayer at any available *Ashkenazi minyen*, unless they are studying the daily page of Talmud at the *Kloyz*. But on the eve of the Sabbath and on Sabbath day they all pray with the large congregation at the *Kloyz*, in the *Sephardi* version, as is the custom of Hasidim, and at the close of the Sabbath they usher out the Sabbath Queen with song and dance: with song – to the sweeping melody composed by a Hasidic Tarnów grocer (and destined to become famous the world over as "*Hava Nagila*," though the composer's name and origins are long forgotten); and with dance – either at the *Kloyz* proper, by circling the pulpit arm-in-arm, eyes shut, feet flying, until they are finally deposited onto the plaza in front of the building, or at one of the ten Hasidic courts operating in Tarnów.

The merits of the *Great Kloyz* in the eyes of the town are several-fold: its doors are open day and night, and it remains lit up non-stop, and the melody of *Gemara* embraces the tune of prayer, and both, intertwined, resonate in the space of the hall for twenty-four hours a day. An additional merit is generated by the heating stoves: they work throughout the fall and winter, and while the Maker-of-Wind-and-Downer-of-Rain-and-Snow drives the cold from the Wisła, on the northern border of the District of Tarnów, and sends in frost from the Carpathians in the south, and the two collide midway above the town to deliver a heavy coat of snow and mud onto streets and rooftops, inside the *Kloyz* the atmosphere remains cozy and heartwarming, a tonic for the body and balm for the soul.

And the water kettle on the stove makes the rounds day and night, and the *booheerim*, the *yeshiva* youths, their throats parched from chanting the text, pour themselves hot tea into glass mugs: the tea warming their insides and the glass emitting a pleasant warmth to the palms that cup it. And round and round the stove the town's poor and just plain hangers-on huddle, seeking shelter from the wind, rubbing their frozen hands above the fire, and they too are sometimes even offered a glass of tea by the *booheerim*.

For all that, the young men are governed by iron rules whose violation earns immediate expulsion. A youth, and sometimes a whole class of youths, find themselves expelled from the *Kloyz*, should a "forbidden" book be discovered beneath the *Gemara*, or should the conduct monitors – such as the overseer at the *Kloyz* or *der Roiter Alter* at the bathhouse – catch a young man in the act of "plucking," meaning the attempt to excise a hair from the budding beard on his chin by squeezing it between two coins.

The *Kloyz*, however, is rigid and fanatic with regard to adults as well. Whosoever comes between its gates as a permanent insider quite naturally consents to a whole slew of rules, of "do's" and "don'ts" – including intimate matters. These rules circumscribed one's continued membership in the institution, or the forfeiting of it, and the punishment meted out was presented as divine retribution and therefore not open to appeal. Thus, the *Kloyz* congregation will not tolerate in its midst anyone whose wife does not cover her head with a wig, or whose twin (marriage) beds touch one another, let alone the owners of a double bed, which most certainly and unquestionably deserve to be shunned as "contemptible."

And just as the *Kloyz* people agreed to the restrictions imposed on their private lives, so, too, they accepted the blatantly oligarchic rule that dominated the institution and was reflected in the hall's seating arrangements – especially since a permanent seat was considered a peerless and inestimable asset. Community dignitaries sat around tables placed along the walls – the long tables occupied on weekdays by the *booheerim* studying *Gemara*. At the head of the table sat the rabbi and eminent scholars, flanked along the eastern wall or opposite it by the well-heeled from the entire gamut of Hasidic sects, whether because of wealth (and consequent influence) or because of lineage, and it made little difference which Hasidic *rebbe* earned the admiration of one or another member of the *Kloyz*.

First in order of seating were Aberdam, from the bank; Jakóbowicz, the owner of numerous stone buildings; and Rubin, offspring of that aged matron, Reizl Rubin, who sat at the doorstep of her clothing shop on Szeroka (the Wide Street) like Deborah the Prophetess under the palm tree, managing the affairs of the world at large, while Leizer, her son, and Meilekh Rheinhold, her son-in-law, busied themselves with daily trifles – business negotiations for the sake of a livelihood and *Kloyz* intrigues for the sake of Heaven. After them, sat Wexler, the philanthropist; Engel of the sausages; Getzler, a paper wholesaler and leader of *Mizrahi*, the religious-Zionist movement; Wolf and Burekh, Wexler's sons; and Voftche and Joshe Stiglitz; Unger of the glassware; Jeiger of the feathers; Herzig of the fabrics at the Rynek; and others.

This arrangement, from the close of the second decade of the twentieth century, when the *Kloyz* returned to its routines in the aftermath of the First World War, underwent total alteration in the middle of the third decade, when the seating was shaken up as a result of the economic crisis. The Wexler House lost its assets, and the son, Wolf, a handsome man, well-versed in prayer, who was sometimes called up for cantorial duty, moved (or was moved) to the corner of the table. Engel, the sausage maker, on the other hand, agreed to act as deputy cantor at the *Talmud-Toireh*. His voice, a soft, lyrical tenor, would at such times replace the thunder of the chief cantor, Abish Faust from the grocery, a hefty man with a baby face and a beard half of which was black and the other half white, and a bass voice which, in outright contrast to his soft expression, penetrated to one's innermost parts. The co-opting of Engel to the cantorship at the *Talmud-Toireh* took on added urgency with the appointment of Abish as *gabbai* (beadle) at the Dzikover *Kloyz* in the Jakóbowicz building at *Holzplatz*, at the corner of Grabówka-Lwowska 17.

The Dzikover *Kloyz* venerated the memory of Eliezer Hurvitz, son of the legendary Naphtuli of Ropczyc. Eliezer was the first of the Hurvitzes to settle in Dzików, starting a dynasty there that was named after the town. When the Dzików court moved to Tarnów in the twentieth century, preserving its original name, it came under the great rabbi's great-grandson, Reb Alterl, while other great-grandsons established dynasties of their own. And what a pity that among his many virtues Alterl was not endowed with a singing voice, but had to rely on both regular and occasional prayer leaders; so that Abish, too, often had to leave his post at the *Talmud-Toireh* in the hands of his deputy and speed to his *rebbe's* place of worship, his mouth bearing the gift of a dramatic bass that made Hasidic hearts tremble.

Yom Kippur of 5687 (1926), which fell on a Sabbath, won an eternal place in Jewish-Tarnów mythology and became known as *Abish's Yom Kippur*. The story goes back to a miscalculation on the part of the two regular prayer leaders at the Dzików *Kloyz* who, as always, divided up the holy day's prayer book pages between them. That year, unfortunately, the two cantors lent the prayers a faster and more energetic rhythm. As a result, the afternoon prayers were reached an hour too early, posing a real danger that the day's closing prayer, the *Ne'ila*, would come too soon, long before sunset. Ignominious! In this hour of need, Alterl sent for his beadle at the *Talmud-Toireh* to step into the breach, so as the Yom Kippur fast not be desecrated, God forbid!

Abish surged forth like a lion to the Dzików *Kloyz*, a distance of some hundred paces from the *Talmud-Toireh*, to find a way out of the predicament. His solution hinged on the fact that the day was both Yom Kippur and the Sabbath. Therefore, ignoring the afternoon *minha* prayers that had already been said, Abish began to recite *minha* again, omitting the "*...Impose Thine awe upon all*

Thy works" in the *shminesreh* (the Eighteen Benedictions) of the afternoon Yom Kippur prayers and, instead, briskly launching into the *"Thou art One, and Thy name is One, and who is like unto thy people Israel..."* in the *shminesreh* of the afternoon Sabbath prayers. Thus, in his great wisdom and with the joy of song so stamped in him, Abish bridged the gap in time and swept up the congregation in his joy.

And, wonder of wonders! The fervent melody dissolved the lassitude of the weary fasters and, responding to Abish's vigorous guidance and the vibrations his deep bass voice transmitted to the congregants, a passionate, mighty song erupted from hundreds of Dzikover throats –

"Thou art One/ and Thy name is One/ and who is like unto Thy people/ Israel!" –

– and the melody revolved on its axis, turning, turning, in one round and another, and over and over again, and each round more inspired than the previous one and its beat more fiery, and both rose from sphere to sphere on the ladder of joy, scaling up higher, higher and up, to the Throne of Glory, where He sits, Blessed be He.

And, more wonderful still: through the windows of the Dzików *Kloyz* Abish's *"Thou art One"* made its way down and across Lwowska Street, the street being empty of all conveyance or beast or tram traffic because of the holiness of the day, and the song spread out and swept all the other *Kloyzes* in the area – the Żabner, the Grodzisker, the Boyaner, the Belzer, the three branches of the Bobover, as well as the Santzer and the Pokszywicer – until it smashed against the mighty wall of the "Great Synagogue" which blocked its passage, leaving only one lame echo to crawl laboriously onto Bóżnic Street. Here it was sapped of all strength and, spent, it dropped onto the stairs of the Stutchiner *Kloyz*, the *Kloyz* of the Rabbi of Szczucin, without however ceasing to mumble the tune.

For a split second, the tune rapped at the gates of the Stutchiner *Kloyz* –

"T*hou art One/ and Thy name is One/ and who is like unto Thy people/ Israel!*" – straining, albeit feebly, here, too, to bring the joy of the great day with which Abish managed to animate all the other *Kloyzes*. But in vain. None of the Stutchiner congregants heard the tune's last breath. The tidings of joy, that it sought to transmit to town and *Kloyz*, would have given up their soul on the threshold of the house of God, drowned by the deafening Stutchiner *minha* prayer – had not an unexpected savior suddenly arisen…

3

In the nature of things, absent from the presentation of the *Great Kloyz* in the twenties and thirties were personalities from the previous generation, though even after half a century their names continued to gleam like jewels in the community crown. Several of them still dwelt in town at a ripe old age, their works engraved in letters of gold in the modern mythology of Tarnów Jewry.

These giants had struck Aazik, ever since he had first entered the Tarnów *Kloyz*, as living legends, and he looked to them in holy awe and admiration. At times, he was invited for Sabbath *kiddush* to the home of a wealthy notable. The eyes of the village boy, whose birth and childhood had passed in a shack of bleak dearth, were then opened to a bourgeois standard of living of whose existence he had not known and whose niceties he had certainly never dreamed to share. But plenty, in itself, is no assurance of courage – as Aazik learned from the shaking knees of Zekharye-Mendl Aberdam: though the latter owned many properties, including the building at 1 Goldhammera Street, and though he had founded a bank – the same bank that his son, Avruhm Aberdam, ran after him in the twenties and thirties, so that he too, like his father, sat along the eastern wall of the *Kloyz* – he still lived in fear of the *Kloyz* zealots. Under pressure from them, Aberdam in 1897 had quit his position as treasurer of the society to establish a Galician farming colony in the Galilee and had even withdrawn his membership from the group. Nevertheless, the personal weakness of one individual, however rich, did not dent the respect in which Aazik held the wealthy, nor alter his view as to the twin cornerstones of Jewish society in the past as in the present: the rich and the scholars – they were the pillars supporting the entire edifice.

One of the old-time magnates of Jewish Tarnów in that distant generation was Herschl Wittmayer, an importer of "colonial" spices and fruits and the owner of both a large, stately home on the main square and a seat along the eastern wall of the *Kloyz*. Following on his heels were two ambitious young men – one from afar, the other from an extensive Tarnów family – who advanced with huge strides to occupy powerful positions in the town and community economy. One of these was Reb Eltchi Baron, a private banker and owner of oil wells in Eastern Galicia. Baron arrived in Tarnów to marry Wittmayer's daughter and board with his father-in-law, according to the custom of *kest*. He built his home next to the latter's and lived there until the German invasion. The other, Itche Brandstätter, housed a family of eleven children on an entire floor of the Aberdam building on Goldhammera and, from there, ran a concern that traded in gold, pearls and gems. As long as Tarnów was subject to Austria, the town provided him with a convenient springboard to Vienna, the hub of all commerce in luxuries. When his boys – Avraham, Yaacov and Shmuel – grew up, Itche established branches for them in the capitals of Europe, thereby penetrating the markets to command an unrivaled business empire.

Thanks to their international ties, to their wealth and, very likely, to their personal endowments, the two young moguls, Baron and Brandstätter, rightly enjoyed the respect and even affection of the public at large and soon, by the end of the nineteenth century, each occupied a seat of honor at the eastern wall of the *Great Kloyz* – until a predatory, insatiable, orthodox zealotry got its claws into them, each in turn.

The dizzying rise at the *Kloyz* of "stars" from outside the Santz inner circle was uncommon and uncharacteristic of the normal "changing of the guard" at the institution. The mother of all change at the *Kloyz* was natural rotation, the head of the family passing on his seat to his son by inheritance. This was true of the prosperous Zekharye-Mendl Aberdam – the magnate whom Aazik would not forgive for bowing to the fanatics on the matter of a Galician colony in Eretz Israel – who bequeathed his bank in town (*Towarzystwo Eskontowe*) to his son, Avruhm and, along with it, assured him a place at the eastern wall at the *Kloyz*. And it was equally true of Ephroyim Stiglitz, who handed down his seat to his sons, one of whom, Vofche, in the last decade of the nineteenth century, studied under Reb Moishl Apter. For a year and a half after the appearance of the village boy from Wisłok, Vofche, under instructions from his rabbi, was Aazik's study partner in the daily *lernen* at the *Kloyz*. Years later, Vofche followed his father's example and passed on his seat to his own son, Moishe, who cherished the privileged position until he made *aliyah* to Eretz Israel.

Over a period of many months, prior to his death in Jerusalem, Reb Moishe Stiglitz would meet with Aazik's son and give him a detailed account of affairs at the Tarnów *Kloyz*. In Israel, Moishe's sons with their father's consent Hebraized the family name to "Ariel," and since 1967 their fame as militant rabbis has been bound up with the struggles for a Greater Israel and with Temple research, including the reconstruction of priestly implements and garments in anticipation of the construction of the Third Temple. This zealotry, replanted in the soil of Israel, may well have been absorbed by four generations of Stiglitzes at the Tarnów *Kloyz*, though its objectives have been thoroughly reversed: the new fanaticism became stridently Zionist, in direct contradiction to the *Kloyz* leaders of old, who were avowedly anti-Zionist.

Most of the people at the Tarnów *Kloyz* paralleled, if not in exact detail, such examples of natural rotation. Sometimes, however, time also, took a hand in affairs, sealing the fate of *Kloyz* members and changing the seating arrangements. The watershed in the life of that generation was the First World War. The flight to Vienna in 1914, in face of the Czar's army's advancing on Tarnów, condemned both poor and rich – including the greatest of magnates – to seek refuge in the imperial city, while in their hometown the looting of Jewish property by Poles and Russians alike left a wasteland in its wake. Thus, when rumors of the desolation reached Vienna, one refugee or another, who had prospered in the capital, decided not to return home but to transfer to relatives his only meaningful Tarnów asset that had remained out of reach of the looting *goyim* – his seat at the *Kloyz*.

Gimpel Schnupftabik, who owned many large buildings and was one of Tarnów's main tycoons, acted in this manner. His departure for Vienna in 1914, at the sight of enemy troops poised to conquer the town, placed him at a crossroads and demanded decisions about the future. At the end of the war, Gimpel resolved not to return to Tarnów, the city that had shown no respect for his basic rights and had made free with his possessions, but chose rather to settle in Vienna, the capital, which had smiled on him. At that point, he turned over his seat at the *Kloyz* to his brother-in-law, Hayim-Yoisif Wald, one of the Dzików Hasidim. Wald dealt in pelts from his shop at the Rynek.

Ah, Hayim-Yoisif, that innocent pelt merchant! Not familiar with the community "nobility", whose names and wealth preceded them, he regarded the opportunity presented to him by his wife's brother as a windfall: to sit at the eastern wall with the great men of the world! But he had not reckoned with the raised eyebrows of *Kloyz* zealots, enraged against this new "aristocrat" who dared to sit in sweet gentility next to them, when the misdeeds of his children were an open secret: one of his daughters had strayed into Communism and even stood trial – the Communist movement being banned in Poland at the time and its members operating underground – and three of his grown sons had joined the Zionist *Halutz* organization and planned to leave for Eretz Israel with the Third Aliyah immigration wave. However long was the arm of the *Kloyz* zealots, so was also their patience, and they would pick their time to strike: one day they would lash out at little Wald, just as they would not hesitate to lash out at big magnates, like Baron and Brandstätter, once they decided that they were tainted.

Time took an opposite hand in the affairs of Tarnów's high nabob, Herschl Wittmayer, who, at the head of his family, had fled to Vienna in 1914. Unlike Schnupftabik, who decided to quit Tarnów forever when he heard of the plunder committed by his Polish neighbors, Wittmayer longed for home, come what may. Just as he had been the first to leave, after seeing Russian *kolpaks* at a distance of twenty miles from town, so he was among the first to return when, in mid-1915, the backs of the routed Russians were seen retreating eastward. The Wittmayer couple, moreover, decided to return before the rest of the family in order to restore the home (which, according to rumor had been robbed and perhaps even maliciously vandalized) and prepare the ground for the others. The rumors proved correct. The home had been pillaged and the work of restoration turned out to be arduous, demanding considerably more resources than the elderly couple had anticipated.

At the sight of the ruin dealt them by the war, the Wittmayers had to start from scratch: to breathe new life into the "colonial" fruit and spice trade – the former source of their wealth – even though wartime commerce was fraught with delays and obstacles, and to put things in order in their large home. The interior of the house had suffered most of the damage, and thorough, creative repairs required a huge outlay of funds. But, before the couple could complete the renovations or take pleasure in the rebuilt home and the return of their kin, the afflictions of Job suddenly visited the wife: Herschl was gone! He died in an epidemic that broke out in town and did not differentiate between poor and rich, old and young.

And alas: out of keen eagerness the man had not acted like the seasoned businessman he was but had invested all his capital in the work on the house, so that the widow was now left penniless. Circumstances being what they were, even the sale of her husband's privileged seat at the *Kloyz* did not yield a price that could ensure her a livelihood. Slowly, slowly, hunger began to peer from the eyes of the woman who had fallen from fortune, even as her restored residence continued to gleam in splendor.

The decline of the Wittmayer family, especially the hunger that plagued the lady of the house, greatly moved Aazik's son; his father, who told him the family history, had been attached by ties of love to the two homes on the city square, the Wittmayers' and the Barons' – most particularly to the Barons, which bond was to gain in strength with the years and remain unbroken even in death.

Had it not been for Rosa, that blessed woman, who can say in what state Minna, the daughter, and Eltchi Baron, her husband, would have found the mother and mother-in-law upon returning from Vienna in 1916. Rosa, the orphan, had been embraced by the Wittmayers from childhood and fostered as a daughter, growing up to become the cook in their home until they left Tarnów in apprehension of the war. About a year later, she married Psahye (Ptahya) Blatt, who owned a bakery on Fish Street, and when she saw the desperate straits of her former mistress, she remembered the kindness she had enjoyed at her hands and, every week, stealthily brought her two loaves of bread and a *halleh* for the Sabbath – anonymously, of course, so as not to add insult to injury – thereby saving the matron from the shame of starvation.

4

Apart from the circumstantial changes rooted in the First World War and the period before it, most of the upheavals in the membership at the *Kloyz* were spawned in the contest of conflicting ideologies – ah, the zealotry, the zealotry! Some of these ideologies sprouted in the soil of the nineteenth century, when the *Hibbat Zion* (Love of Zion) movement and the First Aliyah immigration set hearts aquiver; and some sprung up in the *Zeitgeist* of the turn of the century, when a gust of Herzlian Zionism tried to rejuvenate the ossified order of the *Kloyz*. As a result, on countless occasions the *Kloyz* turned into a battleground. Paradoxically, it was its very comprehensive character that fed factional discord, since each group justly regarded the institution as its home.

Alongside the struggles over creed or power, "minor battles" in defense of honor also often broke out at the *Kloyz*. Intolerance and purely arbitrary rule would then hold sway in a variety of fields and heap insult onto insult. Particularly prominent and vicious was the rivalry over being called up to the Torah on the Sabbath. Name-lists were meticulously drawn up by the beadles in charge of Torah reading, Meilekh Rheinhold, Naphtuli-Hersch Irom and Pinhas Templer – spearheads of the militant group – and woe to anyone they wished to slight: there was no end to the baiting and the indignities were legion. Out of respect for both victims and victimizers, and for the institution as a whole, they are better left unmentioned.

The militant group had in fact carried out a coup, holding the Tarnów *Kloyz* hostage, as it were, even though the institution was from the onset meant to be non-partisan and non-factional, and all its members were Hasidim who continued to make individual pilgrimages to their own *rebbes*. The coup was executed by zealots on behalf of the largest and most powerful Hasidic movement in western Galicia, the Santz Hasidim, named after the town of Santz (Nowy Sącz in Polish) to the south of Tarnów. It had been there that Haim Halberstam, the outstanding disciple of the Seer of Lublin and of Naphtuli of Ropczyc, was appointed town rabbi in 1830. For the forty-six years of his reign, until his death at the age of eighty-three, he had built up Santz as the capital of Galician

Hasidism. So complete was the town's identification with its rabbi that the Hebrew spelling of Santz was changed to start with the 'tz' sound of *Tzaddik* – Zans (pronounced Tzans) – as a sign that the generation's holy man dwelt there; and so Jews still call it today.

The sense of power of Zans Hasidism swelled in direct proportion both to the increasing numbers that joined the movement and to the public demonstration of the founding *Tzaddik's* authoritative leadership and that of his heirs, in Zans itself and in the provinces of their realm. This power soon left its stamp on the Tarnów *Kloyz* too, and was translated into a series of acts of aggressive fanaticism. The *balabatim* (property holders), the reasonable and worldly "bourgeoisie," continued, of course, to clothe the *Kloyz* in a dignified mantle of ostensible calm and tolerance, as originally mapped out by the founding fathers; but it was not the stuff of tolerance that the militants had in mind when, by the force of hand and the weight of numbers, they became the local masters. To them, the institution of the *Great Kloyz*, so intrinsically Tarnowian, became first and foremost the bastion of *their* Hasidism, i.e., the Zansian one. Here again, so unchallenged was the identification of the Tarnów *Kloyz* with the Zans' Halberstam family that Zansers and non-Zansers alike commonly referred to it as the *Zanser Kloyz*. Nevertheless, Reb Haim Halberstam did not move to Tarnów, as did many Hasidic *rebbes*, but continued to reign from his court in Zans, as did the *rebbes* who inherited his seat. Only offshoots, led by the *Tzaddik's* grandsons and great-grandsons, found in Tarnów a wide berth for the glorification of Zans.

The *Zanser Kloyz* in Tarnów was ruled by Reb Leibushl Halberstam, grandson of the great *rebbe*. Leibushl guided his flock with love and identified so unequivocally with his Tarnów followers that he was sometimes called Reb Leibushl *Turner*: the Tarnowian. At the start of the twenties, however, he left the scene in mysterious circumstances which for generations the Zanser leaders adjured their adherents not to divulge, and which remained hushed, whether

in fright or in deference to the *rebbe's* good name. And so it remains
to this day – in Brooklyn and Bnei Brak, in Jerusalem and all over
Israel and the Diaspora – wherever Zanser Hasidim dwell.

All queries on the matter to those "in the know" went unan-
swered and, in place of a response, came elusive hints and heavenward eye rolling; still, those intimate with the codes of insider
talk at the *rebbe's* court were persuaded that the disappearance
of Reb Leibushl from Tarnów was connected to worrisome signs
that had manifested themselves in the *rebbe's* conduct and in the
decision of his inner circle to hospitalize him under expert care at
a suitable institution in the big city. To corroborate the presump-
tion of insanity, there were those who pointed to the widespread
marriages among blood relatives concluded within the Halberstam
clan. Not, God forbid, incest, but most likely marriages arranged
out of a desire to keep the full Halberstam potency to themselves.
People also took note of the fact that one of the *rebbe's* daughters
was emotionally disturbed. Some people even recalled that, from
the first, the grandson of the great Zanser *rebbe* had shrunk from
assuming the burden of leadership and, clearly, no sane person flees
from his mission and honors.

The secret was closely guarded for more than sixty years by
eyewitness Moshe Wald (later, Hebraized to "Yaari" in Jerusalem),
for fear of violating the decree of the Zans *gabbaim* not to disclose
the reasons behind the *rebbe's* disappearance. Moshe was ten years
old on that Sabbath of 1924 when he accompanied his father to the
Kloyz as he had done every week since the latter had taken up his
seat along the eastern wall. The memory of the scene that the boy
witnessed that Sabbath was to make his heart flutter for the rest
of his life. Only at an advanced age, after all other witnesses to the
incident had either passed away or perished in the Holocaust, did
Moshe no longer see himself bound by the conspiracy of silence.
What's more, he believed that the cover-up reflected a Diaspora
mentality, and that it was his duty to redeem the *rebbe's* honor.

Moshe described the incident in a written note that he sent to the author of these lines, for he knew that his friend was, among other things, researching the history of the Jews (including, the Hasidic courts) of Tarnów during the half century preceding the Second World War. In his note, Moshe implicitly empowered his friend to make known the truth about the *rebbe*: "I will tell the story about him, as I know it," he wrote, "and you may glean from it whatever you wish."

And this is the story of that Sabbath, a story told here for the first time since 1924, when it was shackled in the chains of secrecy by order of the leaders of all the Zanser *Kloyzes*. That Sabbath, May 3 by the Gregorian calendar, was the national holiday of the new Poland, a day celebrated with festive military parades, especially in the early years after the "Miracle on the Wisła," when the nation showered affection on its fighting forces who, in 1920, had repelled the Red Army at the gates of Warsaw. In Tarnów, too, on that day, the 16th Regiment of Infantry and the 5th Regiment of Cavalry set out from the barracks at the far end of Goldhammera Street and marched towards town along this wholly Jewish street, which was steeped in Sabbath serenity. At the head of the parade were the wind instruments of the military band, its drums rattling the window-panes of the homes on the street with ear-splitting "oom-pa-pa's" and "boom-boom's", tearing into the calm of the holy Sabbath. These were followed by the saddled cavalry, their swords drawn and their horses rebounding on the cobblestones with a measured "taram-tatam," as droppings strewed the route to the beat of the music.

At that precise moment, hundreds of worshipers poured out of the *Kloyz*, bearded and side-locked, with black silk *bekesheh*-robes adorning their bodies and fur-edged *shtreimels* embellishing their heads in honor of the Sabbath. They, too, began to make their way along Goldhammera, but in the opposite direction, to escort their *rebbe* home, totally unaware of the large military force drawing upon them. When they saw and heard the military band, and the horses relieving themselves on the street, defiling the spirit of the Sabbath, the *rebbe* could not contain himself: feeling a mighty jealousy for his God and the Sabbath Queen, his throat released a terrible cry in Polish: "*Polski gnój!*" ("Polish dung!"), it remaining unclear whether he meant the horses, whose defecation carpeted the entire street, or their riders.

Any Jew raised on the tales of pogroms cannot fail to visualize the picture of mayhem that broke out on the street. "You may imagine how we felt at that moment," Moshe shares with his friend the experience of the critical confrontation with the powers of state and army, "when the Poles fell on us to ferret out the person who had called out. We believed the community was doomed." It may have been brave to fight for the honor of the Sabbath (the people involved felt), but it was certainly not prudent, and only a madman would not hesitate to endanger the whole community by such boldness.

Fortunately, the "Great Synagogue" worshipers also walked out just then and, as usual, strode toward Goldhammera – Jews festively attired in elegant European fashion, some of them clean-shaven and all of them speaking fluent Polish. Wasting no time, they immediately intervened on behalf of their Orthodox brethren, managing to explain to the officers and the police that the fellow who had cried out was touched in the head and therefore an unseemly prey for the victorious Polish army. While they were busy calming things down, the Hasidim whisked their *rebbe* off to safety and, on Sunday at daybreak, hastened to convey him to Lwów and from there to the mental institution at nearby Kulparków – and even those who were thoroughly convinced of Leibushl's utter sanity agreed with the measure, so as to establish proof, in the event that his identity became known, that the man had gone mad and was properly committed. Some time later, after the file had been closed and the danger was past, Leibushl covertly returned to Tarnów, though for reasons of caution kept his distance from the *Kloyz* where his son, Nuhim-Ephroyim, had been ensconced in his absence. Instead, he would assemble in his home on Bóżnic Street a "private *minyen*," composed of confidants and Hasidim who, like him, despised the haughty manners of some Hasidic *rebbes* and preferred to devote their time to studying a *Gemara* page with their *rebbe*.

In the end, during the "Days of Repentance" between the New Year and the Day of Atonement of 5687 (1926), the most distinguished Zans *rebbes* convened in Tarnów and persuaded Reb Leibushl to return to the *Kloyz* and preside there as before. From that Yom Kippur on, Reb Leibushl again prayed at the *Kloyz*, and by way of compromise, consented to share the bench with his son who sat to the right of him, both serving as *rebbes*. And so it was, until his summons to the Heavenly Seat in 1930.

Reb Leibushl was the son of Reb Yehezkel of Sieniawa, who became famous for the journey he made to Eretz Israel at the bidding, and on the mission, of his father, the great Hasidic *rebbe* and leader, Reb Haim Halberstam of Zans. The tale is well known and often told – how Reb Yehezkel toured Eretz Israel, spending a few months there, visiting the early farming communities, prostrating himself on the graves of the great *Tzaddikim*, and weeping bitterly over the destruction of the Temple and the fate of the Jewish People.

All this time tens of thousands of Galician Hasidim waited in holy awe for the *Tzaddik*-emissary, desperately yearning for a word from him: some even sold their property and packed up their belongings, confident that the *Tzaddik* would urge them to rise and go up to the Promised Land and there await the coming of the Redeemer. When Reb Yehezkel returned, however, with a single stroke he ripped the expectations woven by hopeful spinners of Redemption, and declared to his followers: "*Yidn, macht eich nisht narish* – Jews, don't be silly! The Land of Israel, indeed! The 'land' is there alright, but 'Israel' is here." Thus, he promptly dashed the hopes and pronouncements of consolation that had taken wing in that generation, situating anew the focus of endeavor, thought and deed "here," in the Diaspora. Because of him, not only did Galician Hasidim fail to achieve Redemption, remaining wretched and impoverished in the bitter exile of interwar Poland, but the *Kloyzes* became centers of rampant, anti-Zionist agitation, persecuting anyone tinged by the brush of Zionism. When Reb Yehezkel paid a visit to his son, Leibushl, in Tarnów and worshiped at the *Zanser Kloyz*, the sermon from his holy lips oozed venom before his bewildered audience and aimed blasphemous arrows at the heads of the *Tzionisten* (Zionists) he so hated; and the Hasidim, upon hearing the sermon, doused their burning hearts in water and, their anguished souls torn between longing for Zion and Hasidic discipline, submitted to the dictum of the *rebbe*.

5

The growing gulf amid *Kloyz* faithful – between the moderate Orthodox, anxiously awaiting tidings of Zion and inclined to see them as the start of Redemption, and the extreme Orthodox and confirmed anti-Zionists of the Zans school – had already gained public exposure in the final decade of the nineteenth century. At that time a number of rabbis and Hasidic leaders, despite tongue lashings from zealots, had supported the *Ahavat Zion* movement then organizing in Tarnów to establish a Galician farming colony in the Upper Galilee. This gulf widened greatly from 1902 on, when Tarnów's wonderful precedent – the participation of rabbis, Hasidic *rebbes* and a young, orthodox public, in general meetings advocating *aliyah* to, and settlement in, Eretz Israel – gained support and became institutionalized: it ultimately won official recognition as part of the Zionist Organization in the form of the *Mizrahi* movement which, alongside its abiding love of Torah and Israel, now added to its traditional platform the precepts of *aliyah* and active settlement in Eretz Israel.

The fact that part of the Orthodox public, on principle, shunned the Halberstam anti-Zionist hate doctrine, was a thorn in the side of the hotheads among the *Kloyz* zealots; so much so, that they freely resorted to force to decide all matters. At this point, even the most staid, respectable "grandees," men of wealth and pillars of the *Kloyz*, were to be caught in the web of the Knights of Zealotry, falling prey to their fanaticism. No one was spared.

The first victim was Itche Brandstätter. Unlike Baron, who was armored by the power of Wittmayer wealth and shielded by his being free of all ideological leaning or factional Hasidic preference, Itche Brandstätter made no bones about publicizing his views and thereby drew fire on all sides from those who bade him ill. In fact, his name alone threw down the gauntlet before doctrinaire zealots, because of his renowned cousin, Mordkhe-Duvid Brandstätter, writer and last of the Fathers of Galicia's Hebrew Enlightenment movement. Born in a small town in the district of Tarnów, Mordkhe-Duvid had moved to Tarnów in the mid-nineteenth century, when, at the age of fourteen, he was betrothed to the daughter of a prosperous Tarnów family, and he lived out his long life there until a decade after the First World War. His imposing figure, his books and, particularly, his sharp wit, which spawned a host of anecdotes, were firmly fixed in the landscape of Jewish Tarnów – for better or for worse. For worse – because generations of later fanatics did not remember that, in his youth, Mordkhe-Duvid had been one of them, and they only lambasted his deeds in the present as a representative of Enlightenment and a provocative heretic (it is said that on Sabbath afternoon he would sit on the balcony of his Wałowa Street flat, amiably smoking from a clay pipe imprinted with the words: "for the Sabbath only"). Indeed, the extremists might have harmed him physically, were it not for fear of the imperial authorities, who had appointed Brandstätter judge and awarded him the honorary title of *Geheimsrat* (Secret Councilor). And for better – because his sympathies for the *Hibbat Zion* movement and, later, for Zionism (though he never formally joined the Zionist establishment) made him a standard-bearer for the young dissenters at the *Kloyz*.

Unlike his cousin, Itche Brandstätter did not turn his back on religion but embodied a new type of Orthodoxy: though as a Boyan Hasid he was meticulously observant, his strict piety and devotion to tradition did not prevent him from remaining open to western culture. Primarily, and above all else, he advocated Hebrew education for his generation and the teaching of *spoken* Hebrew (not *lushen koidesh*, the holy tongue). This was true of his own home as well: he personally supervised the instruction in Hebrew of all members of his household and made sure they all spoke the language fluently. Borrowing the biblical reference to *Safa Berura* (ClearTongue), Brandstätter was among those who conceived the idea of Tarnów's ramified network of Hebrew education, named "Safa Berura," which was active until the German invasion in 1939. Hebrew education was uppermost in his interests, both when he settled in Vienna during the First World War and when he made *aliyah* in 1920, and this same idea propelled his work for the *Mizrahi* organization, which elected him as a delegate to the Zionist Congress.

Despite the bitter failure of the attempts of Tarnów's Zionists to establish a Galician colony in the Upper Galilee, patterned after the early *Hibbat Zion* settlements, the initial news of the arrival of Second Aliyah pioneers in Eretz Israel and of their settling there, kindled hearts and aroused a handful of students at the *Kloyz*, including Reb Itche's two young sons, Yehezkel and Yehoshua, to found in Tarnów a pioneering *aliyah* movement, known as *HaShahar* ("The Dawn"), in honor of the well-known periodical edited by Peretz Smolenskin, the foremost Enlightenment writer in the second half of the nineteenth century, as well as of Mordkhe-Duvid Brandstätter, who served on its editorial board and published his writings in it. The two young Brandstätters practiced what they preached, turning their backs on the petty disputes of the *Kloyz*: Yehezkel made *aliyah* in 1908 and his brother, Yehoshua, followed suit a year later – the two becoming the first pioneers of the Second Aliyah from Tarnów!

So long as the question of Jewish education was the bone of contention among the *Kloyz* factions – the lending of a new Hebrew character to the school network, as espoused by Itche Brandstätter, in contrast to the traditional system – even the most extreme zealots refrained from all-out war. This changed, however, when it became a question of Zionist ideology, especially the call for *aliyah*. The consummate act of pioneering *aliyah* on the part of the young Brandstätters galvanized the entire neighborhood, and the *Kloyz* fanatics, the Lord's self-appointed police and exclusive interpreters of His word, unleashed a torrent of machinations, singling out Brandstätter senior as the chief target of their attack, despite his stature. The acts of vengeance reached a climax on the Sabbath following the departure of the second son for Eretz Israel. Arriving at the *Kloyz* for morning *shahris* prayers, Itche, to his shock, found his permanent seat smeared with tar – a thundering message to the father of the errant sons that he had been sentenced to expulsion from the *Kloyz* by the guardians of the sanctuary, and that he might expect the worst should he attempt to take his place there.

For thirty-five years the hurt and rage continued to sear Reb Itche's living flesh. True, in 1920 he himself made *aliyah* and was followed by the rest of his children, who gathered around him in Eretz Israel; eight in all (bar one daughter), in addition to the first two pioneers who had set down firm roots in Yavniel in the Lower Galilee. But even this sense of gratification could not eradicate the insult dealt him by the Tarnów *Kloyz*, and he remained embittered by it till his dying day in Jerusalem in 1944. What's more, at a distance of thousands of miles and scores of years, the affront carved out a niche in the collective memory of the third and fourth generations of Brandstätters and their spouses, scattered all over Israel, even though Galicia was alien to them, and only a faint echo of Tarnów and its *Kloyz* ever reached their ears, like a vision from another world, one very far away and very strange – the tempestuous, zealous world of their forebears, that was no more.

Nor did the doctrine of zealotry show any mercy for Eltchi Baron. Though his piety could not be faulted, he did not escape the chicaneries of Zans. The incident occurred in April 1914 when his daughter married Dr. Zussman, a distinguished lawyer from Berlin ("*a daitch*, a German, may God preserve us!"). Neither Baron's wealth, his substance, his personal qualities or his lineage, nor the lineage of his father-in-law or the fact of the latter's membership in the Orthodox oligarchy of the community council, could spare him. Arriving at the *Kloyz* on the Sabbath after the wedding, just as he did every week, he found his place of honor smeared with tar – an unmistakable signal from the thugs who sowed terror all around, as if to say: "Apostate, get you to a different synagogue in the land of the Jews, to break bread and worship there with 'your Germans', and do not come to pray again within the House of God, for this is the royal shrine and kingdom of the *Rebbe* of Zans!"

Unlike Itche Brandstätter, who never got over the slap in the face and even passed on his outrage to the next generations, Baron merely shrugged his shoulders at his ill-doers, as though uncon-cerned, and headed straight for the eastern wall of the *bis-medrash* next to his home. Moreover, he bore no grudge against the com-munity institutions, and upon his return from Vienna in 1916, after his father-in-law's death, formally declared his candidacy for the presidency of the community council; and, despite all the protests of the zealots, he was elected, and even nursed the hope that his son would one day be appointed Tarnów's chief rabbi.

It was after these events, when the fortunes of war and exile clearly changed the character and composition of the *Kloyz*, that Gimpel Schnupftabik's brother-in-law, the retiring Dzikover Hasid, Hayim-Yoisif Wald, took his seat at the eastern table in place of the wealthy Gimpel, who had remained in Vienna. Even though the transfer of the seat to Wald had followed proper procedure, the act, for various reasons, stirred up resentment among the new generation of zealots. Despite their wrath, however, the *Kloyz* fanatics practiced restraint this time in consideration of the public sympathy for Wald, who had been attacked on the train by Endeks (members of the Polish Nationalist Party): the latter had amused themselves by yanking out half of Wald's beard. Ashamed of his beardless, non-Jewish appearance, for a whole year Haim-Yoisif wrapped his bare face in a *pichayle* (the red kerchief trailing from the back pocket of a Hasidic *kapotteh*), until his beard grew back. As a result, not even the fanatics dared to harm the victim of local anti-Semitism: the watchful, vengeful arm of the canon of zealotry granted the hurting Wald a stay of execution, lest it be said that Jewish zealots are no better than the Endeks. Wald used to come to the *Kloyz* with Moshe, his youngest son, who, at the start of that period was five years old, while the four big boys – Yudke, Avruhm, Ovadye and Noyekh (Noah) – though they still wore traditional garb and sprouted beards and side-curls – did not join their father at the *Kloyz*. They preferred to pass the Sabbath at the "Great Synagogue" – some two hundred yards away, where they reveled in the sweet melodies of Cantor Zvi-Hersch Weinman, so much so that Yudke, who had a fine voice, joined the synagogue choir along with his friend, Ben Zion, the cantor's son. The two, in time, found their vocations – the former in Hebrew prose, the latter in Hebrew poetry and painting – and though their paths diverged in the end, the memory of Zvi-Hersch's tunes continued to resound in their hearts ever after.

Yudke pioneered the Third Aliyah from Tarnów, being the first member of the Wald family to immigrate to Eretz Israel. In the autumn of 1919 he set out on foot at the head of a group of *HaShomer HaTza'ir* members, arriving in Vienna in 1920. Further on in the journey, he shaved off his beard and side-locks and donned worker's clothes, and, at the end of the year, while Ben Zion waited his turn at Ellis Island for an entry visa to the United States, Yudke kissed the soil of Eretz Israel, joined the movement's organ *Kehiliyateinu* ("Our Community," which occupies a proud place in the pioneering annals of Eretz Israel), and Hebraized his name to "Yaari," which was to be adopted by the rest of the Walds when they came on *aliyah*.

Abraham, the brother of the writer-kibbutz member, arrived in Eretz Israel a year later and enrolled in the teachers' seminary in Jerusalem. After obtaining a librarian's degree in London, he became a first-rank bibliographer and was appointed to a top position in this field at the National and University Library in Jerusalem. He published important studies on the subject of books and Hebrew printing, as well as anthologies of texts from bygone generations. In 1927, Abraham returned to Tarnów on his initial stint of duty as a Zionist emissary. His first stop was at Mordkhe-Duvid Brandstätter's. The writer questioned him for a good while and, when Abraham described his excursions in Eretz Israel and told him that he planned to climb up Moses' Mountain in Sinai, the old man, who had lost not a jot of his irreverent wit, pulled a copy of the Pentateuch from the shelf and placed it in Abraham's hands: "When you get there," he said, "give this back to Him." Upon Abraham's return to Tarnów in 1928, the old man was no longer alive. His funeral procession was thronged with the Orthodox (so Abraham was told), not out of respect for the apostate but to make sure that the earth swallowed him up.

Every Sabbath, the emissary from Eretz Israel gathered about him in the "Safa Berura" schoolyard scores of young Zionists, thirsty for conversation and discourse in the spoken Hebrew of Eretz Israel and hoping to learn a new Hebrew song and to dance the *Hora* into the night. On the Sabbath of *Shabbat Hazon*, which fell on the Ninth of Av itself, an invitation was posted on the notice boards "to a talk by the Zionist emissary, Avraham Wald-Yaari."

Wald senior, of course, knew nothing about it. When he arrived for worship at the *Kloyz*, as he did every Sabbath with his youngest son, who had been *bar-mitzvah* by now, he found his

seat smeared with tar. Whether he understood the message and ignored it or whether it did not occur to him at all that he had been
targeted, he sat down at a different seat. At the sight of Wald's unexpected obliviousness, the patience of the zealots snapped. If the
tar treatment did not show this outsider that the son's brazenness
had jeopardized the father's place at the *Kloyz*, the time had come
to avenge the transgressions of all the Walds: the daughter's communism, the *aliyah* of the two sons, and the return of the apostate
son to Tarnów in the service of Zionist propaganda. Consequently,
before the Torah reading could begin, one of the loudmouths went
up to the pulpit, banged three times on the lectern where the Torah
scroll lay open, and shouted: "Sha!" ("Silence!").

The Wald father and son did not yet grasp that the matter concerned them, but they knew very well that a delay in prayers or
Torah reading was a time-honored custom that allowed anyone
who so desired to lodge a complaint before the congregation. When
the worshipers fell silent and stillness descended on the hall and
all ears attended, the accuser began (Moshe, the son, to his dying
day never forgot what the man said, and he repeated it to his friend,
word for word):

"*Yidn!* Jews!" – a battle cry rang out in the hall – "We face a predicament! A young man, whose father sits at the eastern wall of our
Kloyz, has gone astray and descended to *Palestina*, and now, in sheer
audacity, he is back in town and dares to rally our youth around
him, even on this holy *Shabbat Hazon*, and to preach *Tziyonism* to
them, God preserve us!"

The diehard adjured the congregation on the open Torah – so
Moshe related – to prepare a fitting "reception" for the agitator and
instigator with stones and brambles, for the law in such cases demands death by stoning! That afternoon, therefore, enflamed bigots
appeared near "Safa Berura", carrying stones in their hands.

Waiting for them at the gates of the schoolyard with sticks and
with fists were members of *HeHalutz*, of *HaShomer HaTza'ir*, and of

other Zionist pioneering youth movements who had been alerted in advance, and they trounced the trespassers roundly, pursuing them all the way up Wałowa Street until the latter took refuge inside the *Great Kloyz*, which the Zionist pursuers did not wish to enter. It goes without saying that, from that Sabbath on, the zealots did not dare to approach the fence of "Safa Berura" schoolyard, and the Sabbath activities continued there undisturbed.

For days, the brawl was a heated topic among beaters and beaten alike, but the real victim of the incident was Wald, the father, and the double expulsion from the *Kloyz* – the tar treatment and the public shame of delayed worship – cost him dearly. True, esteemed Zionists, including the head of *Mizrahi*, Wolf Getzler, who also had a seat at the eastern wall, came to comfort him, but, like Brandstätter twenty years earlier, Wald was inconsolable. His *aliyah* to Eretz Israel with the rest of his sons and daughters eased the pain somewhat, but he carried the insult in his heart for as long as he lived.

When Wolf Getzler came to Hayim-Yoisif Wald's home to help raise his spirits, he certainly never imagined that in five to six years' time, he, too, would find himself on a collision course with the Zans hotheads. Reb Wolf, who owned a store for wrapping-paper (*Pak Papier*) on Wałowa Street, lived with his large family in a spacious flat on Goldhammera Street, opposite Bau's Music School. A distinguished figure with a convincing public-speaking style unsoiled by the usual demagogic brimstone, he had come to Tarnów from his native town of Jasło as a well-to-do adult and, despite his outsider status, for the thirty years that he lived in Tarnów he was among the most respected and best-liked community leaders, enjoying a place of honor at the eastern wall and even donating a Torah scroll that stood in the *Kloyz* Ark. His meticulous observance of every dot in both Written and Oral Law did not stop him from being a liberal and befriending non-observers as well, so long as they were decent folk, and he certainly felt sufficiently ordained to bring the tidings of *Mizrahi*'s form of religious Zionism to Orthodox circles.

This respected figure, whose ways were all pleasing and whose piety, in the spirit of the times and without reservation, rested on Zionist ideology and on the call for *aliyah*, was not to the taste of the fanatic battalion of watchmen at the *Kloyz* – Ahrin Maurer, Pinhas Templer and Meilekh Rheinhold. The hooligans decreed that the man was not fit to sit at the eastern wall and serve as an example to the young, and to everyone's astonishment they marked him as the next victim of the canon of zealotry. When Getzler's son, Moshe (who, along with his brother, Zeilig, had studied with Reb Aazik in the Twenties), made *aliyah* in 1934, and the daughter, Hanka, followed suit with her husband a year later, the blow was not long in coming – a double blow this time: on the Sabbath after their departure, Getzler found himself banished from the *Kloyz* by the tar treatment. Were this not enough, on the next Monday and business day (shops being closed by law in Poland on Sundays), one of the thugs entered Getzler's store and slapped the old man across the face. Moshe, the son, living in Nahariya today, told Aazik's son that it was Maurer who had committed the act. Thus, the collective violence, which had failed in the Wald affair, was now topped off by stark individual violence.

Unlike Brandstätter and Wald, but rather in the style of Baron, who had ignored the intended affront and moved to the *bis-me-drash*, Getzler too dismissed the matter and moved instead to the eastern wall of the *Talmud-Toireh*, an institution that he had supported for years and whose modern building on Lwowska Street he had helped establish. Over and above that, a year later he himself embarked on a ship and sailed to Eretz Israel, ostensibly to attend the birth of his granddaughter, Hanka's child, but also in order to check the possibility of his own *aliyah* and of settling there permanently. Sadly, the efforts to liquidate his business affairs in Tarnów took longer than expected. On September 7, 1939, Getzler found himself under German occupation and, on June 11, 1942, the day of the first murderous German *akzia* (action), he kneeled, as ordered, alongside ten thousand of his brethren and comrades-in-sorrow on the pavement of the Rynek, exposed to the whips of the Nazi soldiers who that day slaughtered about half the town's Jewish population. And yet: the Lord of Death, who works in mysterious ways, took pity on him and stilled his heart before the tyrant's hand could deal him a death blow. His companions in the back rows, at their own risk, dragged their leader's body out – and brought Wolf Getzler to proper burial in Tarnów's Jewish cemetery.

*

However bitter and offensive the internal disputes of the *Kloyz* may have been, and however painful and intrinsic to Jewish experience the contests between the Redemption-thirsty and the Zans school of anti-Zionism – all were overlaid by prayer-leader Mandl's mellifluous voice, his small sons trilling sweetly in accompaniment.

At that Sabbath hour, all quarrels were forgotten and eyes shut, and the world of the Master of the Universe grew lovelier and lovelier, and Jewish poverty seemed to vanish, as did the inner and outer degradation, and all suffering was dissolved and eradicated.

And every Jew was a king and a son of a king,
and his hut a royal mansion,
and his sons, princes in their father's palace.

And every Hasidic *shtetl* (little village) was the capital of an entire realm, even if it comprised but a single narrow street with a handful of shacks at either end.

And Żabno and Dzików,
Zans and Szczucin,
Bełz and Bobowa,
Rymanów and Lezhansk – holy all,
even if not featured on national maps,

equaled in splendor to the cities of Warsaw and Moscow,
Vienna and Budapest,
Paris and New York –

But this, no outsider could ever understand…

CHAPTER EIGHT

The Wages of Zealotry: The Home

1

AT THE TWILIGHT HOUR preceding Yom Kippur's closing *Ne'ila* prayer of the Jewish year 5687 (1926), as a lone memorial candle flickered on the windowsill, soon to run its course and expire, three of Reb Leibushl's four daughters – Hanneh-Ruh'l, Dineh and Rivke-Henneh – sat at the Halberstam home in Tarnów, reflecting aloud on the Halberstam experience of tribal "togetherness." The experience was particularly sharp this fast day, for their father was once again taking part in the prayers of the holy day at the *Great Kloyz* after a mysterious absence of two years. Oblivious of the rise and fall of Abish's *Minha* tune on the street where they lived, the three women eagerly awaited the moment when the *rebbe* would emerge from the gates of the *Kloyz* in the company of hundreds of joyful Zans Hasidim, with his three sons at his side – Nuh'm-Ephroyim, Haim-Burekh and Yehezkel. All would make their way home to break the fast together with them and affix the first stake of the *succah* (tabernacle), a time-honored custom practiced by Jewish faithful at the close of Yom Kippur day.

Only Miriamche, the fourth and youngest of the daughters, openly spurned the snuggling warmth of the tribal experience. The

older of the neighborhood women never tired of praising the radiant beauty, grace and gaiety of Miriamche's younger years, as well
as her boy-like proficiency in *Mishna* and *Poskim* (legal rabbinic
pronouncements), even though she had not been directly included
in the studies but absorbed their content and chant merely by listening to her brothers' lessons from the sidelines. In her twentieth
year, however, she had undergone a personal crisis to which neighbors alluded with a deafening silence and which had resulted, for
the past fifteen years, in an altered disposition. Irate, wild-haired
and deliberately slovenly, Miriamche had fallen into the habit of
pacing madly up and down Bóżnic Street, up and down, up and
down, while plucking her hair and ripping her dress, her face dis-
torted by a dark alien rage that torched her eyes with the fright of
a stalked animal or, alternately, with a defiant human aggression,
which bias willfully defined as bestial. Little wonder then, that on
one hand, the conduct of this changed Miriamche invited open animosity and, on the other, it aroused compassion and a terrible sense
of loss.

Even after creeping stealthily downstairs and out of doors to
greet the morning of this special Yom Kippur day, the woman fell
into her compulsive, characteristic gait, her palms blocking her ears
in an attempt to stifle the obsessive buzzing that nestled in a niche
in her temples and drove her mad without lull or let-up, as if determined to drill a hole through the shell of her skull. Worse still: this
day, too – the holiest of all and set aside for the pardoning of wrongs
men commit against one another – showed no pity for the *rebbe*'s
daughter. Allowed not a moment's grace, she seemed sentenced to
serve as a constant punch bag for the fists of the wicked who took
the law into their own hands to judge her eccentric behavior as insane and punish her for it. Her welfare and safety were in jeopardy
and there was no refuge, neither from the jeers nor from the hail of
stones that the neighborhood youngsters – street louts and decent
lads alike – rained down on her until they drew blood.

A sense of self-preservation, however, must have honed Miriamche's auditory faculties to a degree far beyond the norm. Vigilance trained her to be aware of every breath, every whisper, whether flung directly in her face or brewed behind her back. Thus, she not only grew immune to the jibes aimed at stripping her of her sanity, but shared a secret with a latent voice in her heart: *The voice of her personal God, a voice of love.*

On that well-remembered Yom Kippur morning of 5687 (1926), after escaping taunts and torment, and exhausted from fasting and blows, Miriamche took advantage of the respite to gaze about her, while resting her back against the gate of the yard of Shloime Kotchker, the wagon driver, who stabled a horse and a *fiacre* there. Her observation point from the corner of the gate was only a street's width away from the homes opposite at 7–9 Bóżnic Street: the site of the Stutchiner *Kloyz* and the Rosner Building, where the Wróbel family lived.

Miriamche considered the gate her personal possession. In moments of bitter despair, when her "sixth sense" perceived that the frustrated walking held no solution to her troubles, she would emerge from her corner to plant her legs squarely at mid-gate and, giving free rein to her tongue, spew rivers of denunciation on the disturbers of her peace: "I demand vengeance and retribution!" – her voice reverberated from one end of the street to the other: vengeance for the persecution she suffered at the hands of the youths, and retribution – for the sins of their elders who did not stop the youngsters from persecuting her. She imagined herself grasping the jambs of the gate, like Samson of old, and toppling them, along with all the houses in the street, on to the heads of the residents. But as her rage bubbled and boiled, a strange blend of two contrary odors wafted from the depths of the yard. Her "sixth sense" serving her once again, she deconstructed the blend into its components: subtracting the stench of horse droppings and urine rising from the stable in the yard, she inhaled the sharp, intoxicating aroma of

Blaustein's *kaveh brennerei* – (coffee roasting factory) – which was also situated in the yard.

The coffee factory had changed Miriamche's life irreversibly. Captivated by the aroma of roasting, she was ultimately trapped in its net. Thus, in the course of her daily striding back and forth, amid anger and pain and assaults of hostility, she took repeated solace in lingering near the factory, relinquishing her ears to the rhythm of the machines Blaustein had imported from Vienna, and opening her lungs to the different stages of the roasting process, deriving a sensual pleasure from each and every one. So obvious was the daily addiction of the *rebbe*'s daughter to the fragrance of roasted coffee that some of the neighbors considered the exposure to an overdose of caffeine a factor in her "mental confusion." Her addiction, in any case, was a fact and, even on Yom Kippur, when both horse and roasting machines rested from work, the air remained imbued with the fragrance of coffee, albeit from old roastings, and the young woman was inebriated by the essence of its aroma.

Miriamche shut her weary eyes and leaned against Kotchker's gate, succumbing to the enchanted coffee fragrance, a scent pungent and stirring and yet simultaneously soothing. For a brief moment – no doubt, a flash of the genetic Halberstam discipline – fear crept into her heart that by submitting on this holy fast day to the influence of coffee, she was perhaps violating one of Yom Kippur's severe prohibitions. She did not, however, have the strength to deny herself the aroma that caressed every limb of her body and lent this magical hour at the day's close the flavor of an undefined craving and an alert anticipation of something larger than both herself and her world.

At the same time, her ears detected faint sounds from the yard: Shloime's mare, which along with the *fiacre* had been forced into idleness by the sanctity of the day, began to stamp its hooves to broadcast a reminder of its existence. Perhaps it sensed the familiar presence of the anonymous woman who passed the gate several times a day and paused at the *brennerei*; or, maybe, it wished to draw its master's attention to the fact that it was exempt from the observance of fasting, even though employed by Jews. Miriamche instantly expunged the faint sounds of stamping from her consciousness, just as she generally disregarded the stable smells. Instead, she totally immersed herself in the stunning bouquet of roasted coffee, allowing it free passage up the canals of her nose to sneak beneath her forehead and, there, sweetly and pleasurably, to stupefy her senses. Suddenly, as she glided, spellbound, on the waves of scent, hundreds of Hasidic Stutchiner throats from across the street rent the serene thrall as they broke into the afternoon *Minha* prayers of Yom Kippur:

"Now therefore, O Lord our God, impose thy awe upon all thy works."

"Thy awe?" The *rebbe*'s daughter was not yet ready to cast the spell from her shuttered eyes. "Thy awe?" Can God be asking this of her as well? Her entire life was but one long succession of awe: not of God, Heaven forbid, but of man. No, the personal God in her heart could not possibly mean that. He, like her, celebrated love. Her ears, more sensitive than all others in the whole world, at once perked up as if on command, though she had as yet no idea as to the force that commanded her, paralyzed her, rooted her feet to the ground and compelled her to listen.

She listens. Her sharp ears discern the thinnest of threads of a different tune and different words penetrating the texture of Stutchiner choral voices – a thread creeping covertly towards her and obstinately twining itself around her consciousness. And it seems to her that both the tune and the words reach her from a faraway, infinite, unbounded horizon, as if whispering into her ear a secret with which only she is entrusted. Little does Miriamche know that the whispered song has actually come from a great distance, having thrillingly managed to penetrate all the *Kloyzes* in town to reach this, the final lap of its journey. Here, here it drops helplessly onto the Stutchiner stairs – only paces away from where she stands – in an effort to scale the last *Kloyz* on its route, and though it is still breathing, its voice, barely audible, is about to be snuffed out like a candle in the dark. And the woman feels with all her might that whatever the source of the song and whatever its final destination, she, and she alone, hears its tune and its words. Yes, only she can save it from its ultimate end, if only she could relieve its back of the heavy, oppressive, predatory burden of the Stutchiner choral block; if she could isolate the tune, in all its purity and innate clarity, from the tumult of wild, stormy voices; if she could channel it via the sensitized receptors of her ears to the speakers of her tongue and lips. This alone will redeem both herself and the tune – her own voice breathing life into it, not the voice of fear that is booming across the street, but the dulcet, clement, velvety, alluring voice of the Divine, the only voice of love:

"*Thou art One/ and Thy name is One/*
  and who is like unto Thy people/ Israel"

Here, then, the secret tune rises up from within her, as if spilling like fine wine from a goblet of the ear to a goblet of the mouth. With eyes still shut as before, her lips, aroused now, begin to murmur the words; at first soundlessly and tonelessly, then, slowly, slowly, joining letter to letter, word to word, note to note – until the tune bursts forth from her mouth in all its might:

"*Thou art One/* goteniu zisser / *and Thy name is One/*
  goteniu lieber / *One – One /* goteniu mein/
  One – One – and Thy name is One – "

During her song-prayer-confession, Miriamche crosses her arms, right palm embraces left shoulder and left palm encloses right shoulder, as if a trembling body were caught within – the body of the child she had never borne? The body of the man who had never clasped her to him? Or, perhaps, her personal God, the one and only, loved and loving, who, she learned, "*has no bodily form, and is not a body,*" yet rests near, very near to her own. And she feels His breath and senses His warmth suffusing her organs and she grips Him to her heart with a passion she has never known:

"*Thou art One*/ goteniu zisser/
One – One and there is none other/
And Thou art within me/ oh, goteniu mein/
Within me – Within me – "

Bit by bit, at the end of the Stutchiner *Minha* prayers and at the sound of the strange singing by the *rebbe's* daughter next to Kotchker's gate, juvenile worshipers begin to pour out onto the *Kloyz* stairs, some of them to stare silently at the sad scene across the street, some to titter in embarrassment, and some to grit their teeth and clench threatening fists. All at once, a cry fills the air and rends the silence, washing over the congregants with waves of laughter and scorn: "*Di meshiggeneh!*"

"*Di meshiggeneh, di meshiggeneh!*" – fanatic voices echo the first trouble-maker amid vociferous declarations: "Scandalous!", "What a disgrace!", "Such desecration, the Lord preserve us!" Miriamche ignores the voices or, perhaps, does not even hear them. Eyelids closed, mouth still singing, only her crossed arms stir now to open wide and high, higher, as if she would fly on the wings of her song to the abode of her God. Then, without warning, a stone lands on her arm. In panic, her eyes fly open to find an ominous crowd poised on the stairway opposite her. Another stone is thrown, and yet another. Miriamche does not defend herself. The song dies on her lips as she curls up in a corner of the gate, shielding her head with her hands and submitting to the stones rolling all over her body...

The lynching – even though not quite murder – was complete. The doctrine of zealotry had triumphed!

2

Ten measures of rage descended on Bóżnic Street in the Jewish neighborhood of Tarnów; nine were inhaled by Leibushl's daughter when she was proclaimed "crazy." In keeping with the observance of the Sabbath and holidays, the woman was careful to carry nothing in her hands on those days, even though this meant consciously laying herself open to ill-wishers by having no form of protection with which to pre-empt their blows or repay the wicked assailants as they deserved. Indeed, on that mythological Yom Kippur her shield was noticeably lacking. On weekdays, in contrast, Miriamche's manic strides were accompanied by a fair-sized carpet beater in her hands, fashioned of a plait of pliable bamboo cane and used for the beating of large carpets. Thus, force of circumstance drew a sharp dividing line on the street. The western side – where, in time, the soles of the *rebbe*'s daughter had trodden out a private path, from the corner of the barracks to Pod Dębem Square – was the mad woman's entire "daytime kingdom." From this point on, woe to the lad who crossed the line and neared her path, even if accidentally and with no hostile intent: the bamboo would lash out at him with all the rage that the carpet beater wielder could muster. And double woe to the girl who found herself in a similar situation – grabbing her hair in her left hand, Miriamche would roll her head back and forth until she was spinning, while the carpet beater in her right hand thrashed and flayed, laying merciless blows on the girl's whole body, in total disregard of her vital organs. It is thus hardly surprising that the little terrors chose to fling their stones at her from the safe distance of the eastern side of the street, with only the ostensibly brave scheming to creep up on the "queen of the street" from behind. Some even managed to pull her scarf from the nape of her neck or, with the edge of a stick, lift the bottom of her dress and expose her underwear, to the glee of the other young hellions.

The violent modes of self-defense developed by Miriamche against the street caused even the morally scrupulous to keep their distance from her, and only the son of Aazik and Golda applauded her defiance and sought a way to approach her. He, too, was careful not to cross her path, lest she fail to differentiate between the "good" and the "bad" and do him injury; but he never took part in the exploits against her, identifying with her pain and actions even if these were considered raving madness. For, strangely enough, the tighter the collar of street clashes closed around Miriamche's neck, the more radiant her sanity, which glowed like a transparent crystal. Her entreaty to "*goteniu*" was couched in terrifying clarity, showing the *rebbe's* daughter to be conscious of her condition and praying to God to be delivered from His punishment.

"His punishment?" Yes, His punishment. Thus, at the end of an exhausting day of confrontations, when things became unbearable, Miriamche would raise her bruised arms upwards and in a heart-rending, clear cry address her beloved *goteniu* – not in complaint, God forbid, or as an accusation, nor even with a demand for justice such as Levi-Yitzhik of Berdichev had uttered, and certainly not in heresy – but as an innocent question, shockingly simple and maddeningly sane:

"*Goteniu lieber, goteniu zisser, goteniu mein, farvus host du mikh geshtruft?*

(Dear, sweet God of mine, why have you punished me?)"

Not for a moment did she doubt the justice of the punishment. She merely wished to know the nature of her sin. But no response was forthcoming, and the *dybbuk* (possessing spirit) of guilt took the place of rational, logical analysis. Confusion seemed to whisper in her ear that the mystery of her sin was related to the measure of mercy that her *goteniu* exercised towards her in his great kindness, whereas it was not kindness she sought but law, for only due process might rid her mind of the dross of ignorance and cleanse her conscience. And if her *goteniu* were not prepared to judge her harshly, it was incumbent upon her personally to do so in His stead and punish herself in His name. Consequently, Miriamche would grip the handle of the carpet beater with both hands and swing the weapon at her head over and over again, dealing blows to her forehead, temples and cheeks until she bled, all the while crying:

"Goteniu lieber, goteniu zisser, I deserve the punishment; I beg you, consent to it, accept it as the gift of my love, and grant my ailing spirit peace!"

True, the self-flagellation was not a frequent occurrence, but it was certainly seen as even more bizarre than the routinely bizarre behavior of the *rebbe*'s daughter. And when it did occur, it so alarmed everyone that even the unbridled youngsters, whose mischief had pushed the poor woman beyond endurance and caused her to turn her violence on herself, were seen to beat a retreat in panic.

The worshipers' stoning of the *rebbe*'s daughter, which Golda and Aazik's son observed on the street where he lived, right near his home, on a day that the boy had been taught to regard as the holiest in the Jewish calendar, was only a late installment of an earlier act that preceded the stoning by two months. The earlier act, too, had fallen on a day that the boy had learned to respect as unique to his people's history: the Ninth of Av, the day of the destruction of the Second Temple. What's more, on the previous occasion, he, himself, had turned from an onlooker into an actor in the drama.

The Ninth of Av, more so than any other day, was disposed to find Miriamche despondent. Just as in the week of Purim the community was resigned to boyish pranks, including the setting of fire-caps beneath the feet of innocents, which startled the elderly and women, so the public accepted the *Tisha B'Av* tradition which permitted youths to play at targeting passers-by with *bobkes* (prickly burrs). The burrs would adhere to clothing, to exposed skin and, above all, to girls' hair (much to the boys' wildly voluble delight), and their removal from the hair would be slow, laborious and painful; sometimes, whole strands had to be cut to be rid of the inextricably entangled nettle nuisance.

Her daily, permanent and foreknown route made Miriamche a predictable target for the bombardment of burrs on *Tisha B'Av*, the "marked woman" having not a chance of escaping the sharpshooters' missiles. The barrage of *bobkes* released from ambushes on the eastern path blinded the "walker" and disorientated her. Drained and submitting to her fate, she fell to her knees midway on the western path, the layer of burrs making her a green hillock on the street's landscape, and she yielded her right to self-defense just as she was to submit when attacked two months later on Yom Kippur. Her capitulation not only failed to arouse mercy, but egged on her tormentors to further audacity. This was the state of defeat in which the boy found her on the Ninth of Av 5686 (1926), when he sped to her rescue.

The boy finds it difficult today to reconstruct exactly what he felt seventy years ago when, out of a desire to rescue Miriamche from suffering, he did the seemingly imprudent at the time, crossing the street and stepping onto the western path – Miriamche's path. He remembers only that, unlike the other boys, he was not at all afraid, his eagerness for the adventure of communication with the mad woman overriding all caution. His basic honesty told him that no real attempt had ever been made to understand her "madness," and that he – and maybe she, as well – might benefit from such an encounter. Thus, without fear, though also with no word of greeting, he walked over to the spot where Miriam was kneeling, tearfully enclosed in sorrow. Being somewhat taller than she in this position, the boy placed a hand on her head. Then, not waiting for a reaction, he slowly and deliberately began to pull the burrs from the mesh of her hair, one by one, gently but firmly dislodging the clinging tendrils of the *bobkes*. Miriamche, the whole while, raised no protest until, exhausted from the procedure, she merely rested her head on his chest and wrapped her arms around his knees.

So engrossed was the boy in nettle duty that he did not realize that Miriamche had spoken to him. The surprise lay not in the content of the message, which the boy did not even absorb initially, but in the fact of the address itself, and even more so – in the melodic quality of the voice, totally unlike the grating screeches she would emit in her wrath. Receiving no reply from her savior, the woman surmised that he had not even heard her and repeated her words in the same singular timbre that now imbued them with meaning: "*Du bist Reb Aazik's a zin* (You are a son of Reb Aazik's)!" She was not asking, she was stating a fact, simply, and with the assurance of knowledge.

And lest her first two applications to him were not enough, she confirmed the fact a third time, even repeating the name, "*Reb Aazik, Reb Aazik*" several times, as if deriving a peculiar pleasure from its mere utterance or, perhaps, to bolster the son's trust in her by implicitly evoking a long-term acquaintanceship and warmly singing the father's praises:

"*A tayerer yid, Reb Aazik, a tayerer yid...* (A dear man, Reb Aazik, a dear man)" – and this, too, in a surprisingly dulcet tone, in stark contrast to the harsh cry she reserved for the street.

Miriamche's words were a shock to Aazik's son. For the first time, the madwoman of Bóżnic Street ceased being a local curiosity – tragic in some views, ridiculous in others – in order to become a subject that personally concerned him and his father. Objectively, the *rebbe*'s daughter certainly had reason to recognize Aazik and his son: since from her vantage point at Kotchker's gate, Miriamche would gaze at the building across the street where the Wróbel family lived, and thus became quite familiar with the faces of the people coming and going. And yet, it was not as obvious as all that: in the absence of communication between herself and the neighbors, how did she come to know such details as name, relationship, or cause for praise, and what was the basis of the transparent, deliberate hint at a prior acquaintance?

Sirens went off in the son's memory: could the madwoman of now be his rabbi's daughter of then? The one that used to peer through the cracks at the tall, destitute young man who, the girls whispered, had come from a faraway village? Or was it the *rebbe*'s daughter who brought him plates of leftovers from her father's kitchen along with bundles of clothing from the charity stocks? Was she the girl who had sustained him, body and soul, for nine whole years, feeling with justice that, thanks to her, he had stayed the course to become the town prodigy? The son's imagination is eager to race ahead to later events, but prudence decrees patience: his reconstruction may be no more than a general assumption, the fruit of errant fancy. On the other hand, the supposition *is* highly reasonable. Might it have been the hand of fate that propelled him onto the western side of the street to discover the truth?

Imagination would not let go and, years later, when the son was to look back on that early time, it was to erupt unchecked once more: nine years of peering through the cracks must have meant nine years of lovesick yearning, more and more filling the heart of the growing girl who had eyes for no one but him. Ah, how breathtaking to discover a youthful love of Father's, hers for him and, perhaps, also his for her! True, in those days, love as such was never spoken of, not by young men and certainly not by young women. Yet, just as certainly, there were circuits of celebration in Halberstam Tarnów, the stuff of which was love: Hanneh-Ruh'l married the town *mohel* (circumciser); Dineh followed her husband, who was appointed local rabbi of some Galician small town; and Rivke-Henneh was sanctified to a *maggid shiur* (study leader) at the *Kloyz* of Leibushl, her father.

Only Miriamche was passed over by the cycles of celebration – confirming the dark face of the wages of zealotry: a Halberstam daughter cannot and will not wed an unknown villager of obscure lineage, even if she is of age and he a prodigy whose name is on every tongue, especially a prodigy who explicates, at face value, the saying of the Sages to "despise the rabbinate" and, doubly so, one who is in league with the *misnagdim*. So it is left to the imagination to spin the denouement of the drama: the tale of a nine-year-long love crushed by a tribal ban with no court of appeal, bringing the lover to the brink of madness. Was this not what the neighbors alluded to when they hemmed and hawed about a breakdown in the girl's life at the age of twenty?

The contact between the boy and the *rebbe's* daughter lasted for a period of some two months after the ill-fated day of the burrs. The son would stop beside Miriamche whenever he took a break from his summer *Gemara* lessons, as well as in September, on his way home from school. Conversely, she would ask after his health and that of his father, a spark of affection lighting up her eyes. Nevertheless, the boy failed in his attempts to draw out the conversation beyond what had passed at the first encounter or to guide Miriamche through the memories of her past. Moreover, all information he brought her of his mother and sisters fell on deaf ears. She seemed to have locked herself up for ever in the orbit of her youthful dreams and, beyond this, time stood still, her consciousness barring entry to new experiences, new persons, new events.

Despite his sympathy for Miriamche and his readiness to come to her aid whenever required, her dual attitude weighed heavily on the son of Aazik and Golda, causing him distinct unease. After all, he could hardly ask his father if the Halberstam rebuff was the reason that he had not married until the age of thirty-two. The boy's discomfort was especially magnified whenever Miriamche greeted him warmly and wound her arms around his neck, but dismissed his attempts to speak of the four people who, in the here and now, shared the life of her youthful idol. Only years later, upon reflecting on the *rebbe's* daughter's one-way closure, did the son conclude that Miriamche, for whom time had stopped, had sought to stop time for her neighbor as well, having no real interest in anybody, not even in Aazik as he grew to be, but merely in his son. Did this transference of her affection represent simple gratitude for the personal assistance the boy had offered her in time of need – the son wondered in his childhood and, even more so, when he recalled the experience as a grown man – or did she, who was doomed to stay single, perhaps see him as someone who might have been her own son had not the way to her heart's desire been blocked? This dire possibility threw the son into confusion, raising questions of dual loyalty with respect to his mother. As a result, he made up his mind to approach Father on the matter – cautiously, of course, so as not to invade his privacy. Thus, one day, as they walked along the eastern side of Bóżnic Street, the boy, catching sight of Miriamche's usual frenzied pace on the western side, plucked up the courage to ask his father about her "madness." The response, in both content and formulation, astonished him:

"*Zi iz nisht meshigge, Herschl* (She is not mad)," Father answered, "*zi iz a geshtrufte* (she is being punished)."

A dozen alarms sounded in the son's heart, his memory rocked by the scene of Miriamche addressing her *goteniu* with a desperate question phrased in the very same terms – "*farvus host du mikh geshtruft?* (Why have you punished me?)."

"Punished? For what?" the boy protested in sheer frustration. "How terrible could her sin have been for the Lord, who, though '*slow to anger and plentiful in mercy*' (as described in Psalms), lost patience with His daughter and withheld His love from her, sentencing her to life imprisonment behind the bars of madness?"

Unlike the boy's vocal remonstrance, the father's reply was muted, a whisper almost. But despite its soft tones, it hit the boy straight in the face: "Miriamche did not sin at all," the father declared, stressing every syllable, yet straining not to disclose his turbulent emotions. This short sentence, and particularly what followed, clearly implied a prior acquaintanceship between Aazik and the *rebbe's* daughter. "The girl was as pure and white as the first snow on the Beskids, spreading calm and serenity all about. No, she did not sin – it was her forefathers who sinned, and the Lord's visitation was for their sins. Did you not learn: '*I... am a jealous God, punishing the iniquity of the fathers upon the children unto the third and fourth generation*'?"

"And her forefathers," the son insisted on getting to the bottom of things, "how did they sin that they brought down such disaster on an innocent offspring, disturbing her mind?"

"One can only guess," the father answered sadly, plainly troubled by the conversation. "Ah, what a pity," he continued, "that there is no way of knowing for whose sin a descendant is chosen to be punished and for whose wickedness he or she will be singled out to atone. It remains a mystery. Only this can be said from observing the conduct of the Halberstams down the generations: the wickedest sin of which they are guilty is zealotry. Spawned by the founder of the dynasty himself, Reb Haim Halberstam, who bequeathed it to his children and grandchildren. And as one rabbi once put it – someone, in fact, who held Reb Haim in the greatest esteem, regarding him as one of the just men of the generation – 'It was a great miracle for Israel that the *Tzaddik* of Zans was not around when the Israelites sinned with the golden calf in the desert, for had he been there, he would have put them all to the sword'."

The explanation did not satisfy the boy. Caught up in tempestuous emotions heretofore unknown to him, and almost forgetting that the purpose of the conversation was to gain information about Miriamche, he refused to make do with blaming the Halberstams, and addressed his prosecution to a different quarter: "But God, Father, God," his heart bellowed, "where was He when the young Miriamche needed Him and where is He now? Where is He, the compassionate and merciful, whose Torah and *Mishna* I study with you every day? What is the point of these if there is no measure of justice in their pages or charity in their legal pronouncements? What value have they against a single tear of Miriamche's and against the tears of all the Miriamches in the world?"

The father was silent, and the longer the silence the greater the rage the son felt: "And worse still, Father, how can He endure the miscarriage of justice that He, himself, inflicted on His daughter? And how can He sit by quietly on His throne, unmoved by the suffering of an innocent woman who has not ceased to love her *go-teniu* despite the troubles He brought down upon her?"

"The concepts of divine justice do not always match human concepts," the father at last broke the silence to counter softly, apologetically. His face was pale and his eyes seemed wearier than ever. Clamming up once more, he trudged on without relish, as if moving his legs against his will and avoiding his son's anguished eyes. Was he surprised by the child's protest, perhaps finding there an echo of his own doubts in his youth? Could he have felt an affinity for the heresy that had burst from his son's lips? Or had he been subdued by memories that he did not wish to recall, which for years had carefully lain undisclosed to anyone – and now, now, were pushing their way out onto the highway of his life and demanding an audience? The boy, too, who so longed for knowledge of his father's youth, was left embarrassed by the turn that his accusations had taken and at a loss as to how to interpret his father's reticence.

At the end of the day a hush descended on them both. They walked home at odds with one another, each sunk in their own reflections. The mental and emotional bridge by which the son hoped to draw closer to his father's youthful experiences had collapsed before it could even be completed. And a terrible sadness overwhelmed him.

3

The daily procession of the "madwoman of Bóżnic Street" had been a permanent feature of the street's landscape for some fifteen years, like the tree or the puddle of mud or the shadow of buildings crouching over the road. It was at the very end of this period that the prospect changed to shift between two poles. On the one hand, neighborhood youngsters continued to torment Miriamche as in the past, treating her as a nameless creature and branding her with the global pariah tag of "*di meshiggeneh*". On the other hand, a warm, personal relationship – albeit short-lived, of a mere two months' duration and ostensibly strange, yet profound and gentle – sprung up between the *rebbe's* daughter and Reb Aazik's son. But after that doleful Yom Kippur of 5687 (1926) something happened: the "crazy woman" stopped going out for her daily walk as had been her habit.

Although her unprecedented absence was a cause for wide-spread wonder, it was days before anyone dared to cross the street to set foot on "her" side. It was generally suspected that the "crazy woman" – her bamboo carpet beater ready for action – lay in wait for her tormentors and that, in a moment, she would sally forth from hiding to rout them. But the days piled up and turned into weeks and there was no sight of the *rebbe's* daughter. Gradually, the realization sunk in that the "monster of madness and rage" (as many called her) or the "sacrificial lamb at the stake" (as her young friend saw her) had escaped from the city by her own devices or with the help of well-wishers, and would never return to live there.

One might suppose that the disappearance of the "crazy woman" was gladly welcomed, both by those who had tasted her wrath and by community leaders who had incessantly blamed the poor woman for giving the community a bad name. Yet, this was not so. After the defeated woman's departure from the neighborhood – whether voluntarily or by force – attitudes towards her changed. All at once a bare and barren air seemed to descend on the street: "*Di meshiggeneh*" was gone.

Old and young alike – including the cheeky scamps who had made her life miserable – were suddenly gripped by a gaping sense of loss, as if the neighborhood had been stripped of a tree that, by common belief, had been planted there to satisfy their whimsies: for them to scale, break its branches, pick its leaves or mutilate its bark while wielding pen-knives to carve out sharp, heart-shaped grooves embellished by their names, heedless of the tree's own life.

The sense of loss was clearly compounded by the lingering

puzzle as to the whereabouts of the *rebbe*'s daughter and the reason for her disappearance. The men, concerned that the incident would reflect badly on Leibushl and the Zans Hasidim, chose to cloak themselves in mystery just as they had done when their *rebbe* had vanished for two years. Not so the women, especially the old-time neighbors who lived nearby. They, in typical fashion, carefully garnered every tidbit of rumor that filtered in from the outside and every stew of gossip cooked up within the inner camp, even though there was no consensus about all the details.

Some of them assumed that the *rebbe*'s daughter had been institutionalized at Kobierzyn near Kraków or in Kulparków near Lwów, where, evil tongues buzzed, Leibushl too had been placed years earlier. The names of these two Galician towns had entered the Polish vernacular as symbols of insane asylums and were euphemisms for "crazy." Other neighbors guessed that Miriamche had been hospitalized in Kraków proper, in the closed ward of the Piyars – a Catholic order that granted shelter even to the most wretched on the ladder of life: the mad. In the absence of a comparable Jewish institution, Jewish mental patients were also brought there, notwithstanding the crucifixes that graced the walls above every bed and in spite of the fear that the Jewish inmates would ultimately be baptized "for the redemption of their souls." For this contingency, too, colloquial Yiddish had devised a respectable expression: "*Ich geih zi di Piyarn* (I'm going to the Piyars)," meaning "I'm going nuts." Both groups of women shared the opinion that the exile of the *rebbe*'s daughter from Tarnów was due to her deteriorating condition. There was a third group, however, that linked Miriamche's disappearance to events within the Halberstam home: without detracting from the severe emotional state of the *rebbe*'s daughter, this camp pointed to Nuh'm-Ephroyim, Leibushl's son – and ironically or sadly enough, Miriamche's favorite brother – as the decisive factor in the removal of his blighted sister from Tarnów.

Still under the reign of his father, Reb Leibushl, Nuh'm-

Ephroyim had opened his own small *Kloyz* at the corner of a wide-open field adjoining the northern wall of the Rosner Building at 9 Bóżnic Street. The area, despite its spaciousness, functioned as a *lokh* to all intents and purposes, serving as a shortcut from Bóżnic to the parallel street of Szpitalna, which housed three Jewish institutions: the hospital (*szpital*, that gave the street its name), an old-age home, and the cemetery. On weekdays, the field was used as a parking lot for country wagons that brought in produce from the northern villages, and the whole area was a mess of piss puddles and dung heaps from dozens of beasts of burden, though the northern, sealed wall of the three-story Rosner Building blocked off the odors and din from the residential section. In gratitude to the Jewish owner who permitted the field to be used during the week, the villagers took turns cleaning up and washing down the area prior to the onset of Sabbath and holidays. Thus, once the temporal defilement was purged, the Divine Presence descended to the small *Kloyz* on the Sabbath and festivals to envelop its adherents in a prayer shawl of pure sanctity.

After Leibushl vanished (or was whisked away) from the neighborhood in 1924, Nuh'm-Ephroyim occupied his father's seat at the *Great Kloyz* in addition to his own small *Kloyz*. The ambitious rabbi managed to endear himself to his Hasidim thanks to the Zans rabbinical affectations that he wisely commanded, in clear antithesis to his father, Leibushl, who shunned rabbinical mannerisms and preferred to cloister himself up with a page of *Gemara*. The rising star's road to success remained unhampered even after his father returned to Tarnów in 1926; the two, father and son, now ruled by mutual agreement at the *Great Kloyz*. But there was a fly in the ointment, and this fly was the "crazy" sister, whose embarrassing presence across from the open field could, Heaven forefend, blemish the name of the *rebbe*-son. She, therefore, had to be removed at once – so the partisans of the third camp of women reconstructed the brother's betrayal of his loving sister – by dispatching her, perhaps, to one of the family branches in Brooklyn where she would fade into blessed anonymity and her turmoil be done with.

Memory is short. The matter of the "vanished madwoman" continued to come up in neighborhood conversations for a little while, but, on the whole, her image grew dimmer and dimmer until it was finally blotted out. Bóżnic Street soon shook off the manacles that had shackled it for a decade and a half, and a new page began in the life of its residents. The invisible line of enforced division between the street's two sides evaporated into thin air and children, from then on, could play with their *szmaciok*-ball across the street's entire width, with no fear that the improvised rag ball would roll onto the path that was once forbidden territory. Also to disappear was the large bamboo carpet beater, the rod of the madwoman's rage, which had filled bystanders with dread. The only carpet beaters now seen were the small domestic ones used by maids on Sabbath and holiday eves to beat the dust out of household rugs strewn over balcony banisters (thereby restoring to carpet beaters their original homey purpose). And, like spring buds, girls now blossomed, strolling along the street at their leisure with colorful ribbons in their hair and braids, unafraid that an arbitrary, vengeful hand would seize them by their hair and shake their heads until it was sore. A new generation arose that knew nothing of Miriamche.

Peace ostensibly descended on the Wróbel home, too, the name of the *rebbe*'s daughter not being mentioned in conversation around the family table. True, the boy wondered if peace had been restored to his father's heart as well, but Father, as usual, was close-mouthed, not revealing his feelings. Only the son, it seems, did not hesitate to reflect on the lost woman who had strayed into his life, although his own experiences, too, gradually grew duller. In his mind, Miriamche's exploits took the form of an abstract model for a phenomenon he was to define much later as "agonized sanity," whereas as a lad he was merely able to discern its tangible components: the expression of dark rage and the shadow of paranoia in her eyes; compulsive pacing to give vent to a maddening physical pain or escape the malice of society; vociferous prosecution of both individuals and the entire universe, on the one hand, and pleading with God, on the other, to put a stop to the torment; and lastly, the physical violence – shaking girls' heads and striking out with the carpet beater – ending in self-flagellation. The vision of the model would now hound the son as a nightmare and, some ten months after his encounter with the *rebbe*'s daughter, events in his own family would cause him to imagine the vision taking on flesh and bone, the horrible nightmare sinking its teeth into the family body for four whole years, without let up, without let up…

4

From the early spring of 1927, the children were gripped by enormous excitement at the prospect of spending the summer at Rabka in the Carpathian Mountains, as Mother had promised them in 1925, when her advanced pregnancy and imminent confinement had made the vacation trip impossible. But, at the start of the summer of 1927, the children, to their astonishment, were told that the plans had been changed and Mother would be leaving for Vienna instead – her first trip abroad after the war – and there she would be staying with her sister, Zippora. The reason for her trip was not explained, nor the urgency for it, apart from an offhand announcement that "this time, Mother would use her sojourn in Vienna for medical tests." Parents, in those days, were not in the habit of providing their children with explanations. Now, however, in a departure from the norm and to make up for the cancellation of the Carpathian journey, the children were informed of the new plan ahead of time.

The breach of the promise made two years earlier was naturally received with disappointment. Nevertheless, the children displayed no jealousy and even shared in Mother's flutters. In their innocence, they interpreted her excitement as emanating from the anticipated return to the haunts of her beloved city – Vienna, Europe's cultural capital! – where she had experienced unforgettable hours of pleasure and freedom in her youth, and unforgotten hours of pleasure and anxiety in the years of her war refuge. In compensation, Mother promised to send them a picture postcard of every site she would visit – Vienna's contribution to the son's collection and proof that the children were uppermost in her joy.

On the designated day, about an hour before dawn, Shloime Kotchker, the wagon driver, and his horse and *fiacre* made their way up the street and stopped at the entrance to 9 Bóżnic in order to drive Golda and Aazik and their three children, along with two suitcases, to the train station. There, all alone on the deserted platform and trembling slightly from the morning chill, the five waited in stillness for the train which, like all express trains, was to stop at Tarnów for three minutes.

How lonely we are here! – the son's glance embraced the four figures who seemed to have strayed unwittingly into the dawn desolation of the long, empty platform: Mala, his older sister of eight and a half, Gunia, the two-year-old toddler, and even Father, despite his strong build, and Mother, in all the elegance of her proud posture – all four struck the son and brother as a band of lost children anxiously hanging on to one another. *Indeed, alone in Poland, with no remedy for the loneliness* – the son silently reiterated his survey of the situation.

We are all five here – this time he included himself in the count, while scanning the platform that was gradually becoming more visible. *Five we are and no more: a dot in the register of the Master of the Universe, a tiny island in the sea of humanity.* He recalled the family tales of his friends: Passover *seder* at the grandparents'; aunts radiating loving chatter and sinking under the weight of presents; smiling cousins wafting perfume, arriving on birthdays in rustling dresses to kiss their cousin on the cheek. *And we, what did we have?* – he was envious of the tellers and, in his despair, "took stock": *Grandmothers, two – both in America; uncles, eight – also in America; and there, too, a whole band of male and female cousins whom we'll never see; and another aunt in Vienna, the one Mother is now traveling to, and the only one we ever met in Tarnów. But in Poland, itself, we have no kin at all! Yes, we are all alone here.*

The sound of a whistle and the metallic clatter of the wheels put an end to his reflections. It is drawing near now, the train, heralded by the white steam of the locomotive. Instantly, the five are alert. In another three minutes Mother will be leaving. How can one say good-bye in three minutes? The children are silent. Father puts the luggage onto the train and, upon returning, makes himself as small as possible next to Mother, like a bashful high-school boy meeting a girl for the first time. Only Mother maintains her calm, behaving and functioning normally.

In another three minutes Mother will be leaving…

Do you know what the life span of three minutes is?

The son, as in a daze, gazes at the large, heavy clock hanging at the center of the platform. It has two faces, the clock does, like the Roman god, Janus, in the story Mother told them, whose two faces looked out in opposite directions. The station clock is just like that: its two visages – number boards – face in opposite directions, one board in front and one board in back. Apart from the pair of black hands to mark hours and minutes, there is a red hand for seconds, bouncing at the rate of one bounce per second. Soon, another sixty bounces will be done, the third minute will be over: Mother is leaving…

Mala, the older sister, a chatterbox in normal circumstances, is also sunk in silence now. It is clear from her face that she is trying not to cry: Mother is leaving…

Even Gunia, the baby, who so far has behaved wonderfully, suddenly bursts into tears. Meaning that even the toddler is aware of an impending change: Mother is leaving...

And Mother, what does she have to say?

"I don't make a fuss over partings" – she had summed up the tenets of her belief when leaving the house, and even at this last moment before departure she does not succumb to hugs or kisses, remaining true to the hardness that has always ruled her. Again, Gunia alone is left out of the orbit of her sternness, earning a kiss and a caress. Next, Mother moves to her "big" daughter and son, delivering final instructions about their conduct in her absence, especially with respect to taking care of Gunia. Her voice transmits an inner calm, a sense of authority and a general air of self-confidence and security.

During the third minute, the son fixes a nervous gaze on Mother's appearance. Was it a heartfelt omen that caused him to well engrave the lines of her face in his memory, lest they change, God forbid? From Mother's figure, his eyes move to the red hand of the platform clock which has mercilessly just bounced for the sixtieth time and completed the final minute: Mother is leaving!

The stationmaster is already at the train car, oozing authority; a four-cornered red cap on his head, a flag in his hand and a whistle between his lips. It is he who will send the train on its way with a wave of the flag and a whistle. At the sight of his waving hand, Mother hurries to the steps of the train car. She puts her right foot first – for good luck! – and places her right hand first on the railing of the stairs – this, too, for luck and blessing!

Ha-ha – the son can't refrain from injecting a trace of a snicker into this moment of sadness – *how many superstitions nestle in that wise head, despite its erudition and broad horizons!*

At the very last second, the shy high-school boy bolts out from hiding, grabs Golda's left, free hand and, wordlessly, plants a long, voracious, intoxicating kiss on it. The children giggle, as children do in such situations. The father, as if caught in the act, lowers his eyes in even greater embarrassment. Golda does not react: she is not bowled over by her husband's emotional outburst nor, however, does she wish to protest. Hard as ever, she is swallowed up in the car as the train starts to pull out. Aazik waves a hesitant hand: Golda – Goldeh – Goldeniu is leaving…

Golda kept her promise. Every four days, starting with the second week after her departure, the postman, Piłsudski's old legionnaire, knocked on the door of the Wróbel home, holding a picture postcard with an Austrian stamp in its upper right corner (in those days, apartment building foyers had no individual mailboxes). The postcards not only enriched the son's collection qualitatively and quantitatively, but, taken all together, constituted an illustrated quasi-guidebook of the Austrian capital. In fact, forty-one years later, on his first trip to his mother's beloved city, the son knew the city not only from the youthful memories which she shared with her children, but also from the postcards she sent in 1927.

In her strong hand, Golda would add to the postcards a few lines written in Polish – whether words of greeting to the children or a further explanation of the picture and warm impressions of the site – but, about herself, she said nothing. To Aazik, on the other hand, she sent a long letter in Yiddish every week, the content of which, as customary then, was kept from the children. Nevertheless, it was enough for the children to glance at Father's clamped face after he read the letter and lovingly folded the page and hid it away in the gloom of his pocket; and it was enough to peek briefly into the black, that suddenly diluted the soft brown of his eyes, to know that sightseeing was only one reason, and not the main one at that, for Mother's trip to Vienna. Indeed, in overhearing conversations Father conducted with acquaintances and with his adult students, the son noticed a frequent mention of the Yiddish word *krebs*, which was unfamiliar to him. Rushing to look it up in his German-Polish Langenscheidt, he almost fell over when he saw the Polish translation.

Cancer was hush-hush in those days, and the Polish word for it, *rak*, was never voiced above a whisper. Doctors, too, at a loss as to treatment, did not help to dispel the clouds of obscurity. Clouds and secrecy! The dimmer the cloud, the heavier the secrecy of *Krebs* and *rak*, and, with it, fear of the unknown, the mere mention of the disease setting hearts atremble.

Adding to the alarm was Aunt Zippora, who, with the best of intentions, decided to write to the children. Zippora, however, did not consult her sister; she did not know that the children had not been informed of their mother's condition and the purpose of her trip. They did know of the visits to the Kraków clinic in the earlier weeks, but they had not been told of the new radium treatment that had been tried on their mother, or of the unnecessary chest surgery she had undergone, which had left her with terrible scabies around the scar, burning into her skin like fire and causing her untold agony. Nor did the agony disappear during Golda's brief spells of respite, for she was gripped by the fear of its imminent resumption. "Mother feels well, but keeps complaining about the itch," Zippora reported. Childless herself, and knowing how dependent her niece and nephew were on their mother, she thought it wise to explain to them that now it was their mother who would be needing a show of understanding. "The tests are finished and in the time that she has left here, she takes strolls in the city all day long. We are all happy to see her so strong and walking, walking everywhere despite the scabies, which is driving her mad."

"*Walking, walking everywhere despite the scabies, which is driving her mad*" – the son echoes the gist of Zippora's letter between gritted teeth. It was her marveling at Golda's walking – an activity in which Zippora discerned the start of her sister's recovery – that filled the son's heart with a dread that thoroughly rattled him and wracked his nerves, even though he had no more than a dim sense

354 CHESTNUTS OF YESTERYEAR: A JEWISH ODYSSEY

of its source and context. His face drained, as if a ghost had intruded between the lines of the letter and fixed its gaze on him. The recesses of his memory dredged up an alternative interpretation for the walking Zippora so welcomed – a subversive interpretation that rejected the activity as a sign of recuperation but saw it rather as the reverse: an ongoing agony and the symptom of a compulsive pacing instinct, cast in the crucible of incurable physical suffering.

'Walking, walking'! Doesn't the robust double verb itself belie the engaging image in the previous line of her 'strolling in the city' to take in the sights? – the boy questions from an instinctive perception beyond his years, while the scenes of manic striding from Tarnów's recent past unintentionally thrust themselves into his field of vision to lodge at a decisive spot in his thoughts.

'Walking, walking'! – the son continues to remonstrate silently with his aunt and perhaps also with himself. *And what if it turns out, contrary to her sister's assessment, that Golda's walking shows not a sense of triumph over the unsettling scabies but submission to it, being driven by a hidden force, in the absence of a cure, to walk and walk in order to escape from herself?*

To his astonishment, the son realizes that he has unwittingly drawn an analogy with "that" Tarnów woman. Appalled by the comparison, he instantly banishes it in anger:

No, no, any similarity between the two is a false impression. There is an abyss of difference between Mother and the other, even if pain was forced on both. So eager is the son to emphasize that the ways of the one will never correspond to the ways of the other, that he is even careful not to explicitly articulate the name of the other woman in the same breath as his mother's.

No, no, not at all, no way! – he again draws a clear line between the two, vowing not to allow any such comparison to ever invade his thoughts again. Little does he know that it will take no more than a week for him to break his vow and that the analogy will be one he was to continue to draw for four long years.

5

From the end of the summer of 1927 until the autumn of 1931 a heavy cloud hung over the Wróbel home, with twin hells, like two great black hounds, crouching at its doorway: the private hell of Mother and the common hell of all. No one probed what the two-year-old experienced until her sixth birthday, but the seven-year-old and the eight-and-a-half-year-old, who at the end of the period would be eleven and twelve-and-a-half respectively, along with their father, came to learn that hell was not an orderly, organized site of suffering, where rows of sinners faced rows of calamities to be meted out to them, but rather a network of grasping canals that bring their victims down to rock bottom at utter random and in total indifference, without bothering to ascertain their names or whether they are saints or sinners.

Yet, worse than the hell of suffering is the hell of fear. And fear has two faces: the intangible one – fear of the unknown – which assailed the children and was nourished on fragments of information absorbed by their young minds from unguarded whispers and soundless sighs bespeaking volumes; and the other fear, that gripped Mother – fear of what she had long known from personal experience. For, to her sorrow, over a period of two years, from 1918 to 1920, she had escorted her father to the Bonifrati clinic in Kraków, and in shock watched him decline unhindered as he was sucked down into an abyss. Now she herself was to be treated at the very same clinic, and for the same disease, she believed, that had taken her father – and the fear deranged her mind. This is what Aazik meant when he remarked, "Death strikes only once, but he who fears death feels it dozens of times."

"The main thing is for us not to upset Mother nor take offence at what she says or does, even if she fumes against us and we consider her anger unjust" – Aazik instructed his children prior to her return – "for the measure of her fury reflects the measure of her fear." As a result, the father decided to swallow his wife's insults and submit to her whims, hoping thereby to calm her raging spirit. Could he have guessed that he, who took care of her and understood her feelings better than anyone else, was to be the first sacrifice on the altar of her outbursts?

From a distance of seventy years, the son examines those four years that followed seven happy years of childhood – the four most miserable years in the life of the family, which, at the very same time, was groaning under the yoke of economic depression that brought Polish Jewry to the brink of starvation. Even today, after most of the representatives of that generation have already passed on, the son of Aazik and Golda – who is himself now ripe in years – cannot shake off the sense of sorrow from that period. All too keenly, the scenes of family crisis in consequence of Mother's condition parade before his eyes, along with the scenes of economic depression wrought by the times. Indeed, had not he, the son, at the end of the four years dared to take the initiative into his own hands even though he was only eleven years old (and feeling a hundred), the dual troubles would have brought down the entire home.

While the suffering was felt by all, there were two main protagonists in the tragedy. Mother's suffering was, without a doubt, unbearable and she featured as the main actress on the four-year stage of crisis. Yet, the more tragic of the two figures rising from the mists of the generation was Father. He – an excellent teacher and top-notch educator, whose straight, strong, proud stature had been likened to an oak – wallowed now, downtrodden and defeated, in the wrath of the woman he loved and admired and who, most probably in her own warped way, still credited him with the springtime of their affections. Under the rod of her anger, Aazik seemed to slowly disintegrate from within, not understanding why he had been singled out as the target for her darts; nevertheless, so as not to exacerbate the groundless confrontations by any unnecessary word or deed, he sealed his lips at the sound of her curses. His body shrank, his eyes dulled, and his back stooped. It was as if he shrank from looking straight at the world in which he had until now walked tall and towering amid admiration and affection. It was as if he would collapse under the weight of questions cast at him from without, or posed voicelessly from within, both in the hearts of his friends and in his own heart.

Oh, the questions, the questions! Like an insistent swarm of bees they continue to whir around the son's ears in buzzing annoyance, returning, like a bad dream, to haunt him for seventy years: why did Mother seek to crush the giant who was her husband of thirteen years and the father of her children? What perverse pleasure did she derive from torturing the man who respected her and respectably provided for her? And worst of all: why did Father allow her to do with him as she pleased and submit to her without struggle? Only years later – in order to write this book and, perhaps, as a personal catharsis – when the son dared to collate his memories with those of his sister and the testimonies of relatives and former students, did he arrive at the notion that he had plumbed the souls of the tragic protagonists and understood the ebb and flow in the tidal relationship of his two parents. Let it be said at once that, initially, the decline in the father's status was not the result of Golda's capriciousness. As incredible as it may seem, it was Aazik himself, as the healthy partner, who, with the intent of curing his spouse by homespun "psychotherapy," willingly and lovingly consented to a process of self-negation in order to encourage his sick wife's self-love. Disturbed by her fears, he sought to restore to her a sense of her own worth, as the only woman in the neighborhood who excelled in languages, literature, history and in the universal nature of her education.

"Perhaps she feels threatened by my achievements in general education, gained over long years as an autodidact," Aazik wondered to himself. To undo any such threat, he banished the picture of the excommunicated Spinoza, which, in his eyes, represented his own struggle with himself, relegated the philosophy books (except for Maimonides) from the front of the bookcase to behind the rabbinical literature and, for his wife's sake, cleared the stage of general culture which she wished to rule alone, while he returned to bend over his *Gemara* as he had done years earlier.

The change demanded that Aazik rewrite the Wróbel saga of the past generation – to conceal his part in the progressive atmosphere at home and attribute its secular culture exclusively to Golda. The "camouflage" was not difficult to carry out. His return to the world symbolized by the *Kloyz* and his reincarnation as a Jewish scholar locked within the four walls of *Halakha* did not seem unbelievable. Once his reversion was accepted as genuine (so he thought), it would seem natural for him to defer to his wife in all matters of secular and modern culture, rather than traditional, Hebrew literature. Thus, the husband/father affirmed before his wife and children Golda's cultural superiority. What's more, in deliberate self-sacrifice, he placed his neck within the noose of her unquestionable dominion over family "togetherness." All this in the hope that these two elements – the rebuilding of her sense of cultural superiority and the conscious reinstatement of Golda's authority in household management – would spawn the antibodies to exterminate her fears of cancer and death.

All too soon, however, Aazik lost control of the process and was crushed beneath the wheels of the machine that he himself had devised and set into motion. So complete and convincing seemed his return to the Talmudic world, that everyone, including the children, accepted the rift between the spiritual world of the bearded and black-garbed Jewish scholar and the world of his liberal wife, not as a pretense but as the real thing, even after the crisis had passed. Sixty years were to elapse before the son, while interviewing one of his father's outstanding student for the archives of Tel Aviv's Diaspora Museum, learned, to his amazement, that his father had secretly studied German while still at the *Kloyz* (Mendelssohn's German, in Hebrew orthography of course), after which – in bar-ter – his student had taught him to read German literature in the original Gothic letters.

This surprising bit of news, gleaned from the interview, solved a riddle that had puzzled the son since his youth. At the end of each high school year, parents were invited to a review of their children's accomplishments. Apart from the dramatization of a play written by the pupils themselves, and a musical performance, the program included the recitation of a poem in one of the languages taught at the school: Hebrew, Polish and German. On two separate occasions, when the son's turn came to recite Schiller's *"Die Bürgschaft"* and *"Das Lied von der Glocke,"* he noticed his father's lips moving soundlessly in the audience, just ahead of the words he recited. Now, after sixty years, he realized that his father had known the poems by heart.

Golda did not comprehend the magnitude of the sacrifice her husband undertook to offer up for her – a sacrifice that was truly anonymous, a gift for the sake of giving, to save her self-image. Fixed on her pain and fears, she viewed the widening gulf between her culture and that of her spouse's as an objective process, rather than as the result of conscious self-negation on Aazik's part for her sake. In the end, in total opposition to her intellectual integrity, she was beguiled into gleaning from the new situation the honey of a perverse pleasure, an egotistically cruel pleasure, showing arrogance towards and contempt of her life partner.

For the first few days after the queen's restoration to her castle there was nothing untoward in her behavior and, despite the scabies, she returned to full functioning, capably performing her pre-Viennese routine chores: gift shopping for the coming holidays, stocking the pantry with goods she bought at the Burek market and at Abish's grocery, preparing family meals on time, keeping the flat clean, taking care of the toddler and, to her son's joy, returning to reading again from the book that had been interrupted by her trip to Vienna.

Under Mother's management, the apartment, too, reverted to its former routine, with the exception of one change that concerned the double-winged glass door between the front room, which housed the kitchen, and the back room, which contained the beds and closets.

The door, which was also the dividing line between the rooms, had until then been left open day and night, thereby, in fact, *merging* the two rooms into one large space. The daily care of Mother's scar, however, restored the door to its original purpose, which was to *separate* the two rooms by its closure. Thus, when the large space was bisected, the back room served as a unit unto itself, protecting privacy until it was reopened. This arrangement was now necessary, since simple flats at the time did not have their own bathrooms. The toilet at the disposal of the Wróbels was separate from the flat and accessed by a door on the balcony; and the laundry tub, once a week, became a bathtub for mother and children (while the father continued to use the *mikveh*). The flat itself, in the front room, had a single tap for running water with a cast iron sink affixed beneath it. This was the only water supply, used for cooking, washing and drinking.

From now on, in the absence of a bathroom, Mala would fill a bowl of hot water in the kitchen each morning, and bring it through to the back room. Golda quickly shut the winged doors behind her and, on the other side, turned her attention to the "growth" that had lodged on her chest. Tearfully, Mala described to her brother the red, somewhat swollen rectangle which had adhered to the mother's skin and obviously looked like a foreign body, with red quasi-antennae sprouting from its four sides. The children had never seen a live crab, but after sketching what Mala had seen and comparing it with the sketch in the nature textbook from a higher school grade, the two agreed that, in truth, "Mother's growth" was similar in form and color to a crab. They assumed, in their innocence, that the similarity in appearance and color was the hallmark of the phenomenon and the reason that it was named cancer. Mala bathed the "growth" with hot water and cooled its tissues with a salicylite solution – a treatment of no therapeutic value which served to reduce the itch and still the scabies. When the door opened once more, Mother would move back and forth between the rooms, as if exploring the route she would require under the onslaught of the "walking obsession."

But, at two-week intervals, Golda had to travel to Kraków for further treatment. At such times, all the scaffolds of restraint with which she normally propped herself up suddenly toppled, as she took to "walking, walking" along the well-known route from the end of the front room to the end of the back room, swearing and cursing in words that had never before been heard in this home and that no one had ever suspected of being part of her Polish or Yiddish vocabulary.

Miriamche! – the son's lips surprised him, involuntarily breaking his vow to defy all comparison between his mother and the Halberstam woman.

He quickly caught himself and proceeded to convince himself of the great difference in the character and situation of the two women. The difference, after all, was of the utmost significance – the son believed – and one should not be misled by incidental similarities that had no basis in fact. Unlike Miriamche, whose anguish (and, some said, madness) had been a chronic, irreversible condition for fifteen years, Golda's problem was specific and recurred only at brief intervals. All the rational analyses, however, lost their meaning one day when Golda, after returning from an especially onerous treatment at the Bonifrati clinic in Kraków, launched into manic pacing back and forth, back and forth, along the length of the two rooms of the flat. This time, as she strode, her lips obsessively mumbled "*Boże mój, Boże mój* (my God, my God)", and the six repetitive Polish syllables sounded like an endless series of long, long sighs. Suddenly, an arrow seemed to pierce her heart and stop her dead in her tracks. Hurting from the train journey to Kraków and back and the difficult medical treatment there, she raised her two arms heavenward and wailed in Polish: *"Boże mój, Boże mój, dlaczegoś mnie tak ukarał?"* ("My God, my God, why have you punished me so?"), and, exhausted, she dropped to the floor.

"Miriamche!" – the son rushed to his mother's aid as a thousand sirens relentlessly screeched in his head. *So the Halberstam woman won, after all,* he acknowledged. From that day on, Miriamche's *"Goteniu lieber, farvus host du mikh geshtruft?"* turned all evasive rationalization into pointless quibbling. All that remained were the memories of 1926 and their inescapable, distracting resemblance to 1927. The frightening logic triumphed over every protest and every excuse, forcing the boy to face facts. Yes, Golda, his mother, and Miriamche, responded to suffering in one and the same way. The color drained from his cheeks. Flinging himself on the bed, the son wept soundlessly and tearlessly.

6

The summer of 1927 passed, and the holidays came and went, bringing with them autumn and falling leaves. Golda's morning treatments behind the shut bedroom doors became a matter of course, although the resumption of school made it difficult for Mala to shoulder the burden; after a few weeks she had no choice but to stop her assistance altogether. More problematic were the scheduled bi-weekly trips to Kraków: it was Golda rather than the doctors who insisted that the check-ups continue, refusing to accept their pronouncement that the situation was stable, the "growth" was apparently not malignant and that they had done all that was in their power to do. Golda interpreted their words euphemistically as lack of hope, an interpretation that fanned her sense of frustration and despair. These feelings were translated into more furious pacing before leaving for Kraków and after her return, accompanied by fiercer charges against God and man.

Aazik helped with the housework, as did the "big" children when they came home from school. The tensions at home did not seem to have an adverse effect on their studies, a surplus of resources from previous years probably granting them immunity. Violin lessons also continued, with only the teachers changing: after early instruction by Rausch, the future Hubermans passed into the hands of the well-known Auber. True, Mala tried the endurance of her listeners by virtuoso departures off every bar and note, so that Auber, in desperation and with tongue in cheek composed a tune for her, which he called "Oy Mala, Oy Mala!"; the Wróbels, however, ignored the broad hint, cleaving to their conviction that son and daughter were to study together, without discrimination!

Although at school their marks may not have suffered, at home the children showed other worrisome symptoms of the prevalent tension. For two long months, Mala could not fall asleep at night, drenching her pillow with bitter tears; and Hesiek – who was now seven-and-a-half and already in the third grade – began to wet his bed again at night. Shut up within herself, Golda did not know how to handle the situation. She never dreamt that it was connected to the son's fears about his mother's fate: the doubts about her chances for recovery on the one hand, and the problem of her resemblance to Miriamche, on the other. The mother did not try – or perhaps in her condition was unable – to decipher the message sent out by her son's behavior, both consciously and unconsciously. Instead, she saw in his renewed bed-wetting a form of shirking of responsibility and she reacted accordingly. As punishment, she included her son among those "deserving" the abominable adjectives she hurled at the world, labeling him with the vulgar Polish tag of *szczoch*, meaning "pisser."

"Come upstairs, *szczochu!*" Golda called one evening to her son who had dawdled in the yard near the chestnut tree with the permanent gang of Bóżnic Street.

"Why do you shame Hesiek in public, Mother?" Mala defied Father's advice of restraint, protesting against the insult that Mother had delivered to her brother. "He is there with his friends. How can he look them in the eye in school tomorrow, when you humiliate him so?"

"Then he had better not wet his bed," replied the personification of obtuseness, ending the discussion.

The hardest thing for the children to bear, however, was Mother's manic pacing, which divulged her fear of the impending check-up in Kraków. As her rage grew, the children learned to dive under the parental twin beds "for cover." Through the narrow strip of air between the height of the bed and the floor, they watched a pair of shoes stride back and forth from room to room, and were trying to calculate when the storm would die down and it would be safe for the "indwellers of darkness and of the shadow of death" (as they romantically invoked a biblical verse to themselves) to crawl out without fear. Little by little, the romantic aspect of the dark hideaway under the beds grew in proportion, opening up before the children an enthralling world – enthralling, even when Mother was her normal self again. The day would come, after four stormy years, when the hideaway beneath the beds would play an important part in resolving the tragedy of the Wróbel home.

As time passed, it became clear that Mother needed help to care for both her person and the housework. The choice fell on the Polish woman who had worked at the Wróbels' in the summer of 1925, when childbirth had confined Mother to her bed. To the surprise of the parents, the children rejected the choice, but would not say why. As a result, Golda dismissed their stance as childish foolishness and hired the woman. From that day on, an evil wind blew through the Wróbel home. And the wind had a name: *ZOŚKA*.

The Zośka episode – which the children had withheld from

their parents – revolved around one Sunday morning in August of 1925, when Zośka had taken Golda's and Aazik's son and daughter for a walk. On the surface, she was doing her mistress a favor, freeing her, after childbirth, of the care of the older children. But this was not the intent of the pious, zealous gentile. To the sound of pealing bells, she led the children of her Jewish employers (a six-and-a-half-year-old girl and a five-year-old boy) to the two-tower Church of the Missionaries at the western entrance to town. The church had been inaugurated during the first decade of the twentieth century, the same period that the silver-domed "Great Synagogue" in the eastern part of Tarnów had been inaugurated by the children's grandfather, Cantor Weinman.

Upon entering the edifice, Zośka removed the cap from the boy's head and, inside, in the stifling darkness, exuding an odor of incense and tallow, she lit two candles on their behalf, a candle for each child's soul, and placed them at the foot of the Virgin. Then she knelt before the Virgin and murmured words of prayer that the children did not manage to understand; both Mala and Hesiek, incidentally, noticed that the church candles were different in color and smell from the candles that Mother lit on the eve of the Sabbath and holidays. She then showed the children the church in detail and, as if letting them in on a secret, warned them not to tell at home what they had seen on their walk. Zośka did not leave matters at that. Upon returning home, she raised the girl, and then the boy, to the *mezuzah* (door scroll) at the entrance to the house, ordered them to touch the *mezuzah* with two fingertips and then place the fingers on their lips like a kiss, and thereby swear not to reveal the secret to anyone. From that time on, the children saw themselves bound by the oath and therefore did not tell their parents the reason for their opposition to the maid who was to keep house for them, even though they were well aware that the disclosure of the secret would have put paid to the plan of hiring Zośka.

Within a day or two, Zośka took over all the various household tasks: cleaning, laundry, going to market to buy vegetables, fruit and all other necessary goods, and, above all, looking after the baby and helping Golda every morning. The new maid, however, spread her protection not only over Golda's home, but also over her soul.

"What chatters' feast keeps them closeted in there for half the day?" Mala turned up her nose upon returning from school with her brother at noon on Zośka's first day in the Wróbel home. She was to repeat the question again and again at the sight of the shut glass doors that were meant to stay open day and night (apart from the brief morning interval to allow Mother privacy to dress the wound), and yet they only opened shortly before noon. Indeed, not before the autumn sun was at its apex in the sky did the maid turn her hand to her tasks, which she did perform most competently. The new order was repeated from then on every day. For the first half of the work-day, the two women sat behind the door, immersed in endless chit-chat as if they were long lost friends. In fact, however, the chasm between them could not have been wider: an illiterate gentile woman, steeped to the neck in Catholic zealotry, and an educated, free-thinking Jewish lady.

"What does that dried-up spinster rattle on about for hours on end, addling Mother's brains?" Hesiek threw in his own irritation. "How is conversation even possible between wise, learned Mother and that utterly uncouth, ignorant woman?" The son thought better of his wonder after years had passed: "In her thirst to talk to someone, Golda no doubt felt that sharing her secrets with the gentile woman offered natural protection from gossip within the Jewish community, which would not have been the case had she unburdened herself before her Jewish neighbors; the armor of her privacy thus made it easier for her to reveal to the *goya*, ignorant as the woman may have been, the darkest recesses of her soul. In the face of her fear of death, which unbalanced her, Golda held on to Zośka as to a lifesaver that had come her way or, at least, as the only spark of comfort in her world that had been laid waste."

"Rasputina," the children began calling her between themselves because of the woman's hypnotic effect on their mother. The image of the ignorant, fanatic monk, who had exercised a demonic control over the Czarina's soul, was still an exciting topic of tales and conversation in eastern Europe, for only twelve years had elapsed since Rasputin's murder and less than a decade since the revolution had done away with the Czar and his family. In the children's eyes, Zośka's fanaticism, self-righteousness and, above all, her ignorance, highlighted the satanic likeness between her and the monk.

Slowly but surely, Rasputina's poison trickled into the convoluted chambers of her mistress's mind, until, by the end of the subversive process, she had destroyed one of the last bastions of Golda's sense of security: her trust in her husband. For no apparent reason – apart from what the children guessed was Zośka's incitement of their mother before the glass doors opened at noon – Golda would erupt from the dimness of the back room and, like a bird of prey, swoop down in body and voice on the front room, where Aazik, at that hour, was bent over his *Gemara,* surrounded by a group of students who had just come from school and whose parents desired them to have an extra hour's instruction in Judaism. Taking deliberate advantage of the young people's presence, Golda would unleash a string of abuse and aspersions, plainly deriving pleasure from insulting her husband in public. It seemed (the son shuddered) as if Miriamche's spirit had possessed Golda's body like a *dybbuk* and was the source of the terrible curses on her tongue, Golda herself lacking the strength to oppose the *dybbuk* or exorcise it from her body. Zośka had evidently discerned her mistress's weakness and a gloating smile shamelessly spread over her cheeks as she listened, while doing the dishes at the sink, to the torrential outpour of slurs that she had so gloriously instigated.

Shocked, the children sought to decode the new expressions that soon colored Golda's daily dose of rage and which she would deliver into the air as soon as the door opened at mid-day. Especially chilling was the Yiddish combination that the children had never heard before – *shiksa-ying* (*shiksa* chaser) – dropped like a stink bomb into the air of the flat. Despite their young years, the Wróbel children sensed that the epithet had "dirty" connotations, though the actions at which it hinted were not made explicit nor was it clear whether it had any basis in fact or were simply a generalized libel. The matter remained a mystery until Mala rose up – yes, Mala, who had a reputation for "understanding these things", being the living spirit in the "sex education classes" that Millek Lauber liked to shower on the building's younger denizens, and having a talent for immediately ferreting out the "juicy" pages in every book (as opposed to her brother who remained an innocent and, until his *bar-mitzvah*, believed that the male objective was the female's belly button). Hurt by her mother's smears, Mala decided to solve the mystery of the *shiksa-ying* and do her father justice.

In the afternoon, she positioned herself in a hidden corner of the dark back corridor that encompassed the four flats on the second story of the building and, seeing but unseen, eavesdropped on the daily meeting of the four *shiksas* who worked on that floor: Anna, Magda, Kasia and Zośka. A "gossip carnival" if there ever was one! Without meaning to, the four imparted to Mala racy sexual lore while sharing with one another their excitements of the previous night with their suitors. None of this diverted Mala from her single-minded purpose: to listen to the gentile girls gossiping about their Jewish employers and the Jewish housewives whom they "fed" information about their husbands' deeds – deeds that either had or hadn't taken place.

The tone of impatience in Zośka's reaction to the tales of conquest of the other girls, all much younger than she, amused Mala: "Religious fanaticism or the jealousy of a middle-aged woman?" But her ears perked up when Zośka bragged about leading her *zhid* (Jew) mistress by the nose: "That fool, who looks down at us because of her so-called wisdom and education, swallowed all the stories with relish," Mala repeated the boasts to her brother. "Lately" – she quoted Zośka – "I provoked her into thinking that her husband is having it on with all the women on this floor and, she, who (at my advice) is 'denying him,' and who knows that 'a man can't do without', almost bursts with jealousy. What a hoo-ha we will soon witness!"

7

The "hoo-ha" was not long in coming. "Aaaaaaaa-aaaaaaaaaa-aaaaaaaa" – a spine-chilling wail pierced the air from the back room where Golda and Zośka, as usual, were closeted till mid-day. And the wail rose and fell and rose and fell again, like the moan of a wounded animal shot by a hunter for pleasure and left in the field to drown in its own blood. The wail was not like the harsh cry the Mother emitted during her walking, and certainly as far removed from her ordinary form of expression in the days when her world was still intact, as heaven is from earth. Like the cruel hunter, Zośka left Golda to bleed after having fed her on vile "information" that destroyed her self-image as wife, while she, Zośka, reaped the fruit of her intrigue.

A split second before the ring of the wail died down, Golda herself burst from the double-doors of the room. Drunk on the poisonous lies Zośka had been serving her for the past few hours, the wife now mustered the last residues of her emotional strength to pull herself together and stand up and, turning the wail into a cry and the cry into billowing squeals, she gave her husband an order which her flushed face and clamped fists left no doubt that she meant him to carry it out:

"Get out of my house, *shiksa-ying*, and never come back!"

And as if she ceased to care "what will the neighbors say?", she repeated Zośka's medley of the husband's escapades, summing up the charges against Aazik in a deliberately loud voice so that the neighbors, too, might support the ban:

"Get out of here, you libertine, go, go to your *kurvas*! See, they're waiting for you, the whores!"

The verbal torment aimed at the husband stretched for long, long minutes. Apparently, she, who had been regarded in the neighborhood as the "literary princess," the "arbiter of good taste," and the "cultural pioneer," enjoyed flinging abuse and dipping in the foul waters of obscenity (to spare the ears of the reader, only the more moderate of her expressions have been cited here). As she sunk to the very bottom of vulgarity, she derided Aazik's fabricated love-mates to the point of the ridiculous: "What did you think? You pinch Anna's *tuhes* – and I will keep quiet? You stroke Magda's bloated *tzitzes* which would disgust a real man – and I will watch from the side and say nothing? You brush against that stinking bag of bones known as Kasia – and I will ignore it? Why, you even tried to start with Zośka, as she herself told me, but she is my friend and fended you off, plain and simple. So go, you miserable filth, and don't defile my home!"

The first to recover from the shock were the children, and three young throats (including little Gunia's, who was now three years old) uttered a dreadful lament, a terrible chorus of three thin voices that quickly merged into a harrowing yowl:

"No, Mother, please, don't send Father away!"

Unwittingly, the children thus ratified the principle that Mother, who, with her foul language, had appropriated exclusive possession of the home, was entitled, without argument or response, to evict Father, or alternatively, to allow him to remain in the flat out of the goodness of her heart. Nor did Aazik appeal the principle, even though the entire property was the fruit of his labors. Golda's sudden attack left him standing frozen at the end of the room, refusing to believe that this was really happening. Only when he saw Zośka slipping out of the back room, did he understand that, this time, it was not another of Golda's spontaneous outbursts, but that Zośka was responsible for what had taken place here before his very eyes and the eyes of his children who were shocked to tears.

"Come now, Goldeniu, enough," Aazik murmured slackly – "you know that this is nothing but a nasty intrigue concocted by that witch who pretends to be your friend; in fact, she behaved in total contradiction to what she told you. This is her revenge for my having pushed her away when she started to dangle about me and rub up against me after you left for Vienna. I swear to you, Goldeniu, on the lives of our children, that's the whole truth. See for yourself. Go ask the other three women if I ever once touched them – whether in the past or the present, whether while you were in Vienna or back here – as that wicked woman claims."

Golda did not go to check the facts, but simply continued to insist Aazik leave the house. The more she railed and insisted, however, the more and more strongly the children clung to their father, linking their arms to embrace him as if to stave off the vile sentence. At that point, Mother pulled out her ultimate card and, with blood-chilling stillness, delivered a final challenge into the faces of the young defenders:

"If that's your decision, it will be as you wish. But, you'd better know one thing: if he stays, I leave! The choice is yours." And, without wasting a moment, she went to the closet to pack her suitcases for her departure.

The threat upturned the plot dramatically, shifting the stage a hundred and eighty degrees. The sobbing children, who at first had supported Father, now, as if by some latent command, directed their weeping against him. And whereas before they had seen his leaving as a disaster, they were now gripped by a hysterical anxiety lest his exit be delayed and Mother carry out her threat instead. As a result, they began to cry and plead and push him towards the door, softly but firmly, urging him to go at once, at once, before it was too late: "Go, Father, please. If you don't, Mother will leave us!"

Golda won. Her manipulative measure ensured that not she,

but the children drive their father from home. Unpardonable manipulation! To his dying day, the son would remember Father's last look prior to his exile from home: it was not a look of grievance or fear, nor of resentment or despair, but of a terrible disappointment, cold as ice, and this, even though he understood that the boy had become a "stubborn and rebellious son" (in the biblical sense of the appellation) against his will. "That look" – the son's agonizing knows no bounds – must have been how Caesar had glanced at Brutus: 'You, too, Herschl'?"

Yes, from the day that Golda put into practice her personal "canon of zealotry" and cast out her husband, the father of her children, from the family home, there began for Aazik a three-year period of painful and desperate exile. In many ways, the physical conditions of his life now resembled the nine-year period long ago that he had spent at the *Kloyz*. Except that then he had been a mere country boy, all alone and virtually ignorant, who had turned up in a strange and alien town at the age of fourteen. And yet, despite the hardship and poverty, the eyes of the lad then had shone like two stars, imbued with a sense of mission and with the glorious dream of Torah. He had been fortunate, and after so many years his reputation had preceded him as a prodigy and sought-after teacher (with a solid income), married to the daughter of the "Great Synagogue" first cantor, an educated woman who gave him three wonderful children. But what good were all these, if after a quarter of a century, at the age of forty-seven, he again had to curl up on a wooden bench as in those days – this time, at the *bis-medrash* to which he had moved his studies in 1914 – left as lonely, if not lonelier, as he had been back then? For now there was no dream and no mission to make the suffering bearable, as it had been in his youth; all that remained now was the estrangement of a woman he adored and would never stop admiring.

From time to time, usually at the start of every month, the father and husband would return to his flat-that-was-not-his-anymore, place on the table the monthly salary that he had received from the school, or payment from someone whose son he had given *bar-mitzvah* lessons, and wait for the queen's dispensation. Sometimes, he was ordered to leave the house at once; at other times, his presence was found tolerable for several days, as if Golda needed a target for her arrows and availed herself of Aazik as the object of her abuse. Once her need was satisfied, she waved her hand at the door to signify that the time of grace was over. Aazik would leave without protest, and the children, too, said nothing, their eyes downcast in shame or in a mute plea for forgiveness that they were unable to articulate. Either way, there was no repetition of the wailing that had accompanied Aazik's initial banishment. Life without Father became a hard fact.

"Poor man," a few self-righteous neighbors clucked, "such a strong man," they chortled shyly, as women will when sharing innuendos about men.

"Poor woman," other neighbors countered, "she's sick, poor thing, and what can she do? But the children, at least, are clean and well cared for, and that's to her credit."

Time did not assuage the rage or pain that ripped Mother's heart to shreds, and, consequently, she did not soften her attitude towards Aazik. On the contrary, little by little, on the days when he was allowed to temporarily return home, it seemed to the children that Mother was about to resort to physical violence against the man who had never raised a hand at his children, let alone at his wife. What was it about Father's behavior that so angered her – the children wondered – or did she perhaps agree to his return with the very intention of torturing him? One day, arriving home from school ahead of time, because class had been dismissed early, the son found his parents confronting one another – Father was at one end of the double room, while Mother, swearing at and cursing him from the opposite end, hurled plates that smashed against his tough body to fall in clanking smithereens on the floor. Aazik neither stirred nor moved, apparently serving as a conscious target, out of the old rationalization that it was necessary to provide his wife with an avenue to vent her rage so that she could calm down. Only when a plate came too close to his head did he bend out of the way or move his head slightly to the right or left to avoid injury. "Enough already, Goldeniu," he repeated his soothing formula, "Enough, in any case I'm leaving now."

It is hard to say how many such incidents occurred over the three years, for the son was made aware of the violent brawl by pure chance, after coming home unexpectedly. They may have been a regular occurrence but, if so, they took place only when the small daughter was at pre-school and the "big" children at school. Still, anyone with eyes in his head could plainly see that the kitchen cupboard had "lost" most of its plates and that the frame above the sink, which held drying crockery, was left bare in shameful loneliness after every altercation.

Worse than the violence, however, was the humiliation, the ultimate weapon in Golda's ever-ready arsenal, which she used unflinchingly. She did so not only by daubing her victim in abuse and broadcasting it to her neighbors via shrieking, but also by acts which she planned in cold blood and unchecked depravity.

The worst, most humiliating, deliberate incident, perhaps, took place one lunch time at the height of a period of grace, when the children returned from kindergarten and school respectively, and Aazik, too, walked in from his daily teaching post at the Baron de Hirsch School. Golda stood at the stove, her back to the door, gazing at the fire, as her hand tended the flame that enwrapped the bottom of the pot in which the mid-day meal was cooking.

"I want a divorce." The sound came from Golda's direction, so hollow and colorless that it was difficult to know whether it was she who had spoken the words, or some nameless thought had suddenly donned a voice to mock them all. The room grew still, careful not to mar the silence. "I said I want a divorce" – yes, it was Golda, impatience and unrestraint beginning to creep into her tone. "Bring me a divorce bill, I said."

As if waking from a deep sleep, Aazik finally understood that the demand, clear now and awesomely transparent, was addressed to him: his beloved wife wished-demanded-insisted-ordered him to give her a divorce.

"*Shoin genig, Goldeniu,*" he began gently and soothingly, as if speaking to a child. "Enough already, Goldeniu."

But Golda couldn't bear it when he treated her like a child. "I want a divorce, and I want it without delay and without excuses."

Aazik tried to appeal to reason: "But why, Goldeniu. We are, in any case, separated, and as far as you're concerned I don't exist."

"I said: bring me a divorce bill, and so you will. Go at once to Yisif-Hayim the *dayan* (religious judge), and have him write out a divorce bill."

The command was unequivocal, yet Aazik still attempted to plead for his life: "Goldeniu, why should I make a fool of myself before Yisif-Hayim, who was my fellow-student at Reb Moishl's and who, even before he married the rabbi's daughter, used to look down on me as a mere 'country bumpkin'?"

"That's your affair," Golda answered dryly, "Go to Yisif-Hayim and bring back a divorce bill."

Oh, Father, you innocent! the son nods to his parent in adult nightmares. *Didn't you understand that whatever the pretext, the name of the game was humiliation? By voicing your fear of self-abasement before the* dayan, *your fellow student of old, you sealed your fate. Not only did you fail to arouse Golda's compassion, but quite the contrary, you gave her what she wanted most of all: to see you brought low and humbled – retribution for the debasement and humiliation you visited on your helpless wife by the secret acts you committed (according to Zośka) in the corridor. Moreover, to debase and humiliate your wife, you enlisted women who in her eyes were* kurvas!

No one can say what went through Aazik's mind when, after leaving the house at his wife's behest, he dragged his feet back – from Yisif-Hayim's house at Pilzno Gate to the Wróbel home on Bóżnic – his back stooped, his eyes dull, and a divorce bill burning through the fabric of his pocket. Did he see his life in ruins at the ruin of his marriage? Or did he, in his heart of hearts, censure all of womankind, believing that he was better off divorced, for no longer would he have to submit to the caprices of a woman and consciously make himself tiny for her sake, but would be free to spread his wings once more?

"I brought you the divorce bill you asked for."

The home was just as it was when he left: Golda gazing at the flames, the children sitting at the table without having touched their food, and the silence only now, for the first time, coming unraveled.

"I brought the divorce." Aazik repeated the message, for fear that Golda failed to absorb it.

"I heard you."

"The bill is not valid until you actually take it into your hands."

"I know."

"Here, it is, then." He stood at her side, the two of them facing the flames, and handed her the bill.

"OK. Now you can take the paper and throw it into the fire!"

"Goldeniu…"

It was over. The humiliation was complete. Golda looked at the fire devouring the Hebrew letters that had been rendered meaningless, and it seemed that the ghost of the spiteful grin that had clung to her face was gone now, jumping to its death in the consuming flames. Aazik, exhausted, dropped onto his chair and wept silently.

8

The remarks of praise uttered by the neighbors about the children being "clean and well cared for" were not idle talk. Between one outburst and another, the lives of the Wróbel youngsters proceeded normally, if more intensely. A higher power seemed to have dealt the children, who had not sinned, added energy to compensate for lost time. Between one outburst and another, the mother took an interest in the children's activities: singing songs and telling stories to the "little one", which, in her opinion, the kindergarten fell short of; suggesting ideas for elective essays the "big" children had to compose at home to read aloud before the whole class, and commenting on style ("Style maketh the man," she would quote Shakespeare). She also encouraged the budding signs of creative writing in her son, and, at the same time, went on instructing him in the French language and French culture. In the evening, Golda read aloud to her children from the collections of modern Hebrew poetry that became available after 1925, when the Kanner-Weinberg Hebrew book store opened on Wałowa Street, and recited from the collections of Polish poetry that she picked out at Seiden's bookstore, also on Wałowa; recitations were popular with audiences at the time, and every school took pride in its declaimers, Golda's son among them.

Between one outburst and another, the mother also strove to broaden musical education: she would take her son to concerts and obtain from Seiden notes of the operas she remembered with nostalgia from her sojourn in Vienna, yearning for her son to play her the arias on his violin – all this in addition to the music literature that he soaked up at Auber's. At times, she hinted – and this was her great dream – that her son, when he grew up, would edit the manuscripts of the works bequeathed to her by her father, the composer, and rescue them from oblivion. "Oblivion is an artist's second death," she said. Alas, this dream would never come true.

But certain things came to a halt during those four miserable years. There were no more climbs up the mountain with Mother or dramatization of historic scenes. Likewise, Golda stopped the train trips with the children to Kraków and, after some time, her own visits to the Bonifrati clinic, even though the fear of cancer and death did not let go of her, setting its mark in her life and the life of the entire family.

The *Gemara* lessons also continued as before, though at a different venue. Every day at dawn, Aazik walked down from Fish Square to meet his son at the corner of Goldhammera and Wałowa, and the two, as before, would make their way to the end of Krakowska; there, at the small *bis-medrash* of Shayeh Silberpfenig, Aazik found a place for his groups in which his son could also take part. After two to three hours of *Gemara* study, the son would take his leave and go to school. The fact that the father came to meet him from the square of the *Great Bis-medrash,* confirmed the children's assumption that that was where he spent his nights, on a wooden bench, as he had done at the *Kloyz* in his youth. "We were so happy that Mother didn't leave us, that, to our shame" – the son agonizes to this day – "we never wondered how Father made out on his own, where he did laundry, where he ate his food, or, if there was someone to prepare at least one hot meal for him a day. He volunteered no information about his life, so as not to worry us, and we, woefully blind and deaf, never asked."

Despite the routine, the situation clearly deteriorated. Father's prolonged absence – for, since the incident of the divorce, he would hand over his salary to his son to pass on to his mother – left its mark on Golda. Her rage-meter steadily rose, seeking alternative outlets for the release of pressure. The "big children" turned out to be a ready target. A new stage began: violence against the children.

It must be said that physical discipline of children – both by parents, for defiance, and by educators at Orthodox *heder* or regular school, for disturbing the class and failure to pay attention or prepare one's homework – was an accepted educational device at the time, used in both the Jewish and general school systems, and neither those who delivered the punishment nor those who received it had any doubt as to its justification. Reb Aazik, of course, never lifted a hand at a pupil or hit his own son (at the most, he may have nudged a shoulder to rouse a student) and, no doubt, there were others who acted as he did. Nevertheless, the saying of the wisest of men in the *Book of Proverbs*, that "he who spares the rod hates his son," lent legitimacy to the violent pedagogic method. On the wall of the *heder*, within arm's reach of the seat of the *melamed* (teacher) or his assistant, the *belfer*, hung the *kainchik*, whether for actual use or as a warning – a miniature whip with long leather strands dropping from its handle. Also Mr. Lieblich, Principal of the Hebrew elementary school, did, despite his well-known liberal views, permanently keep a ruler on his desk, not for measuring or drawing, but in order to deliver two light raps to the back of the outstretched hand of a disruptive pupil whom the teacher had "sent to the Principal." In general, parents and educators agreed on the need for moderate physical discipline of children when called for, and the pupils, too, knew what was expected of them: presenting their bodies or hands for punishment without protest.

What constituted an acceptable beating, and what was considered excessive? Unwritten rules governed the method: corporal punishment was meted out only after a parent or educator had quelled his anger, so as to act out of conscious restraint; it was to be delivered only with a leather implement – such as the *kainchik* or a trouser belt – or a light, wooden ruler; never with a fist or hard instrument, for these could injure a child. If no special object were employed, an open-handed slap to the cheek or the bottom was deemed adequate and proper. Above all: the force used in physical punishment had to be restrained and controlled. Not so Golda, however. Once she embarked on the course of beatings, she grew increasingly more extreme, ignoring the unwritten rules and lashing out at her son and daughter in instantaneous, angry reaction. Her rage clearly boiling, she used all the force in her hand to continue inflicting her lashes. All too soon, she also disregarded the rules governing the implements of punishment, and resorted to objects that were universally deemed improper.

One day, during Mother's regular, demented, invective-spewing pacing – a pacing during which the children learned to stay out of her way along the two-room route – Mala, by mistake, crossed her path and Mother bumped into her. Grabbing hold of Mala's two braids, Golda started pulling her head from side to side with all the might she could gather, and it was quite a few minutes before the poor girl managed to free herself from captivity and, in pain, dive into the comforting "refuge" under the bed.

Miriamche! The son felt his heart pinch as Bóżnic Street's familiar scenes from a few years earlier surfaced to assail his memory in all their horror. But this time, conversely, the comparison was in Miriamche's favor. For the tormented and tormenting *rebbe's* daughter acted in self-defense when young girls or their male peers teased her without let-up; whereas Golda had reacted violently to an accident or a lack of caution that did her no harm, was not premeditated and carried no malicious intent. Worse still: after Mother committed the act once, the plucking of Mala's braids became a common procedure, whether with reason or without. Countless were the times in the coming two years that her daughter's head would be subjected to violent shaking. Yet, despite the pain, Mala neither cried out nor pleaded, merely succumbing, the way her father had succumbed before her, in the belief that this would calm Mother down.

"I'm next." The son made a stab at a sad jest, having decided like his sister that he would submit. "At least Mother's sense of history has not been impaired, keeping chronological track of her children, ha-ha." Her coming act, however, left no room for bravado.

It happened one Friday afternoon. Golda had finished her

cooking and baking for the Sabbath and, in the time that remained before the onset of the day of rest, she decided to clean the small bedroom rug. She hung it over the balcony banister and picked up the carpet beater to beat off the dust that had settled in it. Meanwhile, at the table in the front room – a table that remembered better times, when *Gemaras* had lain open on it, or even that very morning, when Golda had kneaded her dough there for the Sabbath *halles* – the son strained to finish the composition he was writing before candle lighting time.

"Why did you scatter your papers all over the table which was already set for the Sabbath, apart from the candles?" The complaint that came from the balcony door was certainly reasonable, carrying no trace of rebuke or threat. But so absorbed was the son in that last hour in the task of formulating his thoughts, that only after the question was repeated – this time, with impatience and in a demanding tone – did he realize that he had better put things right at once. But before he could even straighten his back, which was hunched over his notebook, he felt a blow land on his back, the likes of which he had never felt before! It was an entirely new experience: not like the friendly wrestling games at recess in the schoolyard, nor like the knocks he had tasted in his encounters with wild Mietek, the *shaygitz* of the school street who never missed an opportunity to thrash the Jewish children he so hated.

Miriamche! The *rebbe*'s daughter reappeared before the son, carpet beater in hand. Defending the path that her feet had paved on the western side of Bóżnic Street to make it her very own, she wielded the carpet beater to chase off all who conspired against her body or plagued her soul. "I so passionately rejected any comparison between Mother and Miriamche" – the son confessed – "to protect Mother's good name. But, despite my love, I must admit that the lesson of the analogy is different from what I had thought. It is Miriamche, the ostracized, who is the saint, for her carpet beater was only used to protect her own 'God's little acre' in a wicked world, whereas Golda, who did not lack for defenses, took up the carpet beater merely to victimize her captive – a captive simply by way of being her son."

The red line had thus been crossed. The first time that Mala's braids were pulled and her head yanked – a painful act, and not without its dangers over time – was followed by a second occurrence, and a third, and many, many more, a type of punishment that became commonplace for Mala. So, too, were the blows dealt to the son's back – a painful and dangerous measure; after two beatings that Sabbath eve, the carpet beater became Mother's right hand. Sometimes, in the son's eyes, the weapon donned the form of Satan's staff, which he had seen in the illustrated book on medieval art that he liked to take from the shelf and peruse. "But why, oh why," the son lamented bitterly, "did Satan have to choose ours, of all homes, in which to test the efficiency of his rod?"

Let there be no mistake, however: even during the hardest times, it never occurred to the son to regard his mother as the loathsome creature depicted in Christian art and folk superstitions. On the contrary, his heart overflowed with unchecked and unconditional love towards her and, secretly, also with compassion because of the snare in which she was caught – secretly, because she abhorred pity, both from neighbors and especially from her children. Above these two paramount sentiments of love and compassion, there always hovered the hope that the days of awe would dissolve like a bad dream and the domestic idyll of old would return to reign in the home.

Meanwhile, however, hope was relegated to the corner like a pupil rebuked, and despair reigned in the home and hearts of its indwellers. When looking at his Mother on the "days of grace," and comparing her image then with her appearance and conduct on the "bad days," he found it hard to believe that this one figure could harbor two such contrary personalities, as utterly different from one another as good is from bad and kind from cruel. As a result, he imagined that some unknown, horrible being had decided to persecute the family: was it God, whose blind cruelty (so he began to think rebelliously of the Master of the Universe) filled the entire earth? Or Satan? Or, perhaps, it was the *dybbuk* who had left the body of the *rebbe*'s daughter and found another abode, the *dybbuk* who was shoving Miriamche's carpet beater into Mother's hand and teaching her to swing it with all her might above her son's head, like the sword of Damocles, and deliver such well-aimed blows?

Three bamboo carpet beaters were broken during the period that Golda beat her son, a feat of no mean consequence, since enormous force had to be used in order for the flexible cane to break. Today, a grandfather himself to youngsters more or less the age he was then, Golda's son wraps the memory of the biting blows of that period in a bag of velvet, and vows to forgive, but not to forget. And so, evermore will he remember how he practiced clamping his lips together and, mouth closed, swallow back his voice, that he might endure the carpet beater blows without uttering a sound. His sister developed her own methods, so that both managed to refrain from weeping or crying out – an accomplishment that they dedicated to their absent father. As his clandestine representatives in the home since the onset of the tragedy, they made sure to conduct themselves in a manner that would be pleasing to him, even if from afar: "Father would be proud to see us show such self-restraint."

But though it may have been possible, with much effort, to choke back an audible reaction to the pain, the son could not erase the furrows grooved by the carpet beater in his back, crisscrossing it every which way. As a result, he shrank from joining the "Bóżnic gang" for a swim in the Biała or the Dunajec, the two rivers close to Tarnów on the west, in order to avoid the need of inventing explanations for the marks on his back. His evasion of swimming then (the son chuckles), may even have been the reason for a subconscious block to his acquisition of the skill to this day.

The difficulty of circumventing group swimming on Biała and

Dunajec applied to no more than the couple of months of summer vacation – and was nothing as compared with the ruses he had to resort to during his first two years of high school. Unlike elementary school, which had no fixed period for gym, each class setting aside only a few minutes every hour for a brief stretch, in high school a whole weekly hour was allotted for gymnastics and sports. The boys would remove their shirts during class and remain only in their shorts. Fearful of stripping down like the rest of the boys, his inventiveness was seriously taxed to come up with a variety of excuses for an exemption from gym so as not to expose his back to strangers.

9

At the start of the new school year in September 1931 (the month that also inaugurated the year 5692 according to the Hebrew calendar), the Wróbel children could be proud of the rapid progress they had made in their studies despite four years of domestic eclipse. Mala entered the fourth grade at the Hebrew high school; the son, entering the third grade, had assured himself a place as an outstanding pupil; and the little sister, too, was enrolled in First Grade of elementary school, having reached the age of six. And as happened at the end of every summer, the friends came together once more at the foot of the chestnut tree, a reunion this time that in some ways was more adult and in other ways still youthful, with discussion revolving around a new book or recently published poem, and the emergence of budding ideological rifts between the tidings flashing in from the eastern border (the Polish underground) and the continued tidings from Eretz Israel, which was recovering from the riots of 1929.

Mother's suffering found no relief as her rage, symbolized by the bamboo carpet beater, continued to rock both her and her home. Until one day, when not finding the carpet beater within reach to vent her fury, another weapon, harder and crueler, came to hand.

"Where is the vase?" Mother cried one morning. "It was standing on the table!"

"Now it's standing to the right of the window. It seems to be comfortable there," the son tried to jest.

"But the vase is empty." Mother was in no mood for jests. "Where are the willow reeds that Zośka brought for my birthday? Everyone so admired the arrangement – a real flower arrangement! – and Mala, typically, stroked the gray, furry 'cat's paws.' She will be very sorry not to find the reeds where they belong. You know how much she likes fur and anything that resembles it."

"Mala won't be sorry. She, herself, helped me get rid of the wretched reeds when she saw what you had inflicted on me with a wet reed. Even horses are flogged only with dry whips!"

Intending to flog her son with the carpet beater one day and not finding it at its permanent place on the wall hook, she suspected that he had removed it. At a signal from Zośka, she withdrew one of the reeds from the water in the vase and brought it down on her son. Unlike the carpet beater, whose weight had a restraining effect on the user, the reed was as light as a feather and could be brandished like a toy, the flogger having no idea exactly where it would land and being unaware of the severity of the blow. This time the reed came down on the son's back and exposed neck. The pain was unbearable, and despite his willpower and firm resolve to utter not a sound at the pain his mother's blows caused him, a terrible cry burst from him.

A childhood memory from Rabka rose unbidden: a wagon driver flogging his horse and raising stinging welts beneath the fur to spread sinuously along the living flesh. The horse reared, neighing sharply in pain and protest. Now, since his own floggings had begun, whenever the son took a *fiacre* – or does so today when traveling in countries that still avail themselves of *fiacres* – he would pay the driver double fare on condition that he refrain from using his whip on the horse.

Mother was not prepared for the son's outcry. She had grown accustomed to seeing him take the carpet beater blows in silence, and she did not understand the different nature of the pain delivered by the two weapons. The broad head of the carpet beater landed on the whole upper back, diffusing the pain over a wide area rather than concentrating it at a specific point. Whiplashing, in contrast, isolated a ribbon of skin and cut into the flesh like a knife until it drew blood. This pain, especially when inflicted by a moist willow reed, was unbearable, and despite the boy's determination, a cry breached the bulwark of his clamped lips. No, this was not a horror one could get used to, and it had to be stopped at once! That evening, after Mala had dressed his wounds with cold compresses, the two conveyed the vase and its contents down to the trash can in the courtyard and dumped the water along with the reeds.

"Who are you to throw away a gift I received or to decide whether or not it belongs in our home? This very day I will ask Zośka for new willow reeds so that everyone may admire the vase arrangement as they did before."

"And I will remove my shirt and show the admirers the other use that has been found for the reeds in this home. And I will do the same at school after the holidays, when gym classes start: I will bare my back before the eyes of the pupils and the gym teacher, and no longer, as in the past, look for excuses to explain my absence from class."

"What is this? Rebellion?" Two black flames charred the blue of Mother's eyes.

"No," the son replied softly, conscious of the need not to burn any bridges. "A son does not rebel against his mother, he only signals to her that he has reached the limits of his endurance and that these limits must not be crossed."

Golda was silent. She surveyed her son at length as if she had not seen him for years. Before her stood not a child, but a youth, eleven and a half years old, though older than his years and certainly strong and hardened and able to manage. How and when – she wondered – did he so develop to take the place of the man who had been banished, while she had been engrossed in herself and her fears? Still, she had not yet grasped the crucial significance of this point in time, nor did she fully comprehend the ruin she had brought upon herself and the entire family.

The son, too, said nothing. *For the initial confrontation, this is enough,* he thought to himself. He had no interest in "defeating" Mother. Intuitively, he sensed that what had happened that day was not the end of the story. One thing was certain: willow reeds were not to enter this home again. But the explosion would come. As often happens, it would come unplanned and maybe even over something trivial and negligible. But when it came, it would be like a small, negligible match capable of sparking a mammoth conflagration.

The match was called into action sooner than expected, igniting and causing an explosion, as the son had guessed, over something trivial. *For some reason, most of the turning points in the life of the Wróbel family seemed to occur at the end of summer or close to Yom Kippur* – the son would think years later when reviewing the history of that period. The present story began with the son accompanying his father to the community slaughterhouse on the banks of the Wątok, the father carrying a pair of Yom Kippur *kappara* (atonement) chickens. Now, six years later, September 1931 brought the plot full circle with the repetition of the rite of atonement. Unlike in 1925, however, it was Mother who now supervised the custom, in Father's place.

On the morning of Yom Kippur eve, Golda summoned her children – a white hen, its feet bound, fluttering in her hand and the prayer book open before her eyes. First, Mother performed the ritual for herself, swinging the terrified chicken over her head so as to cleanse herself of her own sins for her continued role in her children's atonement – in observance of: "he shall come pure to atone for the sinner, not the guilty atoning for the guilty". She hastily repeated the action three times, also mouthing the verse in the prayer book three times, according to custom.

Then she swung the chicken above Gunia's head, this time saying out loud: *This is your substitute, your vicarious offering, your atonement; this hen shall meet death but you shall find a long and pleasant life of peace* – again, three times, and in finishing had the little girl kiss the page in the prayer book. If truth be told, the daughter had answered her mother's summons with a heavy heart: she was afraid that the hen would poke her in the head or relieve itself there. When neither of these things happened, however, she treated the rite as an amusing game.

"Now, it's your turn, Hesiek"; the bound hen was offered to him.

"I am not doing this," the son declared bravely. "The rite of atonement is either based entirely on superstition or is a bad joke. In either case, I will not be party to it."

"What do you mean, a superstition?" Mother was offended. "It is a tradition, and traditions should be kept."

"I am not sure that it's a universally accepted tradition. I learned that there are important rabbis, like Joseph Caro, the Rashba (Rabbi Shlomo ben Adreth) and others, who reject the custom. In any case, my brain tells me that it is physically impossible to transfer sins from one man to another, let alone from man to fowl or any other creature. And my sense of morality tells me that even if the transfer were possible, it is immoral to saddle an innocent, captive fowl with the sins of man."

"So how will you be saved from the fires of hell if the weight of your sins is still on your back?"

"I don't believe in the fires of hell nor do I feel that I have sinned. I may have erred accidentally, but error is not considered a sin. The truth is that it is you-you-you who have sinned – against us all – and instead of expecting the poor hen to free you of responsibility for your actions, it would be far better if you did some soul searching and consulted your conscience. For four years we have suffered and kept quiet in the hope of easing your pain and fears, but you did not appreciate our restraint and repaid our good with bad. The time has come to tell you how we feel: you destroyed a loving family and in its place befriended the devil's daughter who is the source of all our troubles, crushing Father with intrigues and banishment so that he is a shadow of himself today, inflicting cruel pain on myself and Mala – and still you ask what will become of *my* sins? *You* are the sinner, and the atonement rite will not save you from yourself!"

"And you, Mala?" her voice was deceptively soft. "You, at least, will swing the hen above your head as required, and have nothing to do with your impudent brother's slander!"

"No, I agree with every word Hesiek said, and spurn your superstitions."

The son sensed the black rage that was about to spill onto the blue of his mother's eyes – meaning, she had not digested the message delivered out of love and pain. He guessed that the imminent outburst was to be unlike any before, and he quickly dived beneath the bed, followed by Mala.

The first installment of the livid storm found immediate release: incensed to tears, Golda sent the hen flying after the children – the very hen that had ostensibly absorbed all her sins – flinging it into the unknown subterranean darkness beneath the bed. Mother, no doubt, hoped that the baffled fowl with beak and claws would force the two out of hiding, straight into her furious face and the heavy punishment she planned to impose. But a fowl's instincts work otherwise. Equally disobedient, the hen discovered the strip of light between bed and floor and chose this as her berth, without bothering about the objects she was meant to ferret out, scratch and poke in the gloom of the bed's underside.

From that same strip of light, Hesiek and Mala monitored

their mother's footsteps. Amid incessant vituperation, she reached first for the hook on the wall, where the carpet beater always hung. "She took down the carpet beater!" the two whispered. Then, carpet beater in hand, Golda braced herself, legs apart, opposite the bed, just as Miriamche used to plant herself at the center of Kotchker's gate to settle accounts with the entire universe. From this masterful position, Golda launched into a sarcastic rejoinder to her son's accusations:

"You say I have sinned, ha-ha, I, who raised the three of you to the best of my abilities. And, maybe, you're right. If, among the three of you, I have raised a viper who spews venom at his mother's face, then my sin is great indeed and I deserve to be punished accordingly!" Clasping the handle of the carpet beater with both hands, she suddenly swung the weapon up to pummel her forehead with all the force that her long-suffering body could muster.

Miriamche! The son shot out of hiding and, with all his force, locked his mother's elbows with his own, compelling her to drop the carpet beater. "Not that, Mamusiu, just not that, Mamusieńku," he begged. "If fury drives you to lash out, then hit me, Mama, me, not yourself. I will understand, and I won't hide anymore. Just don't hurt yourself!" He allowed the endearments, so deeply hidden in his heart and unused, to surge from his lips on a stormy tide, in total oblivion of the rules that Golda had instituted years ago.

"Let me go," Golda tried to free herself from the vise of his elbows. "You're hurting me."

"You hurt us more, Mother." He spoke quietly, tenderly, looking straight into the blue of the eyes he so loved. How endless the years since he had studied her face so close up! Wrinkles had multiplied at the corners of her mouth and eyes, and the two furrows on her forehead that he had so loved to "iron" with toddler hands, had deepened. Mother! How he longed to embrace her instead of immobilizing her elbows, to cling to her and feel the warmth of her body – a pleasure he had been robbed of at her command even during the "good" years of childhood. But, he realized, he had to collect himself and act firmly, for the opportunity was ripe and might never present itself again.

"Let me go already," she squirmed between his elbows, "you really are hurting me."

"I won't let you go, nor will I free your elbows." He opted for a forced hardness diametrically opposed to the message of love he wished to put across to her in this, their first eye-to-eye contact.

"Stop pressing, already! I'm fainting from pain. What do you want of me?"

"I'm sorry, Ma-aa" – the decision for hardness unheedingly restored the old form of address – "I will not let you move until you solemnly promise to abide by four conditions. This is how it has to be, there is no other way." Golda did not speak. The son correctly took her silence for acquiescence. How many sleepless nights had he spent rehearsing the conditions he would set during the anticipated confrontation! And the confrontation had come. Violently – not as planned – but come it had, and it was here and now.

"Firstly, as of today, Zośka is fired. She will not be permitted to enter this house again." Golda tried to put up adamant resistance: "Impossible! She has worked for me for four years."

"No problem. There are all sorts of ways to compensate an employee for severance, and I rely on you and your fairness to find the right and just solution to terminate her employment." Golda continued to resist, unable to accept that she would be deprived of a companionship she had grown used to.

"But we are such close friends. I really can't live without her."

"That's precisely why she must go," the boy asserted with the authority of an adult. "As for friendship" – he gestured dismissively – "I could tell you things that you would find hard to believe Zośka did behind your back while pretending to be your friend. One day, you will see it for yourself. But right now, there can be no discussion. She is fired – it is over." The mother opened her mouth as if to continue arguing, but the son silenced her. His elbows, this whole time, had not moved from hers. Finally, he agreed to her request to ease her discomfort, relaxing his hold somewhat, and she abandoned all opposition.

"Secondly," he said earnestly, "Father must be brought back home today, never again to be banished. So that we may be a whole family once more."

Golda kept quiet, giving no sign of either consent or refusal. The son took this as acquiescence.

"Thirdly: Mala – no more braid pulling or head shaking or any other punishment.

"And the fourth condition concerns myself: under no circumstances are you to hit me ever again, not with your hand nor with the carpet beater nor with willow reeds. From now on, this is the rule: if you think that one of your children is misbehaving, you will tell us individually what we have done wrong so that we may learn. We are big now, and we will not consent to physical punishment. It is painful, humiliating, and solves nothing. From now on, the carpet beater will remain on the wall hook, to be taken down only to beat the bedroom rug and any other rug that we may acquire. As for willow reeds – their fate has already been sealed by Mala and myself when we threw them into the garbage – never again will they be found or seen in our home."

Worn out, Mother slid down onto a chair as soon as her son finally released his hold. Resting her aching elbows on the table and cupping her head in her hands, she was like someone whose world had just come apart and whose next move was still a puzzle. The son, even though he had been the one to strike the match, understood what she was going through and, creeping up behind her quietly, again in defiance of the old ban, embraced her trembling shoulders and kissed her full hair. Golda did not react. Her head had emptied of all emotion and her body was too drained and subdued to protest.

"And, now, Mother, I have good news," he whispered in her ear, "it will make you very happy."

"Please, just let me be," she pleaded, "I have no strength for news." Her elbows were very sore and she seemed to be on the verge of fainting. But the son, his face a mixture of childish tenderness and manly firmness, ignored her plea and pain and continued: "I didn't want to tell you this before, so that it wouldn't seem as though I were bribing you with promises. Now, that we are in full agreement, please hear me out."

He turned her chair around and helped her to her feet so that he could speak to her at eye level: "Listen, Mama'leh," he underscored every syllable, "you do not have cancer!"

The taboo had been broken. For the first time, the awesome word had been said aloud and reverberated through the apartment, banged against the walls, to the right and to the left, rose up to the ceiling and landed on all those present. And look: the sky did not fall-in, nor the earth open up, and the sun continued to shine.

Golda took in nothing. Eyes glazed, she leaned against the table to support herself.

"You do not have cancer," the son repeated, "and you will live with us for many, many years!"

The mother, as if only now waking from a long coma, seemed to be searching for points of reference in an unfamiliar world. Slowly, slowly, the words began to sink in and her eyes flew up: "I don't…?" she mumbled weakly, dazed, unable to permit the cursed word to pass her lips, "I don't…? I don't, you say, I don't!"

"Yes, Mother, you are healthy and can forget all your fears. A full, enjoyable life still awaits you, just as we had in the past, and the black period will fade away as if it had never happened."

Her energy returned: "I don't have cancer! I don't!" she shouted, relishing in the articulation of the word, like a child who has just learned a dirty expression and is eager to repeat it again and again. But, all at once, she grew sober again: "How do you know?" The son explained that he had described her condition to Dr. Lezer, a former pupil of Father's, who had completed his medical studies abroad and was now back in Tarnów for internship at the Jewish Hospital. Dr. Lezer was, of course, reserving judgment until he had actually examined her (he was to call on her after Yom Kippur), but on the basis of the description, it seemed clear to him that the diagnosis had been mistaken and the surgery unnecessary and the radium treatment sloppy for what had been no more than a growing benign cyst, and it was the scar that had caused the scabies. "The scabies has to be treated, of course, but the problem that frightened you to death does not exist."

Abandoning her characteristic puritan reserve, an exhilarated Golda fell on her son's neck and wept for joy. Nor could the son stem his own tears. For the first time since he had been a small child, he felt the warmth of his mother's body flow into his own. Thus, they stood, in a long embrace, the son comforting the mother as one would a child: "Come, now, Mama'leh, enough now, enough. Everything will be alright. It will be alright, you'll see."

10

No one knows if after two weeks of rest and treatment at the hands of Dr. Lezer, Mother shed the ordeals of the past only outwardly or whether she truly and consciously cleansed her heart of her personal canon of zealotry. In either case, she began to take stock of her surroundings, finding nothing but charred earth left by years of black conflagration. Financially, the family coffers had shrunk. Apart from the universal depression that had thinned out the ranks of Father's students, there were parents who, at the sight of the tattered suit that covered Aazik's body by day and in which he passed his nights on the bench, felt that erudition and experience were not sufficient to make him appropriate to be presented to their children as a role model.

It was clear to Golda that the first thing she had to do was to mend her husband's trampled honor and self-esteem. Aazik returned home as if on tiptoe, finding it hard to believe that his wife's attitude had changed towards him, yet questioning nothing lest he arouse sleeping ghosts from the past. But Golda understood that this was not enough, and that her personal responsibility for all that had happened demanded that she develop an additional source of income to support the family. The skill and basis were already in place: her creativity and fine taste in embroidery had earned her renown, long drawing women to her doorstep for advice and instruction freely given. Now, she was convinced, she had to enhance that knowledge and experience professionally, confident that as long as Jewish women thirsted for ornaments and were eager to adorn their homes, she would not have difficulty finding clients.

As opposed to her proficiency in the art itself, however, the business aspect of the planned concern was a mystery to her: marketing initiatives and displays, pricing techniques, getting in touch with wholesalers of embroidery fabrics, of DMC colored threads, of wool for *kilims*, of tracing paper and accessories for transferring perforated patterns to the fabric to be embroidered, and a host of other details one had to learn and know. Consequently, Golda decided to invest several days in traveling to Kraków to "apprentice" herself to the top expert in the field, Pani Franzblauowa – an old friend from her refugee days in Vienna, who promised to initiate her in all the secrets of the trade free of charge. Every day, Golda boarded the morning train to Kraków, and every evening, she returned home on the late train, just as she had done once a month more than twenty years earlier. Then, however, the trips had been made by a cheerful young woman whose whole future lay before her; whereas, now, she shouldered the weight of family cares, a woman whose face was etched with wrinkles from the past and who set out to rectify, revitalize and remedy her life, which had gone so wrong.

396 CHESTNUTS OF YESTERYEAR: A JEWISH ODYSSEY

On the Sabbath preceding the onset of the planned trips to
Kraków, Golda strayed from the weekly ascent to Mount St. Marcin
in the southern part of town – a custom revived after four years of
the excursion time lying fallow and re-adapted to adolescent children – and now asked her son to accompany her alone in the opposite direction, to a village on the plain to the north of the town.
Autumn had already seized on every tree, ruthlessly stripping it of
its red foliage, and pinching people's cheeks with chill. The fields
that had been plowed and sowed, seemed to be lying in wait for
new life to ripen within them, like pregnant women waiting for the
mystery of awakening life in the recesses of their wombs.

Reaching the village about an hour later, Golda visited with
some of the women whom she had long known, aware that in winter, when no urgent work called them to the fields, they "hibernated"
in their cabins with embroidery work which they performed to
order. The son was sure that this was the sum total of Golda's business in these parts, but Mother proceeded to lead him northwards
until they came to a solitary wooden shack: "Baba Yaga lives here,"
she informed her son of the other reason for the outing. "I doubt
that this is her real name; it may have been borrowed from fairy
tales or folksongs and stuck on to her out of admiration or… fear."

"Baba Yaga is a wise old fortune-teller, who bases her predictions on palm-reading," Mother said simply, as if there were nothing
more natural than to walk two miles on a Sabbath to benefit from
Baba Yaga's sorcery. "Please understand" – she tried to win over her
skeptical son – "I am embarking on a new road, and I must know
what the future holds for me." The son was bewildered. Was there
no end to her superstitions? His initial instinct was to turn on his
heel and head for home on his own; but he knew that he couldn't
abandon Mother in these strange surroundings. There had again
been rumors recently about a serial killer of women, dubbed chill-
ingly by the press as the "Monster of Düsseldorf," who was on the
prowl for prey. Moreover, in history class at school, the boy was now

learning about medieval chivalry. The knight's romantic love for his lady, and the desire to serve and defend her with his life, stirred the imagination of the eleven-and-a-half-year-old boy: he was Mother's knight. Did he not have to make sure that his lady came to no harm, just as his medieval counterparts had done? Consequently, though he would not sully himself by entering the den of iniquity, he stood guard outside for his mother's protection.

News that Pani Wróblowa had opened an embroidery shop in her flat on Bóżnic soon took wing and was followed shortly after by visual corroboration. In the absence of a shop window, a large showcase, ordered from Pasternak, the carpenter, was hung up on the wall of the building at 9 Bóżnic Street near the main entrance, and safeguarded by a large lock. Behind the glass panes of the case, there was a display of embroidery, secular as well as sacred objects in a gamut of colors – all, Golda's splendid handiwork. Every morning, except for the Sabbath and holidays, before setting out for his teaching post at school, Father carefully placed the showcase on his shoulders and carried it down two flights of stairs to the street, and in the evening, he brought the load back up the second floor, via the same staircase. In retrospect, the sight of his father's back, bowing more and more from year to year under the weight of the showcase, evoked for the adult son the Nazarene, "smitten of God and afflicted," carrying the showcase like a cross up his own private *Via Dolorosa*. A sharp instinct urged the son to rush to his father's aid and offer him a shoulder, like the pilgrim of Cyrene who, two thousand years ago, helped the man condemned to crucifixion to bear his cross – but Aazik would not hear of it. It was a mission he insisted on performing by himself. It was a gift of love that he laid every morning at the feet of his adored wife… in silence.

Oh, Father, Father! Shatter the silence and cry out! Cry out for what was done to you! But Father would not speak. And while Mother and the children reverted to their former ways, Aazik could not shake off the nightmares of the past and, like Shloime, his father, and Yitzhik-Eisik, his grandfather, would not raise his voice nor demand justice. "But verily he hath borne our grief, and suffered our sorrows…and opened not his mouth."

Unlike the incurable sorrow that veiled Father's eyes, the prosperity of Mother's commercial venture in which all the Wróbels played a lesser or greater role, restored gladness and self-confidence to the family home. From the first, however, the son claimed that the healing process would not be complete unless they moved to a different flat, one that was innocent of the past deeds, which, in every corner of the current home, continued to sprout thorns of bad memories best forgotten. The new flat would also be connected to the electric grid, thus putting an end to paraffin lamps and candles that concealed more than they illuminated, evoking shadows of "those days." Electric light, moreover, would also make it easier to do homework and more pleasant to read a book or browse through an art album, much to the enjoyment of the youngsters and Mother.

Two months were to pass, however, before it became possible to leave the flat on the second floor in exchange for one next to the stairway on the first floor of the same building – a flat identical to the previous one in size, but more comfortably divided into three smaller rooms. Only during the move itself did the children realize how difficult it was to part with the two old rooms: the front room, sun-drenched, and the back room, where the chestnut tree thrust its arm through the window. True, the flat bore a terrible scar but, basically, for the three Wróbel children it had been the cradle of a happy childhood: there they were born, there they took their first steps, there they learned to read and write, from there they set out for Mount St. Marcin and for Kraków and to there they returned full of adventures; there they learned to respect books and saw the treasure of the bookcase swelling from year to year; there they breathed song and music and learned loyalty and love for parents and for one another through good times and bad. And yet, the flat had been in the past an arena of calamities, and, as such, had to be abandoned. Everyone therefore agreed that only in a new, well-lit flat would the family be able to make a complete break with the traumas of the past and turn over a new leaf.

But there was more. The son who (with justice) saw himself as the architect of the Wróbel renaissance, sought also to enter the labor force at the age of eleven-and-a-half. Parents had been asking him recently to tutor their children and, little by little, Hesiek's private lessons began to take up all the afternoon hours, the reward being far from negligible. Father, on the one hand, was pleased that his mother Zlatte's plan was coming through – to wrench her eldest son from the equestrian cycle of the House of Wróbel and establish in its stead a "dynasty of Torah scholars: first, Aazikl, and after him, his son, and so on in the generations after him" – even though the plan was, as might have been expected, taking a modern form. On the other hand, he would not agree that the monies earned by his young son enrich the family kitty. As a result, it was mutually decided that this money be saved in an *aliyah* box, alongside the Keren Kayemeth Blue Box and the Rabbi Meir Baal HaNess box. From the markings of the new box – its sides the color of chocolate and its floral lettering spelling out "Suchard" on the broad sides – it was clear that the new, rectangular container, four times the size of the others, had started out in the Wróbel home in the role intended for it by the factory: as a cocoa tin. When it was emptied, after countless cups of cocoa forced on the children every morning "because it's healthy," Father took it to Haim, the tinsmith, whose workshop was in the yard. He asked that a narrow slit be cut in the middle of the cover through which coins could be inserted, and that the cover be soldered to the body of the box along all four sides, so that it could not be removed and the box never be opened unless broken. Thus, unintentionally, the Swiss Suchard factory contributed to the savings fund of the House of Wróbel, which was wholly earmarked for the children's *aliyah* to the Hebrew University in Jerusalem.

11

The letter from the high school officials descended on the Wróbels like a bolt from the blue. By order of the Regional Education Inspector in Kraków, Dr. Wierzbicki, and on the basis of the New Education Reform of 1932, the school had been compelled – so the officials regretfully announced – to demote Hesiek Wróbel two grades, because he had begun his school career at the age of five instead of at the age of seven as stipulated by law. It must be said at once that the *Reforma Jędrzejewiczowa* – the new education law, which was named after the person who had conceived it, the then Minister of Education, Jędrzejewicz – was without a doubt the most important measure adopted in the field of education since the state had regained its sovereignty. Among other things, the reform presided over a wide-reaching reshuffling in the structure of the education system, dividing the twelve years that pupils spent within school walls into three, rather than two, periods: elementary school, high school, and lyceum. The structural change reflected defined learning and educational goals for each of the system's components. But, like every ambitious innovation, the execution of this reform, too, was characterized by rigidity, lack of compromise, and pedantic implementation bordering on coercion. Thus, the outstanding pupil was called upon to pay the price of the reform.

The teaching staff at the high school were no less shocked than the parents. Every teacher addressed a detailed letter to the regional Inspector, reporting on the pupil's achievements in the specific subject that teacher taught. The school doctor, Dr. Feig (later to rename himself Pagi in Haifa), remarked on the boy's physical prowess, which did not fall short of that of his peers. But all their efforts proved fruitless. The establishment zealously guarded the regulation, so set upon the promulgation of the reform that there were to be no exceptions.

The bureaucrats charged with implementing the program at every state school never imagined that a mother's zeal to advance her son would triumph over the establishment's zeal to advance its program, particularly when the mother decried the arbitrary trampling of the principles of justice and fairness: "Such glaring injustice!" – the lioness defended her cub who was being made to suffer through no fault of his own. "I can understand a pupil being demoted if he shows no progress or interest in school, or disrupts the class. But to demote an outstanding pupil, who is unanimously commended by his teachers and accepted by his peers, simply because of an arbitrary ordinance devised in some office is a wrong not to be countenanced. For what is the point of all the highfalutin ideals touted by the reform if their practical results sin against a boy for whom a glorious future is predicted?"

Golda's campaign to assure her son's place in school came as no surprise to her acquaintances. What did cause some of them to wonder, however, was that she seemed to have forgotten or repressed the memory of an act that she herself had committed a year earlier (on one of her "bad days") and which could have had far worse consequences than demotion by two grades. That chain of events started with her being "summoned to the Principal" and told that at the end of one of the recesses, her son had placed a gym shoe on the desk of a teacher who was about to enter the classroom. Despite the boy's insistence at the time (and also seventy years later) that he had been falsely charged, the outraged, disgraced mother would not leave things at "being summoned to the Principal," which in itself was considered heavy punishment, but withdrew her son from school, ending his formal education. She then delivered him unto Pasternak, the carpenter (who would build her the showcase) to hire him out as an apprentice.

A special man was Pasternak, with a special workshop. Broadly educated, he had chosen to pursue manual labor for ideological reasons, seeing himself as a student and practitioner of A.D. Gordon's "religion of labor." Moreover, he was the personal friend of Dr. Yeshayahu (Shayek) Spiro in Tarnów, one of the founders of Gordonia, which advocated Gordon's ideas. His expectation of all his employees at the workshop was that they turn out a perfect product regardless of how long it took, for quality, rather than quantity, was the cardinal principal. For four whole days, from morning till evening, Hesiek worked at Pasternak's – sweeping and re-sweeping wood shavings from the floor, sorting nails according to size and, in the evening, putting the tools back in place – he worked and wept. He wept not only over the termination of his studies, but because of the sentence he had received without a hearing or a fair investigation of the incident. The carpenter watched the boy day by day and his heart went out to him. On the fourth working day, he "promoted" the apprentice, entrusting to him the preparation of carpentry glue and its requisite stirring in a bowl. However, when he saw the boy's tears spilling into the glue, he was reminded of Bialik's poem about the tears shed by the poet's mother into the dough she was kneading, and he could no longer watch the boy suffer. At the end of the day, he personally brought the son back to Golda and, under his influence, it was decided that the punishment had run its course to the full and the boy was returned to school. Could Golda have wiped out the affair from her memory, just as she had wiped out everything else that belonged to the "bad days"?

Whether or not she had totally erased it or simply repressed it, the son, in any case, remembered for scores of years the act that almost changed the course of his life. But, above all, he remembered Pasternak and how the latter had treated him as a man, even though he was just a child apprentice. And he was indebted to his mother for the good that had come out of the "bad job," for through her actions he had been fortunate to make the acquaintance of the wonderful Pasternak. The boy's admiration for the man grew deeper and firmer when he himself joined Gordonia and, like Pasternak, also subscribed to A.D. Gordon's teachings. Years later, after the war and Holocaust, the "former apprentice," as the professor liked to refer to himself, learned that Pasternak had survived the inferno of that period and, in his old age, lived in a senior residents home in Williamsburg, Brooklyn. Rushing to the address he had been given, he found that the mere mention of Pasternak's name caused eyes to light up. "He was a real *Tzaddik*. All day long he walked about with his tool case, fixing whatever was broken on the premises, or whatever was worn out and needed repairing." From the phrasing of the sentence, the "apprentice" understood that he had come too late. He asked to see if any of the carpenter's tools remained, secretly nursing the absurd hope that the man had perhaps been able to save one of the implements that he, the apprentice of old, had been charged with returning to their permanent place in the workshop each evening. But a check of the toolbox revealed that all the items, including the box itself, had been bought at the corner shop in Brooklyn. Thus, nothing remained of Pasternak apart from the memories, cherished to this day by those lucky enough to have known him or worked with him – even if only for four days – for they all came to love and admire him.

The new Golda went to war – or, rather, in a topsy-turvy turn of events, the lady of the young knight, who had once defended her, now rose up to defend him with all her soul and all her might. Omitting all attempt to arrange an appointment with the Inspector because she knew that she would not be granted one, Golda took her son one day and traveled to Kraków to demand that he be given an objective test. After lengthy entreaties, the two were ushered into the Inspector's office. A shorthand clerk was called in to record the questions that would be put to the examinee, as well as his answers. Both questions and answers were to be sent on to the Minister for his decision. Actually, only one question was asked and one was answered, taking up a whole hour. Two weeks later, a special dispensation arrived from the Ministry of Education, stating that the pupil, H. Wróbel, born in July 1920, was permitted to sit for his matriculation exams in 1937 at any high school in the state, despite the law's restrictions.

Some sixty years after these events, the son of Golda and Aazik, a professor emeritus by now, began scouring libraries, archives and public collections to locate material he required for the composition of this book. Among other places, he spent long hours at the Joseph Piłsudski Polish Institute in New York, checking and photocopying important Polish documentation.

It was the pleasant custom of the Institute that every morning at 11:30, two Polish ladies would arrive to set a table in the main hall where Institute staff and guest researchers could partake of a light refreshment of tea and biscuits. One day, as everyone sat around the table, the door suddenly opened and a tall man entered the hall, bald and elderly but erect "as a Polish officer." Everyone rose and, amid Polish graces, invited the guest to join them at the table. "This is Minister Jędrzejewicz," one of the women whispered to the Israeli guest, "he is nearly a hundred years old."

The Minister was seated next to the Polish-born researcher and the two found a common language. After learning that his neighbor's mother and her ancestors had hailed from the Ukraine, the Minister told him that he, too, had been born in the Ukraine and now supported himself in exile by teaching Russian and, when there was a demand, also Ukrainian. In high emotion, the Minister went on to speak of his finest hours in the Polish Government prior to the Second World War, quite naturally noting his satisfaction at the reform that he had succeeded in drafting and implementing. "The reform is still in place today, unchanged, even after forty years of Communist rule. The hardest part was our insistence on rejecting requests for exceptional treatment, but, in the end, everyone readily adopted the law."

"No," the Minister quickly amended that sweeping declaration. "There were two pupils for whom I approved a special dispensation. One of these was from the district of Kraków, the district in which you were raised. The boy was tested by Inspector Wierzbicki in a very original manner. He was called up to the map of Poland that hung on the wall, and told: 'You are traveling from Kraków to Warsaw. Tell me everything you know about this route in terms of history, literature, nature, personalities, etc.'

"The answer was brilliant. There were things in the stenogram I received that I remember to this day because we had not known them before, such as the meeting of Jewish writers during the summer months at Kazimierz Dolny, or the Hasidic towns on the banks of the Wisła, like Dzików, for example, which have established rabbinic dynasties over many generations, and so forth and so forth. The answer took more than an hour, and Wierzbicki rightly decided that there was no need for further questions."

Jędrzejewicz ended by sinking into reflection. Then, as if speaking to himself, he added: "I wonder what happened to the boy – boy, ha-ha, he must be seventy already. I often thought of him during the war: did he survive? It was clear to both Wierzbicki and myself that he was made of academic stuff. Did he realize his hopes? But most important of all, is he alive? And, if so, where could he be now?"

"He is sitting right next to you at this very moment, Mr. Minister."

*

And what about Zośka?

Upon being fired, her mouth released a slew of venom. "Maybe, it's better this way," the son thought to himself, "now, Mother will know who her friend was." Then, Rasputina suddenly turned into Cassandra: "You will all die before me, and I will be queen of this house" – and she bolted.

Zośka was not seen again in the Jewish neighborhood and soon faded from memory. No one wished to remember the four "bad years," and the "bad years" were Zośka.

At the end of the war, Mala returned from Siberia where she had been exiled after finding refuge from the Germans in the Soviet zone of conquest. Her first instinct upon her return – so she later told her brother – was to speed to her parents' home, the home of her childhood and adolescence. For every night in the Siberian reaches she had dreamt of it, soaking her pillow in tears, and even though she knew the fate of her parents and sister before returning to Tarnów, she couldn't help but hope for a miracle…

The building frames for the most part were still standing, but bombed out from the inside, without doors or windows, they resembled ghosts. Of the building on the other side of the street – the "Great Synagogue" – only a handful of broken stones remained. David Becker, the sculptor, who had also returned from exile, joined the stones together into a memorial column that was placed in the Jewish cemetery over the common grave of the twenty-five thousand Jews slain in June 1942, and Mala composed a line for it that spoke volumes:

"THE SUN SHONE WITHOUT SHAME."

Mala raced up the stairs to the empty, ruined flat, having no tears left to cry – they had all poured out on the Siberian *taiga*. In the front room, opposite what had once been a window, she saw a woman standing, her back to the entrance. At the sound of approaching footsteps, the woman turned around to look at the uninvited caller with suspicion and open displeasure.

"Who are you? What do you want here? Get out at once!"

It was said that in post-war Tarnów neighbors had broken into empty flats to rip up flooring in order to uncover the "treasures" that the Jews had supposedly buried before being transported. An awesome jealousy split the camp of the birds of prey, each vulture claiming precedence, by virtue of having worked for the Jewish proprietors, or possessing knowledge of the whereabouts of the "hidden treasures."

"I'm Mala. This is my home."

"*Your* home?" Zośka sneered. "I predicted that you would all die before me. And here, you come. But you, too, are like the walking dead: no hair, no teeth, a hump on your back. Who are you? What are you? Nothing, nothing, nothing, less than nothing! Get your filthy corpse out of here at once!" Mala fled as fast as she could, never to return there again.

These were the wages of zealotry earned by the Polish woman, for whom the German conquest posed no danger during the war and in whom it sowed great expectations for the post-war period. She prevailed over the Jewish refugee, her fellow Tarnowite, who had survived and, despite great hardship, managed to make her way back as far as the doorstep. But there, on the threshold of her former home, she was banished.

The Weinman Cantor family in Bar:
Ephraim and Feige, parents of Zvi-Hersch

Zvi-Hersch Weinman and wife Sureh, née Gokhban

CHAPTER NINE

The Wages of Zealotry: The Town

1

ALTHOUGH IT WAS totally unknown to him at first, Aazik, the lad, settled in Tarnów while the Jewish community was being rent by two sets of zealotry. The one was the *Kloyz* arena, where Orthodox Jews, who yearned for immediate Redemption and were willing to participate even in secular, nationalist initiatives, faced off against those who continued to wait for Messianic Redemption. The rift had widened some fifteen years before Herzl's emergence on the scene, when some members of the God-fearing congregation, fired by the appearance of the first colonies in Eretz Israel, began to identify with *Hibbat Zion*, particularly because most of the First Aliyah settlers were from a traditional background. In opposition to them, especially in the last five years of the nineteenth century, the *Kloyz* zealots' struggle against nationalist drives gained in momentum. The period, in fact, brimmed with initiatives: Herzl's star rose in Vienna, whereas, in Galicia, at one and the same time, Tarnów's Abraham Salz established *Ahavat Zion*, the last of the societies patterned on *Hibbat Zion*, which aspired to found a farming community in the Upper Galilee: Mahanayim. This was to be the only colony of the First Aliyah whose members were to hail not from Russia or Rumania, but from Galicia.

Heading the anti-Zionist fanatics was Reb Yehezkel Halberstam of Sieniawa: "There are men among our people, mostly *doktoirim*" – the zealot dispatched an angry letter to Zekharye-Mendl Aberdam in Tarnów, the treasurer of *Ahavat Zion* – "who advocate creating a settlement in Eretz Israel… and lead many distinguished people to stray into their ranks." With the fear of the Zans *Rebbe* upon him, Aberdam quit his position and withdrew from membership in the society. The zealots' charges, however, were rejected by Reb Shraga Feivel Schreier of Bohorodczany, the senior of all Galician rabbis, and by some twenty other rabbis and Hasidic leaders who jealously championed the tidings of Zion. Their written testimonials of support were collected and published by Tarnów's Hebrew teacher, Zekharye-Mendl Schapira.

The other set of zealots erupted within the Zionist camp itself. It was the misfortune of *Ahavat Zion* and Mahanayim to come into the world at the twilight hour between the proto-Zionist *Hibbat Zion* and the Zionist Movement proper.

Those who jealously guarded the Tarnów accomplishment pointed to the inaction and ideological slumber of the rest of the *Hibbat Zion* societies in Galicia, and gloated over the fact that *Ahavat Zion* had made Tarnów a focal point of Zionist work: here the society had established its headquarters; here the form of the future farming colony was planned; the candidates were chosen for *aliyah* and settlement, land was purchased for them, the construction of housing and auxiliary farm structures was organized and, last but not least, Tarnów's own Zygmunt Bromberg was appointed director of the colony.

Bromberg, thirty-three years old at the time – a poet, translator, aesthete and educator, born in eastern Galicia but raised, educated and active in Tarnów, and one of its delegates to the First Zionist Congress – was among the finest, most interesting figures of na-scent Zionism's romanticism. Despite Mahanayim's failure under his management, many (including Reb Aazik), continued to respect his early achievements and refrained from attributing to him any personal blame.

As opposed to the jealous dreamers of a Galician colony, there were some Zionists who, from the outset, saw no point in its establishment, criticizing the handling of the entire affair and the unsuitability of the people chosen to settle on the land. "What will this small, poor settlement help us?" Ahad HaAm objected in 1895, when the idea was first broached. "Better one thriving colony that can endear [Eretz Israel] to the People, than ten shaky ones that need the love for the land to defend their existence." He added further sundry rebukes in 1898, and more strongly so in 1902, when he delivered the final sentence on what he predicted years before: Mahanayim "is dying."

The foremost opposition to Mahanayim, however, came from the camp of Herzlian political Zionism, which rose on the ruins of disillusionment with *Hibbat Zion* and, for as long as Herzl lived, advocated the obtainment of a charter from the Turkish Sultan prior to proceeding with settlement activity.

The reactions and counter-reactions, as well as the vicissitudes of the Mahanayim project, including its initial success and subsequent collapse, provided Aazik, the young man, with a first taste of the tensions that rocked Zionism from within, in parallel to the tensions that the Orthodox forced on it in their struggle from without.

Will I not have to choose one day between lernen on the one hand, and Enlightenment and Zionism, on the other? Aazik wonders anxiously. Be that as it may, he consoled himself, the time had not yet come; meanwhile, he will remain true to the motives that propelled him to Tarnów, the Talmudic wellspring.

During his early years in town, in fact, *lernen* had no rivals for his devotion. He consciously steered clear of all activities that had no direct bearing on study and firmly shut his eyes to all intrigues at the *Kloyz*. The rumors that reached his ears were mere trifles that idle talk dangled in the bathhouse vapor or in the recess between *Minha* and *Maariv* prayers. His instinct for survival at the *Kloyz* directed him, the novice, to totally cut himself off from the internal frictions that soured the atmosphere in the hall, and to muster all his inner strength to sustain his foothold in the world of Torah. Actually, from the moment that he became immersed in a page of *Gemara*, all the fleeting concerns that split the *Kloyz* denizens dissolved away as if by a magic wand, along with the hall tables and the young men poring over their *Gemara* volumes, and the walls of the *Kloyz* melted away in an endless mist, while his own *Gemara* sailed like a boat in mid-sea, its flag at full mast, plowing the waters with all its force to reach the shores of the coveted solution to the problem under discussion. And *blessed be He, who bestowed the Torah, Amen.*

For the sake of accuracy, it must thus be said that the lure of the Enlightenment and Zionism of which *Kloyz* fanatics accused the lad, and which were subsequently to become the hallmarks of his personality, had not yet appeared on the horizon of his life at this time. Aazik's "Enlightenment" and "Zionisation" did not begin before 1897, his third year in Tarnów, when he was already sixteen, and even then they did not detract from his accomplishments in Talmud, as his rabbi attested.

Nevertheless, even during the early years, when every day and every minute were given over purely to *Gemara*, there was no escaping the outside world. Like mighty breakers, events forced themselves on one and all, some welcome, others casting a pall over everything, and Aazik did not consider himself excused from relating to or confronting them. He arrived in Tarnów just as the Dreyfus Affair burst powerfully into the arena and his life.

The Dreyfus Affair did not only stir up the political and literary salons of the secular Jewish intelligentsia in town, but also wagged the tongues of the permanent cadre of folk-debaters ruling the *mikveh*, whose commentaries were the daily fare of Aazik and of the other bathers at morning ablutions. The Affair gave rise to hasty, mundane chats snatched before and after prayers, primarily within the *Kloyz*, but also at smaller *minyunim* and *shtiblakh*, and freely eradicated any other topic sprouting at shop counters and kiosks. Weightily, the subject crept in between every quick "*shulim aleikhem/ aleikhem shulim*" exchanged in greeting by passing Jews on the street, forcing them to stop for a moment and discuss it. It, the anti-Dreyfus plot, proved once again that Jews – including those who openly defined themselves as conscious assimilators and believed themselves protected from persecution – were, merely by being Jews, at a constant disadvantage and exposed to the basest conspiracies. Look, even France, that most progressive of nations – neither that nation nor its military were in fact immune to prejudice and the plague of anti-Semitism.

But, while everyone agreed that Jews are defenseless among *goyim*, even in a liberal country, and even at the price of complete assimilation – as the conspiracy against Dreyfus, that complete assimilationist, would show – the ultra-Orthodox repeatedly strummed on the anti-Zionist chords sounded by Yehezkel of Sieniawa, and a spate of malicious *pashkvils* (smear pamphlets) struck dread into anyone who sought to hasten the messianic era. Others, however, countered that "every cloud has a silver lining," and "that all things are for the good," and by turning towards the refreshing winds blowing from Vienna, they marveled at Herzl's *Judenstaat*, which in 1896 had just come hot off the presses, in German. Unlike the Ukraine, where mass enthusiasm had to wait for Russian and Hebrew translations, most of the adult Jews in Galicia, where German was the official language, had no difficulty reading the work in the original. As for the young men at the *Kloyz* (Aazik included) and at other *yeshivas*, who were acquainted with spoken German because of their knowledge of Yiddish, yet had no experience of literary German (especially if written in a non-Hebrew alphabet), a solution was found: that February, Sokolow, editor of *HaZefira*, published in his Hebrew newspaper a preliminary summary of the program and, that summer, a full Hebrew translation appeared in Warsaw.

Conversely, for those who had learned pure German with the help of the German translation of the Bible published more than a century earlier by Mendelssohn and colleagues in the Hebrew alphabet – a "Mendelssohnian" version (meaning, pure German in Hebrew letters) of Herzl's *Judenstaat* was brought out in September of 1896. Apart from its inherent importance, this edition aroused in young Aazik a longing to familiarize himself with the earlier biblical translation and, through it, perhaps acquire a knowledge of pure German (as opposed to Yiddish), just as many had done before him.

No matter whether in the original or in translation, readers regarded Herzl's message as the practical and prophetic lesson of the Dreyfus Affair, especially as it came from someone who, until then, had believed in assimilation as a way of life. Yet, after realizing the error of his ways in the course of the Dreyfus Affair, the very same man had arisen and offered a radical solution to the Jewish question and even dared to utter its explicit name: a sovereign state for Jews!

Yes, a new wind was blowing in from Vienna, washing over the entire Jewish world and all its outposts, including the Tarnów *Kloyz*, with electrifying tidings on its wings:

"*Judenstaat!*" – it whispered in the ear of Tarnów's Jewish intellectuals.

"*Medinat Yehudim!*" – it stroked the eyes of both Enlightened Hebraists and *yeshiva* students.

"*A Yiddishe medineh!*" – it jolted the masses with its clear, direct language.

True, not all the young men at the *Kloyz* who pored over their

Gemara day after day discerned the drift of the new wind, even though it dropped down to twirl their side-locks and caress their brows with a kiss. Out of habit, they buried their wan faces in the square Hebrew letters – indifferent, skeptical, fanatical. The indifferent took refuge within a wizened apathy, never even raising their heads as the wind moved past them. The skeptical, as usual, spawned a thousand doubts, mocking both message and messenger. Whereas the fanatics of the old order dug into the antique, worn-out trenches of yesterday's battles as they declared war on all who would precipitate the end of days. Nevertheless, there were also young *yeshiva* men for whom the new wind and the tidings it bore spelled a breakthrough into dormant reaches of consciousness, arousing thoughts that only now did they dare to convey from heart to lips. The program, however, did not yet call for any personal steps to realize the idea.

The new current also shook Aazik, the youth, with all its might. The Herzlian tidings gave him wings and filled his heart with pride and a sense of gratification at being witness to momentous events unfolding before his eyes, events too momentous to be either contained by his imagination or dressed in concrete form. Even Herzl, who had lit the luminous fire with his writing in order to focus the eyes of the Jewish People on the target, refused to translate his message into patterns of *aliyah* and settlement. In any case, Aazik saw no justification for perceiving the tidings of the *Judenstaat* as contrary to the routine of *lernen* to which he had sworn allegiance, or to see it as channeling *his* lifestyle towards pathways outside of the *Great Kloyz*.

And then came *Ahavat Zion*.

It had been bubbling beneath the surface for a year and perhaps more – and he, Aazik, had not known. Young men at the *Kloyz* whispered its name from ear to ear, mentioning in the same breath the names of Torah scholars who lent it their support or had joined it personally – the foremost among them being Reb Feivel Schreier of Bohorodczany, along with Reb Asher Hurvitz, rabbi of Rymanów, and others – and he, Aazik, had failed to understand it. Now, here it was, *Ahavat Zion*, come with great fanfare and out in the open. Like a queen before her subjects, it announced the founding assembly of a movement that was to embrace all of Galicia! And the assembly was to take place soon, very soon – on the thirty-second and thirty-third days of the counting of the *Omer*, 5657 (May 19 and 20, 1897) – convening and organizing right here, in Tarnów.

For the village boy, who until then had not been tempted to even glance at any event or assembly outside the walls of the *Kloyz*, the *Ahavat Zion* assembly was a revelation, an experience that was to remain with him throughout his life, a second *bar-mitzvah* celebration at which he assumed commandments of a different nature. It was a turning point. All of a sudden, everything was so close, familiar, obvious, all but homespun. For the flap of wings brought by the new current did not emanate from faraway Vienna, but from his own town, Tarnów! And while the tidings of Herzl's *Judenstaat* continued to hover in the background in all their force and enchantment, Tarnów's tidings raised another flag to the top of the pole: "Mahanayim!"

Ostensibly, the motto seemed to shrink the vision of the *Judenstaat*, translating into "small change" the dream of a Jewish state that Herzl described in his book and on whose behalf he called on the Jewish People to enlist. But this small change was real, palpable, countable, its ring familiar, its currency common and safe. Not the grand kingdom of David whose flame torched hearts, but a small, simple national village, close and in the present! A dirt road, trodden by bare feet, descending to the Jordan River. A cabin, or stone house with a shady palm tree in front of it. A vegetable garden, with the biblical Seven Species. A cow and chickens in the yard. An unsaddled horse, just waiting to be ridden. A well dug by Jewish hands. Furrows of wheat, stretching into the horizon. Wisłok!

Yes, Wisłok in the cornfields of Galilee. Between Rosh Pina

and Mishmar HaYarden. But, this time, it was totally Jewish, with a biblical name, the one and only, and no other like it! And its land was not the dregs dispensed from imperial assets, such as had been given to his grandfather, but a land of milk and honey as promised by the God of Israel to His people! This Wisłok, and another like it, and another still, and dozens and hundreds of similar ones that were to join it, would bring about the *Judenstaat*, "speedily and in our own times." In truth, they – they in the present and not far off somewhere in the future – already were the *Judenstaat*!

2

Yes, it was a turning point.

"Look, Herschl," Aazik points to the Aberdam home at 1 Goldhammera Street, the second floor of which had once housed the Zoldinger Hotel where the first, fondly-remembered assembly of *Ahavat Zion* had taken place. "This is where my Zionism was born." Forty years, a whole generation in biblical terms, had elapsed since those wonderful days of May 1897. Now the Father feels a need to draw his son closer and sow in him a sense of continuity with the events of that era; especially now, in May 1937, after the son has just sat his matriculation exams, and is soon to depart for Eretz Israel.

"Unlike most of my generation in Galicia and Lithuania, including important writers, for whom the Enlightenment had been a corridor to Zionism, my Zionist experience preceded my 'Enlightenment' for the simple reason that *Ahavat Zion* succeeded in recruiting both modern-educated and Orthodox." Spinning the threads of memory, Aazik deliberately sets out to stroll with his son at dusk along Goldhammera Street. At the end of the nineteenth century, when Aazik had arrived here as a boy, this street in Austrian Tarnów had brought together the two wings of Jewish *baal-batishkeit* (the "bourgeoisie"), secular as well as Orthodox. Also in the twentieth century, after Tarnów's restoration to the bosom of

Poland at the end of the First World War, the street, with its wealthy homes and residents, had continued – while Aazik's son was a young boy – to exude the same quality of dual *baal-batishkeit*.

"*Ahavat Zion*'s tidings descended on me like a divine revelation – so excited was I that I hardly knew what to do with myself. And, all of this, because of two people. The better known still lives on this street and every day, at dusk, takes a walk along it just as he used to do back then; in fact, I have especially brought you here at this hour so that you might see him. There he is now, about twenty steps ahead of us: erect, bareheaded, bald and clean-shaven and, recently, curiously enough, without his famous moustache. That red moustache was the hallmark of his youth. Its pointy ends lent him the look of a Polish *shaygitz*, much to the open disgust of the black-bearded, elegant, aristocratic Herzl. Today, he must be at least sixty; yet he carries his head as high as ever, as if seeking divine inspiration, and his hands still grip a short, ivory-tipped cane – not as a walking stick, but in deference to men's fashion as it was then."

"That's him, Dr. Abraham Salz of Tarnów!" Aazik's eyes sparkle. "I never mustered the courage to approach him; I was too minor to walk up to the doctor as he strolled on the street and introduce myself as an intellectual follower of his" – the words of the village boy spill from the throat of the adult Reb Aazik, who still shrinks from striking up a conversation with his spiritual mentor, as if the latter were a rare and fragile archeological remnant, or a mythological figure segregated from reality by an enchanted aura.

"After all, how could I, a mere *yeshiva* boy, unschooled in adult conversation, bother him with my questions – he, the illustrious leader who corresponded with Herzl himself, who spoke with Herzl face to face as a friend, and even dared to disagree with him?! To Salz, Rothschild's door was always open and he even managed to persuade the Baron to sell *Ahavat Zion* a piece of the lands he owned in Galilee for the sake of establishing Mahanayim! And Herzl, himself, chose Salz to be his deputy at the First Zionist Congress in Basel!

"In my youth I learned wonderful things about this native son of Tarnów." The father gleans isolated memories from the coffers of his experience to display before his son. "While still a student in Vienna, his name went before him as a great organiser; and, after his return to Tarnów as a qualified attorney; and, following his address at the Maccabee gala in 1890 in Lwów, he became known as a fiery orator as well. As a result, from the first pan-Galician conference of *Hibbat Zion* in 1893, he – the Zionist leader of little Tarnów – suddenly, at the mere age of twenty-nine, found himself the foremost representative of Galician Zionism as a whole!"

After a moment's silence, a grin spread across Aazik's face as he cast his mind back to an old joke. "Indeed" – he decided to share one of the period's jests with his son – "people quipped that Salz had managed to push Lwów, the capital of Galicia, and Vienna, the imperial capital, into the backdrop, while turning the provincial town of Tarnów into the capital of Zionist action! But, you know something, Herschl? It wasn't a joke at all. Because, for at least three years – given the ineffectiveness of *Hibbat Zion* leaders in Lwów and the opposition of Herzl to any settlement endeavor prior to the procurement of a political charter from the Sultan – Tarnów really was the only protagonist of Zionist action.

"I was about a year younger than you are today, Herschl, when *Ahavat Zion* convened in Tarnów," the father continues his reminiscences, "and when I caught snatches of conversation in the conference hallways, or when I imbibed the spirit of the assembly and the spirit of its speakers, I discovered how much my study of Talmud, despite its value and despite the satisfaction I derived from it, had limited me to a single plane of Jewish thought and deprived me of all contact with modern nationalist doctrine. And though from personal experience at the *Kloyz* I was familiar with the topics of friction and sources of antagonism inside the Orthodox camp, it was difficult for me to find my way amid the conflicts meandering through the nationalist camp – conflicts between so-called practical

Zionism and political Zionism, that sharpened at the end of the century.

"The truth is that as far as I was concerned, my ideological ignorance also had its advantages" – Aazik chaffed at himself, while his son discerned that the use of the word "ignorance" causes his learned father almost a sense of relish. "My *Ahavat Zion*, my love of Zion as I understood it in its simplistic form, ideologically connected both: the old *Hibbat Zion* movement, whose sun seemed to be waning, and Herzl's new Zionism, whose sun was then rising and shining.

"In embracing the photographs of the first colonies in Judea and Galilee, my personal love of Zion rang out with the biblical poetry of their names – Petah Tikva, Rishon LeZion, Rosh Pina, Yesod HaMaala. And beneath the roof of my love of Zion the old colonies dwelt in peace alongside Herzl and his Congresses, and I saw no essential difference, let alone contradiction, between the two elements. Only five years later was I to come to understand the tension between the two and, oh, how fatal the fanatic insistence on one of them, and how bitter the end of *Ahavat Zion* and Mahanayim, as if decreed by fate to sprout up in the twilight zone between two eras and two ideologies.

"In those days I also discovered the extent to which Eastern European Zionism – as opposed to the Viennese sort – was tied by an umbilical cord to the Hebrew literature of Lithuania and Galicia. Thus, on that very first evening, to my surprise, I learned that for the past forty years, the champions of the Hebrew Enlightenment had cherished a novel written by Abraham Mapu of Lithuania, its biblical language and plot being set in the free land of the Jewish People during the First Temple period. It was only natural to conclude that what had won the hearts of the readers was not only the novel's content and biblical style, but its title: *Ahavat Zion*. Happy the People (I told myself) whose children cleave to books and adopt the title of a book for the name of a movement!"

3

His son at his side, Reb Aazik returns to reflect on the doubts that had plagued him prior to the conference, and the liberating moment when he made the decision to participate in it. Indeed, it was the first time since his arrival in Tarnów two years previously that he found himself abandoning his lectern on the *Kloyz* platform and going out in the company of a handful of other *yeshiva* students, all from old Tarnów families, to the Zoldinger Hotel on Goldhammera Street, which had been hired to host the assembly.

The young men attended the conference at the invitation of their friend, Shol (Saul) Spitz. Shol and Vofche Stiglitz, had, at the bidding of their rabbi, Reb Moishl, two years earlier, taken the Wisłok village boy under their wings; in time, Aazik and Shol became fast friends. Shol's father, Leib, who had issued the invitation, was a member of the *Ahavat Zion* Committee in Tarnów and Salz's right-hand man. His flat was in the Wittmayer building at the Rynek, the very same premises from which he managed Wittmayer's shop of colonial spices and fruit and, where, after his patron's death, he opened a grocery store of his own. A prominent figure, Spitz enjoyed the trust of both the Orthodox and the modern-educated (the former called him Reb Leibtche, the latter – *Herr* Leon Spitz). Alive to the duality of Galician Jewry, Salz, the freethinker, had chosen Spitz to act as an intermediary between himself and the Orthodox faction. And even though the intermediary failed to draw Reb Yehezkel of Sieniawa into the Mahanayim project, the latter remaining entrenched in his zealotry and hostility, Spitz was universally regarded as the architect of the unprecedented covenant between the two camps – a covenant between Orthodox and modern-educated who remained miles apart in outlook, but were prepared to join hands for the sake of establishing the colony.

Aazik's eyes, which had never before seen the inside of a hotel, eagerly caressed the set tables at which the forty-eight delegates of Jewish communities sat with the emissary from Vienna who had come expressly to represent Herzl. Happy emphasis was placed on the fact that in January 1897, during the very first month of the association's functioning, Herzl had been sent Share No. 1 in the sum of five gulden, an acquisition he had confirmed.

Aazik gazed in admiration at the faces of the delegates, though only a handful were known to him. But he managed, at least, to learn the names of the communities they represented at the conference and to roll them over off his tongue in pleasure: Lwów, Kraków, Przemyśl, Dębica, Kołomyja, Borysław, Drohobycz, Tuchów, Bohorodczany, Rzeszów, Tarnobrzeg, Zbaraż, Mielec, Wieliczka, Jarosław, Podgórze, Jaworzno, Łańcut, Rohatyn, Ropczyce and Czernowitz – and these were soon to be joined by another eighty branches! And though, as the saying goes, "in the multitude of people is the king's glory," of all the towns blessed be Tarnów, the one and only – for from Tarnów issued the teaching of *Ahavat Zion* and from it the word of Mahanayim's founding would go forth to all of Galicia!

"I'll never forget the sight of the presidential podium on that first night of the assembly. The two men who sat at the head of the table were total opposites. On the one hand, Reb Feivel Schreier of Bohorodczany, eighty years old, his white beard overflowing, but his eyes smiling beneath the fur of his high *spodik;* the rabbi, disregarding his advanced age, had lovingly submitted to the jerks and jolts of the journey and agreed to travel to Tarnów. And on the other hand, Dr. Salz, thirty-three years old, who, notwithstanding the presence of many Orthodox people, sat next to the rabbi bareheaded and clean-shaven, except for his telling Polish moustache, its copper hue competing with the copper gleam of the huge, Salz bald pate. The two leaders, despite the difference in age and appearance, and despite the difference in garments and lifestyle, conducted the evening in exemplary amiability.

"How happy I was that night to count dozens of long black *kapottehs* disobeying Reb Yehezkel of Sienawa by flocking to the hotel doors, along with the modern-educated, wearing (Germanic) short-jacketed suits," Reb Aazik re-explored the far reaches of rec-ollection with his son. "And how wonderful it was, as a counter-weight to the Zans power, to hear the warm note of support sent by Reb Itzhik Shmelkis, the rabbi of Lwów, and the message of the rabbi of Rymanów. At the end of the evening, the elderly Reb Feivel Schreier himself delivered an impassioned address in praise of till-ing the soil in the Holy Land! In view of the fantastic showing of the Orthodox, I also felt a mighty gust rising from the assembly to jolt my very existence and command me as well to stand up and be counted: 'Here I am'.

"Ah, who can restore to Tarnów those exalted days, the *Lag Ba'Omer* joy of forty years ago that radiated from the assembly onto the entire Jewish community?" Father sighs, casting a final glance at the Aberdam Building, which seems to have shut itself up with nightfall. Does the sigh divulge hopes and disappointments woven into each and every one of those forty years?

"Yes, where are those days of great hope, when holiday can-dles, like traditional *Hanukka* candles, graced all the windows of the homes down Lwowska Street as far as the Grabówka junction, in honor of the event? The lighting was particularly vivid at 14 Lwowska, *Ahavat Zion*'s office premises, whereas at the hotel on Goldhammera the whole length of the floor was lit up, so that even from afar, the eyes of the entire town, Jewish and non-Jewish alike, could witness the defeat of Orthodox zealotry and the vision of Mahanayim donning flesh and bones for the glory of Tarnów and all Galicia.

"A great miracle took place here." At the corner of Goldhammera, in May 1937, Aazik unfurled before his son the tale of the amaz-ing *Lag Ba'Omer* he experienced at the very same corner in May 1897. Can it be (the son wonders in view of the *Hanukka* twist that the tale has suddenly taken) that Father's dreamy eyes still see the hundreds of lit candles, as if the winter Festival of Lights had been advanced to early summer in honor of the Maccabees of our own generation?

"Yes," the Father reiterates his recollection, seemingly unaware of how strange it sounded to dress *Lag Ba'Omer* in the language of *Hanukka* – "a great miracle took place here, and it is the merit of both Tarnów and Mahanayim which stood us in good stead, that we might witness the miracle as it happened!"

Reb Aazik, it seems, notwithstanding the passing decades, continues to cleave to the unity demonstrated that evening and, as then, hears his own voice again reply fearlessly (in floral *lushn koidish*) to a question, also in the holy tongue, put to the *yeshiva* students in the hall by Shol Spitz's father and an unknown guest at his side, who were interested in hearing their impressions. Spitz, as opposed to the Zans zealots, sought to steer the young, including his own son, Shol, and the latter's friends, towards a course that saw no inherent contradiction between an Orthodox Jewish lifestyle and the Enlightenment and Zionism.

Forty years later, Aazik still remembers the question asked in *Ashkenazi* Hebrew by the two gentlemen, who did not address any particular *yeshiva* student. Likewise, he remembers his own shock when, as the youngest and poorest and loneliest of the lot, he found himself (of all people) daring to tackle the question and reply, loud and clear, with the natural ease of one who had always spoken Hebrew. And what's more, even now, when mature in years, he can repeat from memory, word for word, the high-sounding sentence that, ostensibly, had sprung of itself from brain to throat to issue from his mouth unfalteringly:

"Who could have foreseen and who could have guessed" – young Aazik's admiration related more to the general picture of the evening than to its ideological foundation – "that the day would come when rabbis and *doktoirim*, *baalbatim* ('worthy citizens') and writers, Enlightened and Hasidim, would sit at one table, in fraternal togetherness?!"

And he remembers well: as soon as the Hebrew words escaped into the air, embarrassment silenced him and raised a warm blush on his face. For, suddenly, the simple though surprising fact penetrated his consciousness that after two years of intensive, unflagging study of more than eighteen hours a day, and after absorbing hundreds of pages of "dead" texts written in Hebrew and Aramaic, here, for the first time, external circumstances had impelled him to grab a handful of grains from his cache of knowledge of *lushn koidish* and sow them in the wind, his breath breathing life into words buried deep in his mind and ordering them to serve him here and now, independent of their literary source and context.

This new awareness of his ability to use the knowledge stored in the recesses of his brain – knowledge that had lain undisturbed for two years and had never been summoned for secular purposes – thoroughly changed Aazik's mood by the end of the evening: his initial embarrassment gave way to satisfaction and even pride, and a free, calm smile banished the blush that had earlier suffused his cheeks. Reb Leibtche and his companion (who remained unidentified), believing the boy's smile to be meant for them, responded in kind, and they took their leave of the *yeshiva* students in good spirits and moved off to mingle with the crowd.

Aazik remained glued to the spot briefly, trying to fathom the excitement that gripped him. He sensed ripples of pleasure course through him, from the top of his head to the tips of his toes, banding together to envelop his body like a soft mantle. A voice whispered to him that the evening was fateful, not merely for the *Ahavat Zion* movement but for him personally. He guessed that the two gentlemen were connected with it in some way, though he did not yet understand how or why. After all, what did he know of the two men who had suddenly appeared in his life? Leibtche, his friend's father, he did know from before, having been invited to *kiddush* at his home, but he had never really talked to him apart from polite exchanges, which had not been in Hebrew. Leibtche's companion,

however, remained a puzzle. The boy had never seen him at the
Kloyz and all the signs pointed to his not being a resident of Tarnów.
The stranger's identity, and the position he filled, were a mystery to
Leibtche's son as well, although he had seen his father walking in
his company in the past and according him obvious respect. Either
way, it was clear to Aazik that his relationship with the two men,
especially with Leibtche Spitz, was likely to be cemented and, perhaps, engender a change in his life.

Meanwhile, Leibtche did not rest on his laurels. The secular-
Orthodox alliance of the 1897 assembly he had personally labored
to achieve – more so, perhaps, than anyone else in his circle – by
repeated visits to Reb Feivel and Reb Shmelkis and Reb Asher
Hurvitz and their adherents. In no way, however, did the success
of the assembly put an end to his efforts as the bridgehead to the
Orthodox camp and as Dr. Salz's envoy to the camp's leaders. On
the contrary: now that the success had become public knowledge,
it would be easier for him to expand his activities!

Thus, less than two weeks after the assembly, Spitz again set out
on his campaign trips. As he had guessed, many Jewish scholars now
joined the movement, the jewel in the crown of his latter recruits
being Reb Moishe-Duvid Friedman, the *Tzaddik* of Czortków! The
enlistment of the renowned Hasidic *rebbe* – the last of the sons of
Reb Israel of Rozhin – in the cause of settling Eretz Israel brought
with it fervent enrollment from the small towns around Czortków,
including declarations of membership in *Ahavat Zion* and participation in the initiative to establish a colony in Galilee.

4

Leibtche Spitz's glowing impression of both the response to his
question and the character of the responder was not a matter of
that moment alone. He knew from his son, Shol, that since Passover –
the start of the school year's "second period" at the *Kloyz* – Reb

Moishl had elevated the "Rutenian" from his place at the table to the privileged corner on the platform, where, as was customary, the lad had been given a lectern of his own for his *Gemara*. To be sure, there were those who raised angry eyebrows at the sight of this blatant favoritism for the stranger, the *pshivlik*, over the sons of privileged families that had resided in Tarnów for generations. Their grumbling, however, was nipped in the bud by one wrathful look of censure from the rabbi: yes, he, too, Moishl Yekels Apter, had come from the ranks of the poor, and claims of privilege and wealth or any other pressures had never daunted him or clouded his judgment.

Reb Leibtche's interest in Aazik was heightened by the ongoing accounts he heard from Shol of his rural friend's tenacity in study, including his practice of standing barefoot on the cold floor after midnight to counter the lure of sleep. This, while his own son, Shol, returned home after prayers every evening to a warm meal in a loving family and a soft, cozy bed of white linen. Himself an erstwhile *yeshiva* student and now the father of one, Leibtche did not feel that his son's friendship with Aazik was sufficient unto itself, but that it behooved him as well to do something for the boy. He remembered how his own rabbi, an inspired scholar, had guided him by personal example to intertwine the dual fibers of his life, faith and Enlightenment, into a single thread, and how he, Leibtche, had reinforced the two, as an adult, by adding a third fiber, that of Zionism (which in his rabbi's day had not yet been an institutionalized framework). The time had come for him to repay the kindness he had received at his mentor's hands: he would "adopt" the *ilui* (prodigy), and guide him and Shol along the course that he had chosen. Unlike the zealots, who deemed any departure from routine as sheer wantonness, Leibtche knew from personal experience that his road would not be detrimental to the sacred studies of the two lads.

Again it was Shol, at his father's behest, who served as

messenger, relaying to Aazik an invitation to the Spitz home for the next Sabbath *kiddush*. As indicated by the messenger's secretive wink, however, Aazik guessed that this was no ordinary invitation, but one imbued with galvanizing import. Indeed, much to his confusion, when he entered the handsome, spacious dining room, he found Leibtche sitting relaxed at the table, which was covered with a white Sabbath cloth, in contrast to the regular Sabbath *kiddush*, when everybody stood about. Moreover, again in contrast to his previous visits, only family members occupied the room; guests were nowhere to be seen.

"I haven't invited anyone but you this time," the head of the family said in reply to the unspoken question. The words were delivered in *lushn koidish*, of course. "Please join us for the Sabbath meal for I have something to discuss with you, which I think you will find interesting. But seeing as the table is not yet set, let's go into the next room where we can talk quietly." Reb Leibtche pushed open a side door, and the youth was bowled over by the sight that greeted his eyes. He suddenly discovered a chamber no less spacious than the dining room and also containing a large, heavy table in the middle, though this one had no cloth cover, and walls – walls that were upholstered by books, books and more books. "This is my library," Leibtche declared ceremoniously, making no attempt to conceal his pride. "This is where I am meant to spend my free time. Except that the need to make a living demands thought and effort," he sighed, "and does not leave me any free time. In addition, as you know, I have been charged with a public role and, in public life, one knows when the work begins but never when it reaches completion; and no matter how hard one seeks rest of body and mind, it will ever be elusive. As a result, the room stands empty, and the books wait for readers. If you like, you may have free use of my library."

Aazik (as he told his son years later) was stunned. He was not accustomed to being addressed by an adult as an equal and, here, for the first time, an adult was imparting to him his thoughts, his difficulties, his doubts. The boy realized that his intuition on the night of the assembly had been right: his acquaintance with Leibtche was to signal a turning point in his life. In time, when Aazik first told his son about the two people who had shaped his course, he had mentioned only Salz by name as having served as his ideological mentor, even though he was not personally acquainted with him. Now, here was the second: Leibtche, who, by opening his library to him, had opened the world!

Elated by the sight of the book-laden shelves, Aazik was eager to approach, to touch and to feel them. All at once his glance fell on a large, Hebrew newspaper lying open on the table. "I left the newspaper out especially for you, Aazik. It is *HaMaggid*, a Hebrew weekly which, since its purchase by Shmuel Fuchs in 1891, is being published every Thursday in Kraków. The editor has placed the paper at the disposal of *Ahavat Zion* and even serves on the *Ahavat Zion* committee. These are the running issues of the Sixth Volume, from 1897 on, and here is the last paper, Number 21, of May 27, that is, a week after the assembly. And indeed, on pages 165–166, there is a full account of the convention. You may glance at the whole article later. Right now, I'd like you to read the section I marked in red ink. Read it out loud!"

Aazik picked up the newspaper not knowing what to expect. The first idea that sprang to mind concerned the size of the pages. "They're like a *Gemara* tractate" – he bit back an impish smile. "How easily the newspaper can be hidden beneath a *Gemara* volume!" He visualized the figure of the *Kloyz* overseer, his eyes ablaze, apprehending a student with *HaMaggid* or another Enlightenment composition beneath his *Gemara*. "At least, not under an ordinary volume," the delinquent would jest, "but the *Avoda Zara* ("Idol Worship") tractate, ha-ha, most fitting for the occasion." The overseer would not be amused.

"Read it out loud," Leibtche roused Aazik from his reveries. The lad did so, embarrassed: "Who could have foreseen years ago that the day would come when rabbis and *doktoirim, baalbatim* and writers, Enlightened and Hasidim, would all sit around one table, in fraternal togetherness?!"

"You remember the words and who said them?" Spitz bantered at the sight of the blush on Aazik's cheeks. "The truth is, you phrased it better. But that's how editors are: they borrow from anything at hand, without quoting the source precisely as they should, and, because of the pressures of printing deadlines, they commit inaccuracies galore. I know the question that's on the tip of your tongue: how did your words reach *HaMaggid*'s editor? No, no, I had nothing to do with it as you suspect. The editor heard them with his own ears. The man who was with me at the assembly was none other than *HaMaggid*'s editor himself, Fuchs."

In the long run, the unattributed quote in *HaMaggid*'s article was, at best, a subject of jest between Leibtche and Aazik, especially since Fuchs, busy stirring the political brews of the times, seemed to have forgotten all about the lad whose words he had incorporated in his article. The two, in any case, had not met again since the assembly.

Leibtche's opening of his library to Aazik was no momentary whim, but the realization of a long-term plan he had recently conceived and now decided to set into motion: to make his versatile literary trove available to the *ilui* who, though fired by the flame of the modern Enlightenment and Zionism, was submerged exclusively in traditional scholarship and totally unfamiliar with the vibrant, intellectual life of recent generations and the creative fruits that they produced, and that the *Kloyz* has spurned. It was Leibtche's hope that not only Aazik, but also Shol, would profit from the project; even though he, the father, was sharp enough to discern that his son, as talented and diligent as he might be, was apparently not made of that rare, remarkable stuff that turned out serious students and *iluis*, researchers and thinkers, artists, authors and virtuosos.

From that day on and for the next seven years, in parallel with his studies at the *Kloyz*, Aazik was to implement his patron's program by taking over Reb Leibtche's library on his one free day in the week – every Sabbath – from the end of the *Musaf* prayer until well after *Havdala*. Leibtche was more than willing to lend Aazik books, but since the youth had no home of his own and he could not possibly bring the type of material he was now learning into the *Kloyz*, the only choice left to him, with the consent of Leibtche and Leibtche's household, was to closet himself in the chamber off the dining room and draw inspiration from the splendid rows of books for present progress and future planning. There was no doubt about his remaining an autodidact till the end.

"When the day comes that I will have a home of my own, not a spacious one like Leibtche's, but at least with one large room for books, I, too, will create a library where I will sit and study," Aazik promised himself, his eyes rapt with the dream of education, "and should my son have no interest in my library, I, too, will open it up to a capable lad, hungry for knowledge."

Since the sanctity of the Sabbath did not allow Aazik to accompany his reading with penciled comments, he developed a method of retention that fashioned his memory into what the Sages characterized as a "sealed cistern that lost not a drop." Only now did he understand the mysterious concept of Oral Law, and the borne-out conviction in the early ages, that so-called memorizers made Oral Law no less valid than Written Law.

Three things caught Aazik's eyes that very first Sabbath as he sat alone in Reb Leibtche's library, dazzled by the titles of the books on the shelves: *HaMaggid* demanded primacy, despite the fact that it was not on a shelf but always awaited him on the table. Apart from the newspaper, Aazik knew that, as soon as possible, he had to read another item that beckoned to him from the opposite shelf, Mapu's *Ahavat Zion*. Yet a strange reluctance suddenly gripped him, not because of the language, but because he was about to embark, for the first time, on reading a literary work! In time, he was to make his way through the entire Enlightenment literature, including the *Me'asfim* (first modern Hebrew anthologies) and literary journals. And, though his initial reluctance would vanish, he would never read a book for plain enjoyment, but would "study" it, analyze its style, subject it, as it were, to *lernen*. As for the third category – a set of books bound in brown leather and embossed in gold on the spine – he knew that he was destined to spend long years in its company, for this was Mendelssohn's Hebrew-lettered translation of the Bible into German, from which he hoped to learn the language as hundreds and thousands of *yeshiva* students before him had done. Until the end of his days, in fact, Aazik continued to write a Yiddish that was actually German dressed in the Hebrew alphabet, which his siblings in America, with whom he corresponded by mail, were probably unable to understand. The problem was not only the orthography, but the displacement of Yiddish folk idioms. Thus, for example, his correspondence never contained the common Yiddish-Hebrew form *im yirzeh haShem* (God willing), but the German *gebe Gott*, even spelled with two "*tet*"s to represent the double "t" in "real" German.

Aazik's Sabbath day was circumscribed by strict discipline: beginning with *HaMaggid*, he picked out items of news on *Ahavat Zion* and Mahanayim and committed them to memory; then he swallowed up the Hebrew-lettered German, spending hours upon hours studying the language; and finally, for dessert, he dipped into a selection of prose and poetry.

HaMaggid's first four years in Aazik's hands made for exciting if, at times, also frustrating reading. Again and again Aazik re-read the reports of important developments, which built up into a two-pronged, quasi-diary of the heart: the history of Mahanayim as it appeared from the decisions made by the "top brass" in Tarnów, and the actual chronicle of its budding, blossoming and withering. He felt as though he was a part of the entire process: exulting in every joy of the colony's, and commiserating with every drought, every setback, and every case of a member's abandoning the colony. In his mind, he built together with the settlers the first house, sowed and reaped upon the land, dug the first well, grew embittered at the delayed receipt of funds from the society in Tarnów, and rejoiced at each addition of manpower. At the same time, he participated in every *Ahavat Zion* gathering and function in Tarnów without worrying about "what the *Kloyz* zealots would say."

Here, for instance, is *HaMaggid*, August 1897: in anticipation of the First Zionist Congress, debate sharpens over fundamentals – whether the movement's aim was the establishment of a "Jewish government," or the ever-growing "settlement of Eretz Israel."

HaMaggid, September 1897: Two issues are devoted to the Zionist Congress. The second carries a headline about the purchase of land for a colony "between Rosh Pina and Mishmar HaYarden." Salz, much to Herzl's displeasure, traveled straight from the Congress to Rothschild in Paris. He dispatched a telegram to Tarnów noting that the transaction had been signed. "The day we have hoped for has come" – Fuchs exults.

HaMaggid, January 1898: The *Tzaddik* of Czortków formally joins *Ahavat Zion*. Kudos to Leibtche Spitz! Zionist Tarnów is proud of your achievements!

HaMaggid, February 1898: On *Rosh Hodesh* of the month of Nissan, a lottery is held and the first settlers chosen. The colony is to be established this very year!

HaMaggid, May 1898: Fuchs against Herzl's school of thought. We must return to practical Zionism!

HaMaggid, June 1898: Tarnów celebrates the departure of Bromberg, the director of the colony, to prepare the groundwork.

An item appears about colonists who had not waited, but are already in Eretz Israel.

HaMaggid, July 1898: Convention of Galician *Hibbat Zion* in Kołomyja. Salz is chairman. At his side is Rabbi Schreier. Herzl telegraphs greetings, but it is Salz whom students raise on their shoulders as the father of the Galician movement for active colonization of Eretz Israel. Salz prudently affirms that he agrees with political Zionism, ostensibly achieving a compromise between his school of practical Zionism and Herzl's political Zionism.

HaMaggid, 21 November 1898: The first eleven pioneers set out for Mahanayim (Fuchs, in his address, likens them to *Ahad-Asar Kokhvaya*, the eleven astral bodies cited in the Passover *Haggada*). Formal farewells are made at the train station. Many weep. (This is where Aazik was apparently spotted, and then reported to the *Kloyz*.)

HaMaggid, end of November 1898: Rabbi Schreier dies.

HaMaggid, mid-December 1898: Reb Yehezkel of Sieniawa dies. What irony! Because of the proximity of the deaths, the two rivals are eulogized together!

HaMaggid, 25–26 April 1899: A second *Ahavat Zion* assembly in Tarnów. Salz closes the assembly with the words, "Next year in Jerusalem."

HaMaggid, 1899: Letters from Matityahu Tzinder at Mahanayim. A house is inaugurated. A second well dug. Description of the settlers: Hasidim with side-locks and *shtreimels*. A photograph of the early settlers, shown with Bromberg. At the end of December 1899, Bromberg is photographed wearing a *kaffiya* on his head.

HaMaggid, March 1900: Farewell parties for Zekharye-Mendl Schapira, the Tarnów Hebrew teacher who was to practice his profession at Mahanayim. Mordkhe Leibel of Tarnów is given approval for a house and a grocery store in the colony. Also Abba Neimark of Tarnów, an ironsmith, makes *aliyah* to Mahanayim. There are already ninety-three people settled on the land. Twenty-seven buildings. Experienced Jewish farmers from Galicia are sent to Mahanayim. Salz seeks to buy himself 25 acres of land in the colony that he established. Another photograph and enthusiastic letter from a Tarnów emissary: "Only a year has passed, and the wasteland has become a heavenly garden."

Here (Aazik surmises) is where the initial sound judgment became carried away by success. On the third anniversary of *Ahavat Zion*, the society provocatively suggested that an additional colony be founded, flying in the face of Herzl, whose policies were opposed to the first settlement as well. Internal Zionist zealotry now moves into action in all its ruthlessness. *HaMaggid*, until then the organ of practical Zionism, is unexpectedly transferred to Vienna, Herzl's base. Why? – Aazik objects. Indeed, for five and a half months, Fuchs finds no spot for Tarnowian Zionism. Not a single word is printed on Mahanayim or *Ahavat Zion* activities.

HaMaggid, April 18 and 25, 1901: Abruptly, in a two-part article, Fuchs publishes a eulogy, "On the grave of the Galician society, *Ahavat Zion*." Outraged, Salz is galvanized to condemn the villainy, protesting, in an article in Drohobycz, *HaMaggid*'s hasty burial of *Ahavat Zion*. Equally suddenly, the colony finds itself financially strapped even though it was thriving only a year before. This, too, may not be accidental. In great pain the settlers leave the dissolved colony and scatter in all directions. Mordkhe Leibel returns to Tarnów to dream of making *aliyah* once more and reviving Mahanayim, except that his death comes first. His son, Pinhas, unable to carry out his father's wishes, joins the founders of Kfar Yehezkel. Tzinder moves to America (where his name is pronounced Zinder). Forty years later he returns to settle in Rehovot, having kept alive the memory of Mahanayim of old. In his old age, he writes a memoir of those times. When his son lends the memoir to the author of this book, a note drops out of its pages – the inscription on the tombstone, desired by the man who had remained true to Mahanayim:

<u>Inscription on my headstone:</u>
<u>Here lies Matityahu Zinder</u>
<u>Son of Rabbi Abraham Shmuel Tzinder</u>
The first of five founders of the colony of Mahanayim
An ardent Zionist. Strove, worked and gave for the country.
A plea and a demand: Write no less, no more. Honor the dead
father.

Mahanayim was dead. It did not die at the hands of the Orthodox, the arch-enemies of its founders, but it was the Zionist movement itself that brought about the colony's downfall, whether inadvertently or with clear intent. Over the years, five attempts to resettle the land in the Upper Galilee "between Rosh Pina and Mishmar HaYarden" were made by various groups, some of them including offspring of the original founders. The final attempt bore fruit, and the site dreamed of by Tarnów Zionists for the building of their home, is now graced by an established kibbutz.

And should you walk up to two or three of the early homes and peel off several centimeters of the plaster which later residents applied to the houses, you will discover the stones that the Tzinder family and the Leibel family put in place with so much love and hope for the future. Indeed, the last residents are to be commended for commemorating the early pioneers, and those who repeatedly returned after them to cherish the land of Mahanayim: at the entrance to the community, kibbutz members installed a Founders Boulevard with engraved wooden plaques, identifying the aspiring settlement groups one by one. The first plaque is dedicated to the Zionists of Tarnów.

As for Dr. Salz, who had hoped to settle there on the twenty-five acres of land he purchased with his own money – his plans were thwarted. He perished at the Rynek, along with the majority of Tarnów's Jews, in the bloody Nazi *akzia* of June 1942.

5

Mahanayim's tragedy was the tragedy of all Tarnów. Just as the budding of this single Galician colony crowned Tarnów in laurels and enshrined it as the capital of Galician Zionism – whose leadership surpassed that of larger, more important towns, such as Kraków and Lwów – so its withering, even though due to external causes beyond the control of the Tarnów committee, was laid at the door of Tarnów's conscience. It was seven years since the awakening of Tarnów's intellectuals (called *doktoirim*, whether out of respect or in contempt) and their banding together with naive Hasidim and practically inclined Orthodox to share the dream of an agricultural colony in the Upper Galilee.

Except that, after two pioneering years of suffering and satisfaction, the dream shattered on the rocks of reality, leaving only scars and pain, a burden of debts, mutual recriminations and gloom. Stricken, through no fault of their own, those who had longed to be valiant farmers in Eretz Israel were cast into despair, remaining locked within their sorrow no matter where they turned. Mottl Leibel, who moved back with his family to Tarnów, walked about as if his world has been destroyed, so much so, that Aazik, who had been among those who saw him off at the train station at his departure, now averts his glance in shame and grief whenever he passes him.

The personal pain of those who sought to dedicate their bodies and souls to the soil of Eretz Israel does not, however, stop the *Kloyz* fanatics from mudslinging. They, ironically, do not differentiate between practical and political Zionists. Just as they blame the practical Zionists for the crisis of the veteran colonies, so they now gloat over the misfortune of the youngest colony, Mahanayim. They view its collapse as divine retribution for heeding the call of Rabbi Schreier, rather than obeying Reb Yehezkel of Sieniawa. On the other hand, no less than at Mahanayim's failure, the zealots sneer at Herzl's political machinations: his meetings with the Kaiser, his feelers in the Sultan's court, his talks at the Vatican, his intercession with Plehve, the Russian minister – in all these he had failed, having done more harm than good.

The doctrine of zealotry knew no rest. Zans libels and lampoons continued to intimidate the public, accompanying Herzl's diplomatic travels with heathen fire and open ridicule. Nor did young Aazik escape the *Kloyz* slanderers, even though his part in the Movement was that of a sympathetic onlooker only and his *lernen* remained unaffected. He could feel the noose tightening around his neck, with only Rabbi Apter standing between himself and expulsion from the *Kloyz*. The animosity the fanatics bore him was for having openly participated since the age of sixteen in public assemblies for *Ahavat Zion* and for having escorted the emigrants to the train station! What's more, even today, at the age of twenty-three, he readily acknowledged that he has no regrets, and claims that it is not the idea itself that failed, but that circumstances and human weakness had defeated it! Be that as it may, sorrows came fast on the heels of one another. Before Aazik could even begin to recover from the collapse of Mahanayim, personal disaster struck again, leaving him inconsolable.

During the Days of Awe of 5673 (1902) Moishl Apter was summoned to the heavenly assembly and Aazik, the *ilui*, was orphaned not only of a great teacher and rabbi but of his only protector at the hostile *Kloyz*. Ah, how sad that Reb Moishl, who was only sixty at his death, did not live to see his Talmudic innovations in print, notwithstanding the fact that the manuscript had lain ready and arranged for twenty years, his desk piling up with endorsements from noted scholars, as customary in the publication of rabbinical literature. The wealthy, however, whose financial support would have made possible the publication of his book, had never had any genuine sympathy for the rabbi because of his inferior origins, and he, for his part, refused to genuflect to their mammon.

Reb Moishl's coffin was laid out at the *Kloyz*, the house of his worship and the site of self-*lernen* by his top students. A painful silence cloaked the huge crowd (including representatives of the Austrian government) that thronged the hall from end to end during the eulogies. The homage was simultaneously broadcast, through the open, eastern windows, to the masses huddled in the square due to lack of space inside, straining their ears not to miss a word. The panegyrics in German (in deference to the state officials present) were delivered by the town rabbi, Reb Abbaleh Schnur, followed, in Yiddish, by Abraham Orschitzer, a judge at Tarnów's rabbinical court.

After the memorial service at the *Kloyz*, the entire Jewish community set out to escort the coffin to its final resting place. In the sad, chestnut leaf fall of Tarnów's autumn chill, the funeral procession wound its way slowly along the usual route to the cemetery: leftwards, from the *Kloyz* lane to Wałowa Street, where waiting crowds at Pod Dębem Square joined the cortège, and from there, to Pilzno Gate, where the deceased had lived. Here the procession halted, and was joined by two women who came down from the first floor of the building: the widow, Rekh'l, a pale, modest woman, who had never uttered a sound in public, and the Apter daughter, who was married to Yisif-Haim Kirschenboim, the rabbi's student and heir at the rabbinical court. Both the son-in-law and the deceased's son, Yehezkel, recited the *kaddish*, and the procession moved on down Lwowska, where shopkeepers shuttered their stores and joined the cortège for the rest of the way, and youths and young men from the entire gamut of *heders*, *yeshivas* and *kleizlakh* stepped outside to join the congregants.

Just before the Grabówka junction, the procession turned left onto Szpitalna Street, passed the Jewish community hospital and, after crossing another junction, arrived at the gates of the Jewish cemetery. Most of the entourage remained outside the gates, filling the street, since the grave of the departed rabbi had been dug in the rabbinical patch next to the gate itself, facing the street. Bit by bit and in silence, the mourners filed past the grave, led by the city rabbis and public figures, and, trailing behind them, came the deceased's pupils and other *yeshiva* students and, finally, in no particular order, the rest of the mourners crowded and pushed their way past. When Aazik's turn came to wield the shovel and toss a clod of Tarnów earth into the open grave, he sensed all too palpably that he was covering not only the grave of his teacher and benefactor, who had treated him like a son and whom Aazik cherished as if Moishl were his real father, but that he was sealing a decisive chapter in his life. The tombstones that rose from the ridged ground seemed to him like question marks, standing upright and wondering at what the future held in store. Ah, where was the wise man in 1902, who could foresee two world wars and the Holocaust that were to visit this land in the next forty years, leaving in their wake no more than the funereal monuments of this grand Jewish community?

For a whole year after the death of the great rabbi, things remained more or less the same, the select circle of his students continuing to hold together. The living spirit behind this unity and the person who set a clear, defined goal before the young men who cherished the memory of their rabbi was Rekh'l, the rabbi's widow. She invested all her emotional strength and powers of persuasion – which until then, neither she nor anyone else knew existed – in the effort to publish the book that her husband had not lived to see in print. The editing task was placed on the shoulders of the son, Yehezkel, and son-in-law, Yisif-Haim, while the others all helped by running errands to the printer's, proofreading, and performing the dozens of other minutiae involved in the hallowed work of transforming a manuscript into a book. Throughout, the students continued to meet at the home of the Apter family at Pilzno Gate, where the work was done under the all-seeing eye of Rekh'l, who supervised each and every detail, advancing the mission with vigorous strides. Thus, on 16 Av 5663 (August 19, 1903), after a ten-month, concerted effort, the printing of Part One of Apter's *Imrei Moshe* ("The Sayings of Moshe") was completed; the other parts have not been published to this day. All that was left was to bind the pages and it was done.

And, look, on that very day itself, 16 Av 5663, her hopes having been realized in full, Rekh'l gave up the ghost. It was as if publishing her husband's manuscript concluded the role of the faithful wife on earth; or, perhaps, it was the finger of God clearly showing who deserved praise and thanks for unlocking the immense treasure of wisdom before the scholarly community. In view of this development, at the last minute the editors added a two to three line acknowledgment for the ascent of Rekh'l's saintly soul.

At the end of the seven-day *shiva* mourning and before the onset of the *selichot* Prayers of Penitence in the month of Elul, which heralded the approach of the New Year, Reb Moishl's elite group of students stopped meeting at his flat and ceased to exist as a corporate entity. The flat passed into the hands of Yisif-Haim, who was appointed a *dayan* (judge), at Tarnów's rabbinical court, in place of his father-in-law, and he was to live there with his family for forty years until the German conquest, when in 1942, along with the rest of Tarnów's martyrs, he would be banished to the ghetto and transported on his final path.

During all the months of shared work on the rabbi's book, as well as the following year, Aazik continued to cherish the *Kloyz* as his sole home and occupied his place on the platform, his *Gemara*, as always, open on the lectern, and the hidden bench at the end of the hall waiting to grant his body brief rest in the wee hours of the night. But two years after the passing of the great rabbi, and as his aura increasingly faded, his Wisłok student found himself exposed to the whims of the zealots and the *Kloyz* revealed itself in all its wickedness.

"His self-study reeks of Enlightenment," the keepers of the faith pronounced.

"His excessive delving into Maimonides is not right," others grumbled.

Actually, there was nothing wrong in studying Maimonides as such. In fact, it was rumored that old Reb Haim Halberstam himself, the father of Zans Hasidism – whose wisdom was hailed in the *Kloyz* not only as Haim's "living words" (expressed by the title of his book, *Divrei Haim*), but as the words of the living God – used to shut himself up in his room on Yom Kippur night to study Maimonides' *Moreh Nevukhim* ("Guide for the Perplexed"). Moreover, it was to the special credit of a *Kloyz* student to be able to resolve a difficulty or contradiction in the sayings of the Sages by quoting from Maimonides. But the combination of Maimonides' philosophy and the ideas of the Hebrew Enlightenment struck *Kloyz* zealots as a highly dangerous, explosive mixture.

It was to become clear to the *ilui* from Wisłok, who had fixed the *Kloyz* as his permanent seat during his rabbi's lifetime and even after he was left bereft in Tarnów (apart from the Sabbaths, which he secretly spent in the quiet of Leibtche's library), that the venerable institution, which until now had given him of its honey, was preparing to give him a taste of its sting. He was to feel now, first-hand, the penalty for the sin of having an independent mind: the cadre of those who only yesterday had praised him would shred him very thin, while the others would turn their backs on him, not wasting even a pinch of tobacco on his behalf. Indeed, his rabbi's death was the breaking point. Nine years had passed during which time the "wayfarer of Wisłok" had become the "*ilui* of Tarnów," betrothed to his place of honor on the *Kloyz* platform. In his innocence, he had imagined that – as in the text of a marriage contract – the place was betrothed to him forever: not only "in kindness and mercy" on the part of its *gabbaim*, but "in righteousness and in judgment" for his true scholarship and intellectual integrity. Yet, upon the death of his rabbi, circumstances had placed him at a crossroads.

On the one hand, where was he to go? In the absence of the

voice of good counsel of his rabbi and mentor, Aazik's course in his further *lernen* was insufficiently clear to him and he was at a loss as to the direction his independent self-study should take. On the other hand, the physical framework of his life – he had just turned twenty-three – also required re-examination. Even if he were to continue to harden his heart and deny himself, as before, outlets that had been suppressed and longings that had been nipped in the bud for nine years on "bread and water," must now pose questions about the future; and though there may not have been any answers, the questioner was not absolved from mulling over them. All this was in contrast to the case of his *Gemara* partner, Yisif-Haim. Now, here were two young Torah scholars whom fate bound together for nine years – both endowed with brilliant talents and destined for greatness – yet, how different the stuff of which each was made and the tracks along which they were to propel the carts of their lives in the future!

6

Yisif-Haim's road was paved for him in terms of both the direction of his further studies and the practical aspects of his life. As regards study and scholarship, his is the king's highway, a path beaten out by the soles of many good men before him, leading directly from *Mishna* and *Poskim* (late legislators) to the *Shulhan Arukh* and its commentators. From there, a handful of tracks branch upward, which only a few students would manage to navigate and by which only a few would arrive at the height of the ridge, the throne of *dayanut* – the rabbinical judiciary. But from that *dayanut* throne only a single, narrow trail leads to the peak, to the high seat of the town rabbinate, and only one person would be privileged to scale it. As for what would lie at the end of the trail – who could foretell? Now, just as Yisif-Haim's future study plan is laid out for him, so, too, the blueprint for his personal life contains no foreseeable shocks. All the circumstances are in his favor, without the shadow of a reason to prevent him from taking full advantage of them. He has at his disposal a spacious flat, inherited by his spouse after the death of her parents, Reb Moishl and Rekh'l Apter, and what possible cause could there be for him to pledge his troth to a celibate corner at the *Kloyz* for the sake of study or to take possession of a section of a wooden bench next to the hapless *schlemiel* from Wisłok?

Happy and fortunate is the lot of Yisif-Haim, who pledged his troth to the daughter of the rabbi himself and wed her "in righteousness and in judgment and in kindness and in mercy," and now his path is doubly laid out for him. Look, he has just been appointed the town *dayan*. And what's more, he has picked up the writer's pen and composed a handsome pamphlet on the laws governing *mikvehs, Kav Mayim Haim* ("A Measure of Living Water"), appending it to the "Novel Viewpoints on the Talmud" by his rabbi and father-in-law, and the two books were published in a single volume at the end of 5663 at Zvi Eliezer Lehrhaupt's press in Tarnów – with a note on the kinship between the two men, of course. Indeed, Yisif-Haim's road is solidly paved – and you, Aazik of Wisłok, country bumpkin that you are, who put all your trust in *lernen* for its own sake rather than its practical considerations, and were not wise enough to see what was happening around nor, in any case, to score any of the pragmatic coups that your colleague managed – you must certainly not grumble at or question his deeds or motives. No matter how you judge them, they all are pure, free of the least shred of doubt, and all are honest; all were born in sanctity, and all, without exception, were for the sake of heaven! Could it be otherwise?

Though Yisif-Haim's actions may enjoy due respect, it has been clear to Aazik ever since he entered the *Kloyz* that the royal road to the top, chosen by his peer and others like him, was not his road, and this conviction has only grown stronger with the passage of years. He interprets at face value the maxim of the Sages in *The*

Sayings of the Fathers to "despise the rabbinate," and firmly rejects
the slightest hint of his possible appointment – as Reb Moishl's outstanding student – to the high rabbinical court of the holy community of Tarnów. Far better, he decides, to make his living by teaching
Torah to the children of wealthy *baalbatim*, or doing other errands
for them, rather than be dependent on the public kitty.

And just as in Aazik's eyes, the establishment road symbolized by Yisif-Haim is inconsistent with his own desires and doubts
about the future, so his relationship with the Apter home, which
he so loved, has increasingly cooled since that home became Yisif-
Haim's residence. For what connection can he have with the house
now? The rabbi is gone, and a stranger fills his seat. Yes, none other
than Reb Yoseph-Haim the *dayan*, his former fellow-student and
the son-in-law and heir of Reb Moishl, now relaxes in the modest armchair Aazik remembers so well, the arms of which have no
doubt been repaired and reupholstered according to the wishes of
the new woman of the house and the lofty status of the ensconced
scholar!

Since the passing of the saintly Rekh'l, Aazik has vowed never
to go up again to the flat that occupies such an important place in
his youthful memories, nor to sit opposite the armchair in which
his rabbi once sat. He was not to know, he could not know that,
one day, in the late Twenties, he would, against his will, again have
to cross the threshold of the flat and sit opposite Yisif-Haim. The
reason for the unexpected encounter was to cause Aazik untold
agony, a sense of failure and of terrible humiliation, but, as always,
he would accept the decree and bear the insult in mute pain, without complaint, or words, or rancor...

To be free – this was now Aazik's only desire – yes, free to endlessly continue with all his might his *lernen-lernen-lernen*, just as
he had done at the corner of the *Kloyz* platform for more than nine
years, and to spend his Sabbaths in Leibtche's library. But realizing
this ambition was not so simple: the atmosphere at the *Kloyz* was

446 CHESTNUTS OF YESTERYEAR: A JEWISH ODYSSEY

becoming more and more difficult, more and more tense, almost unendurable, as dissension and controversy sharpened. The monster of Orthodox zealotry – the fanaticism which Aazik believed to be rooted in shameless, uncouth ignorance and which spewed a heathen fire under the pretence of offering up a holy one – lay in wait for him day and night, ready to burn him alive with its flaming breath. How, then, was he to chart his course? *Ah, who can restore you to me, Reb Moishl, my rabbi, who can restore you, father mine?* his lips murmur in speechless sorrow. *It is your guiding hand I need, like a support for the blind, through the confusion in which our community is caught!*

Aazik, who in 1904 is poised before numerous questions and, from his vantage point in the corner, looks out on the *Kloyz* and the clashes between Orthodox Zionists and zealots, now firmly identifies with the Zionists. In his heart of hearts, he sketches the type of home he would like to set up when the time comes for him to build a family. The Meir Baal HaNess collection box will surely be flanked by the new blue box, that of Keren Kayemeth Le Yisrael, the fund established three years earlier by the Zionist Organization, and recently distributed in Jewish communities. The first such box had already reached Tarnów and people did not stop speaking of how attractive it was.

Similarly, he imagines his children attending a modern Hebrew school, alongside the traditional study of *Gemara*, and speaking fluent Hebrew in the Sephardi vocalization, like the pioneers in Eretz Israel, rather than his own Ashkenazi pronunciation. True, the latter's wealth and beauty is indisputable. Even Bialik composed his poems in this form, including *"Be'Ir HaHareiga"* (In the City of Killing) on the Kishinev pogrom, which had just appeared under the title of *"Masa Nemirov,"* ostensibly for fear of censorship, and pretending to hark back to the pogroms of the seventeenth century. Nevertheless, the Ashkenazi dialect sounded, so Aazik felt, as if it bore the entire weight of Ashkenaz exile on its back. It was clear to Aazik, that the new generation, born into freedom, would wash their hands of it. Last but not least – should he be privileged to re-alize all this – perhaps fate would grant him one more kindness and allow him to set up home in Eretz Israel?

*

Except that one hot Tammuz day in 1904, a telegram arrived from Vienna that thoroughly jolted the Jewish public. As if a floe of ice had suddenly intruded on mid-summer, freezing blood and heart. It is not clear to Aazik's son today, nor, perhaps did Aazik himself know then, how long he would have continued to wallow in the mire of doubt and wander in the maze of uncertainty before decid-ing about his future at the *Kloyz* – had it not been for the news that arrived from Vienna. The scene of the gaping abyss that opened at the *Kloyz* on the 20th of Tammuz of 1904, upon receipt of the ter-rible announcement of Herzl's death, drove home to Aazik that his generation of Jews was rent into two camps and that there were moments when even someone like himself, who kept himself to himself and lived in utter humility, had to stand up and be counted with one camp or the other. For, while the one camp was stricken with an immeasurable grief that orphaned every man and woman, old and young alike, the other camp burst into wicked and spiteful rejoicing, upsetting the delicate equilibrium that most of the *Kloyz* regulars had worked so hard to preserve for the sake of peace.

"The time has come to act!" Aazik heard himself declare out loud, and he shut his *Gemara*. And heedless of the looks of his companions who sat at the tables, he unwaveringly abandoned his privileged lectern at the corner of the platform and strode briskly out of the *Kloyz*...